Angels Sing At Sunset

Pam Warren

Published in 2015 by FeedARead.com Publishing

The sun set. The vivid orange ball of fire ignited the waves momentarily, then was extinguished in the ocean. A majestic line of pelicans swooped westward. Hannah pulled the elastic band from her hair and shook her head, releasing the long braid. The repetitive slap and whoosh of waves was soothing. She stretched her legs; resting her head on the back of the park bench. Her hair draped behind her shoulders, almost touching the sand. She closed her eyes and inhaled the tranquility of the newborn evening. Even with her eyes shut, she knew when he'd arrived.

Funny thing; that knowing. She couldn't smell him, didn't hear his footsteps. He didn't touch her or say a word. But she knew he was there. Him. Everyday this week, he'd watched her. From the far side of the lobby, he'd watched as she dabbed paint on her mural at the State Employees' Credit Union. Of course, she'd noticed him watching.

She was used to people observing her at work. A fresco artist is a curiosity- folks watch for a few minutes, perhaps ask a question, then move on. But, this guy returned day after day. Initially she'd thought he might be an artists' agent or a gallery owner.

3

Yesterday, it seemed that he had all the time in the world. No hurry; he'd just stood across the room for more than an hour to watch her paint. Although he hadn't spoken to her, he did smile when he'd caught her looking at him. Funny thing, how that grin had made her heart race. Talk about a dazzling smile! The man could pose for toothpaste commercials.

Dressed all in black, he looked exotic with dark grey eyes and his long hair pulled back at his nape. It wasn't that his presence at the credit union was intimidating; only that she was cautiously curious about him. Just last night she'd wondered about him while she swept the floor after dinner. She didn't think he was Italian or Mexican; middle Eastern maybe? No, she didn't think so.

Weird how the hairs on her arms prickled when he sat down on the opposite end of the bench. In the warmth of a North Carolina spring evening, she'd shivered. She felt as if someone had whispered in her ear, cool breaths that tickled her neck.

Eyes still closed, she had turned in his direction and asked, "Can you hear it?"

His voice was like corduroy – warm and soft, but a little wrinkled. It was a very soothing voice and it fit him well. "The sunset music? It's almost over now; but yeah, I hear it. "

Her green eyes popped open in surprise. "Do you really?"

He was relaxed with arms akimbo and legs sprawled. "Sure."

She arched her back, jutting her shoulders forward. "My grandmother told me that the angels sing at sunset."

He closed his eyes and rotated his head, flexing his shoulders. "Your grandmother is a smart lady."

"Was. Gram was smart; but she was a dreamer."

"Dreamers are the people who leave a mark on the Earth."

"Dreamers are the people who write faerie tales."

"True enough. You've got a nice smile. You should use it more often."

"I smile plenty."

"Do you?"

Hannah shrugged her shoulders and dropped her head so that a curtain of hair covered her smile. He slid a bit closer to her end of the wooden bench.

"I'm Gabe."

"Gabe? Gabriel? Like the archangel?"

"I'm no angel."

"No, I don't suppose you are. In paintings, Gabriel is blonde, not dark like you." She tilted her head to the side, studying his face. "Those grey eyes are mysterious, maybe even mystical, though."

"Hmm." He gouged his thumbnail into letters carved on the bench. "I wonder if Marv still loves Helen."

"Probably not. Young love needs to be documented on our overpasses, toilet stalls and park benches so that a record remains long after the burst of white-hot lust has faded."

"You're a cynic, Hannah."

She hunched her shoulders and giggled. "So, you know my name. I've seen you watching me."

"Do I make you nervous?"

"No. Fresco painters are used to an audience."

"You're talented."

"Thanks."

"Pay good?"

"Pay's all right, when there is pay. Problem is a shortage of commissions. Do you work close by?"

"Actually, I work out my home."

"And home is…close?"

"Close enough. I happened by, saw you at work and decided to stay in Beaufort for awhile."

"Just like that, huh? Just decided to stay?"

"Yeah. Just like that."

"Are you independently wealthy or are you on the run from a wife and twelve children?"

He rubbed his left elbow and flexed his fingers. "I don't need much. Money isn't particularly important to me."

"Oh?"

"I grow some vegetables. Like I said, I don't need much."

Hannah glanced at her watch, stuffed her sketchpad back into her pack and stood up. She held her hand out to him. "Nice talking to you, Gabe."

She thought her hand seemed small compared to his. Her fingers tingled when they touched his palm. He generated an intense heat, like the space heater Gram had kept in her bathroom to warm the cold ceramic floor tiles during winter.

"Can I come watch you paint again?"

"Sure. I'll look forward to it."

"Tomorrow?"

Hannah nodded and turned away. "Until tomorrow, then."

He was there the next day.

He neither stood close to her nor said a word while she worked. He remained on the opposite side of the bank lobby; casually lounging on a bench the color of unsalted butter. However, his presence was as disturbing as if he had breathed on her neck and whispered in her ear. What was her problem? It was almost impossible to concentrate while a handsome stranger stared at her.

A muralist generates an audience, Hannah reminded herself. At least that's what she'd told the manager when he commissioned the project. I'm used to people touching the wet paint and asking goofy questions. She sneaked a peak over her left shoulder, watched him rub his index finger back and forth over his upper lip. Why does this particular man distract me? She saw him catch the tip of that finger between his teeth and touch his nail with his tongue. Hannah sucked a breath between her own teeth and ran her tongue over her bottom lip. The next time she glanced over, he was gone.

8

But, he reappeared, outside the revolving door, when she left the building.

"It's Friday. Going back to the park today?"

"I go everyday. It's a good place to unwind."

He nodded towards the bulging backpack she had slung over her shoulder. "And to sketch bird studies for your watercolors?"

"Something like that."

"I've seen your watercolors. Down at the gallery on the wharf."

"Just happened by Pierside Peddler and decided to browse?"

"Something like that."

He grinned and she chuckled.

"Your work is good."

She smiled and dipped her head. "I know."

He moved like a leopard on the prowl. Although his normal strides were long and smooth; he'd slowed his pace to walk beside her. Gabe seemed comfortable with the quiet; but Hannah searched the shaded sidewalk, hoping for something worthy of conversation. No luck! Usually there were children on the sidewalks. Bikes and skates

and hoola hoops. Why weren't a few kids riding bicycles this afternoon? And where were the squirrels? Could she rely on one to
scamper down the big oak tree and retrieve an acorn?

"Brought you a present." He held up a pink and green striped
peppermint stick.

"Trying to woo me with extravagant gifts?" she laughed.

"Something like that."

"Might work."

After sleeping late on Sunday morning, Hannah sailed her skiff
over to Carrot Shoals, where she sketched the wild horses that roam
the dunes. At dusk, she returned to Beaufort. The first star appeared
while she cleated the bowline at the neighborhood dock. As she furled
the sail, a familiar voice called out.

"Nice boat."

Gabe set his grocery bag on the sidewalk and walked down the
dock. He extended a hand to help her climb out of the boat.

Hannah laughed, "Yeah, it's not a yacht, but I like it! I never
have to worry about finding crew."

Gabe touched her cheek with his finger. "Ahh, another one of your smiles. They could prove to be habit-forming."

Maybe his voice was more like velvet than corduroy, Hannah decided. Dark purple velvet like Gram's goosedown quilt. A bedroom voice. She'd always thought it a strange description; but now she understood the definition.

"Hungry?" Gabe asked.

Her stomach rumbled in response. "Yeah, I guess I am."

"I'm headed over to the diner for a Spanish omelet. Wanna join me?"

Hannah tipped her head towards the paper sack he'd left on the sidewalk. "What about your groceries?"

"A can of roasted cashews and a six pack of apple juice."

"Not a well-rounded diet."

"Just snacks. I eat out a lot."

"I see."

"Do you?"

"No, but I'll ask questions while we eat."

They'd had fun, laughing while they ate fluffy omelets oozing cheese and spicy salsa. The diner was empty except for one elderly couple in a booth at the back of the room. Each of them was small. Very small. Both peeked over the table, like toddlers without booster seats.

The man was dressed in an unusual suit the color of dirt. Hannah guessed it was made of chamois. His red hair was tangled and stuck out in odd spikes. He was quite animated; gesturing with broad florid motions.

In contrast, the woman was huddled in the folds of a black hooded cloak with red satin lining. She moved slowly, with a graceful measured rhythm. She appeared to be at least a hundred years old; her face was incredibly wrinkled. Hannah was reminded of the shriveled figures carved from apples that she'd seen at Appalachian craft fairs.

The odd pair shuffled past her table as they left the diner. Hannah thought that the woman winked at Gabe. But, he assured her she'd been mistaken.

Monday was the last day of her commission. Hannah had been surprised when Gabe didn't show up at the Credit Union. A tall man dressed in a dark suit sat on the butter-colored bench and she'd spun around with a smile. But he wasn't Gabe. She turned back to the fresco and dabbed three random splotches of pale blue in the right-hand corner of her painting. She studied her palette, swiped another camel's hair brush into burnt sienna, and then swirled it in a fleck of umber. She touched the fresco with her brush, carefully stippling small dots into the shadows of her composition.

The bank's manager approached from behind her. "It's great!"

Hannah jumped as though his words were electrically-charged. "What? …Oh. Thanks." She stepped away from the painting and cocked her head. She nibbled the wooden tip of her brush. "It is nice, isn't it?"

"Yes, it is. What made you think of leprechauns?"

Hannah shrugged. "Oh, I dunno. I don't know much about finance. Nasdaq and mutual funds are riddles to me. Legends say the Wee Folk use riddles as clues for finding their hidden pots of gold." She scratched the bridge of her nose and smiled at him. "Somehow it was a sensible analogy to me!"

The banker patted his head, in an attempt to tame the few springy strands of hair that sprouted at his crown. "Well, unlike the faery folk, the bank honors its debts." He pulled a white envelope from the breast pocket of his navy silk jacket. "For a job well-done."

Hannah tucked the envelope into her backpack. She glanced over her left shoulder, to the spot where Gabe should have been.

"Hmmm," she mumbled, "Easy-come, easy-go."

There was work to be done. She still had to clean up; wash her brushes and scrape any paint drops off the marble floor. After all, the bank was hosting a grand-opening celebration tomorrow morning at nine.

A little less than two hours later, she kicked off her sandals and scrunched her toes in the warm wet sand. She really liked this little strip of beach park, conveniently near her house. Her backpack lay open beside her, broken pieces of charcoal and conte crayons were strewn among the seashells in the tide line at her feet. She chewed the eraser of her pencil while she inspected the drawing on her pad.

"More faery sketches?" he asked.

"Not this time," she smiled. "Sometimes I draw devils." She flipped the pad and he grinned at the sketch of himself, fingering his upper lip and looking quite perplexed.

"Ah, but a handsome devil!" He held his hand out to her. "Come. Walk with me for a while."

Hannah stood, then retreated a step. She stooped to gather her belongings. "Umm. No. Thanks, though."

"Got other plans?"

"Nooo. Not for awhile yet."

He reached towards her shoulder, but his hand only hovered; he never touched her.

"Short walk. Come on."

She giggled and he took three strides, heading towards the pier about two miles down the beach. He turned his head and called out, "Coming?"

Hannah hiked the backpack over her shoulder and sprinted to keep up with his long paces. "Yeah, for a while."

They walked together in silence for a minute, maybe two. Pelicans soared overhead, screeching and occasionally diving into the shallow surf. Sandpipers scurried out of reach of each swell that crashed to shore, then tiptoed forward to search for food dislodged by the receding wave.

Gabe tipped his head towards the tiny birds, tottering on long spindly legs. "That's you."

"Pardon?"

"You skidder out, explore quickly, then retreat."

Hannah halted in mid-step. Feet firmly planted, toes anchored into the sand, she raised her hand to shake a finger in his face.

"How can you say that? You don't know me."

"Am I wrong, then?"

"Yes!" She wrapped her arms at her waist, took a step back. "No," she murmured, almost in a whisper. "I've learned to be independent. And cautious. Fewer disappointments."

"Well, take a chance here," he said. He gestured towards the sand dune and sat. "Let's talk."

Hannah moved her foot back and forth, swiping an arc in the damp sand. "Umm, I dunno."

Gabe patted the ground at his side and motioned her forward with a nod. "C'mon."

She placed the backpack as a wedge between them.

"Tell me about yourself. How did you end up here, painting walls in a bank lobby?"

"Just sort of a natural progression from childhood Crayola scribbles to art school to selling my talent."

"Impressive. I'll bet you were a good student."

16

"I worked hard."

"And you set out to make your mark on the art world?"

"It's more of a dent than an actual mark, though," she giggled, tucking her bare feet under her long skirt. " I haven't really hit the big time yet!"

"Hungry for the mega-bucks?"

"Well, I've eaten my share of saltines with peanut butter. The majority of my money used to go towards brushes, canvas and paints. I still wear clothes from the Salvation Army."

He tugged the hem of her colorful gypsy skirt. "Eclectic styling. The look agrees with you."

She snickered and shook her head.

"My first commission was a huge thirty-foot wall at the Salvation Army in downtown Boston. One of the major donors offered me a chance. He wanted something colorful, something whimsical."

"So you painted faeries?"

"How'd you know that?"

"I've seen your sketchpad, remember?"

Hannah arched her brows and grinned. "Yep. I painted the faeries from Gram's stories."

Gabe picked up a small pebble, studied it for moment, then tossed it into the water. "I suppose your Gram was proud of your accomplishments."

Hannah rubbed her eyebrow. "She would have been my biggest fan. Her refrigerator used to be covered with my drawings." Hannah massaged her temples, stretching her hand over her eyes. "Cancer. She died during my freshman year at college. Then I was an orphan again."

"Again?" Gabe touched her shoulder. His palm was warm and comforting.

She scraped at a speck of paint on her thumbnail. Took a deep breath. "Yeah. My parents were killed in car accident when I was a kid. That's when I went to live with Gram in a little town outside Boston."

"So, how did you move from inner city Boston to the coast of North Carolina?"

"While I was painting faeries cavorting across that thirty-foot long wall at Salvation Army, a corporate VIP hurried into the building for a meeting. He was distracted by my fresco. He glanced at his watch, reached into his briefcase, found a business card and dropped it on my palette. Neglected to introduce himself, but he said my work showed great promise. Told me to contact him. I shoved the card into a pocket. Days later I discovered it while loading the washer at the Laundromat."

"Did you call him?"

"Of course. He led me to a couple of jobs."

"So you amassed a fortune and retired here, to live in relative obscurity?" he teased.

"One commission was for the new Port Authority building over there," She pointed towards the causeway. "across the bridge in Morehead City. Beaufort charmed me."

"Been here long?"

"No, not really. Less than a year."

"Still settling in, making a niche for yourself?"

"Something like that. I don't make friends easily. "

"Could have fooled me."

"I have business contacts. Not friends. If I don't make any friends, I can't suffer another loss. The losing is too hard."

Hannah shuffled through the shells half-buried in the sand at her feet. She put a fractured Scotch Bonnet shell on his knee. Even through the denim of his jeans, she could feel his heat. She closed her fingers and hid them in her lap.

"What about you? What kind of farm do you have?"

"I grow herbs."

"Herbs? Like basil and oregano, you mean?"

"Among other things."

"And you can make a living with that?"

"Enough."

"Yeah. Sure thing."

"I'm an herbalist."

"Sounds like the name of a new age religion."

"I lived with my godmother for years. She distills her own medicines using herbs and wild plants. Some of my earliest memories revolve around the smells of herbs drying in the kitchen. I guess it's only natural that I'm fascinated with herbs and natural remedies."

"What brings a farmer to town?"

"Even farmers take time off."

"Really?"

"I was bored, lonely. I needed something...more..." He shrugged his shoulders, spread his empty hands.

"So…did you find it?"

"Maybe…I hope so."

A breeze teased Hannah's hair. Errant strands tickled her cheeks and nose. She swiped her fingers over her eyes and brushed her nose. Gabe tucked a stray lock of hair behind her ear.

"Time you were heading back home," Gabe said. "You don't want to keep the folks at Shady Arms waiting."

"Are you stalking me? How did you know I teach at Shady Arms on Monday nights?"

"Whoa! I'm an innocent man." Gabe chuckled and held his hands over his shoulders. "I confess I've asked a few questions. You're a fascinating woman. Beaufort's a small town. I admired your watercolors and the woman at the gallery …"

"Miranda."

"Yeah, Miranda said that you are not only talented, but beautiful." He winked at her. "I agreed with her; told her that I took you to dinner."

"Dutch treat," she reminded him.

"Miranda wished me luck. She said that her nephew works as an orderly at Shady Arms. Said he'd asked you out several times and that you always say no."

"I don't do well with commitments."

"Dinner and a movie don't necessarily lead to binding contracts, Hannah."

"Yeah, well…enough about me. Tell me about your herbs. I don't know much about herbal cures, except that garlic is a surefire precaution against vampires…or is it werewolves?"

"Well, that's a beginning!" He lay back, propped up on his elbows, legs extended straight out. "When you peel an orange, what is it that you smell?" He arched one eyebrow when she hunched her shoulders. "It's the essential oils that give spices, flowers, fruits their specific perfume. Did you know that it takes one ton of rose petals to produce a small bottle of rose oil?"

"No wonder perfume is so darned expensive, huh?"

"See, you're learning the economics of herbalogy."

Hannah saluted and smiled. "I appreciate the education." She stood and shook her skirt, sprinkling him with sand. "It's late. I do have to go."

"After the watercolor lessons, I'll buy you dinner."

"No."

"Walk you home now?"

"I think not."

"As far as the park, then?"

"Okay."

"Do you live close to the park?"

"Uh uh. No clever girl gives a strange man her address."

Gabe threw up his hands in surrender. "No address, then. Do you have a house? Live in an apartment?"

"The realtor called it a bungalow, actually."

"Sounds nice."

"It is. I spent most of my money repairing the roof and re-wiring the electrical, so the décor is Spartan. But, it's mine."

"I'd love to see it."

They had reached the park. Hannah stepped into her sandals and held her hand out to him. Gabe sandwiched her hand between his, barely touching, yet definitely warming her.

"Thank you. I enjoyed our walk," she admitted.

"Until next time, then."

"But I'm finished with the fresco."

"I know. But, I'll see you around. Beaufort is a small community, remember? Sleep well."

Tuesday, she had stayed at home, scrubbing the bathroom and doing laundry. Periodically, she'd peek out the windows, halfway expecting to see him strolling down the beach. On Wednesday, while she was at the grocery store, she had looked for him as she thumped cantaloupes in the vegetable section.

"Oh, get over it, Hannah. You don't even know the man's last name. Gabe. Gabe from somewhere close enough. He could be a mass murderer. Or a con man. No. You don't believe that because he never asked you for anything but conversation."

Although her refrigerator hummed cheerfully, she shoved the produce into the frost-proof drawers and slammed the door shut. "You trusted him, didn't you? You idiot! I thought you'd learned not to depend on anyone. Independence; that's the key."

More frustrated than hungry, Hannah opted for a long walk on the beach before dinner.

"…Stupid maybe; but I enjoyed being with him. He made me feel good about myself. A person can't live in a vacuum. I need companionship, don't I? What if I never talk to strangers? Then I'll never know anybody. Nobody will ever know me. I'll live and die and my total legacy will be a stack of paintings."

Her pockets bulged with auger shells when she finally collapsed in a chair on the deck. The angelic song was short that evening. Purple clouds loomed, turning the pink sky ashen. Angelic voices modulated, then fell silent. The clouds massed on the horizon, and the evening turned dead-calm. Quiet. A little bit eerie. Not a branch twitched. She leaned back in the chair, propping her feet on the porch railing. She enjoyed the light rain that sprinkled her cheeks. She drifted to sleep, but she was jolted awake by violent claps of thunder.

The sky strobed with garish lightning bolts! Abusive winds hurled the neighbors' beach furniture against the seawall. Hannah rushed through the pelting rain down to the shore to collect any unbroken chairs. Furious claps of thunder chased giant fireballs through the sky's black void.

Lightning struck her roof; a brilliant white-hot flash that illuminated the whole yard momentarily. A piece of gutter ripped off the house, clanging as it hit the grill on her porch. For a second, a thin blue stream spilled from the nozzle of the gas cylinder. Unbelieving, she watched as flames burst from the propane tank, quickly leaping to the clapboard siding. She was thrown to the ground and temporarily deafened by an explosion. Thick clouds of dark smoke undulated on the roof. An oily, pungent odor scorched her nose and throat. Her eyes stung and streamed tears. She could actually taste the devastation permeating the smoke-filled air.

It was a nightmare! She watched the flames flash with piercing beauty. On the dunes, sea oats caught fire and sizzled like Fourth of July sparklers, charring the sand. Only a dull roar echoed in her ears. She felt the percussion of her own rapid heartbeats throbbing.

Red lights flashed as the fire trucks arrived. Neighbors surged from their homes, anxious to watch the spectacle of destruction. They raced past her, shouting soundlessly to one another and motioning to the firemen who wore respirators. Dressed in a housecoat, her hair in pin curls, Mrs. McReedy clutched Hannah's arm and mouthed silent questions. She dabbed at Hannah's forehead with a wadded tissue; but turned to watch the kitchen walls collapse. Dazed, Hannah wandered away from her wasted house. She needed to breathe clean air. She'd feel better if she walked for a few minutes.

The rain slackened to become a fine mist. Muffled sounds returned, but Hannah's ears still buzzed like a swarm of mosquitoes. Her footsteps created muddy ripples in the puddles. Her feet and legs had been splashed with oily gray ooze. An increasing fog hung in the still air, softening the streetlamps to a glimmering haze; the arc of a lamp silhouetted a tall figure at the end of the block.

"Gabe."

She reached out to grasp his outstretched hand. She felt a spark in her quivering fingertips!

"God in heaven!" she whispered.

"No. Just a man."

She reached for him, a drowning swimmer pulling ferociously towards safety. It was as if a strong magnetism compelled her to him. The air crackled and her scalp tingled, making her feel electric.

"Are you hurt?" Gabe asked.

Hannah breathed in the vegetative wetness of the evening. She shook her head slowly. "I don't think so." She pushed against her right ear and moved her jaws side-to-side.

With a feather-like touch, he stroked her neck and shoulders, trailed his fingertips down her wet arms. She shivered pleasantly. Slowly, he retraced his path along the sensitive skin of her arms. Every pore of her body tingled. She could not look away. Hannah reveled in her emotional nakedness. She felt as if he could see into her soul.

She wet her lips with her tongue. All of the night sounds were amplified while she stood transfixed, immobile but intensely alive, throbbing. She made a soft hissing sound, sucking in a much-needed breath. He hugged her body to his.

She flinched and tried to push him away.

"Easy now. You're with me now, Hannah. You're safe. I won't let you get hurt."

He rubbed his face against her neck, beginning at the base of her throat, where her pulse beat in staccato rhythms, ending at her right ear.

She had a vague impression that he was marking her with his scent, like an animal marks his mate. She started to lift her hand to fondle his head. But she stopped. When his tongue traced her collar-bone, her knees buckled. She slumped. Hannah realized he held her in place tight against him, chest-to-chest, thigh-to-thigh. She was tethered to his body.

"I think I'm flammable!" she stammered stupidly. Her voice cracked in ragged whispers.

"No. Just human," he said, smiling. "Come with me. Come stay with me."

She blinked, startled and speechless.

Using his forefinger, he touched her chin, closing her gaping mouth. He smiled at her again.

"Trust me. Trust in yourself."

She was seduced by his gentle voice, enthralled. He recaptured her hand, gently enfolding it in his firm grip, sharing his warmth. He grinned at her, and she returned a tentative smile.

"What is your last name anyway?"

"Murray."

"Gabriel Murray."

"Gabriel Edward Murray, at your service."

"Hannah Marie Everette. Pleased to meet ...."

Gabe's face blurred. It was as if she were looking at him through Jello. His edges were gelatinous. She reached out to grasp his arm, but swayed instead. She opened her mouth to speak, but formed sounds rather than words. Not exactly a hiccup, not a sob or laughter. Maybe a hybrid of the three. Hannah was chilly…and overheated. Sweating and shivering at the same time.

"I'm a mess."

Gabe led her to a brick wall that lined the parking lot on the corner. He sat down and tugged her close, wrapping his arms over hers. "It's obvious you've had a rough night. Want to tell me about it?"

Hannah's eyes drifted shut. Her head drooped forward, chin to chest. "I've lost everything…or I'm pretty sure I have."

Gabe rubbed the knob of her spine, right at the base of her neck.

His hands were warm, like bread fresh from the oven. Her tense muscles melted like butter. She felt safe.

"What happened?"

"A fire. My house caught on fire!" She was in tears again.

"Do you know how the fire started?"

"Lightning. It was like watching a movie. Bright, bright flash of light. Seems like it almost moved in slow motion for a few seconds, you know? Something fell from the roof; a board or a chunk of gutter or something. I think the propane tank dripped gas and a fire started-burning in a blue stream at first. Then, there was an explosion and the neighbors came to look and I couldn't hear and I think I just wandered away and then you found me."

Gabe brushed the hair off her forehead. He held her face in his hands, stroking her cheeks with his thumbs. "But you're not hurt?"

Her bottom lip quivered, but Hannah shook her head. "No, I'm fine," she whispered. "I can hear you now; but it sounds like you're talking in a tunnel."

He squeezed her right shoulder, asking, "Are you frightened, then?"

"Tonight my house and all of my possessions exploded." She giggled with an almost hysterical urgency. "My closest companion is a virtual stranger. Shouldn't I be frightened?"

"Do you want to call someone else?"

She shook her head quickly.

"No. Amazingly I'm not really afraid. You're here. Didn't you promise to protect me?"

"Of course I did."

"And I trust you for some reason I don't understand."

"Good. It's settled then."

"Settled?"

"Yes. We'll leave tomorrow afternoon."

"Leave?"

"You should come home with me. Stay there a while. Get your bearings. Recuperate."

"I…er…I don't know…I can't just leave."

"Do you have friends who can take you in for a while? How about Miranda?"

Hannah scraped her teeth over her lower lip. "No. I keep to myself most of the time. I could rent a room somewhere, I guess. Of course it's pretty late tonight. Beaufort pulls up the sidewalks at eight o'clock."

Gabe stood and pulled her to her feet.

32

"Well, you don't have anywhere to sleep tonight. My motel room has two beds." He tugged at the oily, wet curl that stuck to her arm. "And a hot shower."

Hannah crossed her arms at her waist and hunched forward, touching her forehead to her knees. "I can't stay in your motel room!"

"Do you have a better suggestion? I can take you to Miranda's house. Can't you call a neighbor?"

Hannah forced a chuckle. "Oddly enough, I know more about you than about anyone else in town. Perhaps my isolationist theory has a few fallacies." She held her empty arms out. "If your offer stands, I could use a rest stop tonight. I'll consider plans for my future in the daylight!"

"Then do you consider us friends?"

"I'll figure that out in the daylight, too."

"It's not a long walk to the Shady Rest Motel," Gabe promised.

"My room is small; but the shower is stocked with lots of those tiny bottles of shampoo and bath gel." He led her through an attractive courtyard where crepe myrtles had littered the bricked walkway with pink blossoms.

In his room, Hannah was relieved to find two double beds separated by a nightstand attached to the wall. She stood alongside the chair upholstered with an unfortunate selection of patterned chintz. Gabe smiled at her and flipped on the light in the bathroom.

"Why don't you take a leisurely bath?"

While she filled the bathroom with steam and soap bubbles, he perused the merchandise in a nearby shop offering tourist novelties. He held up a black shirt emblazoned with a pirate Jolly Roger and the claim *'I survived the graveyard of the Atlantic'*.

"Is this the best you have to offer as a woman's nightgown?"

The clerk stuffed a dog-eared magazine under the counter and shrugged. "Fraid so, honey. Nowadays girls sleep in tees all the time. Bigger the better." She scanned the barcode on the price tag. "This all?"

Gabe pulled a hanger from the closest rack and inspected a dress, rubbing the gauzy fabric against his cheek.

The clerk shook her head and chuckled. "My experience proves most good-looking men are darned accurate guessing a woman's size!" She took the dress from him and held the straps at her own shoulders. "That look about right?" She moved her hips, swishing the flared skirt side-to-side.

"Maybe a little smaller. Shorter."

Five minutes later he left the shop replete with a modest wardrobe stuffed in a bright yellow plastic bag. Besides the graveyard nightshirt, he'd selected a zippered jacket with a hood, a pair of gray sweatpants with a hot pink drawstring, the sundress and a pair of rubber flip-flops.

Hannah turned off the shower and wiped circles on the foggy mirror with her hand. She finger-combed her wet tangles. Water dripped down her back and soaked the towel wrapped around her. Although the door to the bathroom was locked, she jumped when Gabe knocked and called out, "Feeling better?"

"Huh? Oh, yeah. Smell better, too, I'll bet!" She wondered if he'd noticed the quiver in her voice. The face in the mirror blinked two red, swollen eyes. She threaded her fingers in her hair, pushing at her temples with her palms. "Steady, Hannah. Just breathe," she mumbled.

"I got you a few things," he said. "Selection wasn't great; but…"

He stroked the laminate on the door as if it were her skin. "They're out here in the chair. Have a look. I'll be back in a few minutes."

When he returned, he brought sustenance. "Pizza," he an-

nounced, holding the cardboard box in his right hand. "And salad!"

She reached for the bag in his other hand.

"Here, let me help you." Hannah unpacked two tubs of Caesar

salad, plastic forks and a handful of paper napkins, laying everything

out on one of the beds. "Now THIS smells great!"

He stood directly behind her; but he didn't touch her. Hannah's

bare toes curled to clutch the loops in the carpet. She was swaddled in

the gigantic tee. The shirt fit like a tent - the neckline bared a glimpse

of her collarbone, the hem fell past her knees, and the shoulder seams

practically touched her elbows. She felt gawky and clumsy.

Gabe's breath made her damp scalp tremble. Made goose-

bumps on her arms. Made every single hair on her body stand on end.

"I didn't realize I was hungry until just now." She held the bag

close to her face and stared inside intently as if brown paper held the answer to some mystery of life. "There's only one package of pepper," she blurted, hearing her voice crack when she spoke.

"All yours, then. I don't need any." He stepped back, giving her more space. He paused a second before he sat on one corner of the bed. "It's an indoor picnic."

"At midnight?"

"Sure." He patted the spot beside him. "Come, sit down." He folded a piece of pizza in half length-wise and bit off the tip. "Hmm, good."

Hannah perched on the opposite side of the bed. A fourteen-inch pizza carton and about a quarter pound of melted mozzarella separated them. The room was suffused with the unmistakable aromas of basil and garlic. Gabe arched one eyebrow and reached for another slice.

"Do I scare you, Hannah?" He gestured with the white plastic fork and hurled a small piece of romaine lettuce towards her. It landed in a wet, oily blob next to her hand.

She inched closer to her edge of the bed, realizing that she might slide onto the floor soon.

"Not exactly."

"What exactly?"

"Well, I'm cautious." Hannah swirled her fork through her salad. "With an instinct for survival."

"Not all men are feral."

She rolled her eyes. "I've learned that it's best not to trust people – men or women."

Gabe reached one fingertip towards her cheek. She leaned away infinitesimally; but she knew that he'd noticed.

"Maybe you'll tell me about it one day."

"Maybe." She almost smiled; but she touched her lower lip, fingers hiding any evidence.

Gabe stood, stacking wadded napkins, forks and salad tins into the empty carton.

Hannah drew her legs inside the huge shirt, and rested her chin on her steepled knees. "Thanks for everything. The clothes, the food, the place to stay. I'll pay you back."

"Not necessary."

She looked up at him, but her voice dropped a notch. "Thanks for being here for me."

"Glad to help. There's an extra toothbrush still wrapped in cellophane in the glass beside the sink. You get ready for bed. I'm taking the trash out to the dumpster. Sleep well."

"You too."

Neither of them slept particularly well that night.

Hannah moaned and fought dreams, tangling the bed linens around her feet. Gabe used the complimentary coffee pot to boil water for brewing chamomile tea.

He sat in the chair, watching, while she slept fitfully. He murmured nonsense words and stroked her face with a damp cloth that smelled of jasmine.

"Hush now, Hannah. You're safe now. I'm with you."

Her eyes opened, and she blinked in surprise, startled from sleep; but not fully alert. With a soundless gasp, she sat up. Recognizing Gabe, she slumped against the pillow. "If I'm dreaming, don't wake me."

He offered her a mug of lukewarm tea.

"I always carry chamomile when I travel. It's even better than Advil or Pepto-Bismol."

Hannah inhaled the nearly floral fragrance. "Thanks."

She figured that Gabe's chatter was meant to dispel her dreams.

"For hundreds of years, chamomile's been used to treat tension head-ache, sleeplessness, diarrhea and upset stomach. Damned near to a wonder drug, don't you think?"

"Ahh. The herbalogy lesson continues, yeah?"

He sat on the bed to tip the mug to her lips again. "Something like that."

"Trying to distract me?"

"How am I doing?"

She rubbed her face against his shirt, sucked in a breath. "I feel safe here." Then, tightening her arms around his, "with you beside me."

He rubbed the crown of her head, gentling her with his touch. "Rest now. We'll talk later."

It was almost noon when she woke.

Gabe had already packed most of her new clothing along with his. A black canvas suitcase stood ready at the door. The floral sundress and neon pink flip-flops had been left at the foot of the bed.

Hannah nodded towards the duffle, "Looks like you travel light."

Gabe turned away from the window and let the drapes close. The room was shrouded in shadows again.

"Hi, Sleepyhead. Did the sunlight wake you?"

She shrugged and scrubbed at her cheeks. "I dunno. Maybe. But it's okay." She stretched and considered returning his smile. Instead, she grabbed the dress and sprinted for the bathroom, pulling the door closed behind her.

Five, maybe ten minutes later, she emerged, smile in place.

"I'm very brave generally, only today I happen to have a headache."

Gabe squatted beside the duffle, unzipped it and juggled several small plastic vials.

"Here," he said, holding up a tiny bottle of a pale yellow-green liquid.

"Pardon?"

"It's peppermint oil for your headache. Put just a drop on your tongue. It'll help, I promise."

"I don't really have a headache," she grinned sheepishly. "It was a joke. A lame idea of an icebreaker. I was quoting Tweedledum; you know, Alice's buddy in Through the Looking Glass. Pretty lame, huh?"

Gabe stood just as Hannah took a step forward. His forehead collided with her kneecap. They steadied one another - her hands grabbing his arms, his hands cupping her elbows. Neither said a word; but Hannah was pretty certain that the air conditioner sparked at that same moment.

"Bad night, huh?" His fingertips strummed at her upper arms,

feather light touches that make every nerve in her body tingle.

Hannah curled her shoulders and crossed her arms over her

chest. She turned her back and took a step away. Gabe followed her,

rested his hands on her shoulders.

"I'm a good listener."

"I don't want to talk about it. It's over. Leave it be."

"How can you say that? Over? The work's just begin-

ning."

"Everything's destroyed."

"Do you know that?"

Hannah pursed her lips; squeezed her crossed arms

tighter. "I'm a realist."

"Okay then…have you called your insurance agent?"

"No."

"Have you called your relatives? They'll be worried."

"I don't have relatives. Gran died five years ago. It's only me...now." Hannah turned away from him and faced the bathroom door. She sniffed and dabbed her eyes when the first tears escaped.

Gabe whispered, "Let me help."

She spun around and was furious that her voice cracked when she spoke. "Why? Why would you want to help? What's in it for you?" Tears now ran down her cheeks unchecked.

"Because we're friends."

"Are we?"

"Aren't we?"

"I don't know. I haven't got much experience with friends."

"Hmm. Well then, take it from an expert. We're friends. And friends help friends."

She sat in the chintz chair. Pulling at a tangle in her hair, she asked, "What's in it for you?"

"I don't know what you mean."

"I mean, nobody does anything for nothing. What do you want from me?"

"Companionship. Friendship. Trust."

"I only trust what I can see."

"Yet you paint faeries."

"Hey, I don't have to trust 'em."

"But you believe?"

"I'd like to believe in the stories I heard as a child. In those stories, good and evil were easily identified."

Gabe crouched at her knees, balancing himself with a hand on each arm of her chair. She couldn't help feeling trapped!

"Who hurt you, Hannah Marie Everette?"

She expelled a long breath through her nose and shook her head. "Life. Life is hard and I'm tired of getting knocked down."

"If you get knocked, I'll keep you from falling."

"Promise?"

"Yes."

"Prove it."

"How?"

"Well, that's the puzzle, isn't it?"

Gabe stood. He stared at the ceiling for a few seconds, then he flexed his fingers and rubbed the knuckles of his left hand. He paced the length of the room twice before he spoke.

"Okay. Here's the deal. I'll help you tidy up your affairs here. Then, you come to stay with me for awhile."

Hannah started to stand. She was ready to speak; but he covered her mouth with his fingers.

"You can leave anytime you want."

"No strings?"

"Only one."

"I knew it."

"It's more of a thread than a string, really."

"Okay. Let's hear it."

"You'll stay with me. With me. In my house."

"In my own room?"

"I only have one bedroom."

"Uh huh. I see."

"Do you? You stayed in the same room with me last night. Did you feel compromised?"

"No, but…"

"Don't trust yourself, huh?" He arched an eyebrow and grinned.

"I don't trust you."

"I told you early on…I'm no angel…but I am honest."

She shook her head. Back and forth, back and forth.

"We'll play it a day at a time, if you want."

"Can I have that in writing?"

"Sure." He reached for the notepad next to the phone.

She felt light-headed; uncomfortably warm, but she shivered. She took two steps towards the door. Bolt! She knew she should run. But she wanted to stay.

"Scared?"

"No. Not exactly."

"Good. Consider it a challenge, then. I dare you to come stay with me. Say for a month. I'll bet you'll want to stay for-ever."

She stopped abruptly, as if she'd been zapped with a stun gun.

"Pretty confident aren't you?"

"Wishful. Just wishing and hoping."

Gabe stood up and Hannah backed away. He held his hands at shoulder-level, palms facing her.

51

"Easy. Easy." He sat on the edge of her bed. "It's your decision. I won't pressure you anymore. Your choice."

Hannah took one step, then stumbled. She sat beside him. The mattress creaked – a tiny muffled sound that seemed inordinately loud to her. Why did this man influence every one of her senses?

He brushed her knuckles with his fingers.

"I can help you…if you let me."

Hannah just shook her head.

"I want to be wrapped in cotton balls. I want to be protected; shielded from reality. I want to be coddled. But better yet, I'd like to be strong and unaffected. However I AM affected. I really don't have any idea what I should do." Hot tears ran unchecked. She covered her face with her hands and sobbed.

Gabe reached to take one of her hands in his. She doubted that either of them could speak at that moment.

Hannah dabbed her eyes with the corner of the sheet. "I must look a mess."

"Would you believe me if I told you that you look beautiful?"

"No." She almost grinned. "When do we leave?"

Gabe slapped his leg and stood. "Well, check-out time is one." He checked his watch. "We'll get you squared away here in Beaufort, then we'll head home."

"Home…"

"So, there must be lots to do this afternoon. Where to first?"

Hannah scraped her teeth over her lower lip. "Hmmm, to the bank, I guess. They'll give me money even if I don't have identification, won't they? I remember my account number."

"We'll manage."

The bank manager had heard about the fire on the morning news. He was sympathetic and very helpful. But, the insurance agent asked a thousand questions that Hannah considered pointless; a tedious exercise meant to drive her to the brink of insanity. She fled his office with both fists and her jaws clenched.

"Whoa!" Gabe touched her elbow and guided her to the crosswalk. Lord! She'd almost stepped in front of a truck!

"Sorry," she stammered. "I can't seem to get my thoughts running in a straight line. What did you say?"

"I asked where you want to go now?"

"I dunno." Hannah rolled her eyes and sucked on her knuckle. "At least I've got some cash." She thumped the crisp new denim backpack slung over her left shoulder. "Mr. Markham at the bank told me to call him when I get settled. He'll handle transferring my account."

"How 'bout the gallery that handles your work?"

"I called and told Miranda to hold onto any money from my sales. I'll send her my address later."

"You could give her my address."

"I'll call her later."

Although she hadn't meant to insult him, Hannah thought maybe he'd winced. But, good grief…she couldn't just up and move in with the man. What was he thinking? For crissakes, he was a total stranger. Almost, at least. Frankly, she was amazed she'd stayed in his hotel room last night. What

was she thinking? How could she just up and leave with him?

She didn't even know where he lived."

"Second thoughts?"

"Well..."

He gestured to a bench and sat. They stared past the

sailboats swaying at anchor in the harbor sheltered by the nar-

row spit of land, Shackleford Banks. Dampness in the breeze

promised rain. The tide was low and the marsh smelled salty,

fishy. Hannah sat on the opposite end of the bench. She

dropped the backpack at her feet, but then rearranged it, drap-

ing one strap over her knee. She pushed the cuticle of her left

thumb with the nail of her right.

"I've been thinking."

"So you are having second thoughts?"

Hannah tipped her head. "Maybe I'm reconsidering

what may have been a rash decision."

56

"Ah, I see."

"Do you?"

"No."

Hannah stood quickly and the denim bag crumpled at her feet. "That's my point!"

Gabe crossed his arms, stretched his legs out in front of him and pressed his shoulders against the bench. "What point is that?" He turned his head to wink at her.

"You don't see because you don't know me. You don't know anything about me and I certainly don't know a darned thing about you. We're strangers!"

"You know my name. You felt safe with me last night."

"Yeah, and I know you've got an angel's name but a face that would tempt the Virgin Mary. Other than the fact that you do a little gardening, that's about it."

"I can hear your angels humming at sunset."

"Yeah, well…" Hannah stood, kicking her bag under the bench.

"Hey, every relationship has to start with some common ground."

"True….Is that what we're creating here…a relationship?"

Gabe picked up her bag. He brushed away a grass clipping that stuck to the zipper. His fingers brushed hers when she reached for it. A soft contact, barely there; but the generated heat touched her core. Hannah's cheeks flushed and she stepped back, colliding with the bench. Gabe braced her so that she didn't fall. "Easy, there."

"Nothing in my life is easy right now."

"How about friends?"

"What about 'em?"

"Would you like to call a couple? Say goodbye?"

"Yeah. Do you have a couple I can borrow?" Hannah sat again. "Aside from the laughing gulls I feed every morning, I can't think of anyone who will even notice I'm gone. I'm pretty much a loner." She winced and shook her head quickly.

"Ever notice how *loner* and *loser* are spelled almost the same? I have. Loners have time to ponder quirky stuff like that."

Gabe pulled her to her feet. "How about your house? Let's go see if there anything left to recover."

"Sure. I'm already upset. Why not head straight into to-

tal abysmal depression?"

"Lead the way."

Even though the afternoon was muggy, it was pleasant

walking in the shade of the massive live oaks that lined her

neighborhood. Years ago, roots of those trees had buckled the

sidewalk's concrete squares and now moss grew in the cracks.

Hannah's rubber sandals slapped the spots of sunlight dappling

their path. A pair of butterflies flitted from impatiens to a

patch of marigolds. A light breeze carried the smell of fire,

tainting the perfume of saucer-sized magnolia blossoms.

Hannah covered her mouth and nose with her hand.

"Just follow your nose to my house." The lingering odor was

acrid, stinging her nostrils and eyes. It stank like melting rubber, like burned electrical cords, like the sulphur of fireworks, like burned trash.

"Lucky you were outside last night."

Two walls; one corner remained of her bungalow. The front door hung ajar, the wood above each of the broken windows was charred and a ragged portion of the roof clung to the bent gutter. The doormat was miraculously unscathed, still comically offering welcome. A mattress smoldered under a mound of debris that used to be the ceiling. Sooty, black water puddled on remnants of the pine floor.

"God. It's even worse than I'd imagined. There's nothing left. Nothing."

"Don't be so negative." Gabe prodded a piece of singed sheetrock with the toe of his boot. He pushed the soggy plaster aside and squatted like an archaeologist to examine his artifacts. "Look," he said, holding up a small silver picture frame.

He shook it to dislodge the shards of glass and held it out to Hannah.

"Oh," she gasped. "That's me and my parents. We were at Linville Caverns the summer I was eight." Her lips trembled, but she managed a brief smile.

"You were a cute kid. Very sparkly smile."

"It's the sun reflecting on my braces!"

She dropped the picture frame into her backpack. It clinked against her new possessions – hairbrush, deodorant and wallet.

"Hey now, this is amazing." Gabe stood in her cremated bedroom. He lifted the lid from an enameled box. In the quiet aftermath of destruction, the tinny *plink, plink, plink* of her music box rang out like a pipe organ. *When you wish upon a star, makes no difference who you are. Anything your heart desires will come to you.*

Hannah snatched the box from Gabe and turned her back to him. She hugged the box to her breast.

She touched the blistered glaze on the lid as if it were a sacred relic, turning the box over twice. "A memento from Disney World the summer I was twelve," she mumbled. "Our last vacation together."

On the top, Jiminy Cricket was still visible although discolored. But, the underside was still bright orange. Inside the box, everything was intact – three mismatched white buttons, a brass button from a winter coat she'd discarded years ago, seven straight pins, a spool of black thread that had a needle stuck in it and a picture of a girl with curly pig-tails spinning in a big tea cup with a laughing man in sunglasses. Sniffing back tears, Hannah snapped the lid on the box and slipped it into the bag, too.

"Walk carefully here," Gabe reminded her when glass crunched underfoot.

When the bedroom wall had crumpled, it had fallen across her dresser. Hannah discovered some of the clothes inside to be usable although they reeked of smoke. She stuffed a nightgown, several pairs of underwear, two bras, a couple of pairs of socks and a sweatshirt into her bag. Her gingham purse was ruined. Her wallet was scorched, the leather fell apart like dry leaves. Surprisingly, her driver's license was fine, though. The lamination was singed and curled at one corner; but she could still use it for identification.

They found a cast iron skillet and two copper saucepans in the rubble that used to be her kitchen.

"I don't suppose it makes sense to lug cookware all the way to your house, does it?"

"So you've decided to go?"

"There's nothing left for me here." She searched the debris, hoping to locate some invaluable piece of herself.

"I can offer a new beginning," Gabe said.

"That's something, I guess."

"So, you're ready to go?"

She couldn't honestly say she was ready. Her life had

been shattered. It lay in smoldering bits at her feet.

"Lead on."

Gabe lifted the suitcase in his left hand and took her

hand in his right. It was close to six-thirty when they started

walking towards the setting sun, into the expanding vista of

golden light. Hannah was pleased that he paced his strides to

match her shorter steps. She would need some time to organize

her thoughts.

She worried that she was losing her tenuous grip on

reality, though. She'd taken about seventy paces, when she re-

alized she was lost. Almost magically, they were walking

through warm beams of bright noontime sunshine.

"Where are we? I don't recognize this place." They

were thigh-deep in sea of tall green grasses awash with bright

yellow and orange poppies. She swiveled her head left and

right. She thought she saw a couple of tiny figures dart off

ahead of them.

"What are children doing out here alone?" she mum-

bled.

"Pardon?"

She shaded her eyes against the bright sun and scanned

the area again. No sign of the children. Actually, the figures

she'd seen –or thought she'd seen – had been awfully small. A

child that size would have been too young to toddle, much less

run. She massaged her temples. "Must be getting dizzy in this

heat."

She heard a high-pitched nattering sound; a twittering

giggle. She was sure of it! There they were again! Tiny peo-

ple dressed in unusual outfits peeked through the screen of tall grasses. She saw creatures who had enormous slanted eyes and tapered ears that rose to a point, like the Vulcans on <u>Star Trek</u>.

Hannah pointed to what was now a vacant spot.

"What's going on here?"

"What do you mean?"

"Who was that?"

"Who?"

"That." She jabbed her finger towards another empty space. "Didn't you see them?"

"Who?"

"The little fellows… dressed in brown. You saw them…right?"

"Yes."

"Good."

"But you saw them, Hannah. That's the important part."

"It is?"

"Do you believe what you saw?"

"I dunno. What was it I saw?"

"Sprites. Some people call them pixies."

"Oh, god. I've entered the Twilight Zone."

Gabe draped his long arm across her shoulders and chuckled. He's tall; her head fit comfortably against his collarbone. He smoothed some errant strands of curly hair away from her eyes.

"Your hands are strong; but you've a gentle touch," Hannah whispered. But she neglected to mention that she was fascinated by those entrancing gray eyes.

He squeezed her right shoulder and smiled, asking, "Are you frightened then?"

She shook her head. "No. I don't remember any child-

hood stories of sprites committing mayhem."

"No, they're actually hard-working although they do en-

joy a good laugh now and then. Mostly harmless stuff."

Hannah took a deep breath and let it go in a slow,

smooth stream. Her heart was thumping away, beating a mile a

minute. She squinted up at the sun, high in the sky rather than

setting as it should have been.

"I can identify with how good ole Alice felt when she

tumbled into Wonderland."

Gabe pointed over her left shoulder, to the horizon be-

hind her.

"Do you want to go back? I did promise you could

leave anytime you want."

She crossed her arms, each hand covered the opposite

shoulder. She rubbed her lips against a wrist. "Hmm. To be

honest, I don't know." She took a couple of steps forward, and then a few more. "Let's just hope that curiosity doesn't kill this particular cat."

"That's the spirit!"

"Meow."

They walked for another five or six minutes. Hannah continued to watch for the pixies; but even though she was certain that she heard them, she didn't see them again. She hadn't lied to Gabe. She wasn't really scared; but she was wary. Every twig that snapped underfoot startled her.

A shrill voice called, "I'd be over here!"

Hannah squealed. She dropped her backpack and stumbled. Gabe caught her elbow so that she didn't fall. She gnawed her lower lip while Gabe made formal introductions. Trog was an engaging pint-sized man whose lilting voice sounded as if he had swallowed helium from a child's balloon.

He looked rusty! His skin was tanned and dry. The wrinkles around his eyes were dark, as if filled with dust. His cheeks were stained; windburn, she assumed. Hannah figured he'd had bright orange hair as a child. Now, it was the color of a tarnished penny, surrounding his head in a frizzy copper halo. His wide smile revealed that he could have benefited from good dentistry. Several of his teeth were missing!

Trog jerked her wrist, tugging her to plop beside him on the cushion of matted grass. When she was seated and he stood alongside, they were eye-to-eye. He taught her to extend her arm in the palm-up greeting accepted by the Faeries, showing that she carried neither hidden weapons nor magic.

"Kind of a secret faerie handshake, then?" she asked.

"Something like that," Gabe answered.

Together the three of them walked through the huge field, although she never saw a path. The two men seemed able to navigate unerringly without a trail or map. They never erred although the sun set, plunging them straight from afternoon sunshine into darkness. They approached a forest. Tall, massive elms and oaks had sturdy limbs dropping low. Hannah heard giggling voices that reminded her of squirrels chattering with happy noise.

"So…here we are," Gabe said. "We've arrived."

They'd arrived…but, where were they? What a queer place! Trees as tall as buildings, trees with branches as stout as trunks, trees decorated with tiny sparkles blinking high above her. Granted, the night was dark, but there were patches of light. Off to the left, she could see dim yellow flickers, low to the ground, in three or four different clusters. Lanterns dangled from branches overhead, bouncing in the freshening breeze. More lamps were stuck on a line of short poles, the size of rulers, to make a miniature runway lit with torches. The flames throbbed and shadows dodged. At another time, Hannah might have thought it all quite charming; but that particular night, it was eerie.

She squinted into the darkness, trying to discern the figures that hovered in the mobile shadows. Whispered voices failed to sound human.

"Who is she?"

"I dunno. Must be okay, though. She came with Trog."

"Think she's part pixie?"

"Hmmm…naw. Never saw a freckled pixie. Elfin,

maybe."

"I'm thinking those look like pixie eyes."

"Pointless ears, though."

"Would ya be thinking elfin, then?"

"Nope. Feet are too small."

"Where do you reckon he found her?"

"Awk! There's Gabe. Guess she came with him."

"Mebbe."

"Do you think she's the one?"

"Nice hair."

"Odd shoes."

Hannah turned to Gabe. "All I need now is Toto," she

mumbled under her breath. Both men chuckled.

Gabe nuzzled close to her ear. "There's someone I

want you to meet, Hannah."

Innocent words, but his breath on her neck was flamma-

ble. She felt a flush wander from her neck to her forehead.

What was his power? How had he coerced her to come so far

from her home? Of course, her home had been incinerated.

Hannah blinked and nodded. "Okay."

He touched the small of her back and effortlessly pro-

pelled her to what appeared to be a grassy park. They stood

roughly in the center of a semi circle of massive oaks. At the

base of each tree, camouflaged by clumps of bright green moss

or layers of dry leaves, she could spy miniscule lights, glowing

amber at the entrances of hundreds of homes; little houses no bigger than her fist. Tiny creatures chattered as they flittered above the ground, hovering over mushrooms or acorns.

Trog nudged her shoulder. "Go ahead, Girl. You'll fit right in."

It's like a teeny tiny commune, she decided. "I read...I heard... One book mentioned that primroses can make the invisible, visible. The author said that eating primroses is a sure fire way to see faeries."

Trog did a poor job of hiding his grin. Gabe caught his lower lip with his teeth. His eyes laughed, though.

"Hogwash, right?" Hannah ventured.

"Not necessarily so." Gabe touched her nose with one finger and sent hot chills running through her body. "What do you believe?"

"I've never really thought of faeries living in houses,"

she mumbled more to herself than to anyone else.

She knelt on the springy mat of moss to examine a house well concealed under the hanging branches of a willow. Using both hands she spread the leafy curtain. Deep in the shadows near the gnarled trunk was a dwelling made of bark, roofed with a rectangle of sod. Parallel rows of acorns lined a miniature walkway to a bright green door. Windows were thrown open on all sides of the house and dainty lace curtains billowed. She smelled a fire, and noticed the thinnest stream of smoke rising from a mud chimney.

Other homes were nestled into an embankment, barely discernible except for the gaily-painted doors and windows. She noticed cultivated squares of land. Gardens. There were also shops. She smelled fresh bread and cakes. Metallic pings emanated from what she assumed was the fabled elfin gold-smith's shop. She shook her head, incredulous.

"Amazing," she whispered. "Absolutely beyond my fondest imagination."

She turned to Gabe. "I thought faerieland was protected by a gate with a secret portal." She glanced over her shoulder, crouching under the low-hanging limbs. "Doesn't a person have to hold a bouquet of primroses and touch a faerie rock? Gram warned me that a person must follow special protocol or chance being plunged through the door of doom, rather than the gate of faerieland."

Gabe smiled and nodded. "I've heard that tale myself."

"So, it's not true, then?"

"Now I didn't say that, did I?"

"What? Is it the faerie way to speak in riddles? Like leuprechauns?"

"There are many ways to enter the land of the faerie."

He held out his hand to her. "One way is to be invited."

Tiny winged faeries swirled in circles at her head, frequently dipping low near her ear or eyes, or hovering at her shoulders. Elves, who stood knee-high to squirrels, clapped and capered in an organized swarm around them. Their cartwheels and back handsprings hinted of a carnival atmosphere.

Gabe urged her forward; but Hannah turned to him and whispered, "Won't I step on someone? At five foot-one, I've never felt like a giant before!"

"You'll be fine," he encouraged.

"But…"

"Just believe, Girl. Just believe," Trog assured her.

There was no mist of magician's smoke, no tinkling bells, not even an 'abracadabra'. But suddenly, she did fit!

She'd have to stoop, but she could enter those tiny little houses.

The faeries could light on the palm of her hand; but now the elves were thigh-high and the pixies were only slightly smaller.

"Have we shrunk, or did the miniature village grow?" she asked as she dodged elfin children dancing near her feet.

Trog cleared his throat and rolled his eyes. "It just IS, Girl. Don't try to figure out faerie magic. Just accept that it IS."

Gabe pushed her towards a wizened woman whose small stature was further inhibited by her hunched shoulders and curved spine.

"Hannah, this is Ella."

Ella walked with a slow, bobbling gait. She was huddled in the folds of a large hooded cloak, made of thick black velvet with red satin lining.

"What's going on here?" Hannah demanded in a loud whisper.

"What?"

He told me he was no angel; I should have been ready for tricks, she decided.

"Trog and Ella…they were in Beaufort…at the diner, weren't they?"

"Hmmm, maybe you're right."

"And how did everything get big all of a sudden?"

"Nothing's changed except your perceptions."

Hannah rubbed her temples, trying to ease the throbbing headache that was building.

Sidling close, Ella stood on tiptoe to stroke the partially unbound braid where it dangled near Hannah's waist.

The old woman might have used the same technique to calm a frightened child. It worked. Hannah's shoulders sagged a bit as they relaxed.

"Thank you for the welcome," Hannah said because it seemed that Ella held a matriarchal position in the group.

The woman's skin felt like soft chamois when she slipped her hand into Hannah's.

"You remind me of my Gram."

"Do you miss her?"

"Yes. I loved her."

"We'll get on well, I'm thinking," Ella said with a wink. Hers was a soothing voice, a voice that could have belonged to Hannah's Irish grandmother.

She patted Hannah's back. "Come with me, then. It's a bath and a bed you'll be needing." She turned, ready to lead the way.

"She'll be staying with me."

Although spoken quietly, Gabe's words defied objections. Ella curtly nodded, a glimmer of a smile crinkled her lips, and she backed away.

"So you say, Gabriel?"

His fingers touched Hannah's, snaring one, then another, until he'd captured her whole hand. "She did agree."

Ella arched one brow and looked to Hannah.

"I did agree."

Gabe guided her through the crowd of curious spectators who had now emerged into the light. Hannah tugged on his hand. He stopped. While one child tickled his brother's nose with Hannah's braid, three toddlers lifted the hem of her skirt, inspecting her legs and the silly plastic sandals on her feet.

"Were they waiting for …us…me, I mean?"

"Umm, well, as a matter of fact…," he stammered.

Ella bustled towards them, elbowing her path through the throng. "Gabriel! Can't you see the poor girl is nigh on to exhaustion? Be off with you. Go now, off with you!" Ella dismissed them with a flick of her wrists.

So they were off to Gabe's cottage, that had two doors; one front, one back. The back door opened onto a garden cut into the hillock that curved around the northern perimeter of the commune…? …village?

"What do you call this place? Is it a commune or a village or a hamlet or what?"

"Home. We call it home."

Gabe had designed his house carefully. There were several large windows to provide wonderful sunlight and good cross ventilation for the three rooms. Amazingly enough, the layout reminded Hannah of her own bungalow, now deceased.

"You can set up an easel here," Gabe said gesturing to a corner where a massive chair and ottoman were surrounded by large windows. "The light is perfect."

"Are all of the other people here, are they faeries?"

"No. Actually elves, faeries and sprites all live here in the Village."

"Are we the only humans?"

"Something like that."

Her nostrils twitched with the pleasant odors of the herbs suspended from the arched ceiling.

"I recognize the rosemary…and a hint of spearmint.

And something exotic; curry, maybe?"

"Umm hmm…and cardamom and nutmeg."

"Interesting place." She dropped her denim backpack

on the floor and spun in a lethargic circle. She collided with

his chest. He trembled at her touch, and she shivered. Tiny

rippling spasms thrilled from her fingers, up her arms, and

through her breasts.

"Uhh ohh," she stammered. Giggling nervously, she

tried to step away.

"Why not?" His hand settled at the small of her back.

When he moved his fingers, delicious sensations fluttered up

her spine.

"I have no idea. It just seems…I dunno…hmmm, like a

bad idea. I'm too unsteady. I'm not ready to make any deci-

sions. I, we,… you,… I can't…"

"Shhh." Gabe touched Hannah's cheek. She tilted her head to lean into the touch, and then she lifted a shoulder to trap his hand against her hot cheek. God, was she feverish?

A low growl emanated from deep in his throat; a soft rumbling, purring sound that pleased her for some reason. He swiped his thumb across her lips. He rubbed his cheek against hers.

Oh, yes. Cheek-to-cheek is good.

Hannah's knees turned to gelatin, her eyelids drifted closed. She purred a bit herself. Was she in a trance? She allowed him to lead her to a soft bed piled with colorful pillows and a brown corduroy coverlet. He stroked her hair and pushed her shoulders back onto the bed.

After unzipping and removing her parka, he turned to leave.

"Are you serious?" she asked.

"Very." Then he took another slow step towards the door.

"No!" she whimpered. "Don't leave me."

He turned to speak over his shoulder.

"Never," he swore. Then he left the room and she

thought the light seemed diminished in his absence.

Obviously she'd been exhausted because when she

woke, dawn tinted the room with subdued yellows. She

stretched to sit up, blinking and rubbing her eyes.

Hannah heard a soft, deliberate movement and she

turned. Gabe was lounging on the floor nearby, a dark blue ter-

rycloth robe loosely belted at his waist. Michelangelo's "Da-

vid" could not have commanded more of her attention than

Gabe did. He was long and sleek and powerful; exquisite and

graceful like a jaguar. Even at rest, he dominated the small

room.

"Your eyes are hypnotic." Her words were little more

than a rough whisper that cracked and broke into ragged

breaths.

She licked her lips, hoping that he would touch her.

Where did that thought originate?

He stood and reached out to her, fingers hovering a couple of inches above her wrist.

"I've been watching you sleep. Here you are - willingly in my home, in my bed, and I'm afraid you're going to leave."

"That particular thought has not even crossed my mind."

"Good. Forget I suggested it."

Hannah squeezed his hand. Then, she slid her hand into his sleeve. But, she quickly withdrew her fingers as though she'd tested a hot iron. His skin was smooth and warm. And she flared like kindling at the contact.

"I'm trapped in a waking dream. I can't even predict my own actions. I'm behaving completely unlike the person I've always been."

"Maybe you've always acted like someone else."

"Yeah, well. Maybe." Hannah scrubbed her palms over her face, pressed her fingers into her eye sockets. "Something's bothering me."

"What?"

"You didn't cause it, did you? The fire? The lightning?"

"I want to make the earth shudder under your feet, Hannah; but I can't control the weather."

"Good."

"Good?"

"Yes. Knowing that makes me feel better somehow. I'm still not in control; but then, neither are you!" She giggled and he shook his head.

Holding her arm, Gabe tugged Hannah towards him. He positioned each of her arms around his waist, and she rested her palms against his back. He laid his hand on her head urging it against his chest, just at his heart. She heard the steady pulse. Her own heart skipped and then surged to a staccato beat when he loosened her long braid and massaged her scalp, twisting the curling tendrils around his fingers. They stood together, loosely tethered. Words seemed superfluous.

Her stomach growled. Twice.

"Hungry?"

"Would you believe me if I told you no?"

"I'd believe whatever you told me, Hannah."

Oh Lord! This man could be trouble. He was probably a heartbreak waiting to happen. There had to be a catch. There was always a catch.

"I find this - you and me - very arousing, but terribly confusing," she blurted. "You make it difficult for me to remember to breathe."

She stepped away from him. Crossed her arms over her chest and rubbed her palms up and down her arms.

Gabe grinned and flicked his thumb under her chin.

"Breakfast on the back porch okay with you?"

"Lead the way."

Gabe pared a juicy mango, and offered her a slice.

Hannah hesitated before accepting the fruit. She held the mango slice over her plate and watched the juice splat into a little puddle.

"If I eat something, I'll be trapped here… in this faerie raft, won't I?"

Gabe chuckled. "You really have listened to a lot of faerie tales, haven't you?"

Hannah shrugged.

"Didn't I say that you could leave anytime you want?"

"Yes."

"Well, I won't starve you in the meantime! Eat."

He leaned close, watching her bite the fruit and lick the sticky juice from her fingers. He took her hand in his, spreading her fingers wide apart. Slowly, seductively he drew each finger into his mouth, rolling his tongue around it in a gentle caress.

She was mesmerized by those hypnotic eyes of his. For a second, she thought about looking away. But she'd always won the stare-down contests as a kid. He won't have a chance, she figured. Eyes wide, she propped her elbows on the table and settled in for the contest. Green eyes glared into unblinking gray eyes. Seconds clicked by; one minute, then two. Her nose itched. Her mouth was dry. Gabe smiled, arched his left brow. She squirmed in her seat; her palms were damp.

Gabe made that rumbling, growling noise deep in his throat. Hannah was molten lava; she slumped against cushion of her chair. Her cheeks smoldered. Her blood was warm bubbling syrup. She sighed, or perhaps she moaned.

"You don't play fair. I think I might just faint."

He used the pad of his thumb to catch a droplet of mango nectar just under her bottom lip.

"I told you I'm no angel."

"I'm not a pushover. This place – and you, of course- all of this is an incredible package." She pulled a bit of the soft center from her bagel and rolled little bread balls. "Relationships make me nervous. I'm not in the market for a man. Even if I were, this set-up might be a bit much…" She waved her arms, encompassing the general area around her.

"I'm looking," Gabe answered.

"You?"

"Well, at least, I was."

Hannah's eyes crossed and she smacked her head with the butt of her right palm. She collapsed against the whicker chair. "Great. You went to Beaufort and you came home with a girl from a fire sale!"

"I came home with the perfect woman."

"Good comeback." She pushed away from the table and stood. "Thanks for the breakfast. I'm outta here."

Gabe leaped up, overturning his chair. He skidded to a stop, catching Hannah just as she settled her denim bag on her shoulder. He grabbed her arm and she thrust three twenty-dollar bills in his hand.

"Whoa!"

"That cover what I owe you?"

Gabe looked at the money and let it drop to the floor.

"You don't owe me anything."

"Whatever."

Although he tried to hold her arm, Hannah pulled away from him.

"Wait. You didn't finish breakfast. You didn't even give me a chance to show you around. You didn't give me a chance…"

"To do what?"

"To be a friend. To help you." Gabe edged a 'baby step' closer. She took a 'giant step' backwards.

"Back off."

He stepped away, hands held over his head. "Okay, okay. But I dare you to stay with me for another two days."

"Two days? You crazy? A few hours have me…"

"Have you what?"

"Questioning my own sanity."

"So you're scared to stay? Is that it? We're friends, Hannah."

"Not scared; not really. Confused." She nibbled at a hangnail on her thumb. "It's not like I have anywhere to go, though. And you've already found out that I can't resist a challenge," Hannah answered with a smile. "But there will be ground rules."

"Okay." Gabe replied with a wide grin.

"No more pressure. I'm not going to crawl into bed with you."

"Where will you sleep, then?"

Hannah tipped her head, pursed her lips. "Hmm. Good question." She glanced around the three-room house. "There." She pointed to the corner, to the overstuffed chair and ottoman. Several spots of the charcoal gray fabric had been bleached by the sunlight that streamed through the floor-to-ceiling windows.

"If that's what you want."

She wasn't certain when he'd inched beside her again. How could such a large man move so quietly? How tall was he anyway? When he stood this close, the top of her head fit right under his arm. Darn it! He touched her hand and the sensation spread up her arm and to her head. Even her hair follicles tingled! She jammed both hands into the pockets of her light-weight parka.

"I don't want you to touch me."

"I don't believe you; but I'll go along with you…for now."

"Then what's that big grin all about?"

"I like a good challenge, too."

Hannah plopped down amid the needlepoint pillows piled on the mocha-colored velveteen sofa. She faced a stone fireplace that boasted a mantle made from a rough hewn log. The mantel was cluttered. Two bright blue bottles stood on top of several books stacked haphazardly. Slips of paper with curling edges protruded from some of the books. A coffee mug held slightly drooping daisies. A fistful of spearmint was rooting in the rather cloudy water that remained in a small mason jar.

At the far end of the mantel was a photograph of a young couple, smiling into bright sunlight, shadowed craggy mountains in the distance behind them. The man wore a white shirt, sleeves rolled over muscled biceps. His hair, ruffled by a breeze, glinted red in the sunlight. One arm anchored a slender woman at his side; her head was almost level with the tip of his ear lobe. She was dressed in a gauzy white blouse and a full skirt that the wind had lifted. Just a bit of one calf was exposed. The breeze had caught her long hair so that it swirled like blue-black pennants around her face.

"Tell me something about yourself. Who are they?" Hannah nodded in the direction of the photograph. "Your parents?"

"Yes. Sean and Caillie."

"You took a bit from each of them, didn't you?"

Gabe chuckled. "Guess I did. My mother was a small, delicate woman – just a bit larger than your size, I suppose."

97

He swiped his fingers through his hair. "Although I got my father's height and shoulders, the dark hair is definitely from my mom."

"And the eyes. Look at those eyes! Those are her long lashes and mysterious eyes."

"She was beautiful inside and out."

"Was?"

"She died when I was boy."

"I'm sorry." Hannah put her fingers on his hand. "Your dad?"

"Da lives in Scotland."

"Scotland? Guess you don't see him often."

"We keep in touch. I visit several times a year."

"Lots of frequent flyer points, yeah?"

"Pardon?"

"Never mind."

It probably only lasted for three seconds, but to Hannah, the silence was eternal. She exhaled and the sound of her expelled breath was staggering. She cleared her throat expecting the glasses in the cupboard to rattle. Think of something to say, for crying out loud. Think, Hannah!

"You do needlepoint in your spare time?"

Gabe's eyebrows arched and he grinned. He re-arranged a pillow at his back. "Needlepoint? Me?"

Lame, Hannah. Really lame.

"No. Actually Ella made them for me. She thought my house could use a woman's touch."

"Ahh."

"I'm not sure I needed quite so many pillows; but she's a difficult woman to contradict."

"Ahh."

"What'd you do there?"

Hannah pointed to a long table, built along one entire wall. Two shelves above it were lined with clear plastic boxes and colored glass bottles.

Gabe stood and held out his hand. "I'll show you."

He stood behind her while Hannah investigated. She laid her palms flat on the tabletop, rubbed wide circles on the cool marble. Her fingertips flitted over the mortar and pestle. She aligned the two Bunsen burners. She opened several boxes and smelled the dried herbs inside. Cinnamon and cloves, garlic, ginger, vanilla and pine needles. She uncorked a pale green bottle and sniffed it. Her eyes crossed and she quickly plugged the bottle again. He retrieved the bottle and replaced it on the shelf.

"Blue gum eucalyptus," he said. "Smells like camphor, doesn't it?"

Hannah rubbed her nose. "Yes. It's awful! What's it do?"

"It's great for treating bronchitis or croup."

"Like Vick's Vapo-rub?"

"Exactly. Good for aching joints, too."

Hannah snapped her fingers. "Your own version of Ben Gay!"

Maybe they didn't hear her arrive because they were laughing. Maybe secrecy was just the way of the faeries. But, Hannah was startled when Ella called out.

"Are you ready?"

Hannah flattened her hand over her heart, felt the wild thumping beat subside to a normal *the-thump, the-thump, the-thump*. She turned and tried to smile.

"Ready for what, Ella?"

Ella twirled around, started out the door and called over her shoulder.

"C'mon then. Everyone's waiting!"

Just like the Cheshire Cat, Hannah thought as she followed the waddling elf outside. Grins and riddles rather than real answers.

When Hannah blinked in the bright sunlight, hundreds of hands clapped. The entire population of the Faerie Village must be standing in the park she figured. Cheering voices chanted her name

"Han-nah. Han-nah. Han-nah." The shrill voices got louder; the chant, faster when Gabe stood at her back. "Han-nah. Han-nah. Han-nah. Han-nah."

She waved and hoped that her lips were stretched into a grin rather than a grimace. The boisterous welcome was intimidating. Because her hand was shaking, she clutched her fingers into a fist at her side, wadding her dress into a mass of wrinkles.

Then, someone touched her elbow. Warm fingers covered hers. Gabe was at her side. For the briefest moment, he touched his lips to the top of her head. Amazingly, she calmed.

Sunshine glittered all around her, as if she were on stage in a spotlight. Her cotton sundress sparkled; it was practically iridescent. Elfin magic, she decided. Her toes tingled. She wiggled her toes, not really surprised to find that her vinyl flip-flops were now studded with rhinestones. We're quite a contrast, she thought. Gabe, somber and mysterious -dressed all in black- and me shimmering with elfin magic!

Hannah slipped her hand into his. "Magic." She wasn't certain she'd spoken out loud.

"You're magic," Gabe whispered. "You do something to me. Is my hair standing on end?"

His voice was velvet: deep, thick and luxurious. It made her feel beautiful. Her voice sounded timid in comparison; maybe like gingham.

"I'm no authority on faeries; but is this unusual behavior?"

"It's not difficult to rouse the faeries to a party. Something as simple as daybreak or a beautiful sunset can be cause for a celebration."

The woods reverberated with exuberant cheers. Hannah and Gabe were swept into a whirlwind of faeries. The crowd moved as one huge undulating mass towards the pavilion at the village square.

Hannah threw both arms into the air, waving them in the air. "Whoa! Wait a minute!" Noise subsided to a gentle murmur, the progression stopped.

She stepped to the side of the path. Crooking her finger, she beckoned Gabe. "I think we should have a word... in private."

He shrugged his shoulders, and turned his hands, palm up. "Okay."

Hannah's green eyes flamed. "Do you think me dim-witted?"

"No. What makes you think so?"

She shook a finger at him. "Then am I being Shanghai-ed?"

"Pardon?"

"I am at a distinct disadvantage because you, Trog, Ella; all of the elves and faeries, are privy to the agenda of the day, but I'm not!"

"Ahhh. Then let me explain. We're celebrating."

"What?"

"You. Me. Us."

"There is no *us*."

His head rocked side to side, very, very slowly.

"Giving up so soon?"

She crossed her arms under her breasts. Shoulders rigid; neck stiff.

He touched her elbow again. He leaned close and whispered just above her ear. "The decision is yours. Go. Stay. You decide."

Hannah tapped her lips with her fist.

"You laid out the rules. It's your call."

Two tiny winged creatures danced a ballet overhead, sprinkling Hannah's head and shoulders with a film of gold dust. The bells on their shoes pinged like windchimes.

"Seems a shame to spoil the party." She smiled. Gabe winked.

Trog had maintained a quasi-discreet distance from the couple, watching them closely. Now he pivoted to the throng assembled around the square. Both thumbs were raised and he grinned like a Jack-o-Lantern.

Raucous cheers thundered. "Han-nah, Han-nah!"

Strange lilting music drifted over the hubbub.

Giggling nervously, Hannah quipped, "This scene gives the term 'swept off my feet' a totally new perspective!"

Squeezing her hand gently, Gabe answered quietly, "Everything will be right. I promise."

A series of tiny tittering ladies presented themselves to Hannah. Each curtsied and then spoke her name in a squirrel-like chatter. Hannah nodded, trying to concentrate, although she feared she'd neither recall nor be able to pronounce many of their names.

"I'm Nowatil, the seamstress."

"No-waddle," Hannah repeated.

Others sniggered as a plump elf with hair the color of cotton candy bobbled front and center. Hannah thought that the polka-dot dress she wore would have been better suited for someone younger, more sylphlike. Nowatil wore four large rings – gaudy stones set in tarnished metal. She proudly presented Hannah with a package wrapped in pink tissue paper and tied with a satin ribbon the color of ripe cherries.

"Open it, Girl. We're all waiting!"

"Hurry, hurry," echoed the throng of villagers.

Nowatil reached for the package and ripped open one edge. "Open it, Girl!" Paper and ribbon fell to the ground at Hannah's feet.

"Oh my…Oh my gosh! I've never seen such a lovely dress!"

Hannah held the diaphanous creation to her shoulders. Layer upon layer of sheerest gauze swirled around her ankles.

The gossamer material was opalescent, neither lavender nor blue, but a wonderful compromise of the two.

"It's magic… it's beautiful. Thank you ….um…Thank you so much."

"Say *No Way Til*, dear. Emphasis on the *Way*."

"Thank you, Nowatil." Hannah clutched the dress to her waist and spun once.

"I'm proud of the cloth." Ella elbowed her path through the crowd. "There's an art to weaving faerie dust, you know."

"Why no, I've never considered…You MADE this cloth? With faerie dust?"

"Nothing else would shimmer the same way, now would it?"

Ella brushed at Hannah's shoulder, scattering golden powder.

"I don't suppose so." Hannah rubbed the soft cloth to her cheek. "How did you make it? With magic?"

"Magic. Well, that's easy, now isn't it? Just a snap of the fingers, don't you know?" Ella rocked back on her heels and popped her fingertips together, scattering yet another glittering dust that smelled like cloves. "But, some things are best done with hard work and a good loom."

Several dogs barked. A cat hissed. A blond toddler whined at his mother's knee and a baby cried somewhere in the crowd. The elfin mothers gathered children for breakfast. Musicians tuned instruments, adding strains of discordant harmony to the mix of confusing sounds.

Ella patted Hannah's hand. "Take your time; but don't take too long. Food waits for no man here with the faeries!"

Hannah nodded. "Be right there."

She turned to Gabe, who was leaning against the bandstand rail.

"You look pleased with yourself."

"No, I'm pleased with you."

Hannah spread her arms wide. "This place is amazing!"

"Yep."

"Oh, learning about the faeries is going to be fascinating!" She shook her head, spraying him with faerie dust that had stuck to her hair. "I can't wait to meet everyone. It'll be such an adventure!"

"Whoa, there, Girl!" he coached. "There are a few rules."

"More strings?"

"Maybe a couple...but we both dance to these puppet strings; you and I. The faeries operate under a curious code. Humans need to be cautious and respectful in their realm."

Hands on her hips. "Well naturally." What made him think she needed etiquette lessons?

"No, this is serious," he continued. "No matter their size or character, all faeries have enormous power." Gabe spread his hands in a circle, pantomiming a globe drawn in the air. "Elves, faeries, sprites and lots of other species live together in a faerie raft. Almost all of them are mischievous. Most are kind; but never forget that a few are cruel. Very cruel. Here's the catch. No matter how the faeries behave, they expect only the best behavior from humans."

110

"A double standard, huh?"

"Faeries prefer cheerful, generous humans, especially lovers."

Hannah stuck her chin in the air. "I'm a good person."

"Of course, you are," Gabe soothed. "Be mindful, though, that a faerie can use either crippling pain to punish or amazing good luck to reward."

"Got it." She smoothed the soft opalescent material, folding her magical elfin dress to make a tidy parcel.

Gabe snapped his fingers. "Oh yeah. Don't get your feelings hurt if someone neglects to say 'thank you.' Faeries don't always recognize emotions, so they may not necessarily acknowledge you. It's all whimsy."

"Okay." She shrugged her shoulders. "Be sort of like dealing with young kids. You know…they remember their manners one minute and forget them the next."

"This last bit is very important," he said, tapping her nose. Her eyes crossed as she followed his finger. "Some fae-ries are unquestionably selfish and evil. No amount of human compassion could ever alter their character. Not ever."

"Sounds like you've got someone specific in mind."

"Just remember what I said."

Hannah threw her hands up in surrender. "Okay. Okay."

Gabe rubbed the gauzy material of her new dress between his thumb and middle finger. "Pretty. The color suits you."

"So, Ella makes the fabric and Nowatil sews. Is it like a commune? Everyone does a bit of the work. Everyone shares."

"Pretty much. We have bakers, woodworkers, farmers, weavers; all we need for life. You'll find your own place quickly."

"What's your contribution?"

"I use herbs, logic and a bit of first aid to help."

"Well, it's obvious you live here in the faerie raft, but you don't appear to be a faerie. Are you?"

"No, I'm not."

"Will you tell me about yourself, then?" she asked.

"That depends," he said. "What do you want to know?"

"Well, I do have questions that nag for answers. Why are you one of those rare humans chosen to live among the Faeries?"

His hypnotic gray eyes seemed to probe her brain. "What do you think?" he asked rhetorically.

"I think you're not answering my question."

He asked a question of his own. "The faeries allowed you to enter the village, didn't they?" She nodded. "Ella even invited you to her home, didn't she?"

Hannah caught her bottom lip between her teeth, considering. She nodded quickly and shrugged her shoulders. "Yes, I guess so."

"See. It's not unheard of. Not so rare after all."

"So, how did you come here?"

"Ella brought me here when I was eight years old."

"Wow, so young."

"My mother had died and my father wasn't able to deal with his grief. Ella's my godmother."

"A true faerie godmother, then?"

"Umm hmm." Gabe gnawed on his knuckle, watched as Hannah paced three steps away and marched back again.

She was pretty sure that he'd hypnotized her. That's why he affected her so strangely. Why else would she be so susceptible to his ridiculous suggestions? Maybe he was a psychic – gave her some subliminal suggestion. Why would a sane woman believe that she was surrounded by a band of frolicking faeries?

"No tricks, remember? I told you I'm honest. "

She jumped. "Can you, then? Can you read my mind? Can you steal my private thoughts?"

"No," he chuckled, "I can't read your mind. You have an expressive face. Most of your thoughts are written there!" He tweeked her nose and she swatted at his fingers.

"I do feel like Alice in Wonderland, suddenly thrown into a world where nothing is quite what it seems."

"Does that make Trog the White Rabbit? Or maybe the Cheshire Cat?"

She chewed her bottom lip. She picked at a hangnail. "No, Ella's the Cheshire Cat."

He tipped his head to the side, scrunched up his mouth, rubbed his chin. "I see the resemblance."

"But you...you don't fit into any description. You're a magic man."

"You've got the magic, Hannah. I feel it every time you touch me."

"Pretty words. Seductive. But, I don't want to be a souvenir you brought home from a vacation in North Carolina. A toy you play with for a while, then discard."

His fingers inched closer to hers. Fingertips touched. She shivered. He linked his fingers through hers and squeezed gently.

"You know better than that."

"I don't think I know anything anymore."

The unearthly music began. Wooden flutes piped shrill whistles. Tiny bells jangled and strange horns blatted 'umpahs.' Overall, it was a most festive symphony! Music from pan flutes and loud whistles filled the air as children scrambled to grab her hands, eager to pull the guest of honor to the waiting feast. Hannah and Gabe were applauded yet again. Trog sported flecks of whipped cream in his whiskers when he offered Hannah a steaming mug of cocoa.

"Good stuff, do I say so m'self."

Eyes closed and her nose in the mug of chocolate, Hannah bumped a gangly boy with bright freckles and wispy tuffs of copper hair. She stumbled over the curled toes of his bright green boots. Bits of drying mud clung to the scab on one of his knobby knees. He shoved a plate of food towards her.

"Fer you."

Hannah put her hands over his and together they set the plate on the slightly warped wooden planks that passed as a table. As Hannah found a seat on the bench, she noticed that a sizeable chunk was missing from her slice of cake.

"Yum! Cinnamon streusel. One of my favorites."

"Mine, too."

"Maybe you'd like to share a bit of this with me, then. This is a large portion for one person."

The boy looked around for approval. Slapping the youngster on his shoulder, Gabe said, "This fellow has a hollow leg, Hannah. Never turns down an offer of food."

The boy blushed, clear up to the tips of his pointed ears. But, he kept shoveling coffee cake, cramming his mouth overfull.

"Tobias here lives in the cottage next door to mine. He can smell muffins baking a mile away!"

"Good to meet you, Toby. Maybe you'd like to sample my Gran's recipe for blueberry muffins. "

Toby spritzed her with crumbs when he spoke. "Sure thing! Anytime you want." He wiped his mouth with the back of his hand. "Gotta find a glass of milk. 'Scuse me."

Hannah discovered that a faerie feast meant more than fruit, cheese and crusty wedges of bread slathered with thick creamy butter, dripping blobs of sweet clover honey. It also was loud laughter; songs of love found and lost, happy elfin pranks and hours of enthusiastic dancing.

"No more work scheduled today?" Hannah asked Glendar, the baker who smelled like cinnamon and looked as if his body was made of soufflé. He had puffy red cheeks and a soft, jiggly stomach.

"No schedule any day. Today we celebrate!"

He grabbed Hannah's hands and pulled her up for a rousing spin around the dance area. For such a plump fellow, he moved with incredible vigor. Elves somersaulted, faeries flitted overhead and Hannah was certain she'd not giggled so much since she was in second grade.

When the joyful pandemonium had finally quieted, she and Gabe stood together at the edge of the trampled grass dance area. Mothers shepherded their squirming children off for afternoon naps. A few elder elves gathered in small clusters, chattering like red squirrels. Two gnomes sat alone at the feasting table, whittling small blocks of wood as they enjoyed a shared pipe. The air was redolent of the fragrant smoke that wreathed their bright russet caps.

"You know what, Gabe? I think maybe you're right. Maybe life here will be perfect."

She realized she was getting used to it. The exhilaration when he wrapped his arms around her. She relaxed; her shoulders pressed into his ribs, the top of her head fit snugly under his chin. She propped her hands on his forearms. Yes. This feeling was all right.

Not that she was relinquishing her independence, she reminded herself. She wasn't falling for him or anything. She'd never, never depend on him. He seemed too perfect; there had to be a catch somewhere. But being with him was getting more and more comfortable.

Gabe's voice was low. Velvet, definitely velvet. "We're not quite to perfection yet, but we're making progress."

Yes, Hannah told herself, her life was almost absolutely perfect.

In the morning, she squinted in the pale sunlight when the rooster yodeled to wake his harem and their chicks. She was surprised to find Gabe seated on the ottoman, next to her feet. She pulled the covers to her chin and squirmed to sit up. When she was settled, he smiled and offered her a cup of steaming cocoa topped with a dollop of whipped cream.

"It's hot," she mumbled as she sipped. "How did you know exactly when I'd wake up?"

"No magic involved, Hannah," he laughed. "I'm observant. The past two days, you've gotten up when Chanticleer crows."

"You're amazing." She circled her lips with her tongue, licking the sweet creamy mustache.

"Tell me what you're thinking. I want to know how you feel."

"…how I feel about…?"

"Me. Us. The village."

Hannah tilted her cup, watching the chocolate sediment swirl. She tipped her head to one side and scratched her nose. "Ummm. Well, I've already told you I think you're amazing. Thoughtful."

"Thoughtful? Hardly the stuff of romance. "

Hannah tipped her head to the other side and grinned. "Romance? I thought we were friends."

"Are we?"

"Yes."

"Then that's a good beginning. What do you think of the village?"

She touched her finger in the thick dark cocoa dregs in the bottom of the cup. Her tongue was like a kitten's, testing the chocolate goo with tiny quick flicks. "The village defies definition."

"Let me introduce you around."

Gabe escorted her through the village, pausing at each shop and most of the homes to introduce Hannah to the villagers. At each stop, they were given a gift. Her satchel bulged with two pears, bread, a big wedge of cheddar, her sketchbook, charcoals, paints and brushes.

"Let's lunch, picnic-style, under the low hanging limbs of this

oak," Gabe suggested.

Taking only one bite from her pear, Hannah pulled the sketch-book into her lap. As she watched a group of children at play with a ball, she filled page after page with animated drawings.

"You'll never fatten the girl up if you don't make her eat, Gabriel." Ella pinched his cheek as she waddled past Gabe. She stopped just behind Hannah's shoulder to inspect the latest rendering.

"Mind if I keep one?" Ella asked. "I'll trade you an apple pie."

"I'll be honored for you to have it."

Ella snatched her sketch with a grin. "Good! You eat while I make my selection."

Day five, Hannah visited the bakery to watch Glendar at work. His pies and cakes were the stuff of legends. Elena and Alinore, twin daughters of Mugwor, the cabinetmaker, followed her inside the shop. Glendar supplied each girl with a gingham apron many sizes too large. He set them to work, cracking eggs in a large bowl. They stood on tip-toes, using a bench to reach the countertop. They were quite serious about the business of egg-cracking, taking care to tap the shell once, then twice against the edge of the bowl, letting the yolk free fall with a splattering plop.

Hannah's pencil flew across her pad, capturing the pixies hard at work. She darkened the background to emphasize their pale hair plaited into braids that dangled at shoulder length. Ten or twenty stipples would suffice to indicate the hundreds of freckles dancing across the bridge of each nose. Spindly legs emerged from the voluminous checkered aprons that camouflaged their slender bodies. She couldn't resist adding a cloud of flour floating in the background, just above a pair of knobby elbows. Hannah nodded at the study and slid it into her satchel, patting the bag with satisfaction.

She stood and stretched, tapping the ceiling with her fingertips. She clapped her hands. "Okay, boss. I'm reporting for work. What chore do you have for me?"

For hours, Hannah helped Glendar knead huge batches of dough for brioche. Her arms and shoulders ached, but her taste buds sang when he shared the bread! While Glendar prepared delicate fluted pastry shells, Hannah opened her satchel and quickly captured him with charcoal on paper.

His sleeves were rolled up to reveal well-defined biceps. His eyes gleamed with mischief because he was relating tales from Gabe's boyhood. His pointed ears stuck out through a thatch of uncombed hair. His lopsided chef's hat had been pushed far back off his forehead, and a stripe of flour tattooed the bridge of his nose.

Hannah held her lower lip between her teeth as she filled the page with quick, sure strokes. Using the pad of her finger, she burnished shadows, highlighting Glendar's eyes, and the glints of light that dappled his hair and face. She gnawed her gum eraser absentmindedly, holding the drawing at arm's length. Wrinkling her nose, she added a few faint lines- the laugh lines that framed the baker's wide grin. She wasn't quite satisfied with his hands.

"They're just not right yet," she mumbled under her breath. "Too feminine. Glendar's hands are strong, capable."

"Were you talking to me, then, Hannah?"

"Hmm? No. Just muttering to my muse."

"Oh. I didn't see anyone come in. Has she gone now?"

Hannah looked around the shop, confused. "What? Oh, no. She's not gone, Glendar. " She tapped her chest several times, then thumped her forehead. "I keep her locked inside. Here and here."

"All righty, then." The elf shook his head and smiled at her naivete2.

Hannah used the side of her hand to smear the bold lines she had added. Now the sketch showed the prominent veins on the backs of Glendar's hands. A more few marks widened each knuckle tensed in the large dough ball. Carefully placed shadows intensified the feeling of the power in those hands.

"Yes. That's it!" She jumped up from her perch, toppling the precarious three-legged stool. "That's perfect." She bent to peck a kiss on Glendar's check, just above the ruff of ruddy hair that edged his jaw and chin. "You're just perfect!"

She gathered her satchel and hugged her sketchpad to her chest. She skipped out of the bakeshop, happy as a child on Christmas morning. Glendar watched her through the kitchen window. He slowly shook his head and chuckled, "Humans! Who can figure them?" But he touched his cheek with flour-dusted fingers.

Hannah had lost track of the days. They just slipped by quickly, each filled with a new adventure, like summer vacations or Christmas holidays. It was early evening. The dinner dishes were stacked in warm sudsy water. Although she had already tucked her sheets around the cushions of the chaise where she slept, Hannah wasn't sleepy. She had planned a cozy evening with Gabe, trading stories in the dark, cuddled with pillows before a crackling fire. At least that was the plan until a frantic boy banged on the kitchen door.

"Gabe! Gabe! Oma says come quick! Winnie's been hurt. Bitten by a centipede, she thinks."

Gabe rushed to the door, pushing it open wide to pull a young sprite into the kitchen. "Calm down, now Carwig. Take a deep breath. That's right. Now another." He braced a hand on the boy's trembling shoulder and squatted to look him in the eye. He watched the boy inhale slowly and then puff his cheeks to expel the air in a gush. "All right, now?" Carwig nodded with one decisive bob of his head.

"Now, start again. Your sister; Winnie's been stung?"

Another curt nod. "Yep. She was out back of Oma's house, playing down near the creek, where the path narrows. You know the spot? There's a pile of logs all covered with thick moss. Well, Winnie's always pulling off bits of that moss. Says it makes the loveliest carpet for her doll's house." He stopped to gulp more air, then he plunged back into his narrative.

"Well, alls I know is that she pulled off a big chunk of moss and was scraping dirt off the bottom. She says there was a weird bug; wormlike with a bunch of legs. She says it had pinchers, like a lobster, and it jabbed her finger. Now that finger is swole up something fierce!" He pouffed out another blast of air, gulped a fresh breath and continued.

"Winnie ran back to Oma, crying like the Spriggans were chasing her! Oma told me to run fast as lightning to fetch you. So, here I am!"

With his task accomplished, Carwig looked exhausted. Putting a hand on each of his scrawny shoulders, Hannah turned him towards a chair.

"Sit. Rest yourself. It will take Gabe a minute to collect his bag."

"Yeah. Okay. " Perspiration plastered dark hairs to his forehead. His hazel eyes were wide with worry. "He's gonna fix'er up; right?" Carwig's hands quivered and he jammed them in his pockets.

Hannah brought him a glass of apple juice. "Here. Drink this. You did well. Of course, Gabe will help Winnie." She brushed his hair back from his face. His wide brow was several shades paler than his cheeks. Obviously the cowlick was always in his face.

"Okay. Let's go, then Carwig." Gabe turned to Hannah, quirking an eyebrow. "Coming?"

Hannah grabbed her jacket from the peg by the door, hurrying to catch up.

"How old is Winnie, Carwig? I remember that she was born in Spring. When was that? Three, four years ago?"

"Hmm. Let's see. She's four years younger'n me. I'm nine, so she'd be, umm...."

Hannah pulled the hood of his tunic up to cover his damp hair. "That would make her five. Four plus five is nine."

"Yeah. That's right," he assured her. Smiling, he faced Gabe. "She's five, sir."

Gabe coughed a chuckle into his hand. "Thanks."

The circuitous route to Oma's was well lit. Faeries had heard the news and flitted in wild circles, gossiping. Their innate glow illuminated the path like amber nightlights. In minutes, Carwig led Hannah and Gabe into a vine-covered cottage hidden deep in the branches of a giant fir tree. Hannah stooped to enter the small door. But, Gabe simply materialized inside.

Still bent double as she entered the cozy living room, Hannah bumped her head on his thigh.

"Oooft! Someday you'll have to explain how you do that!" She smiled at him as she rubbed her head.

"What?"

"Teleporting yourself without one of those huge cellular fragmentation machines from Star Trek."

"Someday."

A muffled sniffle drew all attention to the patient. Behind a wooden rocker, carrot-colored ringlets peeked over a quilt mounded in the corner. Gabe slowly moved a corner of the quilt so that he could see Winnie. She huddled; one hand gingerly held the other. Her injured hand was swaddled in wet cloths. A tiny stream of water dripped across the bumps and crevices of the wrinkled quilt. A good-sized puddle was forming at her feet.

"Hi, Winnie," he crooned. She looked up at him, eyes wide.

Hannah nudged Carwig, pushing him to stand next to Gabe. "Hey, Win. This is Gabe. Remember, he made that cherry flavored stuff you drank when you had a sore throat last year?"

"Umm. Yeah, kinda." She sniffed again, and rubbed her nose with the mitt of soggy bandages.

Oma bustled back into the room. Between two thickly padded potholders, she carried a piping hot bowl of foul smelling yellowish brew.

"Man, that stuff stinks, Oma. You're never gonna get Win to drink that junk!" Carwig shouted. In a much more modulated tone, he coached Gabe, "Hope you got something that smells more like that cherry stuff!"

"It's not for drinking, you thick headed clot!" Oma said as she grinned at him. "It's for smelling! This is my own special potion to repel insects. Be still now and let Gabe work!" She set the bowl on a table already littered with bits of paper, nutshells and several dried hydrangea blossoms. Laughing, she swatted at Carwig's head with one of her potholders.

Hannah used the distraction to move closer to Winnie's quilted tepee. She knelt beside the frightened child. With hands cooled by the night chill, she touched the tiny, fevered face. "We're going to make you feel better, Winnie. All right?" Winnie turned her flushed cheek into Hannah's palm and gave a slight nod. A lone tear ran down her cheek, drying before it reached her chin.

She lifted her bandaged hand about an inch, bracing it with her good one. "It hurts bad."

"I know." Hannah lifted the doll-sized child and moved to the rocker. Holding Winnie close, Hannah kissed the crooked part in her hair. "I know, Lovie. I know."

She gave Gabe a nod. He unsnapped his bag and took out two clear vials, a small white jar and a length of gauze. He carefully set them on the floor right at Hannah's feet. He pulled over a sturdy-looking footstool and sat close to the rocking chair.

"May I see you hand, Winnie?"

"Yeah, I guess," she said just above a whisper. "Is this gonna hurt?" She turned to Hannah for the answer.

"Not nearly so much as the bite, Sweetie."

From across the room, Carwig mumbled, "Uh oh! Here we go again! She's gonna start caterwauling again!" He covered his ears and winced.

Winnie burrowed closer to Hannah, hiding her eyes, but extending her hand to Gabe. He removed the cool wet cloths, exposing an inflamed and swollen index finger. Glancing towards Oma, he said, "Good thought; the cold compress."

He tapped the child's chin with his finer. "Can you bend your finger, Winnie?"

She curled the first digit slightly.

"Okay. That's pretty good." He didn't really sound encouraging.

Hannah's forehead rested on Winnie's. She sang "Deedle Deedle Dumpling my son John". Gabe opened both vials. Hannah looked up immediately. Her eyes watered, her nostrils flared.

"That smells like mothballs!"

"Close. It's blue gum eucalyptus oil. It does smell like camphor, but it's an excellent antiseptic, analgesic, antineuralgic that is also a febrifuge."

"Right. Now say that in English!" She smiled at him over Winnie's orange curls.

"It will kill germs, reduces pain, fever and swelling." He winked at Winnie, who had turned to watch him. He lifted the second vial to her nose. She gave a tentative sniff and grinned. "Is that better, you think?"

She nodded enthusiastically.

"What does it smell like?"

"Lemon candies!"

"Pretty close. It's oil, pressed from lemon peels."

"Ohhhh."

"Okay. Let's mix the two." He dripped each of the oils on a small piece of gauze. Gingerly, he rubbed the finger, knuckle to tip and back again.

Opening the white jar, he lifted that to Winnie's nose. "Okay. What does this smell remind you of?"

Winnie wrinkled her mouth and wiggled her lips back and forth, generating an idea. "Pasta sauce!"

"Right."

Carwig jumped up. His squeaky voice cracked in surprise. "Right? Right it smells like pasta sauce?"

"Sort of. It's French Basil. Your Oma probably uses it for cooking. I use it as an antidote to venomous bites." Gabe smiled at Winnie and tousled her curls. Hannah kissed her head again. She rocked slowly, murmuring "Mares Eat Oats and Does Eat Oats."

Gabe scooped a bit of the basil paste out with his pinky. He balanced a tiny mound on Winnie's swollen finger. He put the soiled gauze in his coat pocket and cut a fresh piece, a bit longer this time. He saturated the cloth with the lemony mixture and wrapped it around her finger. Before tying the loose ends, he reached for his bag. Rummaging through the contents, he hummed a little tune. Winnie was curious. She leaned forward to peek over his shoulder.

"Aha! There it is." He pulled a sprig of lavender from an envelope. Brandishing it in the air, he swirled the leaves in a grand flourish, laying it over the gauze on her finger. He tied the bandage with a bow, securing the fragrant leaves in place.

"If your finger pains you during the night, gently squeeze the bandage. That will release a little more of the medicine. Then you can smell the lavender, relax, go back to sleep and dream of wondrous things."

"All right." Winnie nestled back in Hannah's arms, plugged her thumb in her mouth and was sleeping soundly in minutes.

Strolling home at a leisurely pace, Hannah rested her head against Gabe's arm.

"You were very perceptive tonight."

"Oh really?"

"Sure. Winnie was scared. Because you were gentle and patient, you were able to treat her. You have a knack with people."

They walked few more steps. "I manage in most situations; but to be honest, I think children can be difficult." Hannah stopped and turned to face him. Her mouth fell open, but no words fell out. "Give me credit, Hannah. I realize you sent Carwig over to introduce me to Winnie – sort of an emissary." He smiled at her and flicked the tip of her nose.

"Oh, that was nothing."

"You gained her trust in seconds. That was something special!"

"She's a cute kid. Anyone would have done the same."

"No. Not everyone. You have a rare gift, Hannah. Children are drawn to you. They trust you. They enjoy your company, your silly songs."

She smiled. Shy, all of a sudden. "Thank you."

"Thank you for the help tonight." He pecked a kiss on her cheek.

It was late when they returned home. Since she was exhausted, Hannah simply curled the covers around her shoulders and sank into the soft cushions of the large chaise. After turning out the lights, Gabe arranged the quilt to cover her legs. He nudged the ottoman, aligning it with the chair.

"Comfy?"

"Yes. Thanks."

"Thank you for being here. With me. Thank you for loving me."

Hannah jerked to sit up. Red alert! Red alert! That warm syrupy feeling had just turned to molten lava! Back away! Back away from the heat, she told herself.

"I've never said a word about … about…love, Gabe." The whisper floated past her lips and she considered trying to catch the words in her hand.

"But…"

"No buts, we're friends. That's it."

Gabe reached for her hand, laced his fingers through hers. "Well, friend, I love having you here."

They spent the next day tromping through the woods. Gabe taught Hannah to recognize the large hairy angelica plant with its ferny leaves and pom-pom of small white flowers. She helped him collect the aromatic rhizomes that Gabe claimed would be used to make a medicine to stimulate the immune system.

"This is Snakeroot," he told her, pointing to an inconspicuous little plant with a fragile, but hairy stem holding a solitary flower with petals the color of a brown-purple bruise. "It's a wild ginger."

Hannah knelt to inspect the tiny blossom. "It smells good."

"We'll collect the tubers and dry them for distillation," he told her as he dropped the rhizome into a canvas sack attached to his belt.

"Look here," Hannah said as she touched crinkly bright green foliage. "This looks like parsley."

"It is." Gabe squatted next to her. He pulled a few stalks free carefully, bringing up a clump of dirt clinging to delicate thread-like roots. "Trog will be pleased to add this variety to his vegetable gar-den." He dampened his handkerchief with water from his canteen and wrapped the parsley. "To keep it from drying out."

Late that afternoon, Gabe and Hannah sat together in his lawn, watching as the sun set the sky afire. The hills in the distance turned purple. She lay back in the cool damp grass and pointed up, outlining the shimmering edges of a pink cloud.

"Sharing the experience is special, isn't it?"

"Sharing most anything is special, Hannah."

"Yeah, but the sunset – Only Gram could actually hear a sunset with me! You're the only other person."

"So you've missed sharing the music with your grandmother?"

"Well, yes, I miss her; but it's more than that, really. Today; here with you, there's more volume, more brilliant colors." She scratched her nose and turned to watch him answer. "Is it always this way for you?"

"Nothing is quite the same for me since you've been here." He took her hand between both of his. "But, I understand what you mean about the sunset."

He drew their joined hands to his lips and kissed her knuckles even though each wrinkle was trimmed with dirt.

They lay side-by-side, hand-in-hand until the sky turned sooty gray and was dappled with a handful of blinking stars. Lying there, Hannah decided that she had identified the syrupy feeling that bubbled through her veins, made her light-headed, made her feel like she had butterflies trapped in her stomach.

"Contentment."

"What? Did you say something?" he asked.

138

"Contented. I'm contented. The feeling sneaked up on me, and I've only just figured it out!"

"Ah. Well, that's good, then."

"Very good." A little unnerving, she thought, but all-in-all a splendid feeling.

Gabe had cooked dinner, and so Hannah did the dishes. Wiping her hands on a dishtowel, she stopped beside Gabe at his workbench. He was engrossed in a book with curled, yellowing pages. He handled each page carefully since they were brittle; some torn, others spotted with mildew. She stood behind him, damp palms pressed flat against his back.

"What are you reading?"

Marking his place with a sprig of lemon balm, he twisted slightly so that she could read the front cover.

"Yearbook of Pharmacy and Transactions of the British Pharmaceutical Conference, 1907. Wow, enthralling stuff there!"

"Actually, it's fairly dry, but it is informative." He had turned so that she stood facing him as he leaned against the worktable.

"What informative information did you gather?"

"I'm trying to understand a reaction. One of Braedoric's daughters developed a rash that I can't pinpoint."

"Braedoric, the old man who tells the wonderful stories to the children in the square?"

He nodded.

"His daughter, you say? I didn't realize he had a family."

Gabe chuckled. "Quite a large family, to be truthful. He must have twenty or thirty children. He's probably lost count of the grand-children and great grands! This particular daughter is about seven years old."

"What? He looks to be at least a hundred and fifty years old."

Gabe teased her neck with a tendril of hair that had escaped her braid. "You're close. I'd say he's nearer to one hundred-sixty."

"You're kidding, right?"

He shook his head and returned his attentions to her neck.

"Boy. I thought Ella was ancient."

Now Gabe leaned back to look at Hannah. "No. She's a youngster. She's a mere ninety-five."

"Ninety-five! An assisted care facility would go bankrupt here. Elves are certainly long-lived."

"Not compared to the faeries. Faeries are almost eternal. Age just isn't important here."

Hannah chewed the corner of her lip. "How old are you?"

Gabe rubbed his lip with his index finger. He scratched his head, then tapped the end of his nose. Well, I've been here sixteen, no seventeen summers. Ella brought me to the village when I was eight, close to nine. So I'm twenty-seven, almost twenty-eight years old. Why?"

Hannah rubbed the tip of her finger in a circle on the smooth wood of the tabletop. She moved a couple of bottles, aligning them in precise order. "I don't know much about you." She covered her mouth with her hand, almost hiding her yawn. "I was suddenly afraid you would tell me that you are older than Methuselah." Hannah yawned again.

Gabe smiled and tapped his knuckle beneath her chin. "Tired you out today, huh?"

She closed her eyes and covered her mouth with both hands this time. "Think so! Guess I'll get ready for bed."

"Go get your things. I'll help you with the sheets tonight."

Hannah was already moving towards the trunk in the bedroom where she stored her pillow, quilt and sheets. "Okay. Thanks. I'll just be a minute."

Gabe was reaching for his book when someone tapped at the door.

"Are we interrupting?" Ella called as she opened the front door and stepped inside.

"No, of course not." Gabe stooped to kiss her cheek. That's when he spotted the miniscule couple standing in the circle of lamp-light on the porch.

He tipped his head. "Tatiana. Oberon. Welcome, Majesties. My home is always open to the King and Queen of Faeries." He stepped back and the royal couple fluttered into the room.

Oberon was dressed in purple. The curled toes of his boots were decorated with tiny brass bells. His mane of snow-white hair was brushed straight off his face and secured at his nape with a golden lanyard. His queen wore silver, studded with gemstones – amethyst, topaz and sapphires. Her auburn hair was arranged in an intricate design, piled atop her head in precariously looping curls held in place by more sparkling gems.

Hannah came back into the room dressed in her favorite sleeping attire, the huge tee shirt Gabe had bought in Beaufort. Her hair was loose and hung past her waist in rippling waves that almost touched the hem of her shirt. Heading to her alcove, she carried her supplies in a stack topped by a pillow. Surprised by Ella and the two faeries, she clutched the folded linens to her chest and covered one bare foot with the other. "Oh!"

"Exactly," Tatiana commented with a smile. "I'd say we are interrupting something."

"Ah, well…no. No. Come in, come in." Hannah dropped the sheets and pillow on the floor outside the bedroom door. "If you'll excuse me for a second, I can change…"

"Why would we want you to change?" Oberon asked. "If Gabriel is happy with you, we are, too."

Hannah blinked. She gestured towards the tee-shirt and curled the toes of her left foot under the arch of her right foot.

Ella sat on the chaise Hannah used as a bed. She examined a needlepoint pillow, tweaking the silk braid at one corner and plucking at invisible bits of lint. She shook the pillow, kneading it until it was sufficiently plump. Then she tucked it back into its place on the chair. Hannah thought Ella was stalling - trying to avoid conversation for some reason.

"Are you, Gabriel?"

"Am I?"

"Happy with her, of course!" both Tatiana and Oberon answered as they flitted around the room. A shimmer of golden dust trailed behind each of them, marking their flight path.

"Yes." Gabe had closed the door. He leaned a shoulder against it; relaxed, hands in his pockets.

Tatiana hovered in the air, just at Hannah's ear. "How about you, Girl? Are you happy here, living here with Gabriel?"

"Yes." Hannah whispered. "Yes, m'am."

"He treats you well, then?"

Hannah licked her lower lip. She glanced towards Gabe. "He treats me very well. Yes."

Tatiana landed on top of Hannah's pile of linens. The faerie stamped her foot, dimpling the fluffy goosedown pillow. The tiny bells that hung from multi-colored tassels at her waist tinkled like a windchime. The pillowcase was littered with a fine dusting of gold.

"Then why does he have you doing laundry so late at night?"

"Seems unreasonable to me, Gabe," Oberon chided. "Not much moonlight tonight."

Hannah bit the inside of her lip in an attempt to stifle her laughter. She knelt beside Tatiana. "I think you've misunderstood." She held out her palm and the faerie queen stepped onto her fingers. Hannah remembered the times as a child that she'd held butterfly or a beetle. That's what it was like…holding a perfect being; a living, breathing creature who weighed no more than a spider's web!

Hannah walked with Tatiana to the alcove where Ella sat in the big chair with her short legs stretched out, toes pointed to reach the edge of the ottoman. "The sheets are for my bed. I sleep here, on this chair."

Tatiana buzzed three laps around the alcove. She circled Gabe twice. Hands on hips, she confronted him. "You're much too big. How do you fit in such a small space, the two of you?"

145

Gabe swiped his hand across his mouth, but Hannah knew from his eyes that he was smiling.

"I sleep in the bed, Majesty."

"Alone?" Oberon asked.

"Yes."

Tatiana pivoted to question Ella, "Did you know?" But Ella had dozed off. Her head rested on the needlepoint cushion at what seemed to be an uncomfortable angle. Her snores were gentle hisses of air. P'sssst, p'ssst, p'ssst.

"Elves!" Tatiana remarked with a scowl. "Naturally, she wouldn't say anything. She'd want to avoid confrontation. Silly woman," she said to Gabe.

Then, to Hannah, she demanded, "Well, there's nothing to be done. You'll have to leave."

"Leave?" Hannah took a step backwards. "Leave?"

Gabe caught her just before she toppled backwards over the easel set up in corner. He kept one arm at her waist and Hannah thought her legs might have collapsed without his support.

"That's unreasonable, Tatiana," Gabe said. "Oberon, help me out."

"You know the rules, Gabe. "

Hannah touched his hand. "Rules?"

Gabe ignored her question and addressed the King instead.

"She's the one, Majesty."

"You sure about that?" Tatiana interrupted.

"The one for what?" Hannah's voice was shrill and crackled.

"Yes." Gabe's voice was soft, dark velvet.

"But you sleep alone, Gabriel. When was your handfast?"

"Well...um..."

Hannah tugged on the sleeve of his shirt. "What's going on?" she whispered.

"Just let me handle ..."

"You're not handfasted, are you?"

Hannah was surprised by Oberon's roar. How could such a tiny man produce such volume?

"Shame on you, Gabriel." Tatiana shook her head, curls dangling, flinging golden dust particles. Her bells pinged repeatedly.

Angry royalty is intimidating, no matter the size, Hannah decided. But enough was enough! One sharp, shrill whistle stopped all conversation. The only noise in the house was the hum of the refrigerator and the hiss of Ella's snores.

"Wait a minute, Tatiana, Oberon. I don't understand the big problem here. Gabe invited me to stay with him for a while. For crying out loud...my house burned down. I had nowhere to go. He should get your praise, not grief."

"It's okay, Hannah. You don't have to explain to them," Gabe told her.

Hannah turned to him, eyes glaring, hands fisted at her hips. "Maybe I should just go, then. I thought you were different. I thought you'd stick..."

"I'm not talking about leaving. You are."

"Yeah, well." Frustrated, Hannah scrubbed her face with sweaty palms. "Maybe I don't belong here." She tipped her chin towards Tatiana and Oberon. "They obviously want me to go."

"Do you think I want you to go?" Gabe asked.

Hannah shook her head. She touched her nose with her knuckle. Damnit, she would not cry!

"And I thought things were going so well. I thought we..." she sniffed.

"We all thought you two were handfasted," Tatiana interrupted. "Otherwise, we'd never have welcomed you into the village."

Hannah glared at the tiny, but imperious queen. "What the hell is handfast?"

Tatiana turned to glare at Gabe. "You never even explained to her, did you?"

"Old Gaellic custom…"

"…year and a day"

"…just like a married couple"

"…honorable…legitimate children"

They were all speaking at once, and to Hannah, it all sounded like Jabberwocky.

"One at a time, please!"

Gabe cleared his throat and sat on the arm of the sofa. His feet were flat on the floor and his shoulders drooped, arms hanging between his legs. He touched his fingertips together, making an inverted steeple.

"I'm Scots. You know that, right?"

Hannah nodded.

"Well, the faeries respect many of our old Gaellic customs. They take a custom and …well, customize it to fit their own traditions."

Hannah swirled her big toe in the faerie dust scattered on the floor, drawing a curlique. "Go on."

Tatiana hovered at Hannah's shoulder. Her wings moved so quickly, they seemed to disappear. She gestured with her finger, jabbing the air.

"We faeries can't just accept any human who happens to wander into our villages. There's too much at stake. You can understand the dangers, can't you? Humans try to steal our magic. It's happened before."

"Yes, but I don't understand what any of this has to do with Gaellic customs. Ancient Gaellic customs."

Gabe continued, " Handfasting? Do you know the term?"

"Obviously not."

"A couple publicly proclaims their desire to live together for a year and a day…It's kinda like a wedding ceremony."

"A year and a day?"

"At the end of that period, a choice of options are available. The people can marry but either person can disavow the handfasting. There's no dishonor in the relationship, only love. Any child born to the couple is legitimate, even if the parents go separate ways."

"Sort of like an uncontested divorce, but everybody stays friends – right?"

Oberon clapped his hands. "Oh good! She does understand!"

Gabe looked up at Hannah. He held a hand out to her, and she moved a step closer to him. Gabe trailed his fingertip down her arm, from elbow to wrist. The hairs on her arm quivered.

"Handfasting used to be quite expedient in the Highlands where settlements were remote. In those days, the ministers traveled constantly, visiting the many villages in their parish. Most young couples were unwilling to maintain celibacy waiting for his sporadic visits." Gabe smiled sheepishly and winked at Hannah.

"Yes, go on. I still don't see how this affects me…you and me."

Gabe shifted positions. Hannah thought he sounded nervous. "Well, you know that in the old days, men would travel long distances, leaving their homes for several years at a time. Umm, because of war, maybe, or trading or hunting trips. Well, ummm, men far from home, away from family, don't you know, they would …ummm… still have sexual ….urges."

"Ummm hmmm. I can imagine."

"Yes! Exactly!" Oberon interjected. "Through handfasting, these men and women…surely women… form honorable relation-ships. Handfasting offers security, emotional harmony, and a promise of legitimacy to any children created. But, a handfast is a contract with a time restriction. A year and a day. "

"Or…"

Gabe blew out a breath and stared at the ceiling for a moment. "Or the couple would marry when a priest next wandered through the village."

"Okay. That was interesting. But, how does this ancient cus-tom affect me?" Hannah opened her mouth, ready to voice another question. Gabe interrupted, and spoke quickly.

"Oberon and Tatiana want you to handfast with me."

"Faerie pimps! Sounds like they're forcing me to be your whore!" She glared first at Gabe, then Oberon and last at Tatiana.

Gabe stood. He rubbed his palms on the backside of his trousers. Although less than three feet separated them, it took him a very long time to move to Hannah's side. She stood, rigid as a marble statue. Her fists and jaw were clenched. Her eyes were closed. She took a deep breath and blew it out in a steady stream that sounded like a deflating inner tube. Deflated. That's the way she felt. Once again, disappointed by the person she depended on. She shook her head. When would she learn?

"You'd never be my whore, Hannah," Gabe whispered.

"Damned straight," she mumbled.

His breath was soft and warm on her cheek. She opened her eyes and his face was no more than three inches away. She felt like crying.

"I would honor you and respect you. Forever."

He'd captured her hand in his, knitted their fingers together. Damned if he didn't kiss her knuckle. That syrup in her bloodstream was beginning to boil again.

"The year and a day would allow you a grace period to adjust to life in the Faerie realm, to adjust to me."

Hannah jerked her head side-to-side. "Uh uh."

153

He squeezed her fingers. "I can't, or rather I won't, force you to stay here with me. But, in truth, I don't think I'm strong enough to force you to return to the humans. I want you here. With me."

His finger skimmed her chin, sending hot electric chills through her brain.

Tatiana spoke, breaking the spell. "It's your decision, Hannah. If you want to stay here – with the faeries – with Gabriel – you must handfast. We can't allow strangers to stay here, to learn our secrets."

Hannah nodded slowly, shifting her eyes left and right.

"I see."

"Do you? Do you really understand?" Oberon asked. "Like husband and wife. Sharing. Everything."

Now Hannah sat. She perched on the seat of the wooden rocker as if she had been strapped into an electric chair.

"Here I am again. Hannah in Wonderland, where nothing is quite what it seems."

She chewed her bottom lip. She picked at a hang nail.

"Why me?"

His fingers inched closer to hers. Fingertips touched. She shivered. He linked his fingers through hers and squeezed gently.

"You know I want you. I want you to want me."

He massaged the knobby little bone that protruded at her slender wrist. She watched their joined hands. She stared at his profile and licked her bottom lip. She quietly exhaled a stream of air. Closing her eyes, she turned her head to face the ceiling.

"Okay. Maybe, I can see your point."

"Do you, now?" Oberon smiled at his queen.

"Well, yes. I understand what you're saying. Maybe when we've had a while to get to know each other, Gabe and I can discuss handfasting again."

"Fine. Fine!" Tatiana said to Hannah.

"How much time do you need?" Oberon asked Gabe.

"Five…ten minutes?"

Gabe pulled Hannah into the alcove where Ella was dozing. He cupped her chin in his hand.

"Do you still trust me?"

Her answer was less of a whisper than a hiss. "I don't know! You tricked me!"

"From the first, I told you I'm no angel."

155

Curse him, he had the audacity to smile at her. Hannah's resolve started to melt.

"Remember those strings I told you about on your first day here? I told you that we were both puppets, hooked to strings that the faeries control. Remember?"

Hannah shrugged one shoulder. Nodded. Pursed her lips.

"I meant what I said earlier. I do want you to stay. I want you."

"But…"

Gabe brushed her mouth with his fingertips. "But, I should have been honest with you. I knew sooner or later Tatiana and Oberon would confront us – you."

"Can't we just pretend? Tell them that we're handfasted, but continue on as before? Can't we do that?"

Hannah thought Ella's snores seemed louder all of a sudden.

He shook his head. "No. The faerie have ways of rooting out the truth. Trust me on this. You don't want to be caught in a lie by the king and queen of the faeries."

"Oh." Hannah nibbled her lip. "This husband and wife thing. What do they mean? You know, do they mean…"

"Yes."

"…with a stranger?"

"I'm not exactly a stranger, Hannah."

Hannah could have sworn Ella snickered.

"No. I guess you're not."

"This is the twenty-first century. Men and women DO enjoy sex without being married."

Hannah scratched her left shin with her right foot. She rubbed the tip of her nose, twirled a piece of hair around her index finger. "I do trust you. God help me; but I do. And I want to stay. Here. With you. A year and a day. It can't be that bad. Right?"

"Right."

"Right?" Tatiana called.

"Right," both Hannah and Gabe answered.

"Swear it before witnesses, then," Oberon counseled.

Tatiana flew in swooping circles around Ella's inert body. "Wake up, you old elf! You've played possum long enough!"

Ella was laughing when she sat up. She stood on the ottoman to thump Gabe's shoulder. "Good work, Boy."

"I never had a chance, did I?" Hannah asked no one in particular.

"None at all," Tatiana agreed.

"When do we do the swearing ceremony?"

"No time like the present, I always say," Ella chirped.

"You mean *now? Right now?*"

Gabe nodded. "That's exactly what they mean, Hannah."

"But look at me." She gestured at the tee shirt and her bare feet.

"Pfft! Clothing! That's easily remedied!" Ella said with a wave of her hand.

There was no flash of light, no smoke or mirrors. But, Hannah was magically dressed in her beautiful new gown made of faerie dust. The hem fluttered just above her ankles – and her still bare feet. The gown draped loose and low in the back. The neckline was graceful, falling just at her collarbone. She'd never felt quite like this before; beautiful, radiantly beautiful.

Gabe stepped behind her, one hand on each side of her waist. "You look like a faerie princess."

"Okay," Hannah asked, "What's next?"

"Repeat after me," Oberon instructed. "For a year and a day, I give to you my body, my heart, my worldly goods, my protection, and my fidelity. For that term, we will be as one. We are bound by this vow so long as we both agree to live together in harmony."

Hannah reeled from the promise she'd just made. She felt giddy; scared, but happy.

Gabe tilted her chin, raising her face to his. He watched her nervously touch her lip with the tip of her tongue. She swayed a bit, dizzy with anticipation. He pulled her close, wrapping strong arms around her narrow waist. She stood on tiptoe, placed her hands on his shoulders. Hannah heard a soft moan. She was pretty certain it was her own voice. Gabe tasted her lips.

She gasped.

He slid his tongue into her mouth. She melted. Thank goodness he still held her tight. She could feel his heart pounding. She massaged the back of his head, urging him to lower his mouth to hers again. Gabe touched his lips to her jaw, kissed her neck, licked her shoulder.

"Well, I think our job is done here," Oberon said as he ushered Tatiana and Ella outside.

"At least for tonight," Ella agreed with a wink.

Hannah whispered, "I feel like a Roman candle, flaring wild bursts of light into the sky!"

Later that night, they'd bundled together in Gabe's large bed that was somehow covered with hundreds of flower petals. Now, those petals were strewn across the floor, amid the discarded clothing and needlepoint pillows. Hannah nestled against him. Her words were muffled because she spoke with her lips pressed to his skin.

"I think maybe you're right. Maybe life will be perfect."

She fell asleep hoping that Gabe slept joyously happy that night, cradled deep inside her.

Morning sunlight streamed through the windows, glittering dust motes danced in the sunbeams. Hannah woke to discover six faeries darting in one window and out another. The pings from their tiny bells reminded her of the triangle she played in rhythm band back in her nursery school days.

She also remembered that both she and Gabe were quite naked, thank you very much. Nudging him, she tried to discreetly tug more of the top sheet out from under him. Her breasts were covered, but barely.

"They're here to check on us," Gabe tried to explain, waving his hand in the general direction of the swarming faeries.

"To check…?"

"They'll report to Oberon that we did in fact sleep together – as a couple – in my bed."

Hannah slid down to crouch under the sheet. "How embarrass- ing!"

"It's a customized version of displaying the virginal marriage bedsheets, I think."

"How can you joke about this?"

She tried to maintain her furor; but Gabe destroyed the mood when he pulled the cover over his head, too.

"Did you ever make sheet tents when you were a kid?" he asked.

"No."

"Well, then, tonight we'll have to build a grand tent; like the nomadic sultans. You can be the bellydancer! And we'll eat grapes and drink from a wineskin."

Hannah couldn't help it. She smiled.

"You're outrageous!"

"I've only got a year to convince you to stay forever. I have to be creative."

Breakfast was delivered to the porch. Tobias arrived with a big tray covered by a white linen cloth. A single long-stemmed red rose lay across the cloth. Since he needed both of his hands to balance the heavy tray, Toby kicked the front door and yelled "Help!" Hannah pulled on Gabe's terrycloth bathrobe and hurried to answer his urgent calls.

"I'm coming, Toby. Is there a problem?" She was struggling with the latch.

"S'fer you."

The boy pushed the tray into her hands. His pointed ears were as flushed as his cheeks. He reminded Hannah of a colt wobbling on unstable legs when he stumbled at the step in his rush to run away.

"Thank you, Toby. Good to see you again!" Hannah called to his rapidly retreating back.

She placed the tray on the kitchen table and held the blossom close to her nose.

"Gabe, come look!"

"What's this?"

"Toby brought us a gift."

"Toby, you say?"

Gabe lifted the linen to discover two sliced bagels, a wedge of cream cheese, a crescent of cantaloupe, a carafe of coffee and … a half-eaten cranberry muffin.

"The breakfast is from Ella, I suspect. But, Toby apparently charged a fee for delivery."

"Did you have a big appetite when you were a boy?"

"Almost ate Ella out of house and home! That woman taught Glendar a thing or two about baking goodies."

"Well, what d'ya know? You have a sweet tooth? I just learned another piece of childhood trivia about you. Keep going. What's your favorite cookie?"

"Oatmeal raisin. But I can eat at least six balloons in one sitting."

"Go on. Balloons?"

"Never had one? It's a doughnut without a hole, really. Rolled in sugar." Gabe rolled his eyes and rubbed his stomach. "Delicious!"

He offered Hannah a bagel. "Want to know one of my weaknesses?"

"Sure. One day I might need that information."

"Blackberry fool."

"Pardon?"

"Berries cooked into a syrup then mixed with whipped cream." Gabe licked his lips. "How about you? Any childhood favorites your mother would fix just for you?"

"My mother didn't cook. She entertained; but she didn't cook. Good hostess, though. My parents threw great parties…lots of food and people in fancy clothes. "

"So you grew up with a taste for canapés."

"Once I moved in Gram, I was a teenager, too conscious of gaining weight to raid the cookie jar often."

"was it difficult to adjust to life with your grandmother?"

164

"My parents were in a plane crash. Daddy died immediately. They rescued my mother. She hung on for three days; but she never regained consciousness."

Gabe scooted his chair closer, facing hers. He pulled Hannah out of her seat and onto his lap. She rested her forehead on his shoulder. She panted, trying to keep her tears at bay. After all the years, she still felt the hot tears under her eyelids and the sobs that burned her throat.

"I'm sorry."

Hannah shook her head.

"It's okay. They were gone a lot the time, anyway. Business travel, that sort of thing. I stayed with Gram lots, anyway. So, it wasn't like it was a big deal to move in permanently, you know?"

"Yeah, I know about changes." He tapped her knee. "But, eat up now. I want to take you somewhere special."

"I thought I'd seen the whole place, met everyone."

Gabe chuckled. "Not by half."

He led Hannah to a clearing in the woods. Crickets chirped a serenade. Two bright orange butterflies landed on a tall ginger plant with pale yellow blooms.

"The flowers look like orchids, the leaves are like cannas, and the fragrance is as sweet as gardenias; my personal favorite."

"Ah. So I should woo you with gardenias!"

"I think you could say you've wooed me already. This place is … Wow!"

Hannah was struck mute by the waterfall at the far end of the clearing. It plunged into a dark pool, falling more than sixty feet, over a rocky bank filled with thousands of ferns. Large flat rocks rimmed one side of the pool, to create a seat just underneath the pounding water as it fell.

"It takes a while to adjust to the noise of the roaring water," Gabe yelled.

A chilly mist blew from the falls across the clearing. They stood in a cloud, cool vapor clinging to their skin.

"It's incredible!" Hannah whispered. "What awesome power."

Gabe slowly unbuttoned her blouse. She shrugged her shoulders and the garment fell to the ground.

"Beautiful. You're perfect."

"You don't have to say that."

"Yes. Yes, I do." Gabe touched her collarbone with his fingertip. She could feel that touch radiate through every cell in her body.

For more years than she'd like to remember, Hannah had segregated herself, afraid to develop any dependent relationships. She'd told herself that she rarely missed the intimacy. Now she admitted the very real possibility that she'd been wrong.

She wasn't certain how Gabe managed to hold her close while he shrugged his own clothes to the ground. But suddenly, he twisted, flopping them both into the pool.

Hannah tensed, grabbing his arm, expecting the shock of a cold bath.

"Several hot springs warm the water," he explained.

"Oh. Of course," Hannah nodded her head, figuring that she looked as incoherent as she sounded.

He reached for a small jar hidden at the water's edge.

"My own private stash," he explained.

Scooping out a large dollop of gel, he massaged her scalp. She swayed; suspended in the dark water with her hair floating around her shoulders in tangled masses.

Ripples stirred the water as a pair of lithesome water sprites broke the surface. They were no larger than Hannah's foot. Both had short curly blonde hair and large, luminous blue eyes. She turned to Gabe, her own green eyes wide, mouth gaping. She was afraid to speak, afraid the creatures would disappear.

"Nix. They are called nix," he said.

She held out her hand to the tiny beings, whose giggles were a musical tinkling sound. Then they clasped hands above their heads and dove in unison, exposing their multi-colored scale-covered legs. The water sparkled green, blue and mauve in the concentric circles as they disappeared. The whole encounter lasted less than thirty seconds; but Hannah was positive she'd remember it for the rest of her life.

"Oh my gosh! Am I dreaming? Nix? What are they?"

"Part fish and part either man or woman."

"Mermaids?"

"Not exactly. Nix are very playful and curious. But, like most tiny beings, they are quite cautious – the small fish steering clear of bigger fish kind of thing."

Hannah nodded.

"Sometimes, they ride equine water sprites called kelpies."

"Seahorses?"

"Sort of. Kelpies are very strong, and very fast, like race-horses. A kelpie's head and upper body are amazingly like a horse's, but his hind-quarters are decidedly aquatic! They live mostly in un-polluted rivers and streams. Look closely beneath the water. Can you see them ?"

He moved his fingers through the water in sweeping arcs. Rip-ples undulated under the flotilla of shampoo bubbles.

"The nix were beautiful. Will they be back?"

He smiled and shrugged his shoulders. "Maybe."

She put her face close to the surface of the dark water, trying to spot the nix.

"Don't get caught up with the nix or the kelpies, Hannah. Their wet faerie world holds both beauty and treachery. The nix are sporting creatures; they host races to rival the most competitive Kentucky derbies. They ride the kelpie, cavorting in the warm springs."

"Sounds like fun."

"You think so? Sometimes the nix encourage an unsuspecting human to mount a kelpie for a ride. And just for the lark of it all, the kelpie dive recklessly, dragging the foolish mortal underwater !"

"Do the people drown?" she whispered.

"Sometimes," he answered. "The Faerie World isn't always beautiful."

Hannah nodded; but she was fascinated and continued to search for the Nix. Only reflected opalescent sparkles gleaming on the surface hinted at the mysteries deep in the pool.

"We can return here often to watch for the Nix, if you'd like. Would that make you happy?"

"Of course. This is amazing. Everything here is fascinating. Will you tell me about all of the magical beings who live here in the Faerie Village?"

"They're not all beautiful – inside or out."

"But you'll tell me?"

"In time, I will."

"In time? We only have a year left."

"We have all the time in the world." He leaned close and nipped her earlobe.

"I wish."

"What? What do you wish?"

"That this was real. You and me. I've never been part of an *us*."

Gabe pulled her close, grabbed her legs and wrapped them around his waist.

"Feels real to me."

With strong kicks, he'd moved them out to the center of the pool.

"You're like an otter or a seal; perfectly at ease in the water. I'm not." Hannah paddled her hands in the water, hoping to keep afloat.

"Do you trust me, Hannah?"

That velvet voice turned her insides to the consistency of warm oatmeal.

"Y-es-ss."

"Then relax. Enjoy. Depend on me to keep you safe."

"I have problems with dependency. Major problems." She pulled a few more strokes through the water.

"I've noticed."

They lay tangled together; sprawled on the thick carpet of moss, naked in the warm sunshine, but kept damp by the constant spray drifting from the waterfall. Hannah brushed her fingers through a healthy clump of violets as she sang, "Mares eat oats and does eat oats. Little lambs eat ivy; a kid'll eat ivy, too. Wouldn't you?" She plucked a purple blossom and dropped it into Gabe's navel.

"Are you like your mother? Did she sing silly songs and cuddle you close?"

"Well, yes. She held me in her lap and sang to me when I was very little. That's what a mother does, Gabe."

"Hmmm. It's hard for me to remember. Elves sing a lot, but they rarely cuddle."

"So, you don't remember your mother?'

"Really only in general terms. I remember her smell. A soft floral smell, like spring flowers, maybe. Da says she sang, but I can't recall any of the songs. I just have memories of a soothing voice and pleasant tunes." He looked past her shoulder, staring into nothingness.

"I think I remember her hugs, though. After so many years, I can almost feel arms wrapped around my back, pinning my own arms to my sides, hands stroking through my hair. That's a vivid memory, even if I manufactured it in my dreams." He took a deep breath and expelled it in a soft whoosh.

Hannah sat up and opened her arms. Gabe moved closer and she pressed his head to her breast. He folded his arms around her ribs and she stroked his thick black hair, crooning a soft lullaby.

"Thank you for being here." He pecked a kiss on her cheek.

"You didn't have to agree to the handfast; but I'm glad you did." He leaned up to peck her cheek again. She turned her face, caught his lips and sucked his tongue into her mouth.

Night shadows settled in the meadow below while she and Gabe climbed a craggy hill. He'd promised her the perfect spot to watch the meteor shower predicted that night. A bevy of faeries flitted zig-zag patterns, their amber glow providing pinpoints of illumination on the path. Gossamer wings reflected like tiny jewels of iridescent light.

"Can you believe I've been here with you for almost a month?"

173

"You fit here. It's been a flawless transition, I'd say."

She reached for his hand. It was as though she were blind, feeling his fingers to memorize the shape. Her fingertips eased over each of his knuckles, tracking the long tapered fingers. She slid the pad of her thumb across his smooth broad nails. She lifted his index finger to her lips.

"I'm living a faerie tale. No one from my old life would believe it. There are times when I miss that life, though."

"I understand about missing friends."

"Do you? You have a world of friends here, Gabe."

"Faeries and elves try, but they just don't understand friendships." He almost whispered. "I do have a true friend back on Skye, though. A good man is Ewan." Gabe looked up and out, past the trees.

Hannah touched his hand, anchoring him to her. "Tell me about him, then."

Gabe tugged on his left earlobe. "Ewan's quick to remind me that he's my elder – older by a full month. His coloring is much like Trog's; all ruddy and spotted."

Hannah interrupted, "You mean he has red hair and freckles?"

Gabe shrugged, "Sure, if that's the way you'd describe Trog. Anyway, the two of us, Ewan and me, have always been around the same size."

"Then you'd hardly confuse Ewan with Trog!"

"Hardly. Anyway, as lads, Ewan and I were always competing. There were contests to determine who could run from my doorstep at the farm to Floddigarry center fastest, or who could coax more milk from a cow, or who could eat the most grasshoppers without puking. Always competing, that was me and Ewan. But, like a true friend, he was always my champion; even when I faced strong opposition! I hate to admit it, even now; but Mairisi, Ewan's kid sister, was the toughest challenger either of us faced. Sometimes it took the both of us to best that scrap of a girl."

"They both sound like wonderful friends."

"And who was your best friend, Hannah?"

"Hmm. Tough question. I've told you that I spent most of my time alone."

"Come on. Everyone has a best friend, a confidante," he teased.

"Then I guess my best childhood friend was my dog, Turnto. I told him the secrets of my soul, and I'm pretty sure he never betrayed my confidence!" She pursed her lips, but she forced a smile. "But, he left me, too. Got hit by a car and died while I was at school."

Gabe squeezed her hand. She appreciated that he waited silently until she was ready to speak again.

"You're my best friend now, though."

"Then stay with me forever. Forget your old life. Stay here."

"There's not much left of my old life, anyway. The house, the newest paintings are gone. Probably no one remembers me or misses me, unless I owed them money!" she giggled.

"I think you're unforgettable."

"But won't you get tired of me, Gabe? How long will I interest you? There are lots of more beautiful women."

"Do you think me so fickle?"

Closing his hand over hers, he clasped it to his chest. With his other hand he gathered back the fall of curls that shielded her eyes.

"Look at me, Hannah." He nuzzled her neck, trailed his tongue around her ear. "I live in a state of constant arousal." He directed her hand to his crotch; let her fingers trace his erection. With his index finger, he drew a path down the nail of her pinky, across the knuckles, up her ring finger, sending quivering jolts through each of her fingers. "Standing beside you leaves me breathless." He panted dramatically in her ear, sounding more like a Labrador than a breathless lover. She turned to grin and he winked at her.

"You know, I enjoy strawberries. Eating one berry only makes me want another and another. Being with you; loving you is the same." Kissing her, he whispered, "Now for another and another and another."

"I've been thinking…" Hannah turned her back to him as she stretched to switch off the bedside lamp. The room was dimly lit by moonlight.

"Thoughts are over-rated," Gabe tried to tease. Hannah settled against her pillows, propped against the headboard. She noticed that the smile on his lips tensed into a thin, straight line. He caught a lock of her hair and twisted the spiral curl around his finger.

"How have you remained friends with Ewan? When do you see one another?"

Gabe expelled a long, soft breath, rolled his eyes. "Oh! Ewan!" He tugged her curl to his mouth, brushed it across his lips. "I see him when I visit Da. At least three times a year."

"Where does he think you are for the rest of the year?"

Gabe settled back on his clump of pillows, pulling Hannah with him. She was draped across him, not unlike one of Gram's lap quilts.

"Ah, weel now. Ewan's none too bright a lad, mind ye." He chuckled and Hannah joined in.

"Yes? So, Ewan's daft."

"The man's me best friend in the world, woman!" Gabe shook his head. "But, to be truthful, he's never questioned my absences. When I first left Flodigarry, Da put it out that I'd gone to stay with relatives. Ma's relatives."

"Sounds reasonable."

Gabe shrugged a shoulder. Grimaced and rubbed the bridge of his nose.

"I returned at holidays and in the summer; so it was generally accepted that I was on break from school."

"People assumed that you were attending a boarding school?"

"Yeah."

"And you just never corrected the misconception?"

He shrugged again, squished his eyes closed.

"Now Ewan thinks I live in a flat on the far outreaches of Edinburgh, working as a pharmacist."

Hannah giggled. "Now, how would he have gotten that idea?"

"Another misconception?"

"So, your best friend doesn't know that you live in a faerie raft? Somewhere close to the outskirts of nowhere. Doesn't know that you can transport yourself from place to place just like the guys on Star Trek except you don't need Scotty or a laser beam?"

Gabe nodded once, swiped his knuckles across his eyebrows. Nodded again. "That pretty much sums it up; yes. Haven't I told you I'm no angel?"

Hannah steepled her hands under her chin and tapped her fingertips together.

"So, I know for a fact that you do commune with faeries and that you have learned teletransportation, or whatever it's called locally. So, where does that knowledge put me on your friendship quotient, on a scale of 1 to 10?"

"With or without that information, you are definitely a 15-rated friend."

"15 meaning you know what I look like naked?"

"15 meaning I'd trust you completely in any situation." He leaned close, stared at her for a full thirty seconds. Hannah thought about how easy it would be to drown in the depths of his stormy eyes. His words, whispered against her temples, jolted her. Liquid words, like cocoa, warm comfort on her skin, words that sent rippling jolts through her core. "I trust you with my soul."

"How about if I tell you that I'm not certain I understand what's going on?"

"I'd say you're reacting reasonably."

"What if I tell you I'm not even certain I believe in faeries, even though I've eaten the food they've prepared and I've worn the clothes woven from magic and faerie dust? What would you say then?"

"I'd say I love you."

Hannah tapped her hands together in a "T" for timeout.

"Whoa! I'm not asking for empty promises." She crossed her arms across her chest and closed her eyes for a second or two. "But it would be lovely to think that this was real."

Gabe pinched her! A quick, hard pinch that was going to leave a bruise on her thigh!

"Was THAT real, Hannah? Did it hurt like it was real?"

"Damned right," she mumbled, rubbing her leg.

"That hurt's nothing compared to what I feel when you doubt me."

"Be serious."

He grabbed her shoulders and shook her. "I thought you trusted me!"

She was surprised by his outburst; but she wasn't scared. This was Gabe, after all. He might not be an angel. Goodness knows, he reminded her of that fact often enough. But, she could expect him to tell her the truth.

"I do," she whispered. "I do trust you, Gabe. And believe me, trusting anyone is a little bit scary for me."

Gabe skimmed his hands from her shoulders, up her neck. He massaged her jaw with his thumbs. He pushed his fingers through her hair.

"Well, we've begun, then, haven't we?" He pressed a kiss into her hair. "Long journeys begin with a single step. I think we've made major progress – you and I. Go to sleep now, Hannah. Let's do this relationship thing a day at a time."

"A day at a time for a bit less than a year."

"We'll see what tomorrow brings."

Tomorrow began early. At daybreak, the pack of hounds Toby called pets started barking in the yard next door. Barking, howling and growling. It wasn't long before Hannah heard a door slam shut. She giggled at Toby's attempt to quell the racket.

"C'mon guys, break it off now. Mum's threatening to try a recipe she found for puppy stew! You shoulda seen her face, guys. I don't think she's kidding this time."

A couple of the stronger-willed mutts whined; but all was quiet for a moment. Hannah plumped her pillow, adjusted the covers on her shoulder and settled back for another hour's sleep.

That's when Toby started banging on the front door!

"Gabe! Hannah! You guys up yet?"

Gabe struggled to a sitting position, threw his legs over the side of the bed. "This better be good," he muttered as he stumbled to the door.

He'd twisted the doorknob as Toby pushed the door open.

"Toby! What the devil…"

"I think you'd better see this, Gabe!" he panted.

Toby grabbed his hand and tried to pull Gabe outside.

"Hold on, Toby. What's the matter?"

"Feu. See the burned patches, there on the ground?"

Gabe took a step back. He pulled the boy inside and slammed the heavy door.

Hannah stood at the far side of the room, bathrobe lapels held close to her throat. She didn't understand the problem; but any fool could tell it was potentially serious. As she moved closer, her slippers made a shush-slap noise on the hardwood. Gabe tipped his head, watching her over his shoulder. He held up a hand. Stop. Wait. So, she sat on the arm of the sofa.

"Feu Follet?" he asked Toby.

"Looks that way."

"They don't usually come so close to villages."

"That's why I thought you'd want to know."

Gabe rested a hand on the boy's shoulder. "You did well, Toby. Wait here while I dress. Have something to eat." He motioned for Hannah to take Toby to the kitchen.

"We'll get Trog," Gabe called from the bedroom.

"I'll be ready in a second," Hannah said, letting the robe fall to the floor beside the bed.

"This could be a difficult adventure, Hannah. Not a lark," Gabe warned.

"Okay." She struggled with the laces on her boots. "Do you think I'll need a sweater?"

Gabe pulled her to her feet. He grasped each of her arms. "Are you listening to me? This will NOT be a picnic." She stared up at him and he swiped his hand across his mouth. "Grab a sweater. Hurry! We've got to get Trog."

"Why?"

"He's the best tracker in the whole village."

"What are we tracking?"

"Mean little balls of fire."

Trog meandered the uncharted labyrinth of a route, motioning Gabe and Hannah to follow him. "Feu Follet," he explained to Hannah. "Some humans call them 'Will o' the Wisp', but I think it's a stupid name for such vile creatures."

"Oh! I've heard tales of the Will o' the Wisp. I remember something about people following strange lights into a misty forest at dusk, never to be seen again."

"Those of us who live in the village are careful to avoid the Feu," Gabe continued.

"Damned burning chunks of evil intent. No wonder the Feu look like fire; they're Satan's own kin. Spit from his mouth, too noxious for even Lucifer to swallow," Trog grumbled as he stumbled through briars and gnarled tree roots.

Gabe turned to check behind them. "The Feu Follet, appear as curious lights resembling a flame. They lure humans deep into swamps and bayous. No one is certain what happens then. If the humans are ever seen again, they babble about terrifying ordeals. The faeries have no use for such wickedness."

The morning sun was high overhead. Beads of perspiration dotted Hannah's hairline. She figured the dense undergrowth was blocking the gentle breeze they'd enjoyed an hour ago. Her sweater was stowed in her backpack along with a half-full canteen of water. She wished that she'd thought to pack an apple or a bit of bread. Her stomach rumbled and the sound echoed. It was then that she noticed the decided lack of woodland noises.

"Psst, Gabe," she whispered. "Why don't I hear any squirrels or birds?"

He touched her shoulder, leaned very close to her ear. "Sssh."

The air buzzed with the sound of a swarm of angry bees. Suddenly, crackling balls of light, bright like Fourth of July sparklers, bounced around them. The Feu danced, circling Trog. An acrid, white-hot, almost sulfuric smell irritated Hannah's nose. She gasped and covered her mouth with her hands when one of the bundles of light darted close to Trog. There was a flash, then the unmistakable stench of scorched skin. Trog gritted his teeth and clinched his jaw.

"You pesky devils don't intimidate me."

"Nay, na-nay, na-nay, nay, nay!" The Feu circled; balls of sizzling light that bounced ever closer to Trog.

"Trog," she screamed. "Let me help you!"

Gabe held her elbows. "Be still, Hannah." He spoke without moving his lips; he breathed through his nose.

Trog jerked his head in her direction. "Leave me be, Girl!" he shouted.

"A human?" The voice emanating from the flame was shrill, filled with static, almost sounded mechanized. "You two travel with a human?"

"Not just any human, you nitwit," Trog grumbled. "She is Hannah, handfasted to our healer, Gabriel."

"Is this truth, Gabriel?"

Gabe pulled Hannah close, shielding her from view. He maintained a firm grip on both of her wrists. He nodded towards the largest ball of flame. "She is handfast to me."

"We've heard such rumors…" Then, in less than one second, the Feu were gone! Hannah was certain she heard snickering sounds resembling laughter.

"What do you make of that?" she asked Gabe.

Gabe tipped his head towards the elf. "Okay?"

"Be off, both of you."

Gabe tossed her over his shoulder, wrapped both arms around her legs and poof! Hannah thought that her dangling arms might have brushed the top of a cedar tree, and she definitely felt wind flow through her hair, across her face. In less time than it took for those thoughts to register, she and Gabe were once again in their own kitchen.

"We did it, didn't we? We transported. Oh my gosh; how did you do it? What happened?"

"I needed to get you away from the Feu. Didn't I promise to keep you safe?"

"But, the Feu had gone. After you and Trog explained why I was with you, they left. Didn't they?"

"The Feu Follet never do the expected."

Hannah gasped and covered her mouth. "Trog! Is he all right? Was he burned? Where is he? Shouldn't we help him?"

Gabe tucked a tendril of hair behind Hannah's ear. "He's fine; a tad singed; but fine. Right, Trog?"

Trog pushed open the back door and eased inside. "I could use a pint of ale to soothe me parched throat."

While Gabe hung his jacket, Hannah put a mug on the table. "Are you sure that's all you need?"

Trog licked the foam from his moustache and smiled. "Ahh, best medicine ever invented!" He pressed the cold mug against his red cheek.

"Enough chit-chat," Gabe said. He turned a chair backwards and straddled it. Slapping his thighs, he asked, "So wha'd'ya think?"

Trog belched softly and scratched his nose. "Somebody paid the Feu to get information about Hannah."

"Me? Why?"

Gabe locked his fingers behind his head, elbows pointed out, sprouting like wings from his shoulders. "Well, that's the real question, isn't it?"

Their discussion rambled for more than three hours without ever arriving at a viable theory. Trying to follow Trog's convoluted logic was nigh onto impossible ***Hannah decided. She was surprised that Gabe was behaving like some fifteenth century warrior prepared to shield his woman, even if it meant locking her away in a fortress. Her head was pounding and her jaw ached. She realized that she'd been clinching her teeth to keep from yelling at them. Gabe grimaced while Trog was drawing a diagram on a scrap of paper. Hannah stood abruptly, slapping her palms on the table. Both men turned to look at her.

"There is no danger, guys! You play war and make battle plans; but it's all nonsense to me."

"Nonsense for me to want to protect what's mine?"

"But that's part of the problem, Gabe. You don't understand that I'm not yours. I'm my own person."

"Of course you are. But you are my responsibility."

"I'm responsible for myself. You're not my guardian."

"I care about you."

Hannah didn't even realize she'd stored the tears or the frustrations until they broke loose. "Men! It would be nice to have a woman my own age to talk to. Someone with a background similar to mine."

"Human, you mean?" Trog asked.

Her eyelid twitched and her fingers trembled when she touched her lips. God, this conversation was ridiculous. "Someone who'd listen and understand my deepest, darkest, most puzzling questions or desires."

Gabe dropped his hands. He stood. His voice was soft; hesitant. "And I can't do that?"

She hunched her shoulders and wrapped her arms across her waist. "No. There are some things a woman can share only with another woman." She might not have meant to hurt him, but it was obvious she did.

"I understand."

"No. NO you don't. It's not personal. It's biological, I guess. I don't know. I don't know. It just IS. Like Trog said when I first came here to the village. Don't try to understand it, just accept it."

"I want to understand, Hannah. I care."

Hannah was moving around the room. She put Trog's empty mug in the sink, re-arranged the canisters on the counter, and pulled a drooping daisy out of the vase on the shelf of cookbooks. "I've got to get out of here. I'm going for a walk."

"Where are you going?"

Hannah took a deep breath. She shook her fisted hands at her sides. "I don't know. To the waterfall, I guess." Her pacing had brought her to the backdoor. "It's quiet there. I'll soak my feet. Relax for a while. "

"Be careful," Gabe called. But she'd already left. The screen door slammed shut.

Hannah hadn't returned by dark.

"Enough is enough," Gabe said. "I'm going to get her."

Trog stood and rubbed his backside. "Guess I'll come, too. My butt's going to sleep. This body wasn't designed to spend so much time sitting."

A wind wafted through the swaying trees that ringed the waterfall. Trog was winded as he raced to follow Gabe. "Slow down, Boy." He took off his red stocking cap and mopped at the sweat on his face and throat. He tripped over the root of a willow tree that had never before intruded on the path.

"Dag nabbit! Did you ever tell Hannah about the willow trees? Darned nuisance. Blasted trees… keep honest souls like me awake with their whispered insults. No respectable tree would uproot at night to stalk folks alone in the woods."

Trog stopped grumbling to watch Gabe in the small empty clearing. Hannah was missing! Gabe stared at the ground searching for clues in the failing light. He bent to retrieve something from the moss growing at the perimeter of the pool. He lifted Hannah's hair barrette to his lips and closed his eyes, centering his concentration on her.

"Be careful, friend," Trog panted as Gabe crossed his arms over his chest. "Focus. Flying off like this, you might just land in the middle of trouble."

"If trouble's where Hannah is, that's where I need to be."

Wind stirred; yellow and orange leaves drifted from tree branches to float on the pool's dark water.

"You'd fight the devil for her, wouldn't you, Gabe?"

"I'd slaughter demons and rage at all of God's angels if it would help her."

"Then concentrate on your woman and go."

The leaves swirled at his feet, as Gabe lifted off the ground.

"But be wary," Trog called to the sky.

A tiny head emerged from beneath the water's surface. The nix raised her arm, motioning to bring Trog closer. He scrambled to pool's edge, careful not to fall into the inky water. He leaned as far as he dared, cupping his ear because the language of the nix is difficult to decipher. Theirs is a dialect of short words spoken in a tinkling chatter that echoes through the shadows. Trog struggled to piece together her message.

Elbows braced on a mossy stone, he leaned even closer to the water sprite and asked, "The Bogies, you say? What are those sneaky shape-shifters doing here, so close to the Village?"

The nix spoke of curious lights bouncing through the darkened undergrowth. Trog crossed his arms and scrunched his face in a frown.

"Damned Feu Follet, too, huh? Figured they'd be back," he muttered more to himself than to the nix.

He squinted into the deepening twilight.

Meanwhile, Gabe was five or six feet above the hot, humid swamp tucked in a valley on the leeward side of the Hollow Hills, just north of the village. The air smelled of sulfur and rotting vegetation. Cicadas and crickets called to mates, bullfrogs and snapping turtles plunged into the murky waters. From the shore weeds, alligators watched him, with eyes that glowed red in the darkness. He hovered just above the muddy bogs.

In the distance, he heard laughter. Laughter? "Hannah?" he called; but only his echo answered.

He moved towards the sounds he'd heard. Hannah looked up at his approach. Without speaking, she extended her hand to him. Her fingers were loosely wrapped around something held in her palm. Giggling, she opened her fingers to release two fireflies. They circled her head once, then flew into the night. "I used to catch lightning bugs when I was little."

Gabe swallowed and rubbed his throat with both hands.

"I was following the strangest lights."

"Feu," he whispered on an exhaled breath.

"No. These lights weren't angry like this morning. They skidded across the ground like drops of water on a hot griddle!" She tilted her head and shrugged one shoulder. "Can you imagine it?"

"Yes."

"Well, I guess I got lost." She tugged on her bottom lip. "I wasn't afraid, though. Isn't that strange?" She leaned back on her elbows to look up at him. " I figured you'd find me." And she smiled.

"No. It's not strange, Hannah. It's called trust."

He touched her head, stroked her hair away from her face and curled his fingers in the ringlets at the nape of her neck. Hannah thought perhaps his hand was shaking when he fastened her barrette.

"Always," his voice cracked. "I'll always find you and I'll always bring you home."

He closed his eyes. Hannah thought maybe tears dampened his lower lashes. He cupped her elbow and pulled her up. He kissed the dampness at the crown of her head.

"Of course, you realize this escapade scared the ever-loving beejazus out of me, don't you?"

She pulled his face lower and kissed each eyelid, catching the tears from his spiky lashes on her tongue.

"Sorry."

He held her close, one arm wrapped just under her shoulder blades, lifting her off the ground. Barefoot, she stood on the toes of his boots.

"You know, I used to dance standing on my daddy's shoes just like this."

"Did you now?"

"Well, not JUST like this."

She traced his mouth with quick kisses. He parted his lips and her tongue met his. His other hand kneaded her buttocks, wedging their bodies closer together. She felt his erection against her belly. Gabe eased her bare feet to the ground, and then he stepped back.

"Have you been hurt?" he asked.

Hannah lips trembled into a semblance of a smile. She caught her upper lip between her teeth.

"Not a bit. I hurt you, though. I didn't mean to, you know."

Gabe held her chin. "I know."

"Gabe," she murmured, the single word was a caress. "I'm afraid I love you."

Nearby, crickets chirped and bullfrogs belched messages into the dusk.

"Love isn't supposed to be frightening, you know."

Hannah whispered, "But for me it's terrifying."

"It's late. Let's head home."

"Good idea."

"Hang on!" Gabe pulled her close, her face against his chest, arms criss-crossed at one another's waist.

"Think of home," he whispered.

Hannah closed her eyes. A gentle breeze lifted wispy curls that tickled her cheeks. Her skirt fluttered at her ankles. It was a strange sensation. Flying. There was no feeling of speed, really. The ground just melted away beneath her curled toes. One second, she could feel the wet mud; the next, nothing. Although her feet dangled in mid-air, she knew she was safe, tethered to Gabe.

"The songwriters are right. It's just like walking on air. " She nuzzled Gabe's collarbone. "Love is."

Seconds later, they landed with a jarring thump, confined by the clutter of their closet.

"Interesting landing zone," she snickered.

"Hey, you broke my concentration! I was headed for the bed."

The closet door was jerked open. Trog looked like a troll. His face was scrunched in a scowl, his wiry hair sprouted from his head like the quills of an angry porcupine. "What in hell's going on in here?"

"Nothing that needs your help."

Trog stomped into the crowded closet to jerk Gabe's sleeve. "Then leave it for later. We need to talk."

Hannah opened her mouth to speak.

"Now," Trog said as he turned towards the door.

"All right, Trog," Gabe chuckled, sliding his hands to Hannah's waist. He crossed his arms in front of her, each hand gripping the other wrist, manacling their bodies together.

She felt safe. When had she replaced wariness with trust? Trust him, she did, though. So she leaned back, resting her head in the center of his chest. This is the smell, the look, the feel of love she decided.

She latched on to Trog's words mid-sentence. "...Feu Follet and Spriggans to waylay her."

"You think someone from the village employed Spriggans?" Gabe tightened his hold on Hannah's waist. She squirmed a bit and tapped his wrist.

"Calm down, Boy. We don't have the facts yet," Trog urged. He marched back and forth, bumping into the furniture. He plopped down on the edge of the bed and tugged on his scraggly beard.

Hannah's mind whirled in confused circles. She waggled her head, trying to rattle bits of information into a sensible pattern. "Spriggans?" she asked. "Who are the Spriggans and why should they be interested in me?"

Gabe answered. "Spriggans live high in the mountains, deep inside the Hollow Hills, just beyond the Siddhe compound." He pointed in the general direction of the steep bare mountains that predominated the northern horizon beyond the village.

"Siddhe?"

"Don't worry about them," Gabe said. "Pay attention to Trog."

"Originally, the Spriggan's job was to protect the treasure of those hallowed hills. But, greed changed them into evil, grotesque creatures. They've become an infamous band of destructive villains. These days, they're mercenaries. They destroy crops, steal works of art or money, and kidnap children. In short, no act is too vile for a Spriggan to perform, if the price is right."

"But who would pay them to play a trick on me?"

Gabe hunched his shoulders, tapped his thigh with a balled fist.

"You're not listening, Hannah. There was no trick intended. Even though Spriggans are quite small, they have the ability to inflate themselves into gruesome, monstrous shapes. Sort of like a pufferfish, you understand?"

Hannah interrupted him by pressing a palm flat against his mouth. "But, I saw no monstrous creatures. I was following fireflies and teeny-weeny dots of bouncing lights."

Gabe turned away, resting his head against the wall. Trog caught Hannah's arm and pulled her to sit beside him on the bed. "Those fireballs would have been the Feu Follet. They're dark faeries; skilled in luring humans into danger. Didn't it occur to you that they could change appearance?"

Hannah shook her head, chewed her bottom lip.

Gabe moved to stand at her side. "They stir up havoc."

"And they do a helluva job, right Boy?" Trog's ham-shaped elbow jabbed Gabe's side. Then, he spoke to Hannah. "The Feu appear in forest shadows as a flickering flame or a ball of light or even as the pricks of light you saw. Humans have been known to follow them into a dense wood where willow trees mutter obscenities and birch trees bend to touch a person's head." Trog leaned close to Hannah's face and whispered, "You do know that a birch branch can leave a vivid white scar and inflict madness, don't you?"

Hnnah shook her head.

"If the birch branch brushes his heart, the human will die."

Trog's voice had dropped to a soft rasp and he dragged his stubby finger across her collarbone.

Hannah jumped as though she had been branded by his light touch. In flailing, one of her arms bumped Trog's palm. The elf cradled his right hand in his left, cupping it towards his body.

"What's wrong with your hand, Trog?" Gabe asked.

Trog grimaced and shook his head. "Nothing of much consequence."

Hannah touched his wrist. "Are you certain, Trog? We can ..."

Through gritted teeth, Trog muttered, "Make no mistake, Missy. The Feu Follet are evil blighters."

Hannah sat between the men. She turned from one to the other, trying to interpolate their information. "So, you think that the Feu Follet were leading me through the woods to the Spriggans?"

Gabe arched a single brow.

"To hurt me?"

In answer, Trog opened his hand and laid it limp across his leg. The palm was red and blistered, as if he had grabbed the flame of a torch. Gabe hurried to his apothecary shelves and returned with gauze and ointments to dress the injury.

"I managed to snag one of the Feu." Trog winced, closing both eyes. "I…hmm… encouraged him to explain tonight's mystery," he grinned and shrugged. "The blasted creature admitted that they, the Feu, had in fact, been paid to lure you. They were supposed to draw you around the mountain to the swamp. He assumed that the Sprig-gans wanted you. Since he's young, he wasn't told any particulars."

Hannah touched Trog's thumb. "You're a good friend." She nodded towards Gabe and then tapped her own chest. "To both of us."

Gabe moved the lamp closer so that he could examine the elf's injury carefully. "Hmmm, ahhh," he mumbled as he touched the puffy blisters with the tip of one finger.

Hannah fanned Trog's palm while Gabe dabbed the burns with a greasy ointment. Throughout the procedure, Hannah hovered like a protective mother, stroking Trog's bristly hair and rubbing his back en-couragingly.

Task accomplished, the room was awkwardly silent. Trog arched a bushy brow when he looked at Gabe. Gabe shrugged and glanced towards Hannah.

"Gotta love the intrigue!" Trog cleared his throat. "All this bal-du-rah is exciting; right? "

"Good man."

"Time for me to go." Trog jammed his hat low on this forehead. "We'll solve this puzzle, Gabe...for you and your woman. No worries."

Hannah returned the supplies to Gabe's workbench. She tidied the scattered pieces of paper into a pile, securing the stack with a pale pink crystal paperweight. She used the cuff of her sweater to dust the heavy chunk of crystal. She breathed deep, inhaling the tangy potpourri of drying herbs- basil, mint, oregano and fennel -that made her nostrils tingle. She closed her eyes and rotated her head, stretching her neck, once, twice.

Gabe moved silently; but even without seeing him, she knew he stood no more than two feet away. She'd decided it was nice, that knowing. The feeling used to scare her, but now it was a comfort. She reached towards him and he took her hand in his. Kissing his knuckles, she pressed their joined hands between her breasts. "You hold my heart, Gabe, but you can't be my everything."

"I'll take anything you're willing to give."

"Is that fair?"

"Life is seldom fair, is it, Hannah?"

She swiveled back to the workbench to busy herself with dusting the bottles of dried herbs. "No."

"You're scared."

"You bet," she whispered. She shivered when he breathed on her neck.

"I'll keep you safe. Trust me."

"Oh I trust you." Hannah rubbed her knuckle across her lips until they tingled. "That's one of the things that scares me." She blinked and a big tear dripped down her cheek. "You've forced me to recognize all sorts of feelings that absolutely terrify me."

Gabe stepped backwards, held his arms out at his sides. "I scare you?"

Hannah followed him, wrapped her arms at his waist. "Not you. I love you and it's the loving that's scary. I don't know what to do with the new emotions… the dependence, the sharing, the incredible happiness." She squeezed her arms tighter. "Am I making any sense?"

"No, not really. Why would happiness be frightening?"

"I can't really explain it. I just feel…fragile, I guess. I feel like I'm totally filled up. A balloon stretched thin and filled to bursting." She rubbed her face against his chest, breathing in the smell of him. The smell of love. She took another deep breath.

"It might be scary to you; but it feels perfect to me." He kissed the top of her head, crossed his arms over her back. "I could stand here with you forever."

"I need room to breathe, to experience, to create. I need to be more."

"Are you saying that you want to leave me? Do you want me to take you back to North Carolina?"

"Oh God, no." She grabbed his shirt and pulled it loose from his trousers. She pulled him close, squeezing tight, flexing her fingers into his bare back. "No. I want to be with you. I promised you a year, remember?"

"A year and a day."

"Right. And I always keep my promises."

"Good."

"But, I'd like to have some friends nearer my age. Ella is hardly a contemporary, now is she?"

He chuckled, but he sounded as if he were almost gagging. "Don't ever leave me, Hannah."

Hannah woke to the smell of coffee brewing. She could hear Gabe puttering in the kitchen. Because she knew he was trying to be silent, the sounds seemed exaggerated. Smiling she pulled on his robe – a faded blue terrycloth that she had confiscated as her own. The cuffs were rolled several times, yet they still covered all but her fingers. The shoulder seams practically reached her elbows. Weeks ago, Ella had offered to make a robe that would fit properly; but she'd refused the offer. It was nice waking up in a bed still warm from Gabe's body heat, and burying her face in the pillow that held his scent. Just like the bed they shared, his robe was an umbilical cord, securing her to the intimacy of their relationship – those bits of private detail known only to the two of them.

SSSh, slap, sssh, slap. Her fuzzy slippers whispered to the hardwood floor as she headed for the kitchen. Once there, she was astounded. Gabe was plundering the drawer where she'd organized the cooking utensils; spoons, spatulas, whisk and ladles. Almost every cook pot had been removed from the overhead hooks where they usually hung. Most of those once sparkling copper pots now rested in the soapy water spilling over the lip of the sink. A large saucepan bubbled merrily on the back burner, emitting a sweet scorched vanilla steam. Accumulated vapor dripped down the wall.

A pat of butter skittered in a hot sauté pan, turned brown and started to smoke. On the counter between the sink and stove an orderly procession of chopped vegetables marched in neat straight lines. Matchstick-sized carrot slivers cued up next to little half moons of mushrooms. Two mounds of precisely minced purple Bermuda onion opposed perfectly aligned rows of zucchini circles and yellow pepper rings. The large butcher knife had been left atop three crushed, but unpeeled, garlic cloves. The pleasing, but pungent aroma wafted to her. Snowy white drifts of flour surrounded a bowl filled with a yeasty batter beginning to ooze over the edge. Two nutmegs were discarded next to a small mound of grated powder. Gabe turned to watch her over his shoulder. He had one white streak of flour at his temple and a dab of cinnamon on his cheek.

"Good morning." She kissed him and then rubbed his cheek with her thumb. "What's going on?"

"It's a surprise. I've got the whole day planned."

Hannah tipped her head towards the sink. "It'll take a while to clean up; but not the whole day!"

"What?" Gabe waved his hand in dismissal. "Oh. That. Don't worry about it. Sit. We'll eat while I tell you my plans."

Hannah poured coffee and stuck her nose in the mug. "Ah, the smell of morning! What else have you got on the menu?" She stirred the pale yellow custard that bubbled voraciously.

Gabe pushed a pan of fluffy dough into the hot oven and the room was perfumed with cinnamon and nutmeg. "In twenty minutes we'll have brioche and crème anglaise. How about an omelet first?"

"Hungry, are you?"

"Happy. I eat when I'm happy, and these days, I'm ecstatic."

"C'mon. Tell me your plans," Hannah asked as she soaped the last of the copper pots. "You've got a Christmas morning grin, and I'm curious. What's your secret schedule for the day?"

209

Gabe dried a plate and stacked it in the cupboard. He leaned against the counter and propped his elbows on the wooden chopping block. "I've figured out the solution to your problem."

"Oh, really?" Hannah stood between his legs. She smoothed her hands over his chest. "And which problem would that be?"

"I know where your friend lives." Gabe looked awfully proud of himself. She nipped his neck, licked the bite and blew on it, just to watch him shiver. The pulse at the base of his throat sped up.

"Which friend would that be?"

"Oh, you don't know her yet. But, you'll like her. I'm certain."

"One of the elves?"

He turned her towards the door, pushed her shoulders, swatted her bottom when she took a step. "No more information. It's a surprise! Go get dressed. Wear your boots and a thick sweater."

She was in the hall when Gabe called, "Toss a dress and sandals in your backpack. We might go dancing this evening."

Nestled close to Gabe's shoulder, huddled under the large black cape he wore, Hannah barely noticed the differences in temperatures. She did hear the great whoosh of air, not unlike the sensation of a subway train leaving a station. Air was rushing past, being pulled behind them. She sensed neither a feeling of speed nor movement.

There was only the roar of wind, filling her ears without sound. She hadn't yet accustomed to the phenomenon when Gabe opened his arms. Her skin felt chilled without his warmth circling her.

"Oh! Goodness. We're in Scotland, aren't we?"

"So, you've visited before?"

"No. But, it's hard to imagine anywhere else that could be so lush and green, yet forbidding at the same time. The land's just as you described it."

They stood in a field, or was it a glen in Scotland? Craggy, low mountains ranged along the horizon framing wide expanses of purple vegetation growing close to the ground. Lichen-covered boulders dotted the fields, like so many huge unearthed potatoes left to seed future crops. The sky was robin's egg blue. The austere mountains snagged low hanging clouds; the serrated edges of rock cliffs were festooned with billowy white cotton balls.

"Welcome to Skye."

"It's beautiful." She almost whispered it. The serenity of the place was unequalled. She turned slowly, three hundred-sixty degrees. The smell of the sea floated in the damp air. A gentle breeze cooled the moisture that settled on her face and hands. She breathed deep, filling her lungs with air that felt like a humidifier. Vegetative. The air smelled vegetative; full of life. When she circled, she trampled on heather that grew in a dense cushion across the entire landscape. Tiny green leaves were lost among thousands, no millions, of dainty purple flowers incongruous on woody, almost thorny stems.

"Oh, Gabe. How could you bear to leave this place? It's beautiful here!"

"Yes, Scotland is bonny in the summer months. And Skye is Scotland's crown. But can't Winter can be another thing altogether? Then, even the sheep wear bedraggled coats, dirty gray and hanging in thick bits and pieces. Weather's wet and piercing cold, gray sky, gray rocks. But, all the same, I love it here."

"Well, in the summer, it looks like faerieland, to be sure."

"Hmmm. No. It's definitely not faerieland. That portal closed behind us, tight and secure. Here, no human can see Trog else Trog wants it so."

Hannah was surprised when Trog appeared at her side, red stocking cap in his hand. "It's the cap, you see?" He pulled the hat over his head, low on his forehead till it touched his bushy brows. "Makes me invisible to unbelievers!"

Gabe held her shoulders. His thumbs pressed into her arms. His eyes were squinted, his brows drawn close in a serious, straight line.

"Does it matter to you, Hannah, that I keep some secrets from the people here? Even the people I love?"

"Are you truthful with me? Even here in Skye?"

Gabe laid his palm over his heart. "I will always answer your questions truthfully."

"But you lie to people you say you love."

Gabe cocked a brow and shrugged. "I do love them. And I don't lie...not exactly. I just don't correct their misconceptions."

Now Hannah shrugged her shoulders. "It's a matter of vocabulary. But it doesn't matter. I'm not going to ruin our lovely adventure with an argument. I love you, Gabriel Edward Murray."

He pulled her knuckles to his lips and watched her over their joined hands.

He grinned.

"And that's a mouthful!"

Trog shifted his weight, and sniffed the crisp air. He knelt with his ear to the ground. Winking at Gabe, he squeaked out a command. "Go on and steal a kiss. I know it's what you've planned." Hannah giggled and Gabe quirked his eyebrow. "Someone's coming," Trog squealed. "Long hill-walker's strides. He'll be here soon! Go on. Go on. Kiss her. Kiss the girl. Be quick about it."

"Pushy little imp, aren't you?" Even while he was chuckling, Gabe lowered his face to Hannah's and kissed her until she was dizzy.

"Harrumph. I told you to kiss the girl, not to make a production of it!"

Hannah blushed and Gabe swallowed the giggle she had lost in his mouth.

Bright sunlight made her blink. "Do you know him?" Squinting, Gabe did recognize the man loping towards them.

"It's Ewan! I'd know that pace anywhere." Gabe pointed his arm at the figure in the distance. "See how he swings his arms like they are pistons? He drives those long legs over ground with never a missed step. He's always done that, even as a wee boy." He mimicked the man's gait, lifting his left arm and right foot high, then swinging the arm down, raising the opposite arm and leg.

Hannah watched him watch his friend approach, grinning at his clownish imitation.

Ewan traipsed over the hillock. "Ho, Gabe!" He was a tall man with auburn hair. Sunlight glinted bright red on highlights in his hair. He was roughly Gabe's size, maybe a bit thicker around the middle, but certainly not overweight. Then men exchanged the usual male greetings. Gabe punched Ewan's shoulder and Ewan tapped at Gabe's

belly. Both laughed when they simultaneously said, "Good to see you,

man."

"Are you here to stay for a bit, then, Gabe?"

"Only for the day."

"Such a quick trip."

"I wanted everyone to meet Hannah. My fiancée."

Standing with Trog, partially hidden by a rather large boulder,

Hannah jerked and opened her mouth; but she couldn't think of any-

thing to say. Maybe a handfast partner was sort of like a fiancée.

"So, you're going to be married! Some unfortunate lady lassoed

you, did she? The whole of Floddigarry will be surprised by the news.

The lassies will be all aflutter!" He batted his eyes, waved his arms

and pretended to swoon.

Hannah strolled over to stand between the men. "Have I

missed a good joke?"

Ewan caught himself in mid-swoon. His big brown eyes

popped wide open and his mouth hung agape. Gabe pushed his friend's chin with a knuckle. He touched Hannah at the small of her back, nudging her forward a step.

"I didn't think you'd seen her."

"Hannah, is it? You're beautiful." Ewan folded her hand between both of his. Hannah felt the ridge of calluses on his palms. A hard-working man.

"Hannah, this dolt is my friend, Ewan McDonald, feeble excuse that he is. He and his sister, Mairisi, live just the other side of the small loch, near my Da's farm."

Hannah smiled and nodded. "How do you do, Ewan?"

"I'm thinking our Gabe must be a very lucky man."

Hannah blushed. She could feel the heat of the color rise in her cheeks and figured she looked like a clown. She glanced at Gabe with a self-conscious smile. Then she shifted her focus to her wrist, lost under the freckled knuckles and tawny hair on the back of Ewan's hand. Gabe extricated her hand, only to cover it with his own.

"And your Da knows you're coming, then?" Ewan asked.

"Ummm. No. It's to be a bit of a surprise."

"I'll say."

Hannah interrupted, "But a pleasant one, I should hope."

"Oh, never you doubt it, Hannah," Ewan assured her. "Sean'll be delighted!" He shook his head, "How I'd love to be there, invisible like, when you meet him. God, what a surprise! Sean's beginning to think that Gabe will never settle and be married."

She cut her eyes, glancing at one man and then the other. "Oh. Gabe's been quite the ladies' man, then?"

"No. Not exactly." Ewan laughed, his head jerked sideways to bump Gabe's. "Oh, the ladies like him fine, if you take me meaning. It's just that Gabe never really gave the lassies much encouragement. But, I've overheard one or two of Mairisi's friends gossip about this braw young lad, now haven't I?" He winked at Hannah and she nodded. "Because he rarely visits Floddigarry, he's bit of a novelty for the local lasses, I suppose. Several of the girls hinted that they'd be willing to let him catch them should he ever take chase!"

Ewan cuffed Gabe on the shoulder, then he bent double and clutched his side as he howled at his own joke. His face flushed, turning his pale skin beet-red from his ears down into the neck of his forest green sweater.

"At the dances, Gabe is a willing partner, to be sure. But he'll never single out a special girl. Always jumping from one partner to another. Like a bee sampling nectar from each flower, was our Gabe!" He tipped his head to Hannah. "I guess he was looking for that special someone, ma darlin'." He nudged her waist with his elbow. "You know, we blokes always thought he was just running scared!"

"Yeah. Right!" Gabe raised his fists in front of his face, jabbing punches in the air. "The wee lasses might frighten me, but luckily, I'm not scared of you!" The two grown men tussled together like children, rolling in a jovial hodge-podge of arms and long legs.

After a minute or two, Hannah intervened. "Boys, boys. Break it up now!"

Gabe's customary black shirt was smeared with green stains and pinstripes of rust-colored dirt. Ewan's bottom lip was slightly swollen and a slow trickle of blood oozed from a tiny cut. They'd had a fine reunion!

Hannah poked around in her bag until she found a handkerchief. She wrapped a fingertip in the clean linen and touched Ewan's lip gingerly. "There now," she murmured. The two words stretched into six or eight syllables, rising and falling in a song. "It's not bad, but it'll bruise. Best remember to ice it when you get home."

Ewan laid on the ground, straddled by his very fit and obviously unintimidated friend. "I've died and gone to Heaven. A lovely angel's tickling me lips. She's talking nonsense, but I do enjoy the lilt to her voice and all the round, fat vowels." With just the tip of his tongue, he tested his bottom lip. Tinge of blood. There was a slight knot of swelling. Not bad. He stopped her ministrations, holding her wrist between his thumb and finger. He stared at her for a moment, then turned to Gabe. "Oh, yes. You're definitely a lucky man!"

Gabe laughed out loud and bounced to his feet in one motion, as if his knees were spring-loaded. He reached out a hand that Ewan accepted.

"That I am!" He hauled his friend to his feet. "I am the happiest, luckiest guy in the world! Come to the house tonight. We'll celebrate my good fortune."

Ewan nodded. "Oh, right you are. We can celebrate. But, not at Sean's house. There's a dance at the Country House. Everyone will be there. You two have to come."

Hannah had inched close to Gabe. Her fingers crawled into his palm. He glanced at her, smiling. "The Country House is a big old rambling hotel, right next to Flora McDonald's house – you do know about the lengendary Flora , who helped the Bonny Prince escape the Brits?"

Hannah nodded. "We American school girls do learn our history lessons."

"Every so often, the publicans hire a band to play in the bar. There will be music with pipes and accordions. The music's good for business. Dancing creates a powerful thirst, you know!" Gabe draped his arm across her shoulders and pulled her close against his side. "The dances are in circular patterns, in reels. It's sort of like an American square dance. It'll be great fun!"

Hannah shrugged her shoulders. She shifted from one foot to the other. She inspected the slightly frayed hem of her handkerchief, picking tiny white threads loose from one corner. "I dunno. We'll see." Her voice was soft, hesitant, hardly more than an exhale. A couple of curls fell forward, hiding her eyes.

Lifting her chin with his finger, Ewan grinned. "What's to see? Don't tell me you're scared now?"

"Umm, well." She smiled, trying to bluff.

"Don't worry. You'll have two strong guys, one on each arm, there to protect you!"

She grinned. "Not exactly scared. I don't know the dances. I don't want to embarrass Gabe first time I meet people here."

"Weel now. If that's all that's worrying you, you're in the right company!" Ewan grabbed her hands and pulled her forward. He bowed, practically bumping his forehead on his knee. "Only last month Megan MacTavish and I won honorable mention in the dance competition over at Kyle of Lochalsh!" As he spoke, he pointed over his shoulder with his thumb, towards a vague destination in the distance.

Ewan positioned her left hand on his right shoulder and took her right hand in his left. With a warbling whistle, he capably mimicked the whine of a bagpipe. With swooping arms, he swung her into a dance step that combined shuffling, twirling, bouncing and skipping. She never had time to consider her missed steps or awkward turns. Ewan deftly guided her through intricate maneuvers, dodging the stones strewn in their open-air ballroom. She was dizzy when he abruptly stopped whistling and swaying. Gabe's applause and shrill whistle vibrated in her ribcage.

"Well done. Bravo! Well done!"

"Ewan's a wonderful teacher," she panted, flipping her heavy braid over her shoulder.

"Aye. That I am," he responded with a wink. "I thank you for the dance, Mistress Hannah. Be sure to save another for me tonight!"

She curtsied. "By all means, sir."

Gabe knelt to buckle her backpack, stuffing the extra pair of socks and her hairbrush back inside. "We'd best be on our way, Hannah." He cocked his head towards the gray clouds gathering just to the south. "A storm is coming."

Ewan rubbed his knuckle across his upper lip, hiding the trace of a smile. "Already domesticated the man, Hannah."

Even though both men slowed their pace, Hannah trotted to keep up with them. Each of their strides was larger than two of hers. She looked like a frisky puppy bounding alongside their steady pace. The sunlight was filtered; only a yellow radiance was visible behind the cluster of darkening clouds. Hannah squinted towards the golden light and then twisted her wrist to check her watch.

"There are hours yet before sunset."

"But,"

"It's summer in the far north," Gabe chuckled. "It will be light 'til close to midnight. But, Scotland's winter days are frightfully short. Then, it gets dark around teatime."

"Wow. But what a gift the beautiful long days of summer,

right?"

Ewan waited for Hannah to get in step with him. He cradled her elbow in his palm, keeping them apace. "The folks here on Skye are mainly crofters and fishermen, much like always. We have defi-nitely learned to make hay while the sun shines, because quite often it doesn't."

They'd reached a fork in the path. Ewan veered off to the right, Gabe guided Hannah left. "See you at eight," Gabe called.

A fine mist hovered, cooling the thick air. Gabe draped his cloak over Hannah's shoulders. The hem dragged the ground, occasionally snagging in the heather and bracken along the path.

"Aren't you chilly, Gabe?"

"No. You forget that I'm a Scot, born in the cold and the damp. Wee bairns are birthed already climatized."

She smiled. "I like the brogue. It's much more pronounced now that you're home."

"Is it now? I'd not noticed."

"No, you wouldn't. It was the same when I visited cousins in Georgia. My drawl would stretch for a country mile."

He flicked her nose with his index finger. "Ah. Here we are."

They'd stopped at stone pillars. Thousands of rocks were piled without mortar, making an impressive fence that stood level with Hannah's waist. The path wound between the pillars, over a small hill, and snaked its way to a cottage about a quarter mile away. Pink and white clematis bloomed on vines that crawled the walls on the front and side of the house. Surrounding land was a palette of green and yellow. Brilliant yellow squares, like a patchwork design, covered several acres.

"Your father grows flowers commercially?"

"Flowers? No." He looked at her, puzzled, then looked across the fields. "Oh. You mean the rapeseed flowers. Da sells the crop to a processor who makes canola oil from the seeds. Lots of farms in Britain and Scotland grow rapeseed. Makes for lovely fields, don't you think."

"Definitely."

Two black and white Border Collies rushed to meet them, barking and jousting for position. Gabe squatted and held out his hand. "There's a good boy," he murmured, stroking the largest dog. "This is Dubh. That means black. He's at least ten years old now, but he's spry as a pup. Runs the fields all day, everyday, don't you boy?" Dubh inclined his head, allowing better access to his ears, in case anyone wanted to scratch him.

Hannah tucked her fingers and extended her knuckles to the smaller female dog. "And what's this lady's name?"

"Ah, that's Danu, Celtic goddess of luck."

"She's a beauty." Hannah patted the dog's broad shoulders. "It's a fine lass, you are Danu." A long pink tongue darted a wet thanks on Hannah's cheek. Laughing, she stood up and dried her cheek with the sleeve of her sweater. "Oh, you're welcome, girl."

Their ruckus drew an audience. The red enameled door of the cottage opened and a tall man stepped out. "What's the commotion out here?" he called, shielding his eyes and squinting into the glare.

"It's me, Da."

"Gabriel?"

Sean Murray threw wide his arms. His grin stretched from one ear to the other. "Welcome home, son. Welcome home!"

Gabe wrapped an arm around Hannah, and took a step down the path towards his father. Hannah shook her head. "No, you go. Greet your father. I'll wait," she whispered.

One quick nod and he rushed down the walk. The men embraced enthusiastically, thumping one another on the back. They stood locked together for a precious minute. Hannah used the time to study father and son.

Strong gene pool. They were matched in height. The broad shoulders were close to the same size, too. Gabe had inherited his father's stance and mannerisms. But, his ebony hair and penetrating gray eyes must have been gifts from his mother. Sean's short-cropped hair was a dark chestnut, only slightly graying at his temples. His dark brown eyes were bright with happy tears.

She couldn't hear their conversation. Gabe said something that obviously surprised his father. Sean grabbed at his heart and laughed out loud. Both men turned to her. Nervous, Hannah combed through her hair with her fingers. She approached them slowly, trying to hold the long cloak out of the pasty mud settling in the walk.

Sean opened his arms wide again. "Welcome, Hannah. Welcome home!" She found herself enfolded in his arms and pressed to the soft plaid of his work shirt, which smelled of fresh mowed grass, sweat and a hint of lager. Their arrival must have interrupted an after-work pint.

Gripping her biceps, Sean held her at arm's length. "Let me look at you, girl." He did, smiling as his eyes roamed from the top of her head to the laces on her boots. "You're a sight for tired eyes, let me tell you. I'd given up on this boy. I didn't think he'd ever find the right woman!"

Turning to his son, he asked, "You did find the right one, didn't you, boy?"

Curling an arm around Hannah, Gabe kissed the tangled curls tucked behind her ear. "Oh yes sir. I did."

Taking Hannah's hand, Sean turned back towards the house. "Come in and tell me all about yourself, girl." He winked at Gabe. "You can take her bag up to the guest room, top of the stairs, boy."

"We're not staying the night, Da. This is a short visit."

Gabe dropped her backpack at the foot of the stairs. Trog perched on the banister, giggling. "You'd best marry that girl quickly, Boy. I'm thinking your Da is going to insist on separate rooms until the ring's on her finger!" He almost toppled off the railing when his guffaws made him cough.

Gabe gritted his teeth and pulled the elf to the floor. "Come on in. Join our celebration, Trog."

Hannah admired Sean's home. Even now, in the summer when the large stone hearth was cold and swept clean, the very walls smelled of Winter's peat fires. She closed her eyes and inhaled, enjoying the odor of homecoming. How could this stranger's house smell like home to her? The main room was a cozy, cluttered order with books jammed two rows deep in the floor-to-ceiling shelves. Several large volumes were stacked on the dark green carpet beside an inviting red leather chair that had developed big indentations in the seat and back. She also admired the man across the room, busy pulling glasses from his sideboard. She'd bet that those big indentations that would coin-cide with his torso perfectly. He moved like Gabe, exuded the same

225

grace and confidence, certain of his agility. And strength. Obviously, he was strong. Where Gabe's muscles are a young man's, bulging and prominent; Sean's are mature, honed long and taut. She watched Sean, envisioning Gabe in the coming years, black hair showing hints of silver, muscles padded by the slightest trace of fat, scant lines framing his eyes. Laugh lines. She was sure Gabe's would be laugh lines.

Gabe gave her that all-knowing look and smiled. He could probably tell she was daydreaming. "Hamphh," he cleared his throat.

Hannah felt compelled to respond. "Well, look who you found. Hello, Trog."

Sean turned abruptly. "Trog? You can see Trog?"

"Certainly, can't you?"

"Yes, but,"

Gabe jumped into the conversation. "Da, we've lived together; Hannah and I, in the village for close to three months. She knows about me and the faeries." He paused to swallow. "She knows."

"Oh, I see. Well, this really does call for a celebration, doesn't it?" Sean poured generous portions of Scotch into four tumblers. He served the Scotch neat, no ice. He offered the first glass to Hannah.

"This is Talisker, distilled right here on Skye. It's fine stuff!" He passed the crystal tumbler below her nose. The garnet colored whiskey had a pleasant, but potent, aroma - just a trace of peat and tobacco.

Hannah's nostrils flared and her eyes began to water. "I'm, umm, I'm, well, I'm sure it is," she stumbled over her words. "Just a drop, thank you."

With one quick gulp, Sean tossed back his own pour of liquor. Cheeks tanned by the sun, freckled with age, turned beet-red. Chestnut brown eyes glazed with tears. His nostrils flared. He exhaled a huge breath. "Ahhhh. Fine stuff!" He pounded his chest and shook his head so quickly that his hair stood at odd angles. "Okay, go on with your story, son."

"I told you that we have been living together in the village, Da. We've been living there, together. Together in my cave. We were handfast months ago." He reached for Hannah's hand. "I love her." He kissed her knuckles, staring at her eyes, but speaking to his father.

"You plan to marry this girl?" Sean pressed his finger to the center of Gabe's chest.

"Yessir. That's my plan."

Hannah coughed on her tiny sip of Talisker. Trog slapped her on the back and lifted his glass to touch her's.

"Let's drink to matrimony!" His comical voice cracked on the last syllable, becoming a cough, which he drowned with whisky. "The drink of the gods!" he announced, licking his lips.

Gabe chuckled. Hannah brushed at Trog's cowlicks and then pushed gently on his shoulders, encouraging him to sit in the chair she'd just vacated. "Perhaps I could prepare some food to complement your heavenly drink," she teased.

Sean flustered with his shirttail; tucking one side into his trousers. "Food! Dinner. Of course, you're probably hungry." He smacked the side of his head with the heel of his palm. "Where are my manners?" He started through a swinging door, to the kitchen, but he turned back. "Will you help me, then, Hannah?"

"Of course!" She smiled and hurried after him.

Something savory was already bubbling in a casserole in the oven. Sean nodded towards a cutting board on the center island counter. "You can slice what's left of that loaf. Butter's in the fridge." He tapped his temple with his index finger, then pointed to a bowl filled with pears. "Wash and pare some fruit, too. Check the fridge for a bit of cheese. Is Stilton to your liking, Hannah?" He waited to be certain she found everything she needed. Then, he opened the oven and lifted out the caramel brown crockery using a long dishtowel rather than oven mitts. Boiling juices had bubbled around the lid and sealed it shut. Sean edged a small knife in the seam between the pot and its lid. A cloud of fragrant steam fogged the kitchen. "Nothing fancy, I'm afraid. It's only a bean cassoulet."

"It smells delicious," Hannah assured him. Her stomach growled quietly in affirmation.

"Ah, weel, I did add a wee bit of me special flavoring!" He arched one auburn eyebrow and winked as he dangled a bottle of sherry between thumb and forefinger.

The two of them were laughing and murmuring jokes as they shuttled between the kitchen and dining table, carrying food, silverware, plates, bowls and glasses. While Sean called Gabe and Trog to dinner, Hannah stepped out into the yard. In just a minute, she returned with a cluster of flowers arranged in a small vase she'd found in the cupboard. Settling her centerpiece, she sighed, "Oh, Sean, this is all lovely!"

Gabe watched her, rather than the table setting as he agreed, "Yes, lovely."

The meal was delicious; three varieties of beans simmered with garlic, onions, carrots, cloves, pepper and a dollop of Sean's Sherry. Dinner conversation was confusing; Trog concocted what Hannah assumed were wildly exaggerated stories of his childhood. Sean interrupted with questions.

"So, you're an American girl; from the South are you?"

"Yes."

"I've always wanted to see Florida. I hear it's flat and marshy land."

"Hot and humid, with mosquitoes, snakes and alligators too."

"Ah. And where did you grow up?"

"I was born in Georgia... in a small town where everyone knew my family history. My parents died when I was in grade school. My maternal grandmother and I moved to Atlanta...a very large, bustling city. I lived there until her death three years ago."

"And no one knew your history."

Hannah shrugged.

"I'm sorry for your loss."

It was only natural that Sean would be curious about her; but his questions felt imposing. She didn't want anything to dampen the fun she was having today. She stood and gathered her plate and silverware.

"Just leave the dishes on the counter, Hannah." Gabe checked his watch. "Ewan will be here in thirty minutes."

When she nudged the kitchen's swinging door with her shoulder, Gabe turned to his father. "Dancing at the Country House tonight."

Water was splashing in the kitchen sink. "Go up and dress for the dance, lassie. Trog will help me do the washing later," Sean called.

He laid a hand on Gabe's knee. "You stay with me for a moment, son."

Gabe scraped at a speck of mud that was splattered on his pants. He looked at his fingers rather than at his Da.

"Talk to me. You say that Hannah knows a lot... She's been accepted by the faeries... But she doesn't know everything, does she?"

"No sir. Not yet. She's not ready."

"Ah. SHE'S not ready. But you should tell her. How can you withhold truth from someone you love?"

"Funny, she asked me the same question earlier today."

"And how did you answer?"

"I told her that I would answer honestly any question she asked."

Sean shook his head slowly. "It's not exactly the same thing, now is it?"

"It's the best I can do at present. I can't risk losing her, Da."

"Then explain the situation to me. How did you meet her?"

"Fate. Fate brought Hannah to me. In her corner of America, she's earned quite a reputation as a painter. Frescoes. She paints fantastic murals. It wasn't easy; but I convinced her to leave her world and come with me to mine in the Faerie village." Now he did look at his father. He took a deep breath, and squeezed Sean's forearm with both hands.

"You convinced her, did you?"

"Her house caught fire during a storm. I saw my chance and I acted. I had to have her, Da, I knew she was born just for me!"

"Go on."

"Well, she came with me although she had some reservations."

"You told her you live in a faerie raft?"

"Not exactly. But once we were there, I told her that I wouldn't force her to stay. It was always her choice –to stay or to leave."

"So she agreed to handfast?"

"I failed to mention that stipulation to her."

"Ella allowed that?"

Gabe flinched. "Ella never asked questions."

"But Oberon confronted you?"

"Tatiana, actually."

His chair groaned when Sean tipped it back, balancing on two legs. "What was Hannah's response when challenged by Tatiana?"

"Hurt. Embarrassed and hurt. She told me that I'd tricked her."

"You did."

"I was trying to give her time. She's skittish. I wanted her to know me, to care about me. She has some issues with trust."

"Odd way to gain the girl's trust – lying to her. You're lucky she didn't bolt."

Gabe whispered, "I know."

Dubh and Danu barked in answer to a knock the door, cheerfully drooling their welcome. At the same time, Sean produced a decanter.

"And would you be wanting a bit o' Talisker to settle your stomach, man?"

"Ah weel. And it's a fine idea you'll be having, Sean Murray!" Ewan answered. He swirled the whiskey in his glass, inhaling the bouquet as he closed his eyes, somehow enhancing the aroma while sightless. He tipped the glass and relished a penury taste of the scotch.

"So. What do you make of Gabe's news?" Ewan asked Sean.

"Yes, weel now. We can't rush these things."

"I … see," Ewan drawled. He reached over Gabe's shoulder to grab a half-eaten roll from the breadbasket.

"Do you, now?"

"No. Not really. To be truthful, I expected you to be a bit more…exuberant." Ewan settled into the chair Hannah had vacated, rested his elbows on the table.

"They've only just met. It takes time to know a person – really know the person." He thumped his chest.

Gabe nodded. "She was born to be with me."

Sean tipped his head towards the stairs. "Go get dressed, son. You're denying the lassies a chance at Ewan here."

"Yes; go dress for the doings tonight." Ewan asked as he brushed crumbs from the plaid of his kilt. He stood and straightened the sporran that hung at his waist.

Upstairs in a room furnished with twin beds draped with a dark green tartan, Hannah shook out a dress Nowatil had made of three layers of chiffon: one, red; one, yellow; one pink over a flesh-toned slip. She slipped it over her head. The hem brushed just above her knee. The wide neckline dipped to her collarbone and was set with short-capped sleeves. She slipped soft, red slippers on her feet.

"Just a touch of lipstick, maybe." She lined her lips and brushed on a garnet colored gloss. "And perfume." Each wrist and her throat were spritzed with the light floral fragrance Gabe had concocted just for her. A few minutes later, she opened the door, stepped out into the hall. And bumped into Gabe's chest.

"Wonderful."

"I was waiting for you."

"So I see."

"I have something to give you."

"You do?"

He pulled her tight against him, caught her face between both hands. He inhaled. "Ahhh." Although she didn't think it possible, he

233

pressed even closer to her. She put her hands on top of his. "I love you, Hannah."

She reached behind him, cupped his buttocks and pushed her hips against his. "I want to believe you."

He rubbed his neck the length of hers, down and up again. He kissed her cheeks and eyes, her ears and jaw. When he finally found her mouth, both of them were breathing like marathon runners after a race.

The cuckoo cackled downstairs.

Hannah stepped back. Gabe followed her. She halted him with her palm on his chest. "We've got to go."

Gabe shrugged his shoulders, tugged on his cuffs and bowed curtly. "After you," he pointed to the stairs.

"Now did I say that you are altogether wonderful?" she asked, glancing over her shoulder at him.

"Not that I recall."

"Well, I thought it; but I wasn't accurate. Not at all. You, sir, are totally magnificent!" She gestured at him, sweeping her hand from shoulder to toe, encompassing white tuxedo shirt and sporran; blue, green and rust plaid kilt and high socks; the saigan dhu strapped at his calf and the black slippers on his feet. "Totally magnificent," she whispered.

The loud slam of a car door precipitated another fury of barking from Dubh and Danu.

234

The front door was jarred open, banging against the wall as a benign dervish of energy invaded the library.

"Gabriel Edward!" the dynamo exclaimed in a clipped tone.

Gabe was engulfed in a tangle of limbs. Short, muscular arms wrapped around his arms and shoulders. A pair of shapely legs belted his waist.

Just as abruptly as she had arrived, a veritable pixie disengaged her body parts and stood, hands on hips, taunting. "And didn't I tell himself" she pointed generally in Sean's direction, "that I'd be the one you would marry?"

"And did you listen when I told you it would never happen?" Ewan moved close to tug on her carrot-orange ponytail.

The tornado wrinkled her nose, shut her eyes tight and stuck out her tongue.

"Didn't I tell you that no self-respecting man marries a woman who can best him at racing, at fishing and at wrestling. Not at all. Not at all."

For a long moment, everyone stared at everyone else in the room.

"You must be Mairisi," Hannah said as she extended her hand. "I've certainly heard stories about you!"

The woman ignored Hannah's hand. Instead, she spread her feet to widen her stance, squared her shoulders and linked her thumbs through belt loops of her colorful calf-length skirt. Freckles rollicked across the bridge of her nose. Her heart-shaped mouth was drawn into a pout, but her pale blue eyes laughed. Hypnotic eyes, they were. Ice blue, but not ice-cube blue; more like the blue of a glacier. Not that Hannah had ever seen a glacier, but in photos they looked bluish.

"I would be Mairisi," she nodded curtly. "So that would be making you Hannah, aye?"

"Yes. I'm very pleased to meet you." Hannah tried again for a handshake.

Mairisi pushed at Hannah's hand. "Dinna fash about shakin' me hand," she opened her arms wide. *"Ceud mile failte!* A hundred thousand welcomes, Hannah." She whapped Hannah's back with several solid thumps, then stepped back and diverted her attention to Gabe. "Aye. She'll do."

"Aye, she will, indeed." Gabe grinned like Alice's Cheshire cat.

"Aye." Ewan agreed.

Hands on her hips once again, Mairisi lamented, "But won't it be a pathetic wedding celebration, what with me sobbing about loosing the man I'd picked for meself and me brother moonin' 'bout his best friend's new bride!"

Sean guffawed, "Awk! Mairisi, never did I see you sad for long. By the end of the first dance, you'll be in love with a new man!"

Mairisi studied the food remaining on the table. She popped a berry in her mouth. She shrugged one shoulder and winked.

"Aye. Mebbe so."

Sean belched softly and rubbed his stomach. "Be off, then. I've dishes to do." The dishes clattered when he stacked them. A whiff of scotch whiskey followed him through the swinging door to the kitchen.

Music was definitely in the air. From outside the inn, Hannah heard the pipes and she felt the throbbing beats of the bodhran drums in her chest. Inside the Country House, the wide wooden floor planks vibrated. Hannah marveled at the crowd of dancers who moved as figures on a music box, each performing the complicated choreography with practiced abandon.

Gabe pulled her into the throng. He put a hand at her back and swung her into the dance without missing a beat. She let her head fall back as they whirled, enjoying the moment, unconcerned about her performance. Three-quarters of the way through that first dance, Ewan cut in.

Gabe tipped his head and left in search of an ale. Not five minutes later, Ewan joined him at the bar.

"Where's Hannah?"

"Out there," Ewan pointed to the dance floor where three men lined up to watch Hannah dance with another man. "They cued up soon as you left the floor!"

The friends casually leaned against the bar. The smell of lemon oil blended with the Stout and ale being drawn from the taps with careful expertise. "Ah. She'll be having a good time, then."

Ewan scrubbed at his face. "Go on with you, man. Aren't you powerful jealous what with those lads drooling all over your lady?"

"No."

"Go on with you. Me, I'd be clearing the floor right now. Bastards." Ewan bounced on the balls of his feet and took jabs at imaginary opponents.

"They appreciate a beautiful woman. Nothing wrong with that."

"Have you lost your mind, man? They'll try to steal your Hannah, right here, never mind about your claim on her." Sean stabbed his thumb towards the dance floor. "MacNellis over there is probably filling her head with saccharine sweet talk at this very moment. Boasting and flexing his biceps."

Gabe smiled and offered a frosty glass of ale. "I wasn't jealous of you, Ewan. Why would I be jealous of these lads? I know Hannah loves me. I trust her. The attention boosts her confidence."

He pushed Ewan towards the dance floor, "Go on. Dance with her. She'll save the last dance for me." He winked and turned back to his ale, tapping the bar in tune with the music.

Gabe heard Hannah's laughter, distinct from all of the other voices in the crowded room. He didn't turn towards the dance floor. Although he chatted with a couple named Lachlan, who were expecting their first child before Christmas, he watched Hannah's approach in the bar mirror. Ewan trailed a few steps behind, skillfully blocking any admirers who might attempt to intercept her.

Hannah pushed sweaty curls back from her forehead and used a damp cocktail napkin to mop her face. Perspiration glistened across her collarbone. Smiling, she tucked her arm around his waist.

"Great fun! Thank you for bringing me tonight," she said.

"But you're tired and would like to leave soon," he finished.

"Yes," she said, "if you don't mind."

"Give me one dance and I'll take you home," he agreed.

He led her to the center of the floor. Some of the swirling steps were similar to a waltz, but others reminded her of a square dance. Gabe moved more like a jungle cat than an athlete; fluid graceful movements that maneuvered her effortlessly. She felt as if she were floating an inch above the wooden planks.

The song ended, the musicians called for an intermission and boisterous dancers moved en masse towards the bar where the publican was already at the taps building pints of ale. Gabe laced her fingers through his, and led Hannah outside.

"Should we say goodnight to Ewan and Mairisi?"

"No need. We'll see them again soon enough."

Full dark was hours away, but the sun was crouched low behind a soft blanket of downy clouds. Nighttime quiet had finally settled over the sleepy village. She looked across the crowded parking area towards the hushed street. Not a car on the road.

"Shouldn't we phone for a cab?"

"No."

"No?"

Gabe pulled her to the shadowed side of the building, out of range for the pale yellow arc of the street lamp. He motioned her close with a crook of his finger and the slightest of smiles. He drew her, like a fish on a reel, using only his index finger and the dimples she found so alluring. His kiss netted her and she had no intention of an attempt at escape.

"Think of our house. Concentrate on a relaxing bath in warm soapy water. Think of the soft feather comforter on our bed." He kissed her temple and she closed her eyes, imagining. Cool air, like from an electric fan, blew through her hair for a few seconds. She was warm, though, tucked close to his chest. They landed in his garden moments later.

"Everything today has been wonderful; one of the best days ever," she said as they strolled hand-in-hand towards the house.

Two hours later, Gabe rested on his side, reclining on his elbow, head on his palm. Hannah cuddled spoon-style in front of him. He draped his arm across her waist and kissed the top of her head. They were quiet, almost dozing. The sheer curtains at the windows frolicked in the soft breeze that carried the scent of night-blooming jasmine. Outside, late evening noises filled the shadows with high-pitched chirps and basso grunts.

Suddenly, she sat up and reached for the light. "Oh, my goodness!"

Her eyes were huge round saucers; owl eyes. Mouth agape, she clapped her hands to her face. Her fingers dug into her cheeks, her palms butted together under her jaw.

"What?" Gabe jumped out of bed, tangling the sheets at his feet. He squinted into the quiet darkness in their room.

"I forgot about the Children's Hospital!" Whacking her head with the palm of her hand, she continued, "I promised I would paint a mural before Labor Day."

She jumped up to pace back and forth.

"What month is it? It's not the end of August yet, is it? Maybe there is still time."

Gabe touched her hand, anchoring her momentarily.

"Whoa! What are you talking about?"

"The Children's Hospital in Carver's Hollow. I promised them a mural. I can't believe I forgot…"

Gabe sat on the bed, kicked at the turmoil of sheets at his feet. Hannah crossed her legs Indian-style when she sat beside him.

"You don't have to return, you know. Stay here with me and no one could ever find you."

"Yes, that's true enough. No one would know where I was hiding. But, I'd be hiding from my commitment, my promise. How could you ask me to break my word? Promises are sacred. I always uphold my promises. Always."

"That's supposed to mollify me, isn't it? What about the promise you made to me?"

He rubbed lazy circles on her wrist with his thumb.

"I don't want you to go." His voice was a quiet whisper, barely audible. "You may decide to stay in North Carolina. You might not come back to me."

"Don't be ridiculous. Of course I'll come back. I've made a tremendous commitment to you. But, I must go. Don't you understand? I must."

Gabe didn't look at her. He lightly scratched a freckle on her wrist. "It's the 7th of August. How much time will you need?"

Hannah gathered a tumble of long curls over one shoulder and braided it. "Hmmm. That's tough to answer. The work at the Credit Union took me over a month...you were there for most of the fresco process. But, you saw my sketchbook. I'll need tons of preliminary sketches before I can even begin. That can take weeks."

"What about all of the drawings you've done here? Pictures of the elves and faeries at work? Don't you have a whole book of sketches of the children at play?"

"Of course! You're right!" Hannah knelt on the floor, reaching under the bed to pull out her portfolio. The heavy case was filled past its capacity and the leather straps could no longer meet to close. Gabe squatted at her side. He opened one of the six sketchpads.

"Look, Hannah. Page-after-page of studies. All you have to do is put them together in a design."

Hannah rocked back and forth on her knees. "You're right! Kids love fantasies. I can paint the faerie village. What a great idea!" Carefully she tore a page from one book and aligned it next to a page from another book. Within minutes, the bedroom floor was littered with charcoal and pencil sketches and watercolors. Hannah held the tip of her braid in her mouth as she re-arranged the pictures. She selected drawings of the elfin artisans at work, surrounded by giggling pixies and hovering faeries.

Gabe stood up. "Enough for tonight. It's late. Come back to bed."

Hannah started to collect her papers.

"Just leave them." Gabe took her hands in his. "You can go back to work in the morning. Come, sleep with me."

"The children recuperating in the hospital will be delighted with this scene! Can't you share my excitement?"

"Not when it means you're leaving me. I wish I could make you stay."

"Well, you can't. A promise is sacred to me!"

"I'll remember that fact during the long nights I'm here alone."

"I won't be gone long."

"One night is too long."

Hannah stared at the ceiling, closing an eye while she calculated. "Five weeks at most."

Gabe clutched at his heart. "Five weeks! That's ridiculous. Three."

"Four."

"Three and a half. Twenty-five days." Gabe grabbed her arms and pulled her with him when he fell backwards onto the bed. "That's my final offer."

"You win," she giggled. "I'll leave in four days."

Gabe grimaced. "I feel somewhat less than victorious."

During the next days, Trog was a willing apprentice. Hannah taught him to mix paints and seal them in Mason jars. Lucky that Trog was helpful because Gabe was behaving like a disgruntled child.

While she was packing her supply satchel, carefully wrapping sable brushes and palette knives, Gabe stomped in. The front door banged closed and he headed straight for the kitchen. He picked up a dishtowel, folded it in quarters and positioned it on the counter next to the sink.

"Sandwiches again tonight, Hannah?"

"No. Actually I've made a casserole. It's in the fridge, all ready for the oven."

Gabe opened the cabinet, selected a juice glass, examined it in the sunlight and then replaced it on the shelf. "Doesn't really matter. I'm not hungry anyway." He pulled a drawer. Forks, knives and spoons shuffled noisily. He slammed the drawer shut again.

Hannah stood in the doorway, arms crossed at her waist. "You're acting like a spoiled brat!"

"Am not!"

"Are, too."

"Oh yeah?"

She couldn't help it. She had to smile. Here he was – a grown man, all six and a half feet of him, behaving exactly like a two year old. Those dark brows were scrunched together in a straight line. His eyes were squished, almost closed; but still dark and imposing. With the hair that looked like black storm clouds settling around his face and shoulders, Gabe really did resemble an angel… a fallen angel.

"I thought you liked potatoes au gratin."

"That's not it." He wiped the counter top with the folded towel, watching his hand rather than looking at her.

Hannah put her hand on his, stopping the motion. "Talk to me."

Slowly, ever so slowly, his eyes traveled from her wrist, up her arm, past her elbow to her shoulder. He touched her neck with two fingers and she felt as if he'd tickled each hair follicle on her head from inside her skull.

"I love you. I don't want you to go. There's nothing more to say."

"You love me. You...love...me. You've said the words over and over." She pulled out a chair and sat, patting her palms flat on the table. "But love isn't about vocabulary. It's about trust. Love has to be stronger than any doubts. Bottom line, Gabe. If you love me, you trust me. If you trust me to keep my promise, then you know that I'll be back."

Gabe straddled the chair next to hers. He lifted her hands to his lips, closing his eyes like he was praying. "I trust you. I do. I've just got a bad feeling..."

"Because you're disappointed. Life isn't going your way."

Gabe stood and shrugged. "Well, of course I am disappointed; but this feeling's more ominous. I can't explain it." He crouched beside her chair and twirled a curling tendril of her hair around his finger.

She propped her forehead on his shoulder. "Let's not worry about the things we can't explain or change." She drew her fingers through his hair and he sighed. Her hands looked pale, almost porcelain, compared to his darker complexion. She rubbed her freckled cheek against his, savoring the gentle abrasion of his day-old beard.

"I'll be back, Gabe. Nothing in this world can keep me away from you. I'll do everything humanly possible to come back."

"That's one of the problems, don't you see? Human possibilities are so limited."

"What do you want from me? I've given you everything I have to offer. My trust, my love and my promise. You ask too much."

He breathed against her neck, warm damp words that made her shiver. "Too much is sometimes not enough."

It was early Sunday evening when Ella delivered several bulging packages.

"What have you got there?" Hannah laughed.

"Just a few necessities for her trip."

"You look like a peddler, Ella," Gabe teased.

The elf crouched on the floor, opening the smallest canvas pack. "Dried fruits and nuts."

"How about the other two?" Gabe nudged one heavy parcel with his toe.

"Two crocks of fresh butter," Ella answered with a snort.

Hannah cradled the warmth of the last package, sniffing it. "And loaves of wheat bread?"

Ella smiled at her. "And a bit of cheese."

Nowatil shuffled in, bumping the door with her hip. She carried a pottery jug that dripped sloshed cider.

"It's hard, you know," she whispered as she nudged Hannah's side with her elbow.

"Oh. Here. Let me help you." Hannah took the jug to the kitchen counter, then rinsed her sticky hands at the sink.

"Hard cider makes an excellent aphrodisiac, don't you know?"

"Um, no, I didn't realize that. An aphrodisiac, you say?" Hannah winked at the grinning elf. "Do you think we should drink it? I leave at first light."

"Oh yes. Definitely tonight."

Nowatil waddled over to Gabe. Patting his hand, she said, "You're looking tired, my boy– almost quarter to eight. Best get to bed early tonight! Early to bed, wake up wise!" She swatted the seat of Gabe's soft leather trousers and wiggled her eyebrows at Hannah.

With an exaggerated yawn, Nowatil waved goodbye. Hannah overheard the elves mumble something about missed opportunities and baby booties.

The night was dark and quiet. Light from the stars and the fireflies dimmed and brightened like jerky frames in an old slide show when gray clouds wafted past the slivered moon.

"Aphrodisiac? Saltpeter, maybe next week." Gabe muttered as he wandered; touching her hairbrush, then burying his face in her pillow.

Hannah's slippers made gentle whooshing noises when she came to the bedroom; the fur-lined suede spoke to the hardwood floor; shush, slap, shush. As she crossed the braided rug, sounds were muffled. Gabe turned to her abruptly.

"Did I startle you?" she asked.

"I could have heard you even in a vacuum." His dark eyes followed her. "I can feel the air shift when you enter a room."

Hannah carried two flutes of the golden cider. She set the cider on the bedside table. He was sprawled across the bed diagonally, his head on the far side. His eyes gleamed. Did he hold back tears, or was it a trick of the glowing candlelight? He opened his arms to her.

"Come, lay your head, Love."

She knelt on the bed between his knees and inched her way up his body. Her soft breasts brushed his thighs and he hissed out a breath. She kissed his belly and nestled into his side, resting her head just below the tuft of dark hair in the pit of his arm.

"I don't want you to go," he said kissing the top of her head.

He toyed with a strand of her curly hair, pulling it taut and straight, and then allowing it to spring into a corkscrew again.

"We've been through this conversation before. I have to go. I made a promise. It's that simple. I must go. But only for a while."

"I know. I know. My feeling isn't rational, but I have a bad premonition about this separation. My instincts are usually right."

He hugged her closer. "I could come with you." His heart pounded against hers. Hannah's pulse raced in response. Gabe cupped her face in his palms, and she tried to swallow any impatient words.

"You could come. And I would sleep beside you for a few hours every night. But, I've explained that this work will consume every minute of my time for the next three and a half weeks."

"But…"

She sucked his words into her mouth.

"It's a job, Gabe. Not a vacation."

What more could she say? A promise is a promise. Her kiss
was like kindling on a smoldering fire. They made love with a melancholic poignancy that sang like a sad violin. The glasses of Nowatil's
cider remained on the bedside table untouched.

The sky at dawn was a watercolor- a pastel wash of pink and yellow.
Hannah was awake, propped on her elbow. She loved to watch him
sleep; the angel with a devilish grin who was dreaming at her side.
The wrinkled bed linens smelled of her perfume, of laundry soap and
of the musk of their loving. Using a strand of hair, she tickled his
cheek so that she could see his smile.

"I should say 'Good Morning', but it won't be good once
you're gone," he grumbled.

She stretched and reached for his shoulders. He stopped her at
arm's length.

"I won't be going with you this morning, Hannah. Trog will
walk you to the edge of the Faerie Forest. Every human needs a faerie
escort into or out of the village."

He stroked her face, catching a tear as it trailed down her
cheek. "Only a special human is accepted within the elf-mounds."
His finger lingered near her eye. "We've been given a very precious
gift, you and I."

She caught her bottom lip in her teeth because her mouth quivered a bit. She tried to smile. She nodded quickly, then again. "Yes,
yes, I know."

Hannah sniffed once, swiped at her eyes with the back of her hand and forced a smile that almost lasted five seconds. She felt weak - vulnerable. She reached for him with her eyes closed tight.

"Oh, God. I'm going to miss you. I'm leaving a vital part of myself here."

Somehow her sobs got stuck in his throat, too. She could feel his tremors as she clung to him, dripping hot tears on his bare chest. His voice cracked. "I know you have to go; but I can't watch you leave."

She nodded, smearing tears across his shoulder. "Okay."

"I'll be here, waiting for your return, though."

"Promise?"

"Promise."

"Twenty-five days. I'll be here in twenty-five days."

"I love you, Hannah. Come back."

She sniffed and waggled her head, up and down, up and down. "I will." She figured she probably looked like one of those bobbling statues on a car's dash.

They came together like two ponderous storm clouds, each ready to burst. They were thunder and lightning: electric and magnificent. Theirs was a fierce loving. Gabe sucked her neck; a vampire ingesting the salt and sweet flavor of her skin. Hannah bit his shoulder branding him with her teeth. Kisses of savage romance. Each of them wanted an indelible mark, to possess, to be possessed.

There was a soft rap at the door. "Trog's here." She left the bedroom quietly. He watched from the doorway, tenderly rubbing the talisman bruise on his shoulder.

They walked in silence for a while – the scowling elf and the tearful woman. Trog squatted to inspect a cluster of mushrooms at the base of a black oak. "Tell me, Hannah," he squeaked. "What do you see here?" His calloused fingers were short and thick; misshapen and stubby. The wrinkles at his knuckles were tattooed with dirt, liberally flecked with rusty freckles. One finger jabbed towards a large gray mushroom, broken and beginning to decay. Bright orange algae grew in thin hair-like sprouts on the damaged area. This area of the forest was chilly and damp because the broad canopy of ancient oak trees filtered the sunlight. Although the day was still young, it felt like dusk; dim light and long shadows.

She knelt beside him, put her head close to the ground and peered at the clump of mushrooms. Acorn buckets and moldering pine straw brooms were propped against tiny wooden doors. A dilapidated twig bench had been positioned in an overgrown fern garden. Window shutters were closed tight. "Homes. Elfin homes. They've been deserted, though."

"Only a dreamer would see those homes. A realist would see mushrooms gone to spore."

"Gabe's the one who made the dreams come true."

"Unfortunately, the balance of nature decrees that a super-abundance of dreams is paid for by a growing potential for nightmares."

Hannah rocked back on her knees. Grinning, she snatched his cap, tossing it from hand to hand. "Trog, you surprise me. An erudite elf! Quoting Peter Ustinov, no less."

"Elves are smart. We just don't feel the urge to blather our knowledge like you humans do."

"Maybe I should wear your magic hat," she teased, pulling the cap over her hair. "Then no human will see me. Invisible, I could sneak around undetected, causing all sorts of mischief!"

"Take heed, Girl," he snapped, shaking his finger inches from her face. "Watch yourself. Be careful."

"I'm a big girl. I've been on my own for years. I can take care of myself."

Laughing, she ruffled his bristly brown hair, kissed his bearded cheek and plopped his magical cap on his head. Instantly he faded from her human sight. Yep! She was back. Back in what was now an alien world of humans. Weird how quickly her perspective had changed. She hoisted the satchel containing her brushes and paints over one shoulder, and slung her pack of clothing and food over the other.

She wondered if Trog heard her call out, "Watch over Gabe. He'll be lonely without me!"

The Faerie Raft must encompass vast amounts of land. She and Gabe had entered originally through a portal somewhere near Beaufort on the coast. Now, after a short hike, she found herself beside a cornfield on the shoulder of a four-lane highway in the foothills. Not two hundred feet away was a large green highway sign 'Carver's Hollow Next Right ¾ mile.' Oh well, Trog had warned her months ago, don't try to understand it. She adjusted the straps on her packs and jaunted off, down the road to what she hoped would be an exciting project.

The township was small – the main street, Carver Boulevard, was five blocks long with two traffic lights. Children rode bicycles on the sidewalks and dogs ran in the grassy park without leashes. At each corner mounds of multi-colored impatiens spilled from large concrete planters. Their spent blossoms littered the walks like confetti after a jubilee. At the far end of the boulevard was the university campus; a number of imposing Gothic buildings enclosed by a tall stone wall. Hannah was reminded of a medieval castle and its accompanying serfdom. Alongside the entrance drive, a carpet of petunia blossoms spelled *CARVER U* in white on a background of purple. Fat bumble bees buzzed in the hot morning sunshine, methodically visiting each bloom.

A group of giggling co-eds bustled past her. One girl inadvertently bumped Hannah's shoulder and one of her bags almost slipped to the ground. A slender man leaped to catch the heavy satchel.

"Got it!" He grabbed the strap and lifted to her shoulder again.

Hannah noticed his tattoo. Tough to miss it. A snake slithered from the crease in his right elbow, across his forearm. Its mouth opened right at the vee of his thumb. The design was created so that anyone who shook his hand would be positioned for a snakebite.

"Thank you," she forced her eyes away from his hand.

"No problem."

He was tall…well taller than she is…close to six feet, maybe. Thin blonde hair in need of shampoo was tied back in a ponytail. He wore flip-flops and faded denim jeans and a t-shirt that was more hole than shirt.

"I'm looking for the hospital."

"You sick?" He stepped back.

She smiled. "No. I'm going to paint at the Children's Wing."

"Don't look like a painter. It's over there." He pointed to a three-story masonry building flanked by a parking deck and a recent addition made mostly of steel and glass.

The hospital director's staff had arranged a room for her nearby.

"You can't miss it. Dayton Drive, right around the corner."

Adolescent boys whizzed past her on rollerblades; a blur of bright yellow helmets, gangly arms and legs moving with fluid power. The only other traffic on Dayton Drive that morning was on-wing. Birds caught insects and ferried the food to squalling nestlings. Yellow butterflies hovered above the curling morning glory vines at a mailbox. The morning air was thick and humid. Hannah wiped at the perspiration on her brow.

Welcome back to summer in the South!

Magnolia House. The name seems appropriate!

Once she navigated around the enormous magnolia tree that filled the entire yard, she stood at the steps leading to the inn. The house was charming. Painted a reddish-brown, it appeared to be made of gingerbread. The wide porch was decorated with green columns topped with white curlicues. Large wooden rockers stood sentinel on either side of the front door, where a cheerful sign greeted visitors with 'Welcome Back!'

The door opened wide and a mélange of spicy aromas wafted outside. A tall, slender woman smiled and said, "Come in, Come in." She extended her arm towards the inviting reception hall, papered in a delicate pastel floral print. Overhead a fan whirred with a quiet hum, and on a marble-topped table the fern fronds bounced in the gentle breeze.

As she closed the door, she wiped her hands down the ruffled apron tied in a bow at her waist and said, "I'm Maggie. Can I help you?"

Hannah shook the hand Maggie had offered.

"I'm Hannah Everett. I am going to be working on the fresco at the Children's Wing over at University Hospital."

Maggie pumped Hannah's arm with each statement, like punctuation.

"Of course! Of course. That's grand. Just grand."

She patted the plump chintz cushions arranged on the antique love seat. "Sit. Sit." Hannah sat on the edge of the cushion. She was anxious to stow her gear and get back to the hospital to set up for work.

"Maybe some soup would be nice," Maggie said.

"No. No, I just don't think I can eat a thing. Thank you for the thought, though. I need to get to work as soon as possible."

"Later, then. Okay?"

"Whatever you say!"

Maggie led Hannah upstairs. She opened the door to a powdery pink room. Cherubs tiptoed across the headboard of the large bed festooned with layer upon layer of white eyelet ruffles. At the flip of a switch, the white paddles of the ceiling fan began a slow rotation. Maggie tugged on the windowshade and it rolled up, revealing a compact garden at the back of the house. A knobby wisteria vine curled over and around a trellis that led to a narrow lane at the corner of the yard. She opened the French doors and pointed to the miniature balcony. There was barely room for a café table and two chairs.

"You can have breakfast served out here, if you'd like," Maggie announced proudly.

Although she'd been at the Magnolia House for over three weeks, Hannah had never once been served breakfast – neither on the balcony nor in the dining room. Most mornings she was at work by five o'clock. She could get more work accomplished during the quiet hours before the doctors made their rounds and the nursing carts blocked the corridor. The visiting hours were the hardest times. She had become a novel distraction for parents trying desperately to bring a spark of gaiety to their sick or injured children.

A girl named Adelle was twelve; but she was the size of a four year old. Rail thin, she wore a ski cap, a thick cableknit sweater and heavy socks whenever her father would wheel her chair into the hallway. Baby-fine wisps of bright red hair escaped from the cap, curling just above the girl's ears. Her skin was pale. Deathly pale. She reminded Hannah of a plastic anatomy class model whose veins and arteries are plainly visible.

Adelle lifted her arm to point at Hannah's fresco. The sleeve of her sweater slipped back to reveal the series of clear tubes that fueled her depleted body with food and medication intravenously. "Those little creatures with the wings...Are they angels?"

"If you say so," Hannah answered.

"So, is this a picture of heaven, then?"

"It's my idea of heaven, yes."

"I'm going to like it there."

The fresco was finished, and none too soon; merely sixteen hours ahead of schedule. Hannah decided to leave before first light just to be certain that she made it to the rendezvous point on time. How would she know exactly where Trog would wait, invisible as he might be? Maybe he'd remove his magical hat so she could see him. No matter, Gabe would be there. She could close her eyes and find Gabe in a crowded room. Lord, she had missed him. Sometimes at night, she'd wake up thinking that she smelled him – the spearmint leaves that he chewed or his cologne that was a combination of all-spice and sex.

A few days ago, a student had shown her a pedestrian tunnel through the stone wall that surrounded the college. The tunnel exited onto a street in a residential neighborhood near the outskirts of town. But Carver's Hollow was your typical Smallville, USA. No worry. Nothing sinister happened on these streets after dark. She zipped her jacket and tugged each her bags higher on her shoulder.

The tunnel was dark, not pitch dark, but darker than usual. Maybe a bulb had burned out because the tunnel was very dim. Lots of shadows. Each of her footsteps echoed. The sounds bounced off the walls. She heard a commotion, an argument, outside the tunnel. Voices got louder and closer. Frightened, she hid behind one of the pillars, in the shadows. It was a pretty big group of people…fifteen, maybe eighteen people crowded together, pushing and shoving.

Hannah hid her face when the fight broke out. People were shifting positions; ducking punches, each trying to punch someone else. She realized that something was hurled through the air – maybe a dark green bottle glinted in the dim light. Something slammed into her temple. She felt the jolt and saw stars. Maybe she heard the hollow clunk of glass against concrete. After that, nothing.

"Crap! She's passed out again." Hannah could hear the man's voice, but she couldn't concentrate. Every muscle in her body

261

throbbed. She winced, opening her left eye. The right wouldn't cooperate. It seemed to be glued shut. She lay naked on the floor – a dirty floor… somewhere - face-first amid soiled towels and discarded tee-shirts.

Someone grabbed her braid and jerked her up to her feet. Her legs were gelatinous. He shoved her shoulder so that she fell on her stomach across a desk. The man thrust with angry determination, pounding himself into her inert body. For several minutes his grunts were punctuated with curses. He assaulted her with pelvic thrusts rather than his fists, standing behind her, holding her unwilling hips to his groin. With one final grunt, he finished with her.

Perspiration dripped from his forehead onto her back. He scrubbed at his eyes with fisted knuckles, and then stood to zip his pants. She fell to the floor in a lifeless heap.

"Bitch," he mumbled, kicking at her torso. His steel-toed work boots connected with her ribs in a soggy thud. He sneered when she groaned and curled to a fetal position. "Lying, spying bitch!"

Hannah watched, terrified. He fingered the thin white scar that bisected his face, through his upper lip, across his jaw and into his left earlobe. He sniffed loudly and wiped his nose with the tail of his unbuttoned shirt, leaving a shining silver line of mucus that resembled a slug trail. He leaned down and grabbed her hair, pulling her shoulders off the floor. She heard a moan, but didn't recognize it as a human sound. Her head dangled like a marionette, suspended by the thick rope of her braided hair. He spat. The globule of saliva slithered over her eyelid and through her lashes to drip down her cheek. It felt as is she'd been scalded. He slapped her and fine spray of spittle and blood splattered his arm.

"Wake up, Bitch!"

When she didn't respond, he spread his thick fingers wide, releasing her shoulders. Like a child abandoning a broken toy, he left her discarded on the floor. He covered his shaved head with a ragged ball cap that was bleached with use. Motioning to a fellow slumped in a chair across the room; he reached for a bottle of warm beer left on top of the bookcase near the door.

"C'mon. We'll leave the bitch alone. She'll be out of it for awhile."

Her attacker draped his arm over his companion's hunched shoulders, and offered a taste of the stale beer. He snickered and rubbed his nose with the back of his hand.

"Think you killed her?" the other man questioned in a whisper.

"Nah, just taught her some manners. She'll be okay."

Squatting, the smaller man prodded Hannah with one finger. He looked much like a child examining a dead jellyfish; curious, but cautious. The snake tattooed on his hand appeared to be investigating her ear. He pulled his lank blond hair away from his face and secured it into a ponytail with a leather thong. With a thumb, he pulled her bottom eyelid down while raising the upper with his fingers. The pupil of her green eye was dilated. When he exposed it to the bright fluorescent light, the dilation contracted and the eyeball rolled back. He jumped and dropped her head, which bounced as it hit the floor again. He sprang to his feet, rocking off his toes, agile as a ballerina.

"She don't look too good," he stammered, wiping his hands on the back of his faded jeans.

"That's for sure. She looks like a shitty spy. You know what happens to spies. This is war, man. We interrogate spies; make 'em talk. Can't have spies screwing up our plans."

"What if she's not a spy, though? What if we were wrong?"

"Shit. What you been smoking?"

"What if she's innocent? I think I met her on campus the other day. She's a painter or something."

Chuckling, Scar answered caustically, "Well, we both know she's not so innocent anymore!" He cupped his genitals and raised his eyebrows.

"Yeah, well, I was looking through her backpack while you were… while you were, umm, interrogating her. She had a bunch of drawings and sticks of charcoal and paintbrushes and a bunch a little bottles of paint. That don't sound suspicious to me."

Scar chucked him on the chin lightly. "What's d'matter? You getting soft on me? Don't be worried about this bitch? Hey! Buck up. In wartimes, people get hurt. It's a fact."

"Okay. Yeah. You're right. I just wonder who she is, where she came from. Some of the drawings are cute. Like pictures in fairytale book."

He pulled a pad of sketches from the litter piled on the battered table, disturbing a precariously filled ashtray. Several Marlboro butts rolled onto the floor. Ash residue from his fingers left dark prints on the backside of the papers.

"Wanna see? Some of these drawings are good."

"Shit, Leonard! Just take the damned pictures. Let's get some food. I'm hungry."

The men shuffled out the door. Outside, a padlock clicked in place.

The morning sun had passed high noon. Now, it drifted low behind pink clouds in the brilliant pumpkin orange sky. Shadows fell on trash piled in the corners of the small room. Hannah woke suddenly. She blinked in the harsh fluorescent lights and touched her forehead. A golf-ball sized swelling was really tender. Her head throbbed with each rapid heartbeat, making her nauseous. Knife-like pain pierced her left ribs. What in hell had happened to her?

She spied her bright blue tunic, now splotched with bloodstains. It was draped across the seat of a chair. Painfully aware of her nudity, she snatched a sheet from the pile of laundry waddled around her. She wrapped it around her waist, reached for the tunic and pulled it over her head.

Every movement was painful. She was a collage of cuts and scrapes and had a rather deep gash on one knee. At least one rib seemed to be cracked. She prodded the skin under her breast, wincing. The muscles in her neck were drawn so taut, she wondered if her head was strapped in a vise. Warm wetness pooled in the lacerated tenderness between her legs. With trembling fingers she touched herself and flinched. She rubbed her fingers together, smearing the traces of blood in the sticky semen. Where in god's name am I? Her swollen lips were caked with dried blood that tasted metallic. Her tongue irritated raw skin inside her mouth.

She closed her eyes and hot tears streaked down her cheeks. The pressure that pulsed inside her head made it difficult to open her eyes. She looked around the small room, trying to move her eyes while keeping her throbbing head stationary. The walls had been painted garish colors and were covered with posters filled with serpents, devils and Nazi swastikas. Trash; cigarette butts and soda cans, discarded fast food wrappers, littered the floor. Was she trapped in a nightmare?

No, nightmares don't have smells. Foul odors - soiled laundry and rancid food, mildew and sweaty clothing and the cloying greasy smell of stale food. She sat up quickly; clamped her fingers into her scalp. She pressed her temples as though trying to glue together a crack in her skull. Her thoughts refused to run in straight lines. The room continued to morph in and out of focus around her.

Horrible half-recalled memories and distorted pictures flashed through her brain. Creatures with jerky movements shouted in angry babble, pushing and shoving her as bright lights flashed. Oh God! One deep breath and then she leaned back, trying to calm herself. She leaned against a lumpy pillow on the narrow cot that squeaked with each movement. She lost consciousness; maybe she slept.

Later, regaining consciousness, she resisted the urge to cry although she felt the tears welling in her eyes and tingling behind her quivering lids. Swiping at her eyes, she sat up and greedily gulped air.

I'm scared, she whispered. I want to go home. Home? Lightning; fire, smoke. She rubbed her temples. Maybe she was in a nightmare! Home. There was something more; but she couldn't place it. Home. Home?

She hugged the lumpy pillow to her chest. First things, first. Make a plan. Get out of here. Think.

The air conditioning motor rumbled with tinny clicking noises as it began a new cycle. The noises jarred her thoughts. Cool air spilled into the closed room, fluttering candy wrappers and potato chip bags in the litter on the floor.

She heard voices! In the hallway, men and a woman were laughing. There was a loud clamor as if a metal box was being dropped down a stairwell. Maybe it was the men! She crouched defensively in the far corner of the unsteady cot, inanely clutching the pillow to her chest. The noises retreated and her pulse rate slowed.

She waited, unmoving, for a while.

Make a plan, dammit. Can't just sit here and wait for them to come back. They'll kill you.

Slowly, she edged across the room, approaching the door as if it were a sleeping crocodile. Her fingers trembled when she touched the knob. It wouldn't turn. Of course it wouldn't.

Open! Dammnit, open!

She pulled at the knob frantically, shaking the unresponsive door. She heard muted voices in the hallway.

"Help," she wailed. Beating on the wooden panel, she begged, "Help me! Help me please!" Her voice was a ragged whisper, scratched and abused.

The voices retreated and she fell to her knees, continuing to pound the door, calling unheeded entreaties. Sobbing her frustration, she finally collapsed to the floor.

She was dizzy, even lying down. She rolled onto her side, hugging her stomach. Sweat beaded above her top lip. She groaned and gagged. A thin stream of yellow bile drooled from one corner of her mouth. She wiped her chin with shaky fingers.

Time had become a blur. Had she been in this room for hours or for days? It seemed an eternity…a hellish long time.

Hannah had an urgent need to urinate. There was a narrow door adjacent to the wall-hung sink across the room. Hoping that it concealed a toilet, she struggled to stand. Her knees buckled and she almost fell. She grabbed a windowsill; waited for her head to clear. Sparkling dots of color flared before her eyes and a dull roaring sensation filled her ears. Perspiration rolled across her scalp and dripped rivulets through her hair. She leaned forward to rest her head against the cool glass panes and she felt more stable after a few seconds. It was then she looked out the window.

Several floors beneath her, students hurried across a shady campus on bricked walkways, stopping in pairs under oak trees to chat. The University! Carver U. How could I forget? But, what am I doing HERE, in this room? Who are these men?

Her hands trembled, her shoulders ached with almost violent spasms, but she pounded on the window, screaming for help until her voice was gone. Outside the students congregated in small clusters, cars honked at pedestrians and a wild mix of music blared from boom-boxes; but no one heard her pleas! Not even one person looked up to see her framed in the window.

She struggled to open the window. Thick coats of paint had welded the sashes in place permanently. She wrapped her hands in the sheet and pounded the panes, trying to break the glass. The panes buckled and then popped back in place, undisturbed. Plastic?

The room skewed out of focus. She reeled; heard a strange humming, an overwhelming white noise. For a mere nanno-second, she knew she was about to faint. She reached out her arms, like a blind woman grabbing at the air. Her arms felt leaden, her knees buckled. She collapsed to the floor in a graceless curtsey.

It was full dark when she regained consciousness. She pushed up to a sitting position. At least the room was no longer spinning. Slowly, cautiously, she made her way to the toilet and then back to the cot. The twelve-foot trip across the room exhausted her. Sweating as though she had run the Boston Marathon, she crumpled onto the thin mattress. The bedsprings squeaked metallic complaints. She curled on her side.

Paper crackled when she moved. She sat up and smoothed the wrinkled grocery receipt. She found a red pen stuck in a book on the floor beside the bed. Hannah wrote, "SOS. I'm trapped in a room with a padlock. Please help me!" There was little room for more words. She signed her name, "Hannah Everette." She crawled the short distance to the door. Her hand shook almost uncontrollably as she slid her note out into the hall.

Please God, let someone find me.

Her tears increased the mounting pressure squeezing her temples. She felt like her skull was going to crack and break open like a ripe cantaloupe. She scanned the room with a single purpose, searching for water. She saw the sink – across the room, on the far side of the desk. THE desk.

She struggled to stand upright, and held her arm tight against her rib cage as she staggered towards the sink, lurching to her destination. Huge bullets of perspiration dripped into her eyes and mouth. Her hands shook when she braced herself against the cool porcelain. Waves of nausea. She vomited into the basin already striped with rust stains. Leaning a shoulder against the wall, she turned on the cold water tap and cupped her hands to fill them. Leaning down, she gulped greedily at the tepid water, licking her hands to savor each droplet. She splashed water on her face and neck, and soaked a filthy rag to dab between her breasts. Feeling better, she wet the rag again and squeezed water over her head. .

Hannah dabbed the sticky wetness at her crotch. Lightning-fast, white-hot memories jolted her. Images flashed through her mind without sequence. She could remember being forced to her hands and knees, restrained by a leash of her braided hair. Her head was jerked backwards. Cruel hands squeezed and pinched her breasts, pulling her nipples. Four hands reached for her. Dirty hands with ragged nails and swollen lacerated knuckles. One thick wrist was encircled by a snake. She thought it might be a real snake ready to strike. She grimaced. The tattoo seemed familiar...somehow even friendly. She could remember struggling to escape while her body was battered from behind and entered with painful dryness. She had heard an almost feral howling, then realized it had been her own voice.

Hannah remembered harsh laughter and a slippery wetness when one of the assailants ejaculated on her buttocks. She'd smelled beer and semen and her saliva had pooled around the salty metallic flavor of her own blood. Vaguely she remembered garbled, muffled speech. But mostly she could recall her own panicky staccato breaths.

Retching, she leaned over the sink again.

"Maybe they should have killed me."

In a corner, behind a trashcan under the sink, she found her ripped, soiled underpants. She rinsed them in warm water and used them to scrub furiously, trying to wash away the dried, sticky semen, the stale sweaty musk and the reminders of molestation.

Exhausted, Hannah slumped on a nest of dirty laundry beside the sink. She closed her eyes and saw faceless demons pursuing her through a strangely familiar forest, grabbing at her clothes and pulling her hair.

Loud footsteps preceded the voices in the hallway. The door opened and slammed. She was trying hard not to move a muscle.

"Shit, the bitch is still asleep. Does this place look like a Fucking Marriott?"

She peeked out from under a shielding arm. She saw two men, probably students. Both were dressed in baggy jeans. The smaller of the two men; Leonard, the other man had called him Leonard, was slender, with an athlete's long limbs. His long hair was thin; a dull blond, tied with a rawhide strip to trail down his spine in a tail. His hands were graceful; one wrist encircled with the snake she'd remembered. His fingers were littered with gaudy rings.

The other man was stocky, broad and muscular. The long scar across his face made him look like he was always sneering. Of course, he was so cruel and so angry, he probably was always sneering. As he spoke, he moved clumsily around the room, bumping into the chair and shoving a pile of soiled clothes to the floor. Hannah thought that he must be drunk. Tossing his much worn cap to the nearby table, he rubbed his head; shaved clean and shining like the sphere of a brass andiron. Even with the scar that streaked across his face, he might once have been a handsome man. Rocking a chair back on its two rear legs, he propped his feet on the sink above her prone body.

"C'mon, Bitch. I know you're awake. Even a corpse woulda heard us slamming doors. Sit up. Look here. We brought you some food," he poked her shoulder with his boot.

He tossed a grease-soaked paper bag of fried potatoes towards her. Limp, cold French fries joined the debris all around her. Chocolate goo drooled from the straw stuck in a plastic lid from McDonald's. She lowered her arm and pulled at her ripped tunic. She sat, hugging her arms together at her waist. She kept her eyes averted, instead staring at the cluttered floor. She spoke, startling herself with a raspy strained voice.

"Why am I here? Who are you? My friends will be worried."

His sneer stretched to show his teeth, seeming feral. He arched his back, leaning the chair even more precariously. He tugged at the hem of his shirt, and scratched at his hairy stomach, that bulged out of the unbuttoned waistband of his jeans. Shaking a cigarette from his pack, he snapped his fingers, indicating that he needed a match to light it. Hannah flinched when he jerked his hand towards her face. He guffawed at her wild-eyed fear; but he caught the book of matches tossed over her head. Her nostrils flared, inhaling the sulfurous odor of the flame. She attempted to squeeze further back, closer to the wall.

"Hey, where do you think you're going? You talking 'bout leaving? …And after our hospitality and all!"

He slapped his leg, leaned forward in his chair, lowering the front legs to the floor. "Hell - We got food, we got a woman, we got beer-We're gonna have a bang-up party!"

Again, he reached towards her head. This time, he wrapped her long hair around his hand and used it like a lasso to pull her to him. She knelt in front of him, keeping her arms stiff at her sides. Be brave, Hannah, courage, she told herself. She tried to raise her chin, to look straight at his angry eyes. He grunted and yanked her hair again, then laughed cruelly as hot tears quietly streaked her cheeks. Once more, he tilted the chair back, lifting the front legs. He snatched her awkwardly over him, crushed against his crotch. Her face was mottled red.

"Embarrassed, Bitch? Shit, and here I thought we were fucking well acquainted!"

Her head throbbed. Odors surrounded them - her own fear, his sweat and the smoke that curled from his cigarette. She tried to swallow, thought she'd throw up.

Chortling, the man plucked the glowing cigarette from his lips, threw it to the floor, and crushed it with his heel. Surprised by the limited freedom she was afforded, Hannah thrashed wildly, pummeling his chest with her fists and twisting her body side to side in an attempt to escape. Laughing, he hauled her up with a vicious jerk on her hair. He backhanded her mouth. Blinding pain followed flaring white pinpoints of light. Blood dripped from her lips. Hannah hung her head, curled her shoulders and wept.

She whispered, "Why are you keeping me here? What have I done to you? Let me go home. Please. My friends will worry about me."

"Forget your frigging friends! You'll never see them again anyway."

He stood with feet planted and hands fisted, towering above her as she huddled on the floor.

He snarled, "Bitch, you know why you're here. You were in the tunnel waiting for us. Spying on us." He rubbed both hands from his dark eyebrows to the crown of his head. "You were messing around where you didn't belong. The brotherhood of Hell's Wrath is strong and we fight for our rights. You can try to infiltrate, to undermine our efforts. But, it won't work. We'll always fight."

He twisted the cap off a beer. He pressed the cold, wet bottle against his forehead. "Just wait. Soon this crappy little town with its niggers and Japs and Jews and Rag Heads will listen. Damned straight... they'll all hear! The school, the city, the fucking state, the whole damned country'll listen!"

"What...?"

"You know... it's like nature. Planting bulbs in the Fall, get it? Bulbs mature. Spring comes, the timing's right, flowers bloom. Bombs are planted. The timing's right. Then, BOOM! They'll hear Hell's Wrath then!" His words slurred together. His voice quaked with hostility. The fumes of his fury were almost a visible vapor.

In a breathless whisper, she pleaded, "I am not a spy. I'm an artist. I've never even heard of Hell's Wrath. Let me go. Please let me go."

"We already gave you a little souvenir, though, didn't we? A party favor. Bet you'll remember us now!"

Leonard found his voice. "An artist, you say. Who are you then? Why were you waiting for us in the tunnel? Why?"

"My name is Hannah. I'm an artist. I painted a fresco at the Children's Wing of the University Hospital. I was using the tunnel as a shortcut, going to meet my friends. They will be worried about me. Please believe me."

"Well, Bitch, they've got a damned long wait, then."

275

Without warning, Scar hit her again. She sprawled on the floor.

"Lies. All lies. Who sent you? Who are you?"

"Hannah. My name is Hannah," she mumbled just before she found relief in the quiet darkness of unconsciousness.

They'd arrived before daybreak. Trog and Gabe stood watch under the hanging boughs of a mimosa tree loaded with frothy pink powderpuff blossoms. Now, as the sun set, Trog sported several puffs in his wiry thick beard. The bright pink sprigs added a festive look to his dull brown hair.

He scowled and rotated his shoulders, "Darn that girl, anyway. Head hurts so much my eyeballs won't move." He squinted into the shadows.

"She'll come," Gabe said for the twentieth time, although he no longer sounded quite so certain.

"Silly human, no sense of time. Knowing that girl, she's probably still painting. Be just like her to try to find her own way through the woods without a guide." Trog paced; his comic voice was a shrill squeak when he grumbled.

"Wonder if anyone ever told her tales about wee folk captured by humans."

"She's not particularly 'wee', Trog."

"Ah weel, no. But she's one of the Villagers now. She belongs with us."

"That she does."

"It's always the inexperienced ones who get trapped; novice souls are most vulnerable."

"Why would someone capture Hannah?"

Trog shrugged. "How should I know? I'm only an ignorant elf!"

Gabe rolled his eyes and tugged at the collar of his black linen shirt.

"I've heard of young ones who died in captivity. Pined away, they did. Could be Hannah's resourceful enough to escape, though. She's a hard-headed one, that girl."

"Let's not borrow trouble. Maybe she's just running late."

Trog shook his head and scratched his forehead. "There's surely trouble afoot. The hairs of my eyebrows itch - always a clear indicator of serious problems!"

Gabe drew circles in the dirt with the toe of his shoe. "Don't talk about trouble. Last night devilish dreams tormented me. Could have sworn I heard Hannah call to me!" He used both hands to swipe his hair off his face. "Like she was scared – terrified – and needed my help."

"Could be something. Could be nothing."

"Thanks. That's a comforting thought."

"A man that is born falls into a dream like a man who falls into the sea. If he tries to climb out into the air as inexperienced people endeavor to do, he drowns."

Gabe squeezed the bridge of his nose. "Good Lord! Save me from know-it-all elves quoting <u>Lord Jim</u>."

"Hey! Joseph Conrad is one of my personal favorites."

"Maybe love's an addiction and I need a fix. Could be that's why I'm agitated and sweaty." Gabe pressed his sleeve to his forehead.

"This behavior isn't normal for your Hannah. She's usually so thoughtful."

"...and honest. You know what I told her, Trog?"

"No."

"Fool that I am, I never actually thought she'd leave me. I told her that I wouldn't force her to stay with me, nor would I force her to return to the humans. I told her she had to choose freely. Stupid! I should have shackled her here!" He smacked his palm against his thigh.

"That's what you think? Maybe she's decided to stay with them?"

"Be still, friend. I'm already waging an awful shrieking battle with my own imagination." Gabe pressed his head between his hands. "Is it possible for rampaging thoughts to crack a man's skull?"

"The girl told me that she'd be back to you. Just as she left me standing right here." Trog jabbed a finger into the soft earth at his feet. "Said she had to find her own answers. Maybe that's what she's doing now. Looking for answers."

Gabe touched his nose with the tail of his shirt.

"She'd made a promise to the Children's Hospital, and damned if she wasn't bound to keep it!" Words jammed in his throat. "But...dammnit...she made a promise... a big promise...to me, too!"

Trog's shrill words broke into pieces. "Air's crackling. Disaster's coming."

"Disaster's here! Haven't you been listening? She wanted to leave me and I was powerless to stop her!"

"Jeez...talk about melodrama!"

Gabe clutched his shirt, pulling it away from his chest as if the added weight might crush his lungs. His breaths were shallow and quick. He panted greedy breaths. Birds called cheerful greetings from the trees nearby. Bugs lit on drops of water cupped on fragrant mint leaves that grew in the shade of cedar trees. Bees hummed as they hovered over the honeysuckle vines that covered a stump, all that remained of a knobby dogwood.

"How can life go as usual? I feel like I'm having a heart attack."

"Sit down, Gabe. It's anxiety. Calm down, you'll feel better."

Gabe did sit. For a few seconds. "Where is she?" He paced around the huge mimosa, batting at low branches impatiently. "Why doesn't she call?"

Trog leaned one shoulder against the tree trunk, crossed his legs and examined the fingernails he'd chewed to the quick. "Maybe she is calling. Could be your moaning and groaning are drowning out her message. Gabe. Sit down and be quiet."

Gabe stopped pacing. The branch he'd just swatted recoiled to smack his cheek. He tipped his head, listening. Somewhere in the distance a hawk called, squirrels rustled the fallen leaves in search of food. A carpenter bee whirred just to the right of his head, where sawdust fell from a perfectly circular hole in the tree trunk. "I think I heard something! Did you hear it?"

"Nope. But, then why would I? It'd be you she'd call."

Gabe grimaced, as though scrunching his face might make him hear more clearly. "It was soft – sad – but now I don't hear anything."

"Ssh! Violence," Trog expelled the word on a whispered breath. "I feel violence; a black rage." Sniffing, he tested the air in all directions. "Far away, but close at heart. I smell grave danger in the distance."

Gabe's eyes shifted right and left. "There it is again. Keening. Like at an Irish wake." He rubbed a palm over his mouth. "It's… like an eerie caress." He shuddered, again pulling the shirt away from his throat. "It's Hannah."

He smiled.

"How can you smile if the sound is so sad?"

"Because she's calling me."

Gabe's black cloak billowed behind him like a huge vengeful bat. He wrapped the cape tightly around his torso, forming a cocoon. Closing his eyes, he inhaled. "I'll find her."

"Figured you would."

Beads of sweat pearled at his hairline. "I can see her." His nostrils flared, he snarled a low menacing growl. "Dear God, Hannah is huddled on a floor."

"Like I said. Trouble."

Hoping to shield herself from his brutal fists, Hannah covered her head with crossed arms. Scar laughed - a coarse, hoarse rasping chuckle; more of a snort. Spittle dripped from his lips and fell onto her arms. Her shoulders shook with her sobs. Her nose ran; mucus dribbled into her mouth. Sweat dripped down her neck, pooled between her breasts.

"Shit! Gotta love a subservient woman!" Scar grabbed her hair and jerked her head up. "Look at me, Bitch. Let me hear you beg. Beg for me, Bitch. I got something for you, Bitch." He cupped his scrotum.

Then he traced his forefinger down her wet face, and brushed a tendril of hair behind her right ear. A gentle touch, it belied a lover's touch. The other hand rubbed the zipper that bulged with his swollen penis. Horrified, terrified, Hannah watched his masturbation.

She was tottering, close to unconscious oblivion, when he clutched the back of her head. With one hand he unzipped his jeans and pushed them to his knees. His genitals jutted towards her, throbbing, reddened and swollen. Hannah gagged. Saliva welled in her mouth and she tasted bile as she wretched. Laughing, Scar pushed her head even closer to the smell of his musk, his dried sweat.

He closed her fingers around his shaft. Closing his palm around her fingers, he rubbed her hand up and down his penis; over and over, faster and faster until her hand was covered with the sticky semen that spewed.

"Lick it," he growled through gritted teeth. "Take me in your mouth."

Hannah turned her head; tears running freely down her sweaty face, her nose dripping mucus to the floor.

"I can't," she whimpered. "I'm going to be sick."

Scar jerked her hair. "Lick it. Put it in your mouth," he snarled. She touched the tip of his shaft with her tongue.

"I can't," she screamed.

He groaned and closed his hand over hers, forcing her fingers to rub faster. "Again, and again, and again," he groaned as he pulled her hair even tighter. She wished she was bald.

Gabe had kicked the door when he heard Hannah cry out. The room thundered. The door flew open, splintered wood was flung across the room. Part of the doorframe was ripped from the wall and the hinges hung loose; useless. Scar jolted, turning towards the door, dropping Hannah's hand. But he tightened his hold on her hair. Leonard cowered underneath a plastic table stacked precariously high with books, brimming ashtrays and soggy paper cups.

Hannah tried to pull away from Scar, jerking her head, trying to loosen his grip. She folded her arms around herself, trying to shield her exposed breasts. She was swaying with pain, loosing consciousness. She called "Gabe" seconds before she collapsed.

282

Her head was suspended at an awkward angle, held off the floor by the leash of hair wrapped around Scar's hand. Gabe started towards her; two steps, arms outstretched.

"Bitch," Scar spat and kicked Hannah's inert body.

Gabe flinched, gripping his own belly. Scar wiped his nose with his hand. "Piece of shit."

Gabe roared a battle cry.

Scar yanked Hannah's braid, wobbling her head on a limp neck.

"Hell."

"Close enough," Gabe hissed with a voice that sounded demonic. The dark cloak flew out behind him. A tremendous whistling wind filled the room. Small tornadoes picked up cluttered papers and books, whirling them against the walls, flinging litter. Gabe pointed and screamed, "You!" He threw his arm in a wide arc across the room.

Scar was lifted and hurled against the window, propelled into the night with a sea of shattered plexiglass fragments. The wind subsided. A few scraps of paper rustled across the floor like rodents sneaking to a hiding place. His cape lay flat against Gabe's back.

The fellow crouched under the table moaned. Gabe tipped his head towards the mutilated doorway and the man leaped like a gazelle darting to escape. A pool of warm urine marked his ineffective refuge, and damp footprints highlighted his escape route.

Gabe knelt beside Hannah. His hand trembled when he touched her face. "Safe. You're safe now."

Careful of her many injuries, he nuzzled his neck to her shoulder, once again marking her as his. His cloak cocooned them. Although she was dazed, Hannah knew she'd been lifted off the floor. She could hear the steady beat of Gabe's heart when he cradled her close. She reached up to touch his face. Yes. Her fingers knew every plane of that face

"If I'm dreaming, don't wake me."

She sighed, too tired to speak again. Eyes closed, too heavy to open, her hand drooped to his shoulder, but she grasped his hair. She felt soft winds. There was a gentle, reassuring noise – maybe a flutter? Prisms flashed. Were the jewel-tone colors reflections from millions of translucent Faerie wings? Gabe was taking her home!

Elves, dressed in autumn shades of brown and olive green, were clustered in small groups. Except for their high-pitched chatter, they would have been well camouflaged in the forested shadows. They nattered like irritated squirrels watching the path leading from the woods. From his lookout post, Tobias whistled, announcing Gabe's return. Elves jostled for a prime vantage point, elbowing and grumbling. Faeries flitted from one branch to another. Their tiny bells pinged overhead.

"Where was she?"

"Trog said she might have been trying to find her way back alone."

"What happened to her?"

284

"Is she hurt bad?"

"Looks like she tangled with a gorilla."

"Spriggans, you think?"

"All those bruises. Gotta hurt something awful."

"You gonna be able to patch her up okay, Gabe?"

Keeping his cape securely around Hannah's mostly nude body, Gabe marched past the thigh-high throng without speaking. The villagers fell back to allow him an unobstructed passage.

Hannah's head rested in the crook of Gabe's elbow and her braid was a pendulum, swinging back and forth with each of his strides. Trog looped the hair back over Gabe's arm. "You need my help for anything, just say the word."

Gabe nodded and drew his precious cargo closer to his heart. Trog puffed out his chest, thrust back his shoulders. He marched stiff-legged, not unlike a penguin, scuttling ahead and needlessly telling the villagers, "Move aside. Make room."

Dozens of candles glowed golden to light Gabe's cave. The fire was stoked. Ella hummed as she stirred the pot of aromatic broth simmering on the stove.

Gabe knelt on the rug in front of the fire and lowered Hannah to the floor. Closing his eyes, he joined his hands at the thumbs and spread them, wing-like, to hover inches above her bruised face. Inhaling, then exhaling very slowly, he focused his healing warmth to her. She didn't have energy to speak or to move, but she thought she'd managed a tiny smile. Fresh blood oozed from cuts on her lips.

"Ella, bring lavender, star anise, chamomile, spearmint and nutmeg. Maybe some of that rosemary you've chopped. Heat water. We'll make compresses. Get some washcloths, towels, cheesecloth, scissors and blankets. I don't want her to get shocky. She needs warmth from the fire, so we'll work here on the floor."

Ella waddled around the kitchen, rattling pots. She handed a mug of steaming broth to Gabe. "She's unconscious, Ella. She can't eat now."

"The broth is for you, Boy. You're exhausted. Dark rings around your eyes. It'll take strength to help Hannah heal. I can't be nursing both of you! Drink. Now."

Gabe sipped the soup; but almost immediately he put the mug aside. He pressed his fingers to Hannah's wrist. She was dead still, cocooned in his cloak, but there was a rapid, weak pulse. Ella stood behind him, her palms on his back. While he knelt, she was closer to his height. Gabe tipped the mug, dribbling a few drops of broth on Hannah's mouth. Although she didn't open her eyes, she did lick her bottom lip.

Gabe passed the cup to Ella. "Keep feeding her. I'll get things ready."

Rummaging through several packets, he laid aside spikes of lavender. "I'll crush the leaves. Emulsified in oil with allspice, it'll help relieve stress."

He searched his array of colored bottles, selected one of orange flower water. He handed the bright blue bottle to Ella. "Put a few drops in a bowl of warm water. We'll bathe her."

Bottles clattered together and some tipped over as Gabe pushed them aside. He reached for his mortar and pestle, and fell quickly to his routine pulverizing dried herbs. Sandwiching the pungent leaves and seeds in several layers of cheesecloth, he made a compress of star anise and chamomile, spearmint, rosemary and nutmeg gratings. He covered the compress packets with a damp cloth and placed them on the back of the stove to steam. Next, he steeped lavender spikes in a pan over boiling water. "There you go. A vaporizer."

Sitting cross-legged on the floor, Ella looked over her shoulder. "'Bout finished there, are you?"

287

"Yes."

"Help me here, then. I can't get these filthy rags off without hurting her."

Gabe knelt at her side, lifting Hannah's arm to strip the remnants of her tunic. She winced and moaned.

"She's endured …hssst…savage beatings."

Ella rinsed the bloody cloth. She dripped warm, orange-scented water over Hannah's arms and torso. The purple and blue bruises were macabre patterns, ranging from angry red-brown to purple-blue to a jaundiced yellow. Her anus and vagina were lacerated; there were traces of blood and a crusty white residue of dried semen.

"Barbaric."

"Demonic." Gabe touched her buttocks with a fingertip. Hannah groaned and pulled her legs to her chest, fetal-style. "Look here."

"Nooooo…uh…no." It was a whispered plea.

"Easy, Hannah. Easy."

Gabe spread his hands above her hips, above imprints approximating a man's wide grasp. He turned aside and closed his eyes. A single tear tracked through the beard stubbling his cheek.

"Rape. Vicious brutal rape."

Ella touched his trembling hands. "Be strong," she whispered. She handed him a small brown bottle. "Clove buds and geraniums into mineral oil."

He nodded his head, a quick, jerky motion. Without speaking, he massaged the sweet-spicy oil into each of her bruises. Then he applied one of the warm compresses to her ribs, strapping it in place with gauze. He rocked back on his heels, arched his back and dabbed his forehead with his sleeve. Herbaceous steam still billowed from the fireplace where the roaring fire had become orange embers.

"The gash above her right knee is angry – swollen and hot with infection." Ella had cleansed the area and now he gently probed the gash to extrude a trickle of pus. "A plaster of yarrow and ylang ylang will staunch the fresh bleeding and prevent further infection. Can you see to that?"

At his bench Gabe gathered sutures, a sterile needle and a bottle of alcohol. He set about stitching the deep gash closed. Thankfully, Hannah remained unconscious throughout the brief ordeal. Her leg would be painfully sore and stiff for several days, but the infection would be healed.

Dressed in one of her soft nightgowns, Hannah whimpered and flailed in her sleep. Gabe murmured nonsense words and stroked her face with a cloth that smelled of jasmine. Easing his arm behind her shoulder blades, he encouraged her to sit. He offered her a bit of cooled chamomile tea from the mug Ella had left on the bedside table.

Hannah batted at the mug. Pale green tea sloshed over the rumpled sheets she had wrestled during her fitful dreams. She turned her head side-to-side, grunting and bucking against him.

"Hush now, Hannah. You're safe now. I'm with you."

Her eyes were still closed; but she smiled and reached for him. "I knew you'd come."

Seconds stretched into an hour while she hugged him close, touching his neck at the base of his hairline, fingering the silky texture of his hair, exploring his back with hands that remembered each bump of his spine, each muscle corded across his shoulders.

Turning slightly, she touched his jaw with quivering fingers.

"You've fought your own battles, haven't you?"

His eyebrows quirked, twin question marks. She drank in the sight of him, caressed his cheek. "I've missed that…your rough morning beard." He moved his head to kiss the palm of her hand.

Patting the bed, she said. "Come and lay your head, love. I'll rest better knowing you're with me."

He lay beside her, careful not to jostle the bed or jar her injured ribs. "God knows I love you!" he whispered in a croaky voice.

For long minutes Hannah was quiet, lying there beside him. She just wanted to curl herself around him, to be sheltered in his arms. Time was suspended. Speech took too much effort. Her eyelids were weighted and every strand of hair on her head throbbed. She watched her own hand move lethargically. With one finger, she traced his arm, from shoulder past the elbow, following a blue vein to his wrist. Gabe sucked in a stream of air, a low hissing sound. She let her hand rest.

"I thought I'd dreamed of you again," her voice was scratchy, battered like the rest of her body.

Then she snuggled closer, shivering against his welcomed body heat.

"You're safe. I'm here." He rubbed the crown of her head, petting her like a kitten. "Rest now. We'll talk later."

She drifted into a pleasant sleep, assured by his strong arm draped protectively across her waist.

It was near afternoon when she woke. She burrowed deeper into the familiar soft down pillows and pulled the sheet to her nose. She breathed deeply. Even without opening her eyes, she knew she was safe, because she could smell home.

"Gabe?" Her raspy voice was little better than a frog's call.

She closed her eyes again. She heard Trog's high-pitched voice. He was outside, trying unsuccessfully to quiet two of Tobias' dogs while they fought over food scraps. She groaned when she stretched.

Gabe bolted through the doorway, wide-eyed with concern. "Careful with those ribs."

Bathed and shaved, he smelled sinfully enticing. But, Hannah giggled when she saw him. He held a wooden cooking spoon in his right hand and the lid to a saucepan in his left.

Attempting to hide her smile behind her hand, Hannah croaked, her voice a shattered whisper. "Aha! Ever the gallant knight, sword and shield ready to defend the damsel from the fire breathing dragon."

Dragon? Where did that thought originate? She had a glimpse of a memory - remembered an ugly drawing, maybe a poster.

Gabe glanced at his hands and burst into laughter. "You're a strange woman; but I missed you nonetheless." He bent to breathe a kiss on her cheek. "How about a cup of chamomile tea?"

"Sure. Better than Advil, so they say."

"You remembered."

"Oh yeah. I remember."

"I can whip up some food, too. What would you like?"

"What I'd like has nothing to do with food."

292

He sat on the bed beside her. "What can I get for you?" She encircled his waist with her arms. She pressed her brow to his shoulder blade and felt him shudder at her touch.

"I only need to know that you're here," she answered, kissing his shirt. "That's enough." Hannah felt odd – heavy and lethargic; but lighter than air, almost as if she were floating a few inches above the bed.

"I feel like a rag doll... no bones to hold me upright."

"Go back to sleep, then. Let your body heal."

"Wait!" She reached for his hand when he stood. "Something's been nagging at the backside of my brain."

"What?"

"How did you find me?" She surprised herself with the question.

He hung his head, glancing at her from the corner of his eyes. "Now that's a complicated question."

She inched over a bit, affording him room on the bed, and he sat again, sharing the pillow at her back.

"I need to know," she answered.

Gabe lifted his arm above her, and she leaned forward, grunting with the movement, as he dropped the arm behind her. Then she relaxed against him, curling into his side as he drew swirling patterns on her arm with his fingers.

"Either gift or curse, it's a knack I learned from the faeries," he said. "Basically, I picture a person or a place, and I can transport myself there. Like when we visited Scotland. I think of Da, and 'boom' I'm there."

Hannah opened her mouth, as if to speak. Gabe held his finger to her lips.

"Let me finish. Please."

She nodded.

He took her hand, cupping her fingers in his palm. He stared at his thumb as it stroked hers.

"There is a catch to that trick, though." He looked up to find her eyes intent on his face. "If I don't know exactly where to locate a person, I have to clear my head and concentrate. Really concentrate." He shrugged and cocked his head to the side. "Meditate, I guess."

Hannah nodded. "Okay," she murmured.

"Extraneous thoughts will screw up the process."

She wrinkled her brows, but waited for him to continue.

"It's kinda like a faulty radio signal, I suppose. Irrelevant thoughts, like anger or worry, disrupt the connection." He squeezed her fingers. "Understand?"

She lifted her shoulders and let them drop. "I guess I'm with you so far."

Gabe shifted his position on the bed, flexing his neck front to back and side to side. He studied their hands, still joined in Hannah's lap.

"It gets complicated now." He peeked up at her. "When you weren't there to meet me and Trog, I was scared!"

"Yes..."

He lifted her hand to his mouth and rested his lips on her knuckles. His breaths were warm and damp on her skin.

"I doubted you. I thought you'd left me. No goodbye."

"But I'd told you I would be back!"

"I know."

Anger clipped her words, " I.. gave you..my word. My promise. I told you!"

"I know."

She snatched her hand away from him. "What happened to all that trust you like to talk about?" Frustrated, she swiped at her lashes, brushing tears.

Hannah didn't want to touch him. No, that wasn't exactly right. She didn't want to want to touch him. She sat on the bed beside him, felt the mattress adjust to each of his movements.

"How could you doubt me so?" Her voice cracked into scratchy pieces and she swatted his arm.

"I was miserable, Hannah! I doubted you. I doubted myself. I doubted God!" he screamed back. "We'd waited there in the woods for over ten hours for crying out loud."

"Well, sorry to keep you waiting. I was kinda tied up with delegates from hell." Hell? Yeah. Yeah, they were from hell. Some memory was stuck; she couldn't think straight when she was angry.

Gabe stared straight ahead. Hannah toyed with the ribbon laces at the neck of her gown. Both of them panted like marathoners after the last mile.

"How did you finally find me?"

Her hushed question startled him. He flinched as if she'd struck him.

He touched her lips with a finger. "I finally listened with my heart." His thumb tipped to his chest. "I heard you when I listened with my heart."

"I'm glad you did." Her pulse was racing. She took a deep breath. "Thank you… thanks for listening."

"I love you," he said.

"I know," was all she answered.

Gabe stood, wiped his palms on his thighs. "Try to rest."

Telling herself that she was too irritated to be sleepy, Hannah squirmed in the covers. How could he doubt her after preaching about trust and commitment? She stabbed a pillow with a fist. Maybe he's not as strong as he appears. Maybe doubt is a natural human emotion. After all, she'd never really expected him to rush in and save her. But he did. Better than Superman! She slid down to a fully reclining position. Defnitely better than Superman. Tucking her hand underneath the pillow, she curled into a small knot, drawing her feet up like a lazy cat. In seconds, she was sleeping soundly.

Gabe tiptoed into the bedroom. He carried a glass of lemonade for Hannah. She slept. He sat in the ladderback chair, about an arm's length from the bed. The afternoon sun beamed, the heat intensifying the sweet smell of honeysuckle on the trellis outside. At the windows, lace curtains billowed. The glass in his hand was frosted and the condensation dripped on his pants leg. He tilted the front chair legs off the floor, bracing his shoulders on the wall at his back. He gulped the lemonade, watching her. Mostly melted chunks of ice clinked when he rolled the glass between his palms. He rubbed his thumb back and forth on the wet glass, whispered to her as she slept.

"Much as I want to lose myself inside you, I wonder. Could I make you forget?"

She napped for an hour, woke feeling genuinely rested. Gabe was there - arms crossed behind his head with his chair balanced on two rear legs. She shivered. A vague memory frightened her for a second; but she couldn't place it. Why would a chair be scary? She shook her head. He let the chair rest on all four legs and winked at her.

"Hi, handsome," she teased, "Didn't you promise me food?"

The table was piled with food. "Every woman in the village dropped by this morning to bring you a little something." Gabe opened a casserole and sniffed. "Potatoes au gratin, I think." He tried another. "…something Italian; tomatoes and oregano." Hannah swirled her finger in the creamy vanilla frosting of a cupcake decorated with crystallized violet petals.

"Anything will be fine. Something light."

She ate a dish of egg custard, a handful of strawberries and a crusty piece of wheat bread slathered with butter. He just watched.

"Can you forgive me?"

"Forgive you? Forgive you for what?"

"For leaving you, for getting hurt, for worrying you. The list is endless," she said.

Heedless of her broken ribs, Gabe pulled her out of the chair, held her tight against his chest.

"Oh Love, there's nothing to forgive. I was annoyed that you wanted to leave, yes. Given a choice, I'd have kept you here." He shrugged his shoulders, tipped his head. "Yeah, I know. Selfish. But there was the chance that you'd find someone else; some man with fewer…umm, complications." He tugged on the pink ribbon hanging loose at the neck of her gown. "Don't get me wrong… I understood how you feel about your pledge to the Children's Hospital. Doesn't mean I had to react rationally when you left!" He kissed the top of her head.

"I needed to do that painting. Just really needed to do it. It's a good one. Maybe even my best." Her voice cracked. "Too bad because I doubt you'll ever see it." She sniffed. "I missed you terribly." She scrunched his shirt into a wrinkled mess. "I care about you; but I keep my pledges. You should have known I was coming back!" The tears escaped her this time. Now his shirt was wet and wrinkled. He rubbed soothing circles on her back. Circles that radiated tingling sensations down her spine.

"Feel like a short walk?"

"I'll try."

The late afternoon breeze carried a sweet, mellow scent. "Days are getting shorter. Fall's coming."

Hannah tipped her head towards a peony. Saucer-sized blossoms on every branch. "Summer's last hurrah." Leaning on Gabe's arm, she'd managed about a hundred steps. But now, her leg throbbed. "Let's sit down." With a decided lack of grace, she plopped onto the carpet of grass.

"Back in a minute," Gabe said as he sprinted up the back steps. When he returned, she was sitting just where he'd left her; but she'd unwrapped the bandage on her injured knee. She winced although her fingers never really touched the swollen stitches. Crouching beside her, he swabbed an infusion of jasmine and marigold oils around the reddened area.

"Inflammation's down," he encouraged. "The stitches may leave a small scar, though." He kissed her thigh above the last stitch.

She sniffed back a tear.

"Does it hurt so very much?"

Shaking her head, she held up her hands in a 'T' to signal 'timeout.' She wiped her eyes with the sleeve of her robe and pulled the bodice closed at her neck.

"No, the leg will be all right. You're a good doctor. I'm just so happy to be home again. … uncontrollable tears," she tried to explain. "Just hold me, Gabe. Please," she asked in a whisper.

He crossed his legs, Indian-style and pulled her into his lap. Pointing to the sun's position, "The angels are tuning up."

Heads touching, they sat on the damp grass to witness the sunset's brilliant colors, bright pinks, majestic purple and gold. And for them, the angels sang "The Hallelujah Chorus."

It was almost dark. Fireflies winked in the garden. Hannah heard the tiny pings of faerie bells in the trees overhead. Her nose was dusted with glittering powder that fell through the dogwood branches.

When mosquitoes whined at his ears, Gabe carried Hannah inside. Moonlight shone through the cascade of her hair. She was highlighted with gleaming sparkles.

"You look like an angel, all soft and glowing."

"You look feral. Devilish, maybe."

"Never claimed to be an angel."

The evening had a cool bite. Gabe put her on the bed and tugged the blanket around her shoulders.

"Maybe not exactly feral; but definitely comfortable with your body. Do you know since that first day, I've thought you moved like a jungle cat?"

"Oh yeah?"

"Yeah."

"Ever since that first day, I've thought that this is exactly where you belong, Hannah."

"I'm thinking you were right."

Hannah threw back the covers and carefully turned to put her feet on the floor. She hissed as she twisted her torso. "Darned ribs."

"There's not much we can do. Broken ribs just take awhile to knit again." He touched her shoulder. "Can I get something for you?"

"No. I just want to wash up before bed. I'll be all right." Just slow as molasses. Good grief! She felt like arthritic, Ella's age at least. Swaying a bit, she held the edges of the lavatory for balance. That motion gave her a weird hot-cold kind of feeling. Like a bad dream that she couldn't quite remember. She turned on the water and as it warmed, she reached for a washcloth. She held the soap close to her nose – tea rose. Rory, the bow-legged soap and candlemaker made it especially for her. She lathered the cloth and sponged her neck and shoulders. She rinsed the cloth and wiped away the soapy bubbles clustered under her arms. She hummed softly, washing her stomach and between her legs. The soft terry cloth suddenly felt like sandpaper on tender skin. She left the water running and re-wet the cloth again and again, pressing warmth between her legs against the stinging skin. Spreading her feet apart further, she bent her knees and squatted, back pressed against the wall. She dropped the cloth when she saw the elliptical bruise on the inside of her thigh. It was pale blue, striated with angry red marks. Angry red marks suspiciously shaped like a human bite.

Her head rolled back against the wall with a dull thud. She closed her eyes because the room started to loose shape. She sank to the floor. An image flashed! She saw herself naked; forced to her hands and knees. Two angry men. One man slapped her face. The other hit her back and buttocks with something heavy and stiff; a stick.

Her stomach roiled and she gagged. She hovered over the toilet, bracing herself on the seat with shaking arms. Tears mixed with sweat and vomit.

Gabe had stood outside the bathroom door listening to the sounds of running water and Hannah's quiet movements. Hearing her gag, he threw open the door and found Hannah clutching the toilet.

"Hannah."

He touched her head, resting his palm on the nape of her neck. She immediately flinched away from his touch.

"It's all right, Hannah. You're safe now. It's all right."

"Oh, Gabe," she wailed, "things will never be right again. Don't you understand? I must disgust you!"

She curled into a ball on the floor. Her knees partially concealed her face. She wrapped her arms around her legs; head on her kneecaps. Rocking back and forth in that position, she moaned, "I'm filthy." She blew her nose into the tissue he offered. "I'll never be clean again."

She snatched the discarded washcloth and scrubbed furiously, rubbing bright red marks across her breasts, legs and stomach. Gabe reached for her hand, covering it with his own, forcing her to stop. He wrapped his other arm around her shoulders and pulled her close. Her sobs reverberated in the small room.

"There was a rusted sink in that room. I bathed there with my ripped underpants."

Gabe sucked in a hiss of air. "Go on."

She shook her head. Curly strands of hair stuck to her wet face. "I don't think I can bear to remember."

Gabe picked her up as if she were a sick child. She was unresisting when he dressed her in another gown. She rinsed her mouth with water flavored with lemon juice and spearmint. Sniffing, she thanked him with a slight nod. She kept her eyes on the sheets rumpled around her. Gabe lifted her chin with a finger.

"Tell me," he whispered. "Tell me all you can remember."

"I'll disgust you."

He stared into her green eyes that brimmed with tears. "Let me share your pain."

He sat in the chair and held her hand between both of his. She cleared her throat, and tried to begin; but no words would form. Her shoulders shook and she snorted back her tears.

"I can't."

"This is my fault. I should have found you sooner," Gabe mumbled into his hands that were steepled, prayer-like.

"Don't be ridiculous, Gabe."

He sat rigid, back pressed tight against the wooden chair.

"I wasted valuable time, wallowing in my own doubts."

Hannah shifted her weight and swiped at her cheeks to dry them. She cleared her throat and twisted her hands together.

"I was walking in a pedestrian tunnel." She closed her eyes, envisioning the narrow passage, about forty feet long. "I'd just finished the work and I was headed to our meeting place."

Gabe's arms hung limp at his sides; but he flexed his fingers open and closed repeatedly.

She inhaled through her nose, expelled the breath and began again, "I was..umm…was worried….scared… by loud, really loud voices. Lots of cursing, shouting. I …a…decided to…umm, run away. The, umm, the strap … to my …ummm…satchel caught on a railing, I guess. I dropped it and everything spilled out. I ran to hide."

She fidgeted with the lace on the edge of the sheet, spreading it flat and smoothing wrinkles with her fingertips. "…tunnel was dark.

Lots of shadows, columns." Over and over, she pressed the sheet against the mattress, staring at it without really seeing it at all.

"Two men arguing…yelling at each other. Lots of people. Umm, everyone shouting and pushing. I felt trapped…like I was…hmmm… in a coffin. Could barely breathe." She closed her eyes; her eyelids twitched. She swallowed hard. She looked up, moving her eyes, as if viewing a screen superimposed on the ceiling. She swiped her at her nose, buried her face in her hands.

Tears streamed down her cheeks. "I was terrified!" She pushed back against the pillows mounded behind her. She sipped water from the glass on the bedside table. Her throat was so tight, she had trouble swallowing.

"I …I umm don't know what happened next. Something hit my head. Really hard. I remember crumpling. I don't remember hitting the floor."

She shook her head.

"Came to in a filthy room. My clothes were … were torn, shredded. I was naked and I had no idea, no idea where I was."

She lifted her eyes to his again, opened her mouth as if to say more, then quickly looked away. She could read sympathy on his face. There was another emotion, too. But she couldn't identify it.

"I was scared. I couldn't think straight."

She marched her hand in front of her face, trying to pull words from the air, to organize the words of her sentence into a logical order.

"My thoughts were…ahh…confused… disjointed. Snatches," she tried to explain. "I had an awful headache – concussion, maybe. I'd just fade… go blank. I can't put it all together yet. I'm not certain I want to."

She stared at the ceiling, then turned to the shadows outside the window.

"There were two men. They umm, they ahh, umm hurt me, you know. Then, they left for awhile."

In a whisper she sighed, "They…they raped me, I'm sure. I don't remember how many times. I …umm…flash back and see…uhhh…see myself in awful..um…" Her voice became a shadow of a whisper, "Tonight I had a vision, a very clear vision, of … of…umm,er, of violation by both men… simultaneously."

She closed her eyes, forcing out two big tears. With the heel of her palm, she blotted her cheek. She blinked and sniffed, then wiped her nose with her fingers. When she spoke, her voice was flat.

"Nothing's in sequence. What seemed like days might have been less... minutes, even. It's macabre. I float above myself, watching my own humiliation, wanting to fight; but I can't. I can't." She gulped, "I cry instead."

Gabe shifted to sit on the bed, opening his arms. Without any hesitation, Hannah buried her face against his broad shoulder, welcoming the security he offered. He rubbed her neck, shoulders, and back. His fingertips were like Novocain injected straight into her soul.

"Rape is violence, Hannah." He kissed the crown of her head, breathing deep. "Violence motivated by anger and a need for power. You're a victim."

Hannah pushed away from him. "How can you be so nice to me? I'm filthy. Trash." She wiped her palms over her arms. God, would she ever get rid of the dirt? "Why aren't you disgusted?"

"This horrible injustice couldn't make you dirty, *mo nighean mhaiseach.* You're innocent." He pushed hair away from her eyes, tucked a lock behind her ear. "You're the victim of a tragedy. But, remember tragedies can be overcome. Together, we can do it, *mo chride.*"

She sat with her back to him, corralled in the circle of his legs. His hand rested at her nape, warm and settling. The breath she exhaled caught in her throat. Her throat ached and there was a dull pain right behind her eyes. She reached over her left shoulder to touch his wrist.

"Better?" he asked.

"Yes. Maybe." She shrugged her shoulder and turned to watch him. "I do have a few questions for you, though."

"Okay. Ask me anything."

Hannah smiled. Okay, it was only a hesitant vestige of a smile. She twisted a thread of hair around her index finger.

"Who is *mo chride*? And what does *mo luaidh* mean?"

Gabe chuckled. He touched her freckled nose and gently tugged her hair.

"You are *mo chride*, 'my heart.' It's Gaellic. *Mo luaidh* is you, too. That means 'my darling.' You really are my heart, you know." He kissed the top of her head again. "I'll bet you will never guess the meaning of *mo nighean mhaiseach.*"

Hannah slowly sounded out the impossible Gaellic pronunication. "Hum, let me see. 'Mo nee-an vai-sheak'. Well, there's a world of possibilities. Vaisheak sounds rather unflattering. Does it mean 'my shrieking woman'?"

"Not even close, my beautiful girl."

He reached for a curl of her hair. She ducked her head and mumbled.

"Hardly beautiful unless you prefer your women red-eyed and splotchy."

"Always beautiful, *mo chride*. Always beautiful."

He pulled her head against his shoulder. They settled against the pillows and slept for a while.

Dawn arrived, dragging stormy skies that unleashed stiff winds to blow cold rain against the shutters. Rain fell on the tin porch roof. Howling winds wailed.

Hannah woke, clutched the sheet to her throat. "What was that?"

"Wind. It just sounds like a banshee." Gabe pulled her close, brushed a kiss on her forehead as though she were a child.

"Sounds like what?"

"A Banshee – the Gaellic spirits who forewarn of approaching death.

"Great! That's a cheerful thought."

"It's only a tale, Hannah."

"...a faerie tale, right?"

Violent winds blew branches against the window shutters to make an annoying rhythm. Hannah smelled the rich minerals of the rain-soaked earth. The storm raised the hairs on her arms and prickled her scalp.

"Now, Hannah, tell the rest."

"No. No more."

He touched her chin, and she turned towards him. As though he were blind, he traced the shape of her face, memorizing each pore.

"There's more. Tell me. Tell me now, Love."

"It's too awful. You'll hate me."

"Never."

"I wanted to escape. I wanted to die," she confessed. "They..umm, they used me... cruelly. But I couldn't fight them. I was too weak to struggle."

She turned away from him. "I'm pathetic." She let her chin fall towards her chest, picked at a hangnail.

"I called the bald guy 'Scar'. Scar tried to keep me conscious by hurting me. He would slap me, pull my hair or, ummm, twist my, ummm, nipples until I cried."

She covered her breasts with her arms.

"He plunged his fingers deep inside me. I think he was try-ing… trying to get my soul… searching between my legs, looking for my soul."

Gabe groaned, low in his throat. Turbulent winds screamed outside. The shrill, keening of a banshee-wind pierced the stillness in the bedroom. Streaks of lighting illuminated the room in garish flashes, gave Gabe a scary mask made of shadows. Wide-eyed, Han-nah took his face between her two hands, forced him to look at her face.

"He liked for me to cry. He liked hurting me… and he liked hearing…hearing my pain. He would, umm, touch himself…mastur-bate while he hurt me. He made me…made me…" Now she stared over his shoulder, focusing on nothing. She gulped a breath. "He made me hold his penis while he , ummm, while he ejaculated." She exhaled and sucked in another breath. "He came in my mouth, and uhhhh, rubbed my throat until I swallowed."

Her voice was flat and quiet, a dull monotone. "Once he rubbed his semen on my neck, in my hair and over my breasts." Her voice cracked. She covered her mouth with her fist. "Oh God! This is hard!" She spoke through fingers that covered her lips. "He, Scar...

he made the other ... Leonard, the other man's name is Leonard. He

made Leonard lick me clean."

Dropping her hands from her face, she dropped her eyes to her lap. She wiped her sweaty palms on the sheets; trying to clean away the filth she felt.

Gabe gathered her hands into his and pulled them to his lips. Her eyes followed their joined hands. That single tie grounded her although her world was being battered by an emotional hurricane.

"Scar wanted to prove his power, to control you," Gabe told

her. "But he couldn't."

Hannah shook her head, moved to the window, and straightened a pleat in the drapes. The blowing rains slacked. Branches no longer rattled the shutters. Slowly the high clouds floated west.

Gabe stood at her back. "We'll deal with this situation, Han-

nah. Together, we'll be make things right. Believe me," he vowed.

Outside, the sun sparkled through the thin wispy clouds, highlighting water droplets on blades of grass, transforming them to sequins; birds chirped messages to one another, and insects buzzed unscored tunes around the water laden flowers. Three faeries dressed in lilac gowns twirled on the beads of water as though they were musicbox ballerinas.

Wasn't it Disraeli who said "Nature, like man, sometimes weeps from gladness"? Hannah was far from glad; but she did feel less overwhelmed. That was progress, wasn't it? She wouldn't always feel so…so what? So used; so violated; so filthy; so completely and hopelessly shamed. She sniffled and wrapped her arms at her waist.

"Sssh, Love. Quiet now, *'mo chride.'*" He kissed the crown of her head. "I'll protect you, *'mo luaidh.'*" He wrapped his arms around her tighter. She was pliant as modeling clay as he molded her back against his chest.

Why did he care? To be truthful, she knew she wasn't worth the trouble. Her face was bruised and swollen. Her body was a jumble of cuts and breaks. But, most importantly, there were serious holes blown through the emotional barricades she'd constructed. She'd spent lonely years building those reinforcements to protect her self-esteem, her character – her very soul. Now, she was forced to concede that her fortress wasn't as strong as she'd thought. She couldn't stand alone; she needed help and love and support.

Her joints cracked when she turned. He touched her bottom lip with one finger. And she felt the vibrations of that touch in her core. Maybe something of her soul remained intact. "Come back to bed," he

315

said. Hannah's slippers made familiar little 'whoosing' sounds as she crossed the wooden floor.

"You've pampered me long enough, Gabe."

"You need to rest, to regain your strength."

Hannah grabbed the pillow he was fluffing. "After days of lying in bed, I'm rested." Huffing, she tossed it across the room. It hit a vase that wobbled three times before crashing to the floor. Bright yellow coreopsis were scattered in a puddle of water next to her dressing table.

"Do you want to talk about it?" he asked softly.

She shouted, "No. No, I definitely do not want to talk about IT. I want to forget IT."

Scrubbing her forehead with her knuckles, she whispered, "I want to erase all of those disgusting memories."

"But you can't, can you?"

"What do you think?"

"I think you need to talk to a counselor."

Hannah turned her head to the right, then to the left. "I don't see any therapists, do you?" Her hands plopped to her lap in fists.

Gabe left the bedroom and Hannah crossed her arms just under her breasts. She scowled, knowing that she had been spoiling for a fight and that Gabe probably wouldn't give her one. Damn him! Did the man have any idea how infuriating his unwavering patience could be? She knew that she'd been unreasonably cranky; but damnit she had a right. Didn't she?

"Here you go!" Gabe dropped a cardbox box at the foot of the bed.

"You want me to clean out the attic?"

"No. I want you to do a bit of research." He reached into the box and flipped several pamphlets and a few discolored newspaper articles towards her. "Get acquainted with the facts. Realize that you're not the only victim. Come to grips with the situation. Then we'll deal with it. Together." He turned and crossed the room, pulling the door closed as he left.

Hannah reached for one of the yellowed clippings. "That's more like it, Gabe," she muttered. "Show me some of your fire."

She glanced at the piece of newsprint. There was a short article under a blurry photograph of a woman with a black eye. The facts she read were astounding. One in every eight women in the United States is a victim of forcible rape. Over one-third of the rape victims contemplate suicide. Hannah tapped her lips while she read. One in eight women. Good god; she'd had no idea! She'd thought she was the only one. Her fingers closed into a tight fist. She punched her thigh as she read the interview, punctuating each harsh fact with a blow.

"I don't want to know about the constitution of the rapist," the victim had said. "I want to kill him! I don't care if he is white or black, if he is middle-class or poor, if his mother hung him from the clothesline by his balls: I only want to *kill* him! Any woman who has been raped will agree."

"I agree, Diamanda, I agree with you completely," Hannah whispered.

About an hour later, Gabe opened the door just a crack. He peeked inside. "Safe for me to come in?" He nudged the door open with his foot.

"Come here." She patted the mattress. "I want you to read this." She stabbed her index finger at a brochure.

318

"There are more rape victims in the United States than there are combat veterans."

Gabe covered his upper face with his hand; rubbing one eye socket with his thumb, the other with his second finger.

"How can statistics like that be true?" Hannah wanted to know.

"Only 16 out of 100 rapes are reported to the police," Gabe read.

"I can see it - a line of girls and women afraid to report the crime. They could hold hands as their number increases until they've formed a chain to reach around the world, circling the globe time and again."

Gabe smoothed the ripped edges of the next page. "Over half of the college males surveyed stated that they would use force to co-erce a female to have sex if they thought they could escape any pen-alty."

"That's what I allowed; isn't it?"

"I don't think you allowed anything. I think you were beaten senseless and raped."

"But I didn't report the rape."

Gabe laid his fingers over her knuckles. "Is that what you'd like to do?"

"Hell no! There's nothing about this ordeal that's gone the way I'd like, though."

"I'm with you, whatever you decide, Hannah."

She rubbed her eyes, wiped her mouth and chin. "I can't go back there now, Gabe. I can't face it. Not right now."

"I feel like a prisoner released on parole!" Hannah told Trog as she hobbled towards the kitchen.

Gabe followed her. "Well, if you're a prisoner; I'm your parole officer. You behave or I'll slap you back in that bed!"

She banged the teapot on the edge of the sink as she filled it with water. Smiling, she saluted. "Anything you say, Boss."

When the kettle whistled, Hannah was in the pantry, humming a silly limerick.

"Can you check the teapot, Gabe?"

"You've made a remarkable recovery," Gabe muttered. "Did somebody slip you a miracle drug?"

"Nothing to be gained by dwelling on my troubles."

"True enough, Girl," Trog squeaked. "Dwell on mine for a bit!" His stomach grumbled louder than his voice.

She ruffled the unruly hair that his elfin cap had smashed into odd whorls.

The trio sat together on cushions in front of the fire, breakfasting on tea and bread. Licking a drip of honey from her thumb, Hannah said, "Fruit. We need some fruit. Maybe I'll slice some cheese, too. Be right back."

She stood and wiped her hands on her robe. Her movements were economical, each one slow and thriftily spent. But, she walked into the kitchen, whistling. Trog reached for another piece of bread and methodically drizzled honey in neat rows on the slice.

Satisfied with his work, he glanced up at Gabe and with a gleam in his eyes. "I thought the girl was seriously injured. You're a wondrous healer to have cured her so quickly!"

Gabe leaned towards him, pulling the little man closer like a conspirator. "I've cured nothing." He stacked his teacup on his empty plate. "I cleansed the cuts and stitched them. Her body will heal in time. It's her fragile emotions that concern me now." He glanced towards the kitchen. "I'll need your help to watch over her, Trog. I won't let her be hurt again. Between us, we've got to watch out for Hannah."

"You say the word. I'll help." Gabe squeezed the elf's sloping shoulder, and the pact was made. Trog was grim when he nodded. "Aren't elves known to be diligent? Keeping watch on one injured human can't be too difficult a task."

When Hannah returned with her tray of fruit and cheese, the men moved apart, sharing an almost guilty glance. She puzzled over that look briefly, then shook her head and smiled. She was too pleased to worry about their schemes. She hummed another nonsense song and Gabe smiled, touching her back.

"*Cianmar a tha tu, mo chridhe?* How are you, Love?"

"Um,humm, fine," she mumbled, moving deftly out of his reach.

He frowned.

"You really are much more attractive when you smile," she said. She put a fingertip on each of his dimples, pulling his lips up into a crooked smile.

"Talk to me, Hannah," he coaxed. "Your moods are changing faster than the weather."

Hannah sat straighter and pulled her hands together in her lap. "Don't you find a cheerful, capable woman preferable to wailing, useless one?"

He drew in a breath and waited to see if she would say more. She didn't.

"I prefer your honesty. If you're unhappy or frightened, you can share those feelings with me. We are hand-fasted; we're a team, you and I." He rubbed her wrist with his thumb. "Didn't I promise to keep you safe, to share my life with you?"

Hannah pursed her lips and tipped her head to one side.

Gabe tickled her chin. "There's no need for pretense. Not between us, Love."

Hannah looked at the floor, shuffled her weight, glanced to right, carefully evading eye contact. She nodded, the quake in her voice was barely discernible; barely.

"For a year and a day," she whispered.

She chewed on her thumbnail. "I've got to force myself to continue life, Gabe. Don't you see that dwelling on the rape will drive me crazy? I've got to try to get past that pain. To do that, I've got to keep busy."

She reached out to him. He leaned close and she stroked his lips, touched the dimple in his right cheek.

"God knows, I need to keep my mind busy right now. Captain Kangaroo had a song *'Busy hands are happy hands, and that just can't go wrong'*."

"Captain who?"

"He's …he's a character… from childhood television. He had puppet friends; a rabbit and a moose." She waved her hands, erasing the confusing thought. "It's the idea of keeping busy that's important."

Gabe remained seated, though to Hannah, he looked as if he wanted to pace the floor. Instead, he brushed at a speck of dust on the table. His knees bounced.

"You can stay busy right here. The children love your songs and stories. You're a big help to me when I treat a patient."

She hunched her shoulders forward, then back.

"Okay, okay. I understand," Gabe conceded. "Go out and talk to the elves. Help them with their chores. They'll be thrilled with your attention and your help."

Hannah puffed out her cheeks and expelled a big breath.

"Each night you will return here to me, though, Hannah. Promise me."

"For a year and a day… That's the agreement. Yes, all right."

His gray eyes turned black; ebony depths. He exhaled through his nose and growled low in his throat.

"Not just for a year and a day, damnmit. I'll keep you here with me forever, if you'll stay." He spoke through gritted teeth. "I thought we'd been through all this before."

Hannah's shoulders straightened. "A lot has changed since we visited your father on Skye." She stood ready for combat; feet spaced wide, knuckles white on clenched fists at her side. "I'm not a crippled bird you found, Gabe."

"What in blazes is THAT supposed to mean?"

She covered her face with her hands and spoke through the space between her palms. "I don't want to be like the injured starling you found under the willow tree. You feared she'd die if you released her to the wild again. Remember? She became so dependent on you that she wouldn't eat unless you feed her with an eyedropper."

"I remember. That was a bird; not a woman."

"But she died anyway, didn't she?" Hannah persisted. "I need to know that I can make it on my own."

Gabe grabbed her arm. He squeezed so tight that she could barely move her fingers. "You're not going to die, dammit."

"I don't want you to feel honor-bound to keep me."

Gabe lunged to his feet, hands clenched at his sides.

"Does love count for nothing, then?"

She faced him, chin jutted in defiance. Her head matched the level of his heart. She clasped her hands at her back.

"Sometimes, it takes more love to let go rather than to hold on. Sometimes love dies. Or it's murdered."

"Don't spout clichés."

Gabe took a deep breath, then he bent forward to kiss the top of her head.

"A day at a time, Love," he whispered into her hair. "Let's deal with this healing process one day at a time."

Hannah nibbled her swollen lip.

"I wish I could crawl inside your head, Hannah. Maybe I could understand if I could touch your thoughts."

"Oh, you're in my thoughts, Gabe," she told him. What she didn't tell him was that she planned to leave the house to work - somewhere - each day. In the respite of those few hours, she would prepare herself for the coming years without him. She was certain that those years without him would come. At least for a while she would continue to spend nights here, in the house that felt like a home. She planned to watch him sleep, to memorize his smells and tastes. Deep in her heart, she knew he would discard her after the year and a day. What strong man would want to keep an abused woman; damaged goods? Those memories she stored would need to last her whole lifetime.

Gabe raised his hand to touch her shoulder, but let it hover inches above. "You're a victim," he said.

His hand brushed her blouse and floated across her hand, barely touching her fingernails. Something akin to electricity sparked between them.

"And, thank the gods, you're alive." His voice cracked.

"You're a victim," he said. He moved fast, to crush her in a tight hug. "You're alive."

That night Gabe came into the bedroom while Hannah was undressing. She reached over her shoulder to unclasp her hair barrette and shook her long braid free. She hurried to unbutton her blouse and unbuckle her sandals. Shrugging out of her blouse, she grimaced. She squirmed free of her skirt and tried to conceal some of the bruises, but she didn't have enough hands.

Gabe tugged her right elbow.

"Don't," he said, pulling her arm to her side, uncovering the livid yellowing bruise on her right shoulder. "Don't hide from me, Hannah."

She extended both arms out at her sides. "Damaged in shipping, but still operational, I think," she said.

327

She wondered if he noticed the hurt behind her humor.

"Certainly not beyond repair. Looks beautiful to me."

Once she was in bed, Hannah couldn't sleep. Gabe had tucked extra pillows at each side so that she wouldn't hurt her cracked ribs by turning in her sleep. He lay on the other side of the bed. The separation between them seemed as greater than the Grand Canyon. She stared at the ceiling, watched the shadows waiver. She wadded the sheet bunched at her side. Slowly, inch-by-inch, she reached out to touch his shoulder. He jerked at the contact as if she'd zapped him with an electric charge.

"Gabe," she whispered, "I'll love you forever." Then she pulled the covers over her shoulder and closed her eyes.

He turned on his side to watch her. Hours later, in the near dawn quiet, he edged closer to brush a kiss along the arch of Hannah's brow. Then he left her alone in her fortress of feather pillows. He buttoned his shirt while walking towards the garden gate.

Trog called "Morning, Gabe."

"Good morning, Trog. Come with me to see what Glendar has baked today?"

Trog trotted along at Gabe's side, practically skipping in an effort to keep pace. "Let me see your teeth."

Gabe bared his teeth. "What's that mean?"

"Just checking to see if maybe you'd grown a new sweet tooth!"

Gabe chuckled and swatted Trog's cap askew.

"Well, everyday for more than a week now, you're out of bed before the sun, heading towards the bakery before Glendar has taken the first pastries out of his oven."

Gabe rubbed the back of his neck. "I can't stay in bed, watching Hannah sleep. As it is, I lay awake most of the night and count each minute until the sun's arrival."

"If the girl makes you uncomfortable, send her to Ella's place. A fellow's allowed to break a handfast vow, you know. No harm, no foul."

Gabe stopped abruptly and Trog collided with his knees. "You don't understand." He shook his head and *pssshed* out a breath. "Of course, I don't even understand."

"Try to explain it to both of us, then."

"I'd never break my handfast. I want Hannah now more than ever. She's part of me." He rapped his fist on his chest. "But, I'm scared."

"Because she's been raped?"

"Hell, yes, because she's been raped."

"You love her?"

"Stupid question! But she was violated physically and mentally. The physical bruises will fade, but the emotional scars might last forever. She still has horrible nightmares, and I can't help her with those."

"You're helping her. She looks better everyday; bruises fading, the limp isn't nearly so bad as before. She's laughing and singing those silly songs of hers again."

"What if I trigger a flashback if I get too close?"

"You'll never know unless you try, will you?"

Trog cocked his head towards the village, and they resumed their march to the bakery.

"I lie in bed at night and fight my body's responses. Every touch is torture because I want more than she's ready to give. I want... I want...Hannah to want me, and she may never want me – or any man – again."

"Sounds like a problem."

Gabe held the door to Glendar's shop open. Smells of cinnamon, of sugar, and of strong fresh-brewed coffee wafted out.

"I'm driving myself crazy."

Trog winked and pointed to a tray of croissants that oozed strawberry filling. "Let's try to sugar coat your problems, then."

Hannah woke slowly. Her mind registered the noisy morning ritual of the village; but her eyelids were gritty and heavy - refusing to open. The roosters crowed a blustering aria; 'cockle doodles' screeching one after another; a call to reveille for the faeries. Next, the dogs barked messages, crooning both happiness and complaints. She knew that soon elfin children would spill out of doors, whistling for pets as they stuffed bread and fruit into their tunic pockets.

Because she heard the velvet rumble of Gabe's voice and the squawk that passed for Trog's laughter, Hannah pushed back the covers, fighting stiff muscles to climb out of bed. She limped to her closet, massaging her ribs.

Would these blasted ribs never mend? In the bathroom, she splashed her face with cool water and scrubbed her teeth. She brushed her hair without looking in the mirror – that way she didn't have to face the ugly bruises. As she entered the living room, she tied a kerchief around her head, securing a knot under her hair.

"Good morning," she sang, her voice almost lilting.

Both men turned in surprise.

Gabe grinned. "Looked like rain earlier; but you've brought sunshine into the room."

She bobbed her head. "Good."

"Judging from the costume, your schedule must include gardening today," he mused.

"I've spent a long time staring at Trog's garden from the bedroom window. There's work to be done, and it's a lovely day." Smiling she turned towards the front door while patting her pockets, checking to be certain she had her gloves.

"Are you sure you're up to the task?"

"How many days can I hide here, trying to convince myself that nothing has changed?"

"You've been recuperating, Hannah."

"I've been something less than productive, Gabe."

Filling his own pockets with idle hands, Trog mumbled, "This elf isn't going to spend the day toiling in the hot sun without a proper breakfast!" He jutted his chin in a pout, but smiled a crooked grin that pushed his eyes into deep wrinkled crevices.

Tapping the palm of her hand against her forehead, Hannah giggled. "Of course! Breakfast. C'mon to the kitchen. We'll find some food."

Trog's stomach rumbled and he gripped his belly, rolling his eyes heavenward. "Ah, nourishment!" His squeak held a pathetic tremor.

"Your life is dictated by hunger," Hannah teased. "At the last Village dinner, Nowatil grumbled about the giant-sized appetite in your miniscule body."

"...And how did I answer the meddlesome old biddy?" Trog scowled, whiskey-brown eyes glaring under brows that resembled carrot-colored caterpillars. "Great things are hidden in small packages!"

Hannah arranged eggs, bowl and whisk on the counter. She turned to the stove. "While I start coffee, you break the eggs, Trog."

"Done my share already - brought croissants and apple-cinnamon muffins, fresh out of Glendar's oven," Trog squeaked, sticking out his tongue.

Hannah shook her finger at him. "You're acting like a spoiled child."

Gabe laughed, "Oldest darned child I've ever seen."

"I was a man, full grown when you were a bairn, though, wasn't I?"

Hannah crossed her arms, leaned against the cupboard. "So you can tell me tales about Gabe as a boy, can you Trog?"

"Taught the lad all he knows!"

"He's not exaggerating much." Gabe tipped his head. "It was Trog who taught me magic."

Trog rubbed his chin, then pulled on his lower lip. "Not really magic; I just taught you to channel your thoughts."

Gabe waved his right hand above the platter of croissants. One pastry rose and floated just below his fingertips. "To use my mind for transportation." He broke the croissant in two pieces and offered one to Trog.

"Really? That's amazing!" Hannah nodded and whisked a dollop of cream into the eggs. "How did Trog teach you?" Hannah asked.

"With pains-taking care," Trog laughed.

"Awk! He's a taskmaster, is our little Trog."

Gabe wiped his palms on his trousers and then hooked his thumbs in the belt loops.

"The lectures were everlasting! He preached that I needed to concentrate, so I practiced for weeks. Of course, to a young boy, focusing is a difficult task!"

"Weeks? ...years, it seemed to me," Trog interrupted.

"Not an apt student, huh?" Hannah winked.

"Hamph!" Gabe rubbed his forehead. "Trog never told me it would hurt my brain move small objects. There was one pivotal day... I'll never forget that day. I sat on a huge flat stone and stared at a pebble." He circled his thumb and index finger making a circle the size of a quarter. "With every fiber of my being, I willed that blasted pebble to move."

"Yeah, he did," Trog agreed. "A stubborn creature is our Gabriel."

"Anyway…it took a couple of hours. I was getting a headache; but I stared at that pebble. I tried to ignore distractions, like gnats at my ears and heat that soaked my tunic with sweat. I concentrated on the pebble. I had stared so long, my eyes burned and I wanted to close them, just for a second." He took an exaggerated breath. "Trog sat beside the boulder…dozing, whittling, and snacking."

"Hey," the elf snapped, "it was a very long, boring day!"

Gabe ruffled the elf's coarse hair.

"My mind went blank. I was past hunger or thirst. I didn't notice sounds or smells. Sight was my only sense."

Hannah wiped her hands on a dishtowel and moved closer to the table.

Gabe's voice dropped low, "Then,… slowly, …ever so slowly…that pebble turned." He twirled his finger in a circle.

"That little pebble lifted off the surface of the huge rock." He wiggled in fingers inches above the table. "It floated; suspended by my concentration!"

Hannah covered her mouth with her hand. "Telekinesis?"

Trog shrugged and shook his head.

"Then, I was exhausted. I closed my eyes and the pebble fell," Gabe said.

Trog pulled out a chair and climbed into the seat. His legs dangled midway to the floor while he reached for a muffin.

Gabe scowled at the elf for a second. "I scooped up that pebble and ran to Trog."

He turned to Hannah. "Do you know that he was sitting there, feet propped on a tree branch as if he were in a recliner chair? He hadn't even been watching me. He told me he didn't need to see. He knew I could do it.'"

"Talent like his is obvious, Missy. I told the boy that with practice, he could learn to move his body through space to any place he wanted."

"You could tell, just by watching, that Gabe was special?"

Trog screwed up his face, deep in thought. "Umm, yeah; I s'pose."

Hannah twisted the pepper grinder over the pan of steaming fluffy eggs. She watched Trog over her shoulder. "Could you teach anyone, or only the designated few? Could you teach me to do magic?"

Trog jammed his hands in his pockets.

"Why would you be wanting to do magic, Lass?"

Hannah shrugged one shoulder. " I dunno. Haven't given it any thought." She set the platter of eggs on the table beside the basket mounded with pastries. "Do I need a reason?"

"Aw, weel. Be thinking, then girl. We'll talk more later, when you've decided."

Neglecting his napkin, Trog licked remnants of cream from his upper lip, then swiped the same spot with the cuff of his tunic. Draining the last drop of juice from his glass, he slapped the table with the palm of his hand. "Enough time wasted. Chores in my garden. Hurry, girl. Once the sun's burning bright and hot those pesky faeries will be pirouetting on the marigolds and splashing dewdrops on the tomato vines."

Gabe stood and carried a stack of dishes to the sink. "Like I said, Trog's a formidable task master!"

Trog muttered, "Little pests leave dimples on the ripe tomatoes!"

"Don't worry about the dishes here. I'll wash up." Gabe tapped Hannah's hand with one finger. "I've arranged to meet an old friend in the Village, so I'll bring lunch for you two in a few hours."

Hannah limped outside where Trog was collecting a shovel, a trowel and a hoe from the shed beside the back porch. She grabbed the handle of a large watering can and laughed when water sloshed on her feet.

They left the yard, heads bobbing together. They shared an odd, ill-paced gait. Trog's stubby little legs pumped quickly to match Hannah's longer, but more tentative steps. The heavy water can splashed its contents on her trousers and shoes. The elf used his garden tools as walking staffs, to vault himself along the path to keep pace with Hannah.

Once at the garden, they divided the tasks and set to work. Hannah spent about an hour crouching to pull weeds out of the marigold bed and the squash vine hills. The morning sun was pleasantly warm, and she flipped her braid over her shoulder. Being outdoors was therapeutic; she hummed softly as she worked.

Grunting with each motion, Trog hacked at the soil between the rows of corn stalks, working composted manure into the loam. He grumbled about the pesky white flies, the ever-present weeds, the dagburned squash borers and the hungry beetles. His farming technique incorporated organic gardening with abusive language.

"How about some water to cool your temper, Trog?"

He leaned an elbow on the hoe handle and glanced up at her sunburned face.

"Why don't you rest a bit, Girl? You're all red in the face."

"I'm fine. It's good to be outdoors," she told him.

She stood and stretched her cramped back and legs. She pushed at a hair that tickled her cheek, and smeared a long smudge of dirt across her freckles. She glanced at her hands and noticed that each cuticle and nail was outlined with dark soil. She was kneeling at the watering can, dousing her hands and arms when Trog muttered, "Well, it's about time!"

She watched Gabe approach; he moved through the tree-lined path, like a panther with a fluid, feral grace.

Gabe deposited a bulging sack on the large flat tree stump near the garden. Trog wasted no time rummaging through the bag. He held a sandwich to his nose and lifted a corner of the bread. "Peanut butter, honey and bananas?"

Gabe nodded to Trog, but he touched Hannah's flushed cheek. "How are you? You didn't overdo? Should you rest?"

She shook her head and grinned. "It's been marvelous!"

Gabe glanced up, noting the sun's position, and apologized, "The visit took longer than I'd expected. We were childhood buddies, and there were a lot of adventures to relive!"

He looked to Trog, who had stopped eating and seemed ready to speak. Gabe pushed on Hannah's shoulder, urging her to sit on the ground. "Come on. Let's eat. I need to fatten you up, Love."

"What have you got in the bag?"

"If we hurry, there will be plenty of food. If we wait too long, the little weevil will consume our lunch!"

Trog leaned against a picket fence. He licked his fingers, rubbed his slightly distended belly and burped appreciatively. Then he cocked his cap forward to cover his eyes, dropped his chin to his chest and was snoring within a few seconds.

Hannah nibbled at her sandwich. She really wasn't very hungry these days. More often than not, her stomach rebelled if she ate much. Gabe watched to make certain she drank all of the apple juice he'd poured. She brushed the crumbs off her lap and stood.

"Come on, Trog," she called. "Didn't you say you want to plant these potato eyes and pick the Sugar Snaps before we stop work today? Look lively!"

Kissing Gabe's cheek, she chuckled. "Duty calls!"

"True enough. I have patients to check in the village. I'll meet you at home for the sunset, Love."

He blew her a kiss. She caught it and tucked it under her blouse, close to her heart. Her laughter followed his own down the path. He was almost to the curve, in another few seconds she'd lose sight of him.

Two women approached Gabe just as the path started to turn. A woman dressed in red velvet braced against his arm and stood on tiptoe to kiss his cheek. Hannah gritted her teeth when the woman stroked his neck and played with the long hair at his nape.

Both women were dressed more appropriately for cocktails than for a walk in the woods. Hannah couldn't hear their conversation, but she saw Gabe tilt his head towards the woman in red.

"Who are they?" she asked. She hoped that the question sounded casual, although she doubted that it did.

Trog ambled over, awkwardly patted her arm and shook his head. "That," he jerked his head towards Gabe and the women, "that would be trouble."

"Who is she? What do you mean *trouble*?"

"I mean TR-OU-B-L-E."

"Sometimes I don't understand you at all, Trog. I feel like Alice in Wonderland most of the time."

"Don't know Alice."

Hannah planted her fists on her hips. "She's fictional... a character in a story who falls into a magical land where nothing is as it seems."

"Hmmm, place must be run by pixies."

"Soooooo... what do you mean by trouble?"

"That girl, Lynnar; she always delivers trouble. I used to think she was jinxed. But then I decided she's just mean. Likes to brew havoc. Pay her no mind. She's happiest when she makes other women miserable."

He kicked at a bright yellow toadstool. It released spores in a puff of smoke. He cleared his throat.

"Ah, ummm, Well… Now, let's finish with the planting. You look tired. After planting, you go to the pool for a nice bath."

"But…" Obviously Trog considered the conversation over. He'd picked up the hoe and was furiously chopping compost into the soil. She cast one last glance at the three figures disappearing into shadows on the path. Gabe had mentioned a friend. An old buddy. That woman was not exactly what Hannah would describe as either *old* or *buddy-ish.*

For about another hour, they worked together in the garden, speaking infrequently. Trog was a conversational conservationist; saving speech for important matters. At times, Hannah wondered if he had been allotted use of only a certain number of words during his lifetime, and therefore feared wasting any unnecessarily.

"Go on. Bathe." Trog pointed towards the path. "Getting late." He jabbed his thumb towards the sky.

Hannah nodded. "See you later, Trog." She took short cautious steps, all the while rubbing sore muscles low in her back. She grasped the railing alongside the mossy steps leading down the embankment to the pool. Pausing for a breath on the last step, she was surprised to hear voices. The pool belonged to Gabe; it was his special place. To her knowledge, no elf, faerie or sprite would venture into his personal space uninvited.

She heard women giggling. Dulcet laughter. She inched closer, craning her neck to see around the thick screen of foliage. Dry leaves crackled and twigs crunched under her feet. She held her breath, hoping that the two women in the pool hadn't heard her approach.

Naturally she recognized them. These two were the stuff of fairy tales! Gorgeous women with impossibly flawless skin…not all scraped and bruised. Lots of flawless skin covered with lather from the hidden crocks of soap. Old buddies, huh?

"Well, don't just stand there with your mouth flopping open! Either join us, or leave us to finish our bath," a sultry, sophisticated voice exhorted.

Fruitlessly, Hannah brushed at the stains on her clothes. She scrubbed her cheek with the heel of her hand, pulled at her tangled hair. She edged away from the bushes slowly.

"Uhh…Hello," she stammered. "I…ummm, I wasn't expecting anyone here." She coughed and looked at her feet. She knocked the right shoe against the left, spraying flecks of mud bits. "I'm a mess."

The woman who had called out tapped her fingertip against her lips.

"That's obvious, Hannah. Come join us. No, no, don't be shy."

She beckoned Hannah forward. Beads of water glistened like rhinestones on her shoulders. Her long nails were lacquered red. Self conscious, Hannah inspected her own hands. Her nails were trimmed

342

short; but well-formed half moons of dirt showed at each tip. She stuffed her hands deep in her pockets and took a step closer to the pool.

"You know who I am?"

"Oh, for goodness sake, don't be so skiddish. I'm Lynnar, and this is my cousin Trina. We were wards of this Village during our formation years."

Hannah stared at the two women. Darned good formation. Their skin shimmered. Who ever heard of opalescent skin? And those huge brown eyes framed by long dark lashes. Bambi had eyes like that, she thought.

Mahogany highlights glinted in Lynnar's hair, making Trina's deep ebony seem dull by comparison. Although each was a beautiful woman; Lynnar was entrancing; enchanting, compelling. Her every movement was choreographed, like a graceful ballet.

Hannah inched closer to the pond, although she couldn't think of anything intelligent to say. She crossed her arms at her waist and shifted her weight side to side. She felt incompetent and dull; she resolutely promised herself to remain clothed until they left.

The women were snickering, really. At her. She felt the hot blush rise from her collarbone to her cheeks.

"Ummm. Sorry. I didn't hear you." She turned an ear towards Lynnar.

"What ARE you doing here…here in the Village?"

"Oh. Well, umm, that is... Well, truth is, Gabe brought me."

"Ahh. Of course. Gabe." Lynnar and Trinia exchanged glances. "He always did bring home the strangest little damaged creatures."

Lynnar propped her elbows on the rocks bordering the pool, holding her chin in her hands.

"I really can't imagine that he plans to keep you, though. You're more a catch-and-release type."

Hannah jutted her chin forward, rolled her hips back slightly, sucked her stomach flatter and squared her shoulders.

"We're handfasted. Gabe and I."

"How quaint. Handfasted." Lynnar arched her left brow inquisitively. "A year's commitment, isn't it?"

"A year and a day."

"Of course. Can't forget that all important day."

Trinia spoke for the first time. Her voice was unusual. Husky, singsong. Hannah thought of tangerines, sweet, but tangy.

"What a difference a day makes!"

"He says we will get married." Halfheartedly, Hannah tried to turn her scowl to a semblance of a smile. She rubbed the knot at her temple, and grimaced again.

Lynnar let her head loll back. "Well, naturally that's what he said. He wanted to take you to his bed."

Hannah blinked. Her lips formed a silent "O".

"You didn't believe him, did you?" Trinia asked.

Lynnar nodded. "Of course she did." She tapped her lips with a garnet colored nail.

"You're not his first, you know."

"Really?"

"Really."

Hannah touched her throat. She wadded the material at the neckline of her blouse. She was dizzy. Even her ears burned with the heat of her blush.

Lynnar tilted her head. "I was."

Hannah took a deep breath and exhaled through her nose. The sound hissed like a snake. "Oh."

Lynnar was mocking her, Hannah knew it. But she was powerless against the taunts. Lynnar touched the dark areola of her own breast with the tip of her index finger. She snickered and turned to Trinia. "Oh yes, I was his first."

"Pardon?" Hannah croaked past her embarrassment.

Lynnar put her weight on her elbows propped on stones at the edge of the pool. Her legs dangled in the water, swaying side to side. Hannah was reminded of the impossibly long roots that anchored the water lilies in the Southern waterways of her childhood.

"He told me you are 'special.' He didn't mention that you have a learning disability," Lynnar goaded.

"Gabe discussed me with you?" Hannah asked in a breathless voice.

Lynnar jibed, "Apparently he failed to mention me to you, though." Batting her eyes, she added, "I wonder why." She tapped one fingernail against her tooth, then smiled.

"Come on, Trina. We're running late. Remember, we're entertaining tonight."

The cousins paddled to the opposite side of the pond. They giggled and whispered while they dressed. When she stepped into her red velvet skirt, Lynnar turned, eyeing Hannah. She made quite a production of searching for lipgloss in the pocket of her skirt. Then, she slicked her pouty lips with the brilliant red.

Waving goodbye, the cousins left. Hannah huddled on a large boulder near the waterfall. She rested her forehead against her knees and closed her eyes. She fretted with the thong binding her braid and finally tugged it loose, pulling out several strands of hair. With brusque, jerky strokes, she finger-combed the bits of leaves from her hair. Sighing, she lowered herself into the warm bubbling pool while still wearing her clothes.

The soothing waters didn't relieve her tension. She wasn't surprised the water sprites chose to abandon her this evening. She was hardly good company.

She hoisted herself out of the pool and shook like a soaked dog. It was close to sunset when she got home. She lay in the grass, still warmed by the summer sun. A flock of geese wedged through the sky, rudely honking. Hannah tore apart a dahlia, dropping a purple petal in the grass as each of her questions fell on the empty yard..

Where is he? Is he with her? Probably. Didn't she mention that she was expecting guests? Maybe that was just a jibe to worry me. Right? Why isn't he here? ... with me? He made promises to me, too.

The voice of reason tried to answer. He's seeing patients. Complications happen. Just because he's late, that doesn't mean he's with Lynnar.

But her doubts countered. He's been late before; but he's always sent a message. Look at yourself! Why wouldn't he want to be with Lynnar? She's beautiful; not all beaten up. Anyway, she was his first. …First what?

First love? First kiss? First handfast? Ask him. He'll be home soon. Ask him.

Gray clouds shadowed the amber sky and muffled the angelic chorus that night. No wonder. Hannah's mood was almost as gloomy as the sunset. At full dark, she trudged into the house. Shivering in her damp clothes, she lit candles in the kitchen and in the living room, and then she shuffled into the bedroom. She shrugged into Gabe's robe and slid her numb toes into her fuzzy slippers.

She heard noises in the other room.

He was hours late; but Gabe had come back to her! He set his leather satchel on his workbench and called, "Hi. Sorry I'm late, Love."

She rushed to kiss him.

But, she saw the brilliant red smear on his shirt collar. Stung, she snapped, "Apparently, your *old friend* waylaid you again." Then, she turned and stomped out of the room, slamming the door to the bedroom.

Gabe called to her through the door, "What in blazes is going on? Are you angry?"

Hannah crossed her arms and slumped against the backside of the door.

"Are you mad because I'm late? Is that it? I sent a message. Lynnar promised to let you know I'd be delayed. She was going to the waterfall, and I thought you'd meet her there."

She was grinding her teeth; but somehow she answered, "Oh yes, she met me there." She slapped her palm on the door and stood. Her knees felt like Jello, her stomach roiled.

"Good. Then you understand."

She opened and closed drawers with loud banging noises, throwing clothes into a pile on the bed. "Yeah. I guess I do understand."

Gabe pulled the knob, rattling the door. "Open the door, Hannah."

"No."

He shook the door harder. The hinges wobbled. "Hannah! Open this door."

He jostled the knob up and down, pulling it towards him at the same time. There was a tiny 'click'. The old lock gave way. When Gabe burst into the room, she was bundling an armload of skirts and tunics into her canvas tote bag.

"I'm going to stay at Ella's," she grumbled.

"The devil you say! …What's going on? I don't understand."

"At our handfasting ceremony, we promised to trust one another," she said. "I believe my trust was misplaced."

"Trust? Misplaced trust? What's this all about?"

Gabe's fingers were only a few inches from her elbow.

"Don't touch me! You have no right to touch me! I'm not a … a toy …not…a…ummm…not your entertainment!"

Gabe drew his fingers back quickly as if he'd come close to touching fire. "What the hell is that supposed to mean?"

Hannah didn't answer. She jammed a pair of socks into the bag and struggled with the zipper.

"Hannah. Talk to me. This…umm… this ah… there must be a mistake, you'll see." He took a deep breath, then hesitated. "You know you can trust me."

She couldn't bear to look at him. Hot tears scalded her eyes. Her throat constricted as though she'd swallowed lye. She crossed her arms under her breasts and tucked each hand into the opposite armpit. Using every ounce of her self-control, Hannah looked at him. "I trusted you with my heart, Gabe. Promise me your complete honesty in return."

He made a giant "X" over his heart with his finger. "I swear. Honesty always."

Hannah sniffed and rubbed her eyes with the sleeve of his robe.

"There are too many unanswered questions."

"Ask. I'll answer."

She didn't even try to keep the accusation out of her question, "What is your relationship to Lynnar?"

"She's my friend."

Hannah wrapped her arms across her ribs. "And…"

"And nothing. Before this morning, I hadn't seen Lynnar in more than ten years."

"But you've seen her several times today!"

"Lynnar and her brother came here when they were young. Around eleven, twelve maybe. The Faerie provide land on the outskirts of the village for the Siddhe school. Although we were very close as children, I haven't heard from either Lynnar or Aidan since we grew to be adults. We just lost touch."

"You're in touch now."

"We've visited, yes."

"Visited?"

"Yes."

Hannah breathed deep. Words stuck in her dry throat.

"Do you want her still?"

Gabe jerked like he'd been stuck with a sharp knife.

"Want her? Want her? You mean WANT her...sexually?"

"Well, yes, that's exactly what I mean. Do you want her? Do you still love her?"

"Love her? Good God! Where are you getting these ideas?"

He reached for Hannah again; he covered her fidgeting hands with one of his.

"Lynnar's a perfect Siddhe. Do you know about the Siddhe?"

"What's to know? They're beautiful...perfect, maybe."

"Ulysses' Sirens were Siddhe. They taunted Ulysses' sailors; thought nothing of marooning a shipload of men on a deserted island.

Siddhes are notorious flirts, trained to be sensuous game-players. But, I understand those games. Lynnar and I are definitely not lovers."

"But you were lovers, weren't you?"

"We had sex. Once."

"Lynnar said she was your first."

"Well, yes, er, umm. She was the first woman, girl, really, my first…um… partner."

"You made love."

"Not love. We were curious. I think I was thirteen…no fourteen. But love had nothing to do with it. We were experimenting, satisfying teenaged curiosity."

"Was she your first handfast?"

Gabe choked because his words tumbled out so quickly.

"No! NO! We were never…. You are my first handfast… my only handfast."

He scrubbed his eyes with his palm. "Good God, I can't believe this is happening!"

"I thought a handfast pledge meant fidelity," she said.

"It does. I haven't been unfaithful to you, Hannah. Never."

"You weren't with Lynnar tonight, then?"

"No."

"Really?"

"Really."

Hannah paced three steps, then turned to confront him again.

"But, you think she's beautiful…sensual…You're still attracted to her, aren't you?"

"I won't lie to you. Of course, I think Lynnar is beautiful. But, no, I'm not attracted to her. No matter, I would never trust her." His voice dropped. "I love you."

"Some people might say that love and desire are two entirely different things."

"Some might. I don't." Gabe drew a cross over his heart again. "Our lovemaking, yours and mine, is incredible. But… and this is the truth…Even if I never *made* love with you again, I *would* love you forever."

He nodded, and opened his arms to her. She took two small uncertain steps to him, and he gently cocooned her. The odor of musky sandalwood assaulted Hannah. She saw the smeared red streak on his shirt collar.

She tugged the tunic over his head and turned the shirt to show him the stain.

"I told you she's a flirt. That doesn't mean I've been unfaithful to you."

He sat on the edge of the bed, and patted the mattress beside him. Hannah sat next to him, but she kept her arms wrapped at her waist. He stroked her knuckles with his thumb. Her chin quivered, but her lips curved into a tentative smile.

"Okay?"

Blinking a tear from the corner of her eye, she nodded.

"Okay."

His thumb brushed the yellowing bruise at her temple.

"Hurt?"

Hannah shook her head. "I'm okay. Don't try to change the subject! Go on."

"End of story." He leaned back on the bed, propping his head on one hand. With the other hand, he toyed with one of her corkscrew curls. "By the way, there is news from the Village. Rory told me about an accident at Farwe's dairy. One of his sons slipped in mud and ultimately was kicked by an upset milk cow."

"Oh my! Is the boy all right?" Hannah sprang to her feet. "Shouldn't we go check on him? How old is he?" She rubbed her hands together. "Should we take some food? I've got pastries and fruit ready in the kitchen."

She was already headed towards the kitchen when Gabe caught her. "Slow down. It's all right. Everything is fine at Farwe's house tonight."

He took a deep breath. "As soon as I heard about the accident, I came home to gather supplies. While I was packing my satchel, Lynnar and Trinia knocked at the door. They wanted to bathe at the waterfall. I asked them to tell you about the emergency. Then I left. Ella can vouch for me. She and I went to Farwe's dairy together. I came straight home from the farm. I swear." The kiss he left on her cheek was as fleeting as a butterfly's.

"How is the boy? Did he regain consciousness quickly? Did you need to stitch the gash? I'll visit him tomorrow."

"Niall is fine now. He came around soon after we arrived. Ella cleaned his wound and I took a few stitches. I doubt that the accident will give him a noteworthy scar, though. So we bandaged his head in a great turban-style arrangement."

"Who would want a scar?"

"Boys love to boast of their ghastly injuries, you know. Sort of war wounds, if you will. The impressive bit of triage will flavor his tale." He rubbed her lips with the pad of his thumb. "I'll return to check his condition in two days. Why don't you walk with me?"

The following morning began much like its predecessor. With an escort of Toby's extremely vocal dogs, Trog arrived with the dawn to rap the heavy doorknocker impatiently.

"Come in, Trog. Good morning to you, man."

Kicking at a frisky spaniel puppy that gnawed his shoelaces, Trog grumbled, "Don't understand how Toby can live with all these blasted dogs!" He swatted at the large Samoyed who wanted to play fetch with a well-chewed chunk of willow root. "Darned animals demand constant attention!" Brushing a trail of slobber off his pants' leg, he muttered, "Pesky creatures."

"A dog is a man's best friend!"

"Ahh, weel then. There's the rub. Man's best friend, you say. That would be *man* as in *hu-man*. Being an elf, myself, I rely on other elves..." His stomach rumbled. "Good smells coming from the kitchen!"

They followed Trog's nose to a breakfast of fluffy biscuits dripping butter and honey. With his fingertip, Trog collected crumbs that had fallen on his plate.

"Finger licking good … that what you humans say?"

"Yes, something like that," Hannah answered as she ruffled Trog's wiry red hair. "So… you don't mind a *hu-man* breakfast, Trog."

He grimaced and batted at her hand.

"Are you back to the garden today?" Gabe asked.

"No, not today," Hannah answered.

Trog looked up abruptly. "What'd'ya mean? There's work to be done!"

She patted his shoulder and replied, "Then you'll work alone, Trog. Today I'll be with Ella."

Gabe scowled. "I thought we'd settled things last night, Hannah."

"I'm just going to visit, Gabe. I'll be home before dark."

Hannah passed the basket of warm bread to Trog.

Trog cleared his throat dramatically and coughed. A shirt button popped open just above the bulge of his belly. He rubbed the melon-sized mound of his stomach and belched quietly.

"Well, guess I work alone, then. I'll be at the garden if you need me."

Less than an hour later, Hannah followed the elf through the gate. She winced when she put weight on her injured leg; skin around the stitches was still red and puckered. But she whistled on the walk through the forest to Ella's home. This was going to be an interesting day.

More than once, she felt uneasy. Was she being watched? She spun around a couple of times, certain that someone was trailing her. She spied a doe and her fawn grazing along the stream bank. Their large dark eyes followed her as she continued on her way.

She never noticed the figure hidden in the branches just to her left. He paralleled her path until she reached Ella's doorway safely. Then, he settled himself in the bracken to wait. Grunting, he pulled a whittling knife from its scabbard at his ankle and reached for a stout branch fallen on the ground nearby. He shaved curls of wood, all the while covertly watching Ella's doorway.

Hannah rapped on the doorframe, then slowly pushed on the door.

"Ella? You home?"

She thought it strange that Ella referred to her home as a lair. The place was cluttered, but it was so clean that the furnishings almost shimmered. Several multi-paned windows provided bright sunlight required for her weaving. A packrat, Ella kept scraps of material piled in baskets, lengths of thread remnants rolled into balls, boxes of buttons and spare bobbins dangling colorful yarns on a rack of pegs.

Hannah found her bent over a huge loom that almost filled the small back room. The elfin lady worked the wooden pedals with deft motions. Her short, wide fingers with large gnarled knuckles fluidly shuttled the large wooden frames strung with rainbow-hued threads.

She wove the weft threads through the loom's warp threads to create gossamer cloth.

"Sit, sit," she urged Hannah. "I've been expecting you. We'll have tea."

Ella trundled into the kitchen and returned with tea and sweet muffins trailing odors of cinnamon, banana and coconut. She waddled towards a table. Undeterred by the tower of books, skeins of yarn and bits of fabric already perched on that table, Ella simply balanced the tray atop the clutter.

"You came to ask me questions, am I right?"

"You know, it took a while for me to feel comfortable with your unnerving gift." Hannah blushed and picked at a hangnail until it hurt.

"Which gift would that be, dear?"

Ella plopped gracefully on a large cushion on the floor, settling like a swan landing on a still pond. Hair escaped the bun at her nape, and curly gray tendrils fanned around her face when the feather pillow expelled air in a gentle whoosh.

"The uncanny ability to anticipate questions. You usually answer even before my question has been asked."

"Is that a problem?"

"No, not anymore.

Ella tugged Hannah's thick braid. "In the beginning, I loved you because my boy loves you. Now we understand one another, you and I.

Hannah caught the scent of dried rose blossoms, talcum powder and old books-a sweet and comforting aroma. "You remind me of my grandmother, and I loved her very much, too."

"*Gu loeir*! Enough! You'll make me cry!"

Ella poured fragrant tea into delicate porcelain cups decorated with twining morning glories.

"Yes, well," Hannah began. "I do want to ask you a few questions."

"She's trouble, that one," Ella broke in. "I rejoiced years ago when Lynnar left the village. I wanted her and her wicked ideas far away from here ... away from my boy, at any rate."

"You sound like Gabe's still a teenager. I hardly think he'd be easily influenced these days."

"No man's safe from a Siddhe; not if she wants him. It's up to you to protect him from her," Ella spoke in a hush. "She'll trick him with her sex games."

Hannah raised both hands to her face to cover her bruised cheeks.

"I look at myself, then I think of Lynnar's body and I'm depressed by the comparison."

"Oh, buck up, Girl! Don't compare yourself to Lynnar!"

"Hard not to notice the differences!"

"Would you compare the mellow sweetness of a pear to the tart tang of a pomegranate?" Ella pointed to the cushion beside her's. "Sit, girl, sit. I know that leg must pain you still."

Hannah gingerly folded her legs to perch on one of Ella's quilted floor cushions. Fidgeting, she bunched her skirt, then stretched her fingers, releasing damp and wrinkled fabric. She spoke while she attempted to smooth the myriad creases.

"I need to ask you about her. About Lynnar. Precisely, about Lynnar and Gabe." She choked on the words, feeling like a traitor.

Ella stirred tea. "Hmmm, I thought you'd be curious." Her spoon made soft pinging noises inside the dainty cup. Hannah noticed that the arthritic knuckles holding the silver spoon were swollen and misshapen, but strong and somehow graceful.

Ella wondered, "Have you asked him? He'll tell you if you ask."

"I asked some questions. But to be truthful, I was afraid of what he might answer if I asked too much. He did tell me that they were friends. He claims he hasn't even seen her in years. I believe him."

"Ah well, at least you trust him." Ella shifted her position on the cushion, settling to begin her narrative. "First thing, you must understand Lynnar is Siddhe. You've heard of Siddhe?" She arched a brow and rubbed the bridge of her nose. "Powerful faeries are the Siddhe. Tall, young and graceful, most with dark complexions. The Siddhe originated in Tiarnanog, the Land of Eternal Youth, thousands of years ago. Only natural born Siddhe know all the secrets of that land."

"Natural born?"

"We'll get to that in a minute." Ella poured another cup of tea. "The wisdom of the Siddhe is older than the beginning of the world, but they're lazy. Just remember that Siddhe grow to be beautiful young adults; but, they never turn gray or wrinkled. They produce nothing for themselves. They're thieves, tricksters." The elf shook a gnarled finger. "Siddhe desire all that is rare and wonderful."

"So they are covetous. I own nothing, so I can't be a threat to Lynnar."

"Oh, you're wrong, there, Girl. You have Gabe's heart."

Hannah grinned. "But, that heart's a loaner. Mine for a year and a day." She took a deep breath. "Although I love him so much it scares me."

"Pssst! You talk nonsense." Ella crossed her arms and shook her head, scowling.

Hannah squeezed the elf's elbow. "Go on. Please."

Ella poured more tea into her own cup. She tilted the cup back and forth, watching the sediment. "From early childhood, a Siddhe is taught the art of seduction, taught to pamper, to enhance her beauty, to prepare to capture the love of a human man."

"Like a concubine?"

"Sort of. Only the Siddhe are the masters; not the slaves. Siddhe *use* their mortal lovers … for jewelry or money or property. The mortal's love is always discarded and the human lover is left heartbroken. They're a wicked group, those Siddhe."

"Their sole purpose in life is to break a person's heart?"

"Some say so."

"How sad."

"Don't waste sympathy on the Siddhe. They wouldn't appreciate it." Ella swallowed a gulp of tepid tea and poured another serving.
"I know of Siddhe who have stolen a human baby, because it was
beautiful."

"Kidnap a baby?" Hannah gasped. She covered her mouth
with her hands. "That's unthinkable!"

"If she kidnaps a baby, she won't be expected to carry one,
Hannah. I told you the Siddhe are vain. Few of their women will en-
dure the discomfort or disfigurement of pregnancy. But, each woman
is expected to 'produce' a child. So, the woman will bring the stolen
baby to Sidhean, their secret underground faerie mound in Tiarnanog.
The mortal babe is raised with the other Siddhe children in a Tiarnanog commune."

Gabe told me that there is a Siddhe settlement here, outside the
village.

"Yes. A school. At Tiarnanog, days are spent feasting, practicing sex games and making beautiful music. After a few years tutor-
ing, they're sent out into Faerie villages, for fostering, they call it.
Here, the children have scheduled classes in the arts; but mainly they
study seduction, like the concubines you mentioned. Homework, if
you will."

Ella held the sides of the teapot between her hands. She bent
her head over the warm crockery as if it were a crystal ball.

"The heart of a true Siddhe is icy cold, totally incapable of gen-
uine affection. Unfortunately, even the stolen changelings are

thwarted. Most times, they become as selfish and cruel as their Siddhe captors. Lynnar has a changeling brother, a man named Aidan. Like a true-born Siddhe, he seeks only personal gratification and luxury." Ella put the teapot back on its perch high on the precarious stack of books. She selected a muffin and munched on it, nibbling the nuts free of the cake.

"There are tales of Leanan-Siddhe, who lives on the Isle of Man. The Irish say she's the muse of poetry; but legend has it that she literally sucks the blood of life from those men she inspires. They die young and she seeks another victim."

"How can Gabe call Lynnar his friend?"

Ella scuttled around on her cushion. She wiggled her feet, making the curled toes of her boots bounce. "Lynnar was young when she was brought to our village. Her mother had heard about Gabe, the human boy who was my ward. She told Lynnar to practice her budding skills on him. Because he's beautiful, Lynnar was naturally attracted to him. She pretended to be his friend, following him everywhere, feigning interest in his hobbies. Then, as young teens, the two of them devised sex games."

"Sex…games?"

"Umm hmm."

"But Gabe told me they only had sex one time!"

"Define sex!" Ella threw up her hands. "You'll have to ask Gabriel about that! He thought they were friends. Maybe now he understands that she's incapable of real emotions like love, fear or sorrow."

"This is crazy. What can I do to hold him, if Gabe wants to go to Lynnar?" Hannah stood up, arms dangling at her side. "Look at me!"

Ella jerked on Hannah's blouse. "Oh do sit down, Girl! You're trying my patience!"

Hannah hesitated, but eventually she sat.

"Now think! Gabe brought you here, didn't he?"

"Yes. But..."

Ella shook a knobby finger. "No buts about it! You're here, aren't you?"

"Yes."

"He handfasted with you, said he wants to marry you. Have you heard him say different?"

"No. But..."

The twig-like finger shot out again.

"No buts. You just have to be a better player."

It was quiet in the little room. Not even a breeze to ruffle the scraps of cloth and paper on the table. Hannah gulped her cooled tea. Careful not to disturb the delicate balance, she placed the cup and saucer on the tray as she stood.

"Are you good at playing chess, then?" Ella asked.

"No."

"Not much of a competitor, then. Bridge?"

"Not really."

"Hopscotch?"

"Fair."

"Well, you'd best develop a fighting spirit, Girl."

"Oh I'll fight to keep Gabe if he wants to be kept."

"Good, good," Ella murmured. "But, watch yourself, Girl. Like I said, Siddhe are treacherous. With Gabe as Lynnar's latest target, she'll be quick to recognize you as an obstacle to her success. She's not a fool. Siddhes play to win! Watch yourself."

When Hannah had opened Ella's door, the figure watched from the shadows. He dusted the wood shavings from his lap and quickly stuffed the carving into his pocket. Before he followed Hannah, he replaced his knife in the garter on his sock. Hannah's eyes were misty and she walked at an odd pace, as if she were waltzing.

"Strange," he grunted. "Dancing. Must have drunk a warm wine posset."

Hannah spread her arms to embrace an imaginary partner. Then she hummed a lilting tune, twirled and dipped through the forest, nodding to other unseen dancers. She stopped abruptly and turned towards a Hawthorne bush.

"Trog, do you plan to follow me even to the pool for my bath?"

"How did you see me?" Trog grumbled as he crawled out of his hiding place under the bush. Smooth flat leaves and dainty fragrant blossoms stuck in his hair.

"Elves are invisible to human eyes," he chuckled. "Are you a changeling, then?"

She laughed. "Oh, I could smell the orange juice and honey you spilled on your jacket this morning. Besides, a noisy cluster of bees has been tracking you while you trailed me."

"Well, then..." he blustered.

"Tell Gabe that I'm bathing at the pool, won't you?" Saying that, she bent to kiss his cheek and to muss his hair. Then, she spread her arms again and waltzed off towards the waterfall.

"Whoa there, Girl. You can't just wander off on your own!"

Hannah turned, hands on her hips. "I'm going to take a bath! That's hardly *wandering off*."

"Gabriel told me to keep watch over you!"

"Be realistic! I'm safe enough here, a stone's throw from the cave. Don't worry. Go on!"

Trog jammed his hands deep into the pockets of his baggy trousers. "Gonna storm soon, fool woman," he grumped. He stooped to adjust his socks. "Here, take this." He thrust his silver knife into her hand, hunched his shoulders and turned towards Gabe's cave. Thunder rumbled in the distance. After only a few steps, he paused and turned to look back at Hannah.

"Strange behaviour, if you ask me," he muttered. "Women! Wacky, the whole lot of 'em; human or elfin!"

The kitchen door scraped, opening with a loud yawn. Gabe ran into the room, eyes trained on the door that Trog had just closed.

"Your forehead's furrowed like a fresh tilled garden," Trog announced.

"Where is she?" Shaking Trog's shoulders, Gabe insisted, "Where is she?"

Trog blinked and crossed his eyes.

"You were supposed to watch her, dammnit."

"She… is… fine." Trog enunciated each word slowly. "Said she wanted to bathe at the pool. Didn't want me watching. Said to tell you she'll be ready for the dinner at six."

She had run down the mossy path through the woods, unbuttoning her blouse and tossing it onto a bush as she stepped out of her skirt. She repeated silly refrains of *'Singing in the Rain'* while she bathed. The nix appeared; two wide-eyed heads, no larger than the shampoo bubbles floating on the water. They nattered frantically, gestured wildly. Because she couldn't understand the nix language, Hannah assumed that they were warning her about the coming storm. "Thank you." She nodded and they pointed towards the clearing. "Don't be concerned. I'm just leaving." She climbed from the pool and pulled her blouse over her head. Her wet hair dripped in rivulets down her back, chest and shoulders, plastering the thin cotton to her skin, rendering it almost transparent. She stepped into her pants and squatted to gather her shoes.

Someone tugged her hair. Behind her, a man murmured, "Beautiful." He stroked her arm from shoulder to wrist with his index finger.

Hannah jerked, trying to run. But the man wound the length of her hair around his hand as though he were reeling in a fish on a line.

His touch was gentle; he didn't tug her hair nor did he try to hurt her. But, she was terrified. Shivers ran from her scalp to her toes, and her stomach cramped. Tears ached in her throat as if she had swallowed a handful of needles.

One hand on her shoulder, the man turned her to face him. He was tall, almost as tall as Gabe. His shoulders were not so wide, though. He was slender, although quite muscular. Had she not been so frightened, Hannah might have thought the man quite handsome. His hair was a riot of soft golden curls and his eyes were a most arresting color of turquoise blue.

"You really are a confection," he said as he traced her neck, allowing his finger to rest in the hollow above her collarbone. His finger flicked over her breast; a feather-light touch that scalded her skin. His fingertip stopped at her abdomen. With excruciating slowness, his flexed his fingers and laid his palm on her belly. Hannah sucked in a gasp and tried to back away. He spread his fingers to span the width of her hips and gently cupped her stomach.

"It is most unfortunate that you are breeding a selkie pup," he whispered

Hannah inched her hand into her pocket and curled her fingers around Trog's knife. Holding her breath while she moved her hand, she unsnapped the leather sheath and slowly pulled the blade loose. She closed her fingers around the shaft and touched the blade with her thumb, testing its sharpness.

Her terror escaped as hardly a noise, just a high-pitched *h-ahhh-ahh* when he stroked her cheek. It seemed that all of the forest

367

noises had been swallowed as she gulped the air. A roaring silence echoed in her ears. God! Was she going to faint?

Drawing on all of her energies, she screamed and slashed out at the hand that held her hair. She shrieked "No!" and swung the knife menacingly. Her scalp hurt when he yanked his hand, trying to untangle the long wet hair wound around it. "No, no, no," she repeated as she hacked at the hair, releasing each of them.

At quarter past six, Gabe went to the pool looking for Hannah.

From the rocks near the waterfall, a modulated voice taunted him, "Why Gabriel. I can't say that encountering you will improve my day."

"It's my pool, Aidan. Why would you expect to find someone else here?"

"Ever the charming host," Aidan drawled as he lounged casually, leaning against a large boulder. "Rumor has it that a lovely woman bathes here. Long golden hair, eyes the color of perfect emeralds and pale skin dotted with tiny freckles. Maybe you've seen her?" Aidan dragged his forefinger through the water, stirring tiny eddies.

"Don't be coy. Someone told you about Hannah, probably your trouble-making sister."

"Hannah. Lovely name."

"We were handfasted months ago. She's mine."

"For a year and a day, at least." Aidan brushed a bit of dirt off his trousers. "Less than that now."

"I love her. I don't want her to be hurt by any adolescent quarrel between the two of us. Do I make myself clear?"

"Crystal clear." Aidan shrugged. "Of course crystal can be broken easily, you know."

When she'd realized that she was free, Hannah had run mindlessly through the woods, panting and crying. Thunder rumbled. Louder than before. Closer. Her panic increased with the booming sounds. Like warfare. Like she imagined the sounds of bombs would be. Large blobs of rain, maybe some hail, pelted her shoulders. The curious willow trees reached their long branches to tangle in her hair and scratch her face as she ran. She stumbled without a direction, breathlessly gasping each time another willow branch whipped at her. Raising her arms to shield her face, she staggered forward blindly. It was no surprise that she tripped over an exposed root and fell to her knees beneath the rowan tree.

She was panting, hands and knees on the soggy ground. With the sporadic bursts of thunder, the driving rain and flashes of lightning, Hannah thought she'd plunged headfirst into a horror movie - lost and confused in the dark. She was cold and soaking wet; but she had escaped. She rested her forehead on the tree trunk.

The rain slowed to big droplets that plopped on the leaves and bounced when they hit the saturated ground. Bullfrogs called and crickets responded with shrill cries. The giant rowan, protector against evil spirits, waved its berry-laden limbs, whispering "shhh, shhhh, shhh." A woodland lullaby.

Hannah must have slept. Waking, she noticed Trog's knife glittering in her lap. Moonbeams glinted on the blade almost like sequins. She massaged the pulsing muscles along her brows. Absent-mindedly, she combed her hair away from her face with her fingers. Her hands snarled in the massed tangles.

"This hair! Twice now I've been held captive by a rope of my own hair. First, Scar and now this second man. Both coiled my hair around his hand." She gritted her teeth and clinched her fists. "No more! I'm not going to be helpless anymore."

She reached for the shiny blade. Haphazardly she grasped a hank of hair, pulled it taut and used the knife to saw off a length. She felt like a prisoner, snapping the bonds of handcuffs. Soon skeins of hair surrounded her, varying in length from eighteen inches to almost three feet.

Out of the dark shadows, Gabe called softly. "Hannah." He hurried towards her, but stopped to grin when he saw her clearly. Streams of moonlight skittered through the floating canopy of waving branches above her. All around her was a nest of golden hair, glimmering in the moonbeams.

"With those big green eyes, you look like a cherub with a halo of golden ringlets."

"I'm no angel," she answered with a smile.

She pulled at her hair, chewed on her bottom lip. Suddenly, she no longer felt empowered. Instead, she felt like Sampson, cruelly stripped of his strength. She tugged at the scraggly curls that just barely covered her earlobes. Panicky, she covered her exposed neck, feeling nude. *What had she done to herself?*

Gabe crouched in front of her. Placing a hand above each ear, he cradled her head. Tilting her head forward, he kissed her crown, breathing in the honeysuckle smell of her shampoo.

"I like your new look." Using his thumb, he smoothed short corkscrew curls away from her eyes. "All of the faeries will be jealous."

He picked up the knife discarded at Hannah's feet. "Short hair will be the rage," he said as he severed the cue of hair held tight at his nape. The single long dark swath fell like a question mark atop her curls strewn in the damp leaves.

"Why?"

Reaching for her hands, Gabe explained, "Because we're joined; you and me. Whatever affects you, affects me, too."

She fondled the ebony hair that now brushed his cheek. "Your beautiful hair."

With a knuckle under her chin, Gabe tipped her head up. "Did you love me for my long hair?"

"Well, let's say it was part of the complete package."

"Then this is the new abridged edition."

"Ah. Then we're a matched set."

"Exactly."

Gabe held her hand to lead her through the maze of trees. Whispering willows reached, brushing their shoulders with long clinging branches. Pinpricks of light flashed in zigzag patterns - faeries darting in their path. An earthy smell emanated from the wet leaves mounded on the ground. In the distance an owl hooted a melancholic monologue. Unruly hairs brushed her cheeks and tickled her chin.

"It's pleasant here, isn't it Gabe?"

"Some people might have been afraid to be far from home; afraid of the storm and the sighing trees."

"If I'm with you, I am safe. If I'm with you, I'm always at home."

Gabe opened his arms wide, holding the edges of his cloak in each hand. "Let's go to the house, then." He wrapped the cloak around her, she breathed in the scent of his skin and nuzzled her cheek against his chest. Together they rode the gentle breeze.

All was confusion when they returned to his cave. Trog had alerted Ella. In turn, she had notified most of the village, and so a haphazard elfin search for Hannah was in progress. In the nonsensical manner of faeries and elves, everyone had joined the helter-skelter effort. After a reconnoiter at Gabe's, Trog had failed in his attempt to marshall the faeries to work in unison even though he shouted squeaking commands. Three women had brought cakes; another carried a pie and Ella donated a basket of fresh cookies. Aldar, a pixie with a long white beard and a boyish grin, produced a flask of hard cider.

When Gabe and Hannah landed, faeries stood in small groups chatting, drinking and nibbling food. Torches made from thick bamboo stalks illuminated a large circle in the backyard. Toby and his friends ignited flares that shot brilliant rainbow flashes of with trails of sulfurous white smoke. Small boys giggled and dogs yipped while they tussled in the damp grass.

Hannah squirmed to be released from the confines of his cape, so Gabe wrapped his arms around her waist and rested his chin atop her head.

"What's the occasion?" Hannah tipped her head towards the hysterical party-like melee.

"Elves and faeries never really need an occasion."

The crowd was growing louder. Musicians had arrived and they were tuning instruments with discordant screeches and burp-like blats.

"Music. That means dancing." She tugged the cape off his shoulders and draped it over her arm. "Too bulky for dancing! I'll get you a sweater."

Gabe pulled her back. Sliding his hands up and down her arms, he shook his head and mumbled, "I'm fine. They will all be leaving soon."

"That idea is clearly wishful thinking! I believe our guests plan to celebrate for hours."

Gabe spoke close to her ear, warm velvet voice. "I have some thoughts about celebrations of my own." He traced her earlobe with the tip of his tongue.

Laughing, she pushed him into a more erect posture. She held up her hands in a "T", *time out*. "I'll be right back," she said.

Happiness made her giddy; lighter than air. She glided through the kitchen humming with the melody of the musicians' first song. The reverie was squelched abruptly by voices in her bedroom, though.

Recognizing Lynnar's chuckle, Hannah tiptoed through the living room. Luckily, the bedroom door was ajar, allowing her adequate screen for eavesdropping. A dim light flickered in the opening, and Hannah smelled the attar of roses that perfumed her bedside candles. She heard the scrape of drawers being opened.

Lynnar's voice rose to a falsetto. "Oh, how cute! I'd imagine our Gabe must feel like a pedophile when little Hannah prances around in this virginal white gown! Cotton frills… how sexy."

Trina answered with a sultry laugh. "Take off your panties, Lynnar. Hide them in the back of Gabe's drawer. Wedge them there among his clothes. Imagine what the little mouse will do when she finds them!"

Hannah fumed. Mouse indeed!

She heard a rustling of skirt and petticoats. Then a drawer slid open with a quiet scrape. She listened to tittering and snickering, and the sounds of articles being shuffled.

"I heard something. What was that noise?" Lynnar asked in a breathless undertone.

Hannah pushed open the door and stepped into the bedroom. Both Siddhes looked particularly guilty and non-repentant; although their glee had disintegrated to shocked surprise.

"I'd say that noise was the sound of a mouse trapping two alley cats!" Hannah opened Gabe's drawer and tossed a pair of silky red underpants to Lynnar. "Get out." Pointing to the front door, she said, "Take your littermate with you." She smirked watching as the women sidled out.

From the kitchen doorway, Ella chuckled aloud. "Foiled Lynnar's plan, did you?"

"I won this skirmish at least."

Ella rubbed the tip of her nose. "Whatever happened to your hair, Girl?"

"It's a long story."

"It looks nice. Sort of like a pixie."

Hannah brushed her short hair. The humidity had encouraged tight corkscrew curls that defied styling. She dabbed a bit of perfume in the hollow at the base of her throat. She selected her teal sweater because Gabe had once told her the color made her eyes look mysterious. She blew out the candles Lynnar had lit, then she grabbed Gabe's fisherman's knit pullover.

Dancing was in full swing when she went outside. There, in the lawn surrounded by her flowerbeds, Gabe twirled with Lynnar.

Don't panic. Walk slowly, Hannah reminded herself. Smile. Grace and beauty. That's the ticket.

She tapped Lynnar's shoulder and forced herself to smile. "I'm cutting in."

Gabe put his hand at Hannah's waist and together they swirled to the elfin music.

"What took you so long? I was getting worried."

"I was talking to Ella."

"Oh? About what?"

"Battle plans," she answered with a smile. "Kiss me, Gabe."

"Hmmm…is that part of the plan?"

"You betcha!"

They were alone, in a dark corner of the yard. Gabe had forced her to rest. "The stitches on your leg are still healing. Sit for a few minutes, Love."

Hannah sipped at the punch. It was bright pink, fruity and very sweet. "Why were you dancing with Lynnar?"

Gabe shrugged. "She's my friend. She asked, I accepted."

"Should I release you from your handfast vow, Gabe?"

He staggered as if she'd punched him in the stomach. He stared at her, his mouth moving without sound.

Hannah wondered if maybe they both died a little during those seconds.

"Why on earth do you ask that, Hannah? Your mood swings are making me dizzy."

"Then stay away from Lynnar."

Gabe started to speak; but she held up her hand.

"She's trying to cause trouble. I have no idea why, but she wants to make me miserable. Stay away from her."

"If you know she's trying to cause trouble, you shouldn't worry. I'll never cheat you, Hannah."

"Never is a very long time, Gabe. In the past, when I've depended on people, they'd leave me."

"Your parents died in an accident. Your grandmother was an old woman. Just because people die, you can't assume they deserted you. It's not as if they wanted to leave you."

"Nevertheless…Do you promise me? You'll steer clear of Lynnar as long as we're handfasted?"

"Will you trust me when I say yes?"

"Yes."

Gabe patted his chest. "You scared me thoroughly, Love." He tipped his head towards her. "Look, I think I just sprouted six new gray hairs."

"Distinguished looking."

Two hours later, the group of giggling faeries were still dancing. Elves encircled Hannah and Gabe, clapping, stomping feet, jumping and shouting – working up to a frenzy. The villagers' music was a strange, enticing contrast of deep oompa-pas, tinkling bells and twittering flutes. Hannah flung back her head, laughing as she spun with Gabe as though they were children. The sky and trees swirled past; colors collided like a kaleidoscope. Tiny wings fluttered in whorls above the dancers, scattering a fine spray of faerie dust.

"Okay, the party is over for tonight," Gabe called out. The music wound down, ending with a final blatt and a dwindling note on the pan harp. Shuffling into the darkness of the surrounding woods, the gathering split into small groups. The noisy clamor diminished to hushed voices.

In the darkest part of the night, Hannah waked frightened by an unsettling dream. Her nightgown was damp with perspiration and the sheet was twisted at her feet. She reached for Gabe, but found his space in the bed empty.

"I'm here, Hannah." A disembodied voice from the chair on the far side of the bed. "Bad dream again tonight?"

"Did I wake you?" she asked as she climbed out of bed.

"No."

She touched his hand and he linked their fingers. He patted his knee and she curled into his lap.

"When I was a kid, Gran used to rub my back like this when I had bad dreams."

There was a current sparking the air around them. Her skin tingled and she shivered. His fingers sent a mild, almost electrical, charge she felt in her womb and in her breasts.

He sucked in a stream of air, making a *'pssst'* sound.

She purred, rubbed her face against his bare shoulder. "Love me, Gabe. Make love to me here. Now."

He slid to the floor, pulled her down with him. Hannah arched up to him and spread her legs wide. She positioned his penis at her wet center, encouraging, "Now!"

Gripping his buttocks, she forced him inside her and held him tight. She wrapped her legs around his waist and locked her ankles together. They danced again; this time together in the dance as old as mankind.

Gabe pressed his forehead to hers. They were both shuddering. "You blew my plans," he whispered. "My intent had been to love you gently, slowly, cautiously."

Green eyes laughed at his gray eyes.

"Home," she breathed. "I'm home again at last." A single hot tear seeped from the corner of her eye.

Hannah leaned towards him; her head propped on his chest, just under his collarbone. She tickled his armpit and laughed when he squirmed.

"Your giggles are like champagne bubbles that tickle my heart."

"You break my heart with your sweet words," she said. She thought she might just cry.

"What does that mean?"

Hannah shook her head, touched a knuckle to her right eye, then she covered her mouth with her fingers.

"Don't mind me. I'm on an emotional roller coaster these days. It's been…umm…it's been…so… confusing…hmm." She clutched her throat, trying to squeeze the right words into her mouth.

Gabe smoothed his thumb over her eyelids. "Get some sleep, Hannah. Dawn will be here soon."

The sun rose slowly and ushered in a chilly day with puffy white clouds. Subdued sunlight was just beginning to dry the dew as they crossed the meadow at the foot of the hills ringing the Village. Hannah hummed, wading through the tall, damp grasses and dandelions. Gabe squeezed her hand. Birds chirped in the distance, and butterflies circled newly awakened blossoms. Hannah had thought she might have glimpsed a few curious elves scampering through the forest.

He whistled along with her tune. It was an easy hike –a bit over three miles on a well-worn path that meandered over a craggy foothill. They reached a clear stream that bubbled from large gray rocks at the crest of the large faerie mound. Gabe stopped. "We're about halfway to the farm." He indicated a flat-topped boulder with a roll of his arm. "Let's rest here. I brought muffins."

Hannah rubbed her stomach when it rumbled consent. They ate and she touched his lip with her fingertip to remove a clinging crumb. She glanced down to her lap and rubbed her fingers back and forth on her skirt.

"I've missed my period since the rape," she blurted, surprising them both.

"After the ordeal you've been through, that's hardly surprising."

"So, you don't think I could be pregnant, do you?"

"That's not exactly what I said, Hannah."

"I just couldn't be pregnant, could I?"

Gabe stroked his mouth and chin. "Well…"

"Oh God."

He touched her arm and she froze, wild-eyed. "As I recall, we made love five, maybe six times a day during those last few days you were at home." He flicked a fingertip on the tip of her nose. "Remember?"

"Yes."

"Then, of course, it's possible."

She tapped her foot against the base of the boulder.

"How would you feel if I am pregnant?" She was hesitant, uncertain she wanted to know his answer.

Taking both of her hands in his, Gabe turned her palms towards his face, kissing first one, then the other. He answered with a question of his own, "How would you feel?"

"Pregnant… maybe with a rapist's baby?" Hannah looked right, then left; any direction except towards his eyes. "I honestly don't know," she stammered. "I haven't allowed myself to consider the possibility." She gulped a huge breath of air, swallowing the tension that had lodged in her throat. Tears welled in her eyes, and she blinked to clear them. Her jaw quivered with a sob she refused to release.

"Your baby…our baby… would be beautiful," he told her.

With the toe of her shoe, Hannah unearthed a dandelion gone to seed. "I doubt I could force myself to love a child borne of that awful experience." Her voice dropped, and Gabe leaned closer. "Although part of me understands that the baby wouldn't be at fault, I don't think I could forget the possibility of its brutal conception."

"But...," he encouraged her to continue.

"But, I don't think I could ever live with myself if I aborted a baby. I mean...it could be your baby. Couldn't it?" She spread her fingers to span her belly. "Ethically, I believe that there are justifiable reasons to have an abortion. Reasons for other people, though. Decisions are so much easier to validate in theory; not so easy in reality." She pursed her lips and blew out a long stream of air. "But, personally, I know I'd suffer a lifetime of guilt if I killed a child growing inside me." She crossed her arms over her abdomen. "No matter how ill-conceived that child might be." She looked up at him, searching his gray eyes. "Do you understand?" she asked, begging for his comments.

"Oh yes, Love. I understand." He stroked her cheek with his thumb, wiping away the tracks of her tears. "Let's just wait. Don't worry needlessly. If there is a babe, we will deal with it together." He tipped her face to his. "Okay?"

She nodded once.

"No matter what, the baby will be ours to share. There are two of us to share the burdens, the decisions and the joys, Hannah."

She squinted and two more teardrops slid down her cheek. Gabe stood and pulled her to her feet. He stroked her cheek with his thumbs and slipped his hands into her hair, one just above each ear. He drew her forehead towards his chest, and she rested against him, hugging his waist.

"Could you ever forget the rape? In time, could you forgive me?" Her face was pressed against his chest and her words were muffled in his shirt.

"Forgive you? You're not at fault, Hannah. Rape is a violent assault against your body and your soul. You couldn't have stopped the attack. You're the victim." He closed his eyes, and Hannah thought she saw him wince. "It's no wonder that rape is seldom reported."

"Pardon?" Her voice cracked.

"Rape just might be the only crime that brands the victim, rather than the criminal."

"I do feel branded...stigmatized."

"The victim has to prove her good reputation, heal emotionally and regain her self-worth. Those are difficult tasks under any circumstances."

"Does anyone ever get the job done?"

Gabe drew slow circles just under her shoulder blades. "Do you want me to take you home?"

"No." She shook her head and pushed stray hairs off her face. "No. I want to meet Farwe's family. I want to play with the children."

While they continued on towards the dairy farm, Hannah chattered with a forced gaiety. She could smell the composting manure and hear the soft but insistent lowing before she saw cows dotting the horizon. As she and Gabe neared the wooden split rail fence, four young children bounded towards them. Three giggling girls joined hands, tugging their small brother in a snakelike procession that zig-zagged across damp grass dotted with dandelions.

The toddling boy was unable to keep pace with the game of 'crack the whip.' He stumbled and fell to his knees, jerking his sister's hand and pulling her to tumble on top of him.

"Uh oh, Meggie," he said.

Meggie exploded in an angry fury, as only a three-year old can. "Liiiiii-an!" She stood and shook out a much-mended skirt and rubbed furiously at the dark smudge on the faded corduroy. Then she smiled sweetly at Gabe before turning to deliver a swift kick at her brother's backside. The little boy had remained kneeling, dirty, but unhurt by his fall into the soft loam. He shrank into a tight ball, cover-ing his head with his arms and hands to fend off his sister's attack.

Hannah hurled herself between the children, grabbing the boy and cradling him beneath her. "No!" she screamed. Her eyes were wild with fear, and she raised her arms to shield her own head. The three little girls watched in wide-eyed amazement, the two youngest backing away from the wild woman who had captured their brother. The oldest sister cautiously approached Gabe, extending her hand, palm up.

"Meggie didn't mean nuthing. She's jest ticked. Lian' s alwuz pulling on us, tripping us up."

Gabe nodded towards her sisters and tilted his head in the direction of their house.

"Everything's okay. Go now, we'll be along soon to check on your brother, Niall. Go, Mellie. Take Meggie and Margy home. Tell your mother we're coming soon." He spoke to Mellie, but he watched Hannah.

Hannah hugged the frightened boy to her chest, clutching at his back, wadding his shirt as she rocked back and forth, sobbing, "No, no, no." Tears streamed down her cheeks and she stared vacantly past Gabe when he knelt beside her.

He touched her shoulder and she flinched, gasping. Then he said, "Hannah," and she quieted hearing his voice. She released her hold on Lian. The wide-eyed boy jumped to his feet and dashed through the thick grass, following his retreating sisters home.

Hannah grabbed Gabe's shoulders and squeezed until her fingertips turned white. Gabe wrapped his arms around her. His voice was rumpled corduroy. "Together. We'll get through this ordeal together, Love."

Kneeling in the grass, he rocked her, like a mother rocks a restless baby.

Hannah whispered, "I was back in the tunnel. I could hear the chanting, I felt the heat and smelled the sweat!" She opened and closed her fists at her side. Then she lifted one hand and pounded Gabe's left shoulder, releasing an outrage that had been seething since her attack. She leaned her forehead against his chest and cried. Her shoulders shook each time she inhaled.

"Flashbacks are a normal reaction to a violent situation. In time, they'll stop."

"Don't lecture me right now, dammit." She banged her head against his chest. "I don't want to hear about statistics; I want you to understand me!"

Gabe cupped his palm to the back of her head. "Of course you do. I was trying to help you sort things out."

Hannah sniffed, touched a knuckle to her nose. "Okay. Good. Sort away."

"The little girl's aggression sparked some memory for you. Maybe it was a particular movement Meggie made. Maybe it was Lian's response. Maybe neither."

Hannah felt as if her blood was pumping through her body at a furious pace. Her ears roared like a wave breaking on the shore.

"Farwe's family will think I'm a demon. First I tackle little Lian and scare his sisters. Then I dissolve into hysterics. My eyes are red and my nose is running, and...and...and"

"I love you."

"Thank God." She wiped her cheeks with the heels of her palms.

Hannah felt like a plane crash survivor; but, they walked hand-in-hand up the grassy hill to Farwe's sprawling house. A series of rooms had been added to either side, sprouting like unruly arms from the tidy white stucco rectangle in the center. Seven rocking chairs were lined on the wide front porch. She forced herself to breathe

386

evenly although her instinct was to gulp the air. Talk, relax, she told herself.

"The house reminds me of a lop-sided cake my dad and I made for my mother's birthday."

That sounded like normal conversation, didn't it? "The thatched roof is like my frosting that kept sliding off the cake's sagging edges and the chimney is the candle!"

"That cake must have been a thing of beauty!"

Hannah shrugged. "It tasted better than it looked!"

They climbed the steps and before Gabe could raise his hand to knock, the heavy door opened with a loud creaking noise. Margy, the plump five-year old girl, stood in the doorway. Her slanted brown eyes studied Hannah suspiciously, but she curtsied and stepped back, inviting them to enter. Her curls bounced with her bobbing movements and her cheeks dimpled when Hannah winked at her.

Gabe ducked his head to fit through the doorframe designed to accommodate elves. Thankfully, the ceiling soared to almost seven feet, so that he could stand upright. He did have to remember to dodge low-hanging clumps of dried vegetables and herbs suspended from the rafters, though.

Ull, Margy's mother, waddled out of the shadows, wiping her hands on the long white cloth tied apron-style at her thick waist. "So, you're here, are you? Sit. We'll have a bite to eat." Moments later, Farwe was on the doorstep, stomping his boots to dislodge the dark soil before he entered the house.

Hannah immediately liked Niall, a gangly teenager who wore the bandage on his head at a jaunty angle. His wide smile exposed large bucked teeth reminiscent of a beaver or a squirrel. He tickled his younger brother, making Lian squirm and giggle. Niall quickly scooped the toddler under his arm and carried him to a bench, like he would have carried a sack of potatoes or a load of kindling wood.

From her seat at Gabe's elbow, Mellie giggled softly, hiding her smile behind chubby fingers. Margy and Meggie sat on either side of Hannah. Margy had been fingering the soft silk of Hannah's saffron blouse, and now she bent her head to slide her cheek against Hannah's arm. Hannah turned to smile at her and to tousle her tumble of curls. The little girl had been sampling cream and jam with her fingers, immersing her right index finger in the raspberry jam and her left in the thick sweetened cream. She licked the remnants of stolen sweets from her fingers, then she tugged the bright orange ribbon tied at the neck of Hannah's blouse. Hannah grinned and tapped the child's nose.

Somehow Hannah relaxed, even though she was surrounded by the myriad confusions of life in the large family. Meggie and Lian each overturned their bright blue mugs of steaming cocoa, but Ull methodically mopped up the spilled chocolate, her conversation uninterrupted. Farwe reached across the table to catch a stray crumpet before it rolled to the floor. He plopped the bread back onto Mellie's plate and chuckled when she smiled at him, cream dribbling down her chin. When all of the raspberry jam was scraped out of the dish, the last scone eaten and all of the cocoa was either consumed or spilled, the three girls cleared the dishes away. Ull washed the plates and cups and Hannah dried them.

In Niall's bedroom, Gabe checked the boy's injury and applied a clean bandage.

"Hope you've had time to show the impressive bandage to your friends, Niall. This new one is very small; inconsequential really."

Niall shrugged his bony shoulders; his disproportionately large hands dangled from his long skinny arms.

"It's okay, Gabe." He scratched his head and grinned. "To tell the truth, the old one itched!"

Margy was perched on Hannah's hip. She circled Hannah's right ear with one slightly sticky finger. Meggie waved a crayon drawing, crunching the paper against Hannah's arm. "Hey, look at this one! Look. Look at this picture!" Mellie held Hannah's hand.

"Please come back," Ull pleaded while Lian played peek-a-boo, hiding under her skirt. "Tis obvious the girls would enjoy your visit."

"Thank you, I will," Hannah promised.

"But right now, I need to get her home," Gabe said. "She's recovering from an accident herself. I don't want her to overdo."

Outside, he pulled Hannah close, her face to his chest. In less time than it took to call goodbye, they were back at his cave, in the bedroom.

"Tired?" Gabe asked her.

She arched her back, stretching. "A little."

"Lie down, then. Have a rest."

Hannah sat on the bed and patted the space at her side.

"There's something I don't understand." She caught her bottom lip between her teeth.

Gabe sat. He held her elbow, waiting.

"Yesterday, the man…the one I saw at the pool…"

"Aidan. Yes, what about him?"

Hannah noticed that Gabe gritted his teeth.

"He said something puzzling. I'd meant to ask you about it last night; but with the party and all I forgot."

"What'd he say?"

Hannah watched her lap, cupped her hands on either side of her abdomen. "He touched my belly and said it was unfortunate that I'm carrying a selkie whelp. What do you think he meant?"

Gabe sucked in a breath. The sssst sound reminded Hannah of the hiss of a snake. "He said that, did he?"

"Yes."

"And that's what brought up the talk about pregnancy?"

"Well, yes, pretty much. It got me thinking."

"I need to tell you a story, Hannah."

She inched further towards the headboard, propped pillows at her back. "Okay. Sounds ominous."

"No. Just complicated." Gabe stood and started pacing.

"We Scotsmen thrive on stories about the magical seals known as *Selkies*. Although few folks claim to have ever seen one, for centuries the Highlanders have passed tales about the wondrous nights, in the light of a full moon, when a selkie comes to shore."

He glanced at her and Hannah nodded.

"Picture it. Moonlight floating with the inky waves while the selkie swims to shore, shedding her sealskin on the rocks. Whether male or female, while they walk as a human, the selkies are beautiful. They have long blue-black hair and piercing gray eyes."

Gabe turned to watch her. His straight black hair glinted with blue highlights in the afternoon sunlight.

"In this human form, a selkie has two days to find true love. Should she win the heart of a mortal, she can remain on land as his wife. It's said that a selkie adapts well to life on the land. She becomes a good wife if she is well loved. People say that the love between a selkie and a human is an eternal love."

He hesitated, drew a deep breath and sat on the edge of the bed. He turned to look at Hannah and shrugged his shoulders to flex the tension building there.

"Once upon a time, on the northern coast of Skye, there was a young man raised to believe in the faeries who live in the fantastic clouds and mists of the craggy Cuillin Hills at the center of the island."

He reached for her hand. Hannah was surprised that his palm was sweating. He looked at their hands, brushed her wrist with his thumb when he spoke.

"Imagine his surprise when he was searching for a missing lamb but instead found a woman. A beautiful woman wandering through the scrub and heather in the rocky hills at night!"

Hannah thought maybe Gabe's mouth began to curve into a nervous smile, but he shook his head and looked towards the ceiling. He squeezed his eyes shut for a few seconds. Opening his eyes, he continued, "She was beautiful and wet and naked, covered only by a veil of silky black hair that concealed all but her legs. I've been told that she called out, *A charaid.* My friend."

Although he still held her hand, Gabe wasn't looking at Hannah. He stared at the ceiling. Because his lower lip quivered and the muscle just under his left eye twitched, she thought he might cry.

"My father swears that he fell in love with her at that very moment."

"Your father? You've been talking about Sean?"

Gabe nodded.

"He offered her his jacket and helped her into it. He said that she didn't seem to understand how to wear clothing."

Hannah put her free hand on Gabe's arm. Emotional support, she hoped.

"Since she'd spoken to him in Gaellic, Da used the old language. 'Where are you headed *mo nighean dubh?*' My black haired lass?"

Hannah felt inept; but she couldn't think of a single competent thing to say. So, she nodded.

Gabe continued. He didn't seem to be watching her reactions anyway. "Da loved her with all of his soul. They married and within the year, I was born." Now Gabe turned to look at Hannah. He stood up, bent at the waist – sort of a curt bow. "Let me introduce myself to you properly. I am Gabriel Myerson, son of Sean, a farmer and Caillie, a selkie."

Hannah blinked. What did he expect her to say? She covered her mouth with her fingertips, creating a barricade to keep her questions inside.

"We were happy together; the three of us." Gabe closed his eyes slowly, shuttering his emotions. "Quite often, Mother and I would climb down the steep rocky banks to swim in the waves of the cold North Atlantic." He rubbed his upper arms as if even the memory chilled him. "It's a tough walk. Strenuous hiking paths, often shrouded in thick clouds. As a five-year old, I thought it a great adventure."

He turned to look at her, and Hannah hoped her smile was encouraging.

"One day strangers stopped us. Men who smelled of beer and sweat. They didn't pay me much attention. But they circled my mother; pulled her hair loose from its braid and lifted the hem of her skirt. I hid behind Mother's leg, crying." Gabe was pacing- three long strides, then pivoting to take three more strides. "The men laughed. I was pushed to the ground. Mother's blouse was ripped. One of the men shoved her against a tree. He grabbed her neck when she screamed for me to get my Da. I ran. I ran like banshees were at my feet. I ran screaming."

Tears ran down his cheeks. Hannah reached for his hand and pulled him closer to the bed where she sat. He hunched over as if he had stomach cramps. His black hair hung in a sweaty mass, sticking to his face and clinging to his neck. He sat, but it took several minutes before he was ready to speak.

"Da raced as if Lucifer himself was chasing him through the hills. He arrived just as a man dropped my mother's body. She fell to the ground, limp and unmoving. My father yelled at him. '*A mhic an diabhoil*! You son of the devil!' I didn't see my father kill that man; I ran up later, screaming my own outrage. The small round pool of blood sputtering from the dying man's mouth mesmerized me. I noticed that his trousers were unzipped."

Hannah gasped, then clamped her hand over her mouth. She thought of a dozen things to say; but none of them were adequate. She shook her head.

Gabe slipped to the floor, knelt at the side of the bed ; like a child ready for prayers. "My Father knelt over Mother and I joined him." Gabe passed his hand over an imagined body lying on the bed. "She had a strange band of red round her neck and blood pooled around her shoulders. I'll never forget the warm coppery smell of her blood. Da was crying; he rocked back and forth. He just kept repeating, '*Mo chride, mo chride. Mo nighean mhaiseach.* My heart, my heart. My beautiful girl.' After a while, he smoothed her skirts over her legs and used his handkerchief to wipe blood and dirt from her neck and face." Gabe's voice dropped to less than a whisper. "He never noticed I was there. His own grief was too huge for him to remember mine."

"Gabe," she wasn't even certain that she'd spoken. The word floated on an exhaled breath.

"The other men had raped her, but the last man had slit her throat when he was finished."

"Oh, God! Gabe, I'm so sorry." Hannah ached for the child Gabe had been and for the gentle man he had become. She hugged her arms to her sides, hot tears welled in her eyes and burned in her throat.

"What did you do?" she asked.

"Somehow we managed, my father and I. We followed a regimented routine. There was no laughter; only a rhythm of chores, sleep and food."

He turned towards Hannah and reached for her hand again. He squeezed it and rubbed her knuckles with his thumb. He examined her hand from palm to nails.

"One afternoon Ella appeared like the proverbial faerie godmother. She was no taller than I was at the time and she smelled like gingerbread cookies!" Gabe shook his head twice as he remembered. "I loved her immediately!"

"What kid wouldn't?" Hannah asked with a weak smile.

"She arrived at our doorstep, told us she was keeping a promise made to my mother. She filled our home with the aromas of yeasty bread and spicy stew. She darned socks and mended sweaters. She was with us for a month, and I tried to believe that the three of us would remain that way forever."

"I understand how you felt. After my parents died, I latched on the Gran and held on for dear life."

"You probably do understand. You lost both parents; but could depend on your grandmother. My mother died; but I lost my father, too. His grief sucked the life out of him. He became this shell of a man – totally void of emotion. No happiness, no anger, no love. Just a shell." Gabe rubbed his eyes. "I thought he held me responsible for her death."

Hannah knelt on the bed in front of him. She grabbed his arms. "You still think that; don't you? You feel responsible."

Gabe turned his face away from hers.

She squeezed his upper arms, shook him. "You were a boy. A little boy. Listen to your own lectures, Gabe. You were as much a victim as your mother was."

"I know that now."

"Uhh huh," Hannah said. "Sure you do." She smoothed his hair off his forehead.

Gabe stood and picked up a book splayed open on the floor beside his chair. He placed it with other books stacked in a willow basket in the corner of the room. When he pulled the quilt off the foot of the bed, Hannah stood beside him. She took a corner in each hand, and together they neatly folded it. He hugged the quilt close to his chest.

"Ella and my father talked throughout one entire night. I woke sometime after midnight and peeked through the stair rails to see them huddled at the table. They spoke in low murmurs, so I couldn't hear. The next morning Ella offered me a great adventure. She and I would travel to her fantastic faerie village where she promised I would see all sorts of magic. I could return to visit my father whenever I wanted. I was enticed by the thrill of the unknowns; but at the same time, I was frightened."

"Of course you'd be scared. You were only a little boy."

"My father helped me fold my clothes. Then, we pushed a few toys into a backpack. I wanted to collect more toys, but he asked me to leave some for my return trips." Gabe rubbed his finger back and forth across the lip of the vase on the bedside table. The glass squeaked and he stopped. "Da was about ready to cry. I'm pretty sure of it; but he smiled at me and I was reassured."

Hannah clamped both of her lips between her teeth. She wanted to crush Gabe's head against her breasts; but she knew he wouldn't appreciate her sympathy.

After a few seconds, Gabe continued. "Da walked us to the kitchen door. Ella took my hand and we started walking across the yard. I turned to wave goodbye and saw my father wipe tears from his cheek. I dropped her hand, dropped my bag and rushed back to his open arms. He hugged me tight and whispered, *'Mo ghille. Mo chride.* My boy. My heart.' That was all it took. I knew I'd be okay. I said, *'Mo gradh, Athair.* I love you, Father,' then I left on my great adventure."

397

Hannah straightened the rumpled sheets and pillows on their bed, then she sat cross-legged, hands folded loosely in her lap. Gabe stopped pacing and turned to watch her. The large bed creaked when he plopped beside her.

"You would know how confusing and amazing life in the Village seems to a newcomer. Policy in this nonsense community would change slightly whenever I thought I understood the system. It was like trying to play a game with no rules."

"Tell me about it!" she laughed.

"Compared to the tiny villagers, I was like a colt, unsure of my long clumsy legs. My huge hands and large feet seemed totally mismatched to my body. Even though I was horridly large and monstrous, the faeries and elves accepted me, and I made my place among them."

"I find it very difficult to believe that you were ever horrid or monstrous." She traced the curve of his upper lip with her finger.

"When I was about twelve, a Siddhe Queen visited the village. Even though my voice had begun to squeak and break at inopportune times, she wanted to take me to Tiarnanog. Thank goodness, Ella refused the request."

"What would Ella have told your father? Oh, by the way Sean, Gabe's gone to live the life of a gigolo in a faerie mound."

Gabe shrugged. "Well, there was much heated discussion in the Faerie Council. Eventually, the Siddhe Queen conceded defeat. She left in a flurry of soiled faerie dust, spitting threats of vindication in her wake. She swore that I'd be punished because she'd been refused. Although it happened a very long time ago, I thought about that threat when you were missing."

Hannah thought back to her first days in the village. Gabe had tried to tell her that there was ugliness hiding behind the beauty in the faerie village. Maybe now, after so many months, she was beginning to understand. She lay back, pulling him with her. He stretched his arm across the pillows and she nestled into the curve of his body, one hand rested over his heart. She could feel his pulse.

Her other hand spanned her abdomen; thumb just below her navel, pinky just above her pubis. "Was Aidan right, then? Am I carrying a selkie pup?"

"God, Hannah, I don't know."

Her palm cupped his jaw. His beard looked almost blue. It felt like coarse sand paper. Those hypnotic gray eyes watched her, as if they could penetrate her thoughts. He turned his face to kiss her palm. His hand covered her entire stomach, hip-to-hip covered by his five fingers.

"How would you feel? Pregnant with my baby now that you know I'm not exactly human?"

"Blessed. I'd feel very blessed."

They must have dozed, because her body jerked, startling her awake. Flailing her arms, she upset the vase of flowers on the bedside table. Moonlight dappled the room in illuminated splotches.

Gabe propped on one elbow. He caught her wrist, his thumb over her stampeding pulse. "Hannah? You all right?"

"I was drowning." She pushed her hair back from her face with both hands. "I was swimming…swimming with seals."

"Okay."

"It was pleasant. The seals were smiling at me."

"Seals always look like they're smiling." With one finger, he hooked a strand of hair that had caught on her eyelashes. He tucked it behind her ear.

"Well, in my dream, they were happy to have me with them."

"But you started to drown?"

"Yes. Something…someone…grabbed my foot and pulled me to the bottom of the ocean. I found a cave full of explosives; bright red sticks of dynamite like the coyote uses in Road Runner cartoons."

"Underwater?"

"Yes! I was trying to swim back to the surface to warn people … someone … everyone… about the danger; but I got sucked back down. I couldn't get any air. I was drowning." She rubbed her throat, pressed her nightgown to her breasts to blot the perspiration. "What a strange dream."

Gabe brought her a glass of water. "Well, you have every reason to fantasize about seals. It's not an everyday occurrence to realize you're living with the son of a selkie."

"I don't think of you as a seal!"

"Until yesterday you thought of me as a man."

"Now, I think of you as a special man."

Gabe arched both brows, but didn't say anything. He gathered the broken flowers and tossed them in the wastebasket. Hannah dabbed at the spilled water with a washcloth.

"The selkie do have underwater caves full of treasure."

She turned to watch him over her shoulder. "Caves of treasure? Like Ali Babba? That is a faerie tale!"

He sat on the bed. She was squatting, drying the last drops of water on the floor. He toyed with one of her ringlets. "No tale. I saw one. That afternoon my mother died."

She pivoted towards him, balancing with her hands on his knees.

"We'd been swimming. Before I could walk, I could swim. I learned to hold my breath to dive for ten – fifteen minutes at a time. That particular day, Mother took me to the spot where she'd come ashore so many years earlier. She told me it was a secret place – our secret, hers and mine." He set the empty vase on the nightstand. He held Hannah's hand and rubbed his finger back and forth over her thumbnail. "Mother led me to a cave underwater. There was a high ledge we climbed near the entrance. Once I negotiated the rock wall, I could stand. The water only came to my thighs." He brushed his fingertips over his thigh, then he raised his hand above his head. "High up, maybe ten feet high, there was another ledge. That's where she'd stowed a treasure chest full of Spanish dubloons, silverware, goblets and jewels; all gathered from shipwrecks."

Hannah lost her balance and landed on her rump. "What did you do with it? With the treasure chest?"

"Nothing. It's a secret. I've never told anyone about it until now."

"Not even your father?"

"No. There was no need."

"But you told me..."

"Your dream was an omen. It seemed right to tell you."

"What are you going to do now?"

He stood and took her hand, pulling her up. "Well, I'm going back to sleep. Care to join me?"

"I mean what are you going to do about the chest?"

"Nothing." He hugged her. "I have everything I need right here."

Trog arrived for breakfast, a crumpled grease-stained bag of chocolate doughnuts stuffed in his pocket.

"I knew that Aidan was in the Village," Gabe told Trog. "I should have been more diligent about Hannah's safety."

"Hamph," Trog linked his hands behind his head and stretched. "He's never far from that good-for-nothing sister of his. If she's here, makes sense that he'd be here, too."

"He knew I'd search for Hannah. He waited for me at the pool."

Hannah placed a bowl of steaming oatmeal in front of Trog. "To be honest, he wasn't trying to frighten me, Gabe. I just freaked when he grabbed my hair."

402

"Got any more brown sugar?" Trog asked as he stirred the porridge.

Gabe turned his chair backwards, straddled it and rested his elbows on the table. "It's not Aidan's nature to harm you physically, Hannah. However, I'm ready to bet he'll try to seduce you just to spite me."

Trog dragged his spoon around the bowl, scraping out the last morsel of oatmeal. He burped softly and reached for the dish of sliced peaches. "I might have a word or two with the boy." He was swallowing a bite when he pushed away from the table. "Could be he needs a lesson in manners."

The elf jabbed his fists in the air, protecting his face with one hand while punching out with the other.

Hannah hiccupped a laugh as she reached to catch Trog's shirt collar. Gabe cautioned, "Mind your temper. Neither of the Siddhes will take kindly to your interference."

Hannah brought the coffeepot to the table. She filled Gabe's cup and brushed her fingers through his hair. "One person can attempt a seduction," she said. "But, a successful seduction can only be accomplished with two willing partners. I'm your partner. Maybe Aidan should be reminded of that fact."

"Oh, I reminded him the other night. Unfortunately, knowing that I love you will only the contest all the sweeter."

"So I'll tell him," she blustered.

"Lynnar and Aidan are both spiteful and cruel. It's all a game; a championship match to them. They're masters at the game, playing with human emotions. Siddhes are very, very skilled at deceit."

Hannah bent over her mug, alternately blowing into the steaming coffee and slurping sips. "Damnit, Gabe, I'm not a child." She slapped her palm against the tabletop. "Maybe I should be the one to talk to Aidan! You and Trog can't wrap me in a cocoon to protect me from the world. Just because I'm naïve doesn't mean I'm weak."

"I never said you were." Gabe kissed her cheek before he left the cave. "Have a good day, Love. I'll be back before mid-afternoon."

Trog slid out of his chair. "I'll just putter in your nasturtium bed for a bit."

He followed Gabe outside, screen door slamming shut behind him. Tugging Gabe's sleeve, Trog rolled his eyes and tipped his head towards the kitchen door. "Feisty wee bitch, is she no?"

Gabe punched the elf's shoulder and answered, "Ack, aye. And no mistake, she is me own wee bitch, and I'd no change her a whit. You keep an eye to her while I'm away."

Nowatil lived a short distance outside of the village, a stone's throw from the dense forest of evergreens. Her house was almost hidden in the shadows, embraced by long cedar branches. Lichen and mosses grew on her roof tiles. Tiny yellow-green weeds sprouted from cracks in the mortar of her home. Even at midday, the little seamstress sat close to her lantern, squinting at tiny stitches as she worked. Answering Gabe's whistle, she jumped up, smoothing the starched apron at her waist. She touched her hair, patting the graying waves closer to her scalp. She bustled out into the yard. She held both hands out to him in greeting, palms up. "Good day to you, Gabriel. What brings you here?" Short, pudgy fingers clutched her chest just above her heart. She looked over her shoulder and whispered, "Is all well with Hannah?"

"She was smiling when I left her not a hour ago."

"Ahh. It's a favor you'll be needing, then. What can I do for you? Perhaps a new tunic design." She pulled a tape measure from her apron pocket and reached for his arm, stretching her tape from wrist to elbow.

Chuckling, Gabe pulled a folded paper from his pocket. "No. I don't need a new shirt. But, you're close to the mark. I want to surprise Hannah with a dress." He smoothed the crumpled page. "It's a design she admired in a magazine. Can you create something similar for her? Flattering; but simple." He traced the sketch with his finger. "See? Close fitting at the top and sleeves, but with a flowing skirt. Soft, light-as-air material the color of pink pearls. Can you do that?"

"Child's play! Of course I can do that!"

With militant efficiency, the stout elf reached up to brush his shirt at waist level, picking off imaginary lint and straightening unseen wrinkles. "Don't know why you insist on wearing black clothes, Gabriel."

"Selkies are black,Nowatil," he clipped. "Black is fine."

Nowatil clucked as she shook her head. "I'll get started right away. I've got her measurements from the handfasting dress." She cocked her head to the side and winked up at him. "She's not gotten larger anywhere, has she?"

"I think those measurements will do nicely."

"Well, I've heard some talk…"

"Talk's cheap, Nowatil." He bent to kiss her cheek.

A goofy smile stuck to her lips. She massaged her cheek. At the gate, he turned back to her. "Oh, by the way, make the neckline rather low. Maybe to here," he said, using the side of his hand to indicate a position halfway between his clavicle and his sternum. He nodded, approving the idea. Smiling, he waved goodbye and disappeared into the shade of the path.

Hannah was in the kitchen. The chopping block was cluttered with small hills of flour and traces of cinnamon and nutmeg. A trail of raisins ran across the counter to a mound of dough, rising above a ceramic bowl.

Gabe slipped into the room and leaned against the doorframe to watch her as she worked. Her hands were coated in flour, so she used her wrist to brush hair off her face. She crinkled her nose when a curl tickled. She hummed snippets of several songs, all melded together as they passed from her thoughts to her lips. She was whisking eggs into froth, preparing custard to fill the éclair shells cooling on the rack.

"You know, I'm content just looking at you."

She turned towards his voice. The whisk was forgotten in her right hand. Egg dripped from the wires, drooling down the leg of her trousers.

When she raised her arms to hug him, his shoulder and one sleeve of his shirt were slimed with egg yolk.

"Oh bother." She swiped at the gelatinous mess, smearing shimmering swirls on his dark shirt. "Ugh. Sorry about that."

"No worries. It'll wash out."

"You could have a booming career as a cat burglar. Why did you sneak up on me like that?" She stood on tiptoe to kiss him.

"I like to watch you," he said, brushing flour residue off her nose with his thumb. "Touching you is better, though."

"I agree." She kissed him again.

He chuckled. "Phew. A few hours in Floddigarrry and I smell of peat smoke! I'm going to shower."

After a quick towel-drying, Gabe's newly sheared hair stuck out at odd angles, bristling at his crown and above his ears.

Hannah reached up to smooth the soft ebony tufts. "It's amazing that such a large man could look so much like a boy; but you do. You're grinning like a kid with a big secret."

Her palm rested at his jaw. He turned his face to kiss her hand.

"Not a secret. More of an admission."

She immediately went still, cautious.

"Go on."

"I went to see my father this afternoon."

"Oh? Quick trip to Scotland. I didn't even realize you were gone."

"Very quick; but very important trip."

"Really?"

"Really." She thought he enjoyed tweaking her curiosity. He picked up a glass paperweight, held the orb to the light, examining the drops of color held frozen in the crystal. He glanced at her, lifting one brow. "I had to get something from him. Something he was keeping safe for me. Something from my mother."

"Oh?" She spoke, voice as soft as a gentle breeze.

"It's the one thing she took out of the treasure chest. She said I should give it to my wife."

"Oh?" Now her voice was like a shadow.

He slipped his hand into the pocket of his robe. Keeping his surprise hidden, he held a fist just above her shoulder.

"Go on," he encouraged. "Open your hand."

She held out her palm, just below his hand. Slowly he unfurled his fingers, one by one. As he did, a long strand of perfect pale pink pearls slipped from his fingers to hers. She closed her fingers over them, and brought her knuckles to her lips. She was speechless. Couldn't make her mouth form words even if she'd thought of the perfect thing to say. A tear, the size of one of the largest pearls, trickled the length of her nose. She had to remind herself to breathe.

"Oh, Gabe." She tapped her heart, pearls clutched in her hand. "Happiness is painfully wonderful!"

He caught her tear on his tongue. "You can't be surprised. I've made no secret about my intentions. Will you marry me, Hannah? Will you promise to marry me soon?"

"You didn't even need to ask."

"They are as old as the sea," Gabe said, closing her fingers over the long strand of pearls. "Easily damaged and impossible to re-place. Just like love, Mother told me. She promised my wife would care for the pearls, just as she would my heart."

He led her to the big chaise in the corner - the one that Hannah had originally used as a bed. She sat with her back to him and he latched the filigree clasp. Hannah rolled one of the pearls between two fingers. "I've never seen anything so beautiful in my life."

Gabe nuzzled her neck, just above the bump of her spine, right under a corkscrew curl. "I have. Every morning when I wake up and look at you."

"You don't have to overdo the flattery. I've already agreed to marry you," she teased.

"How soon?"

"I don't know." She blinked, shrugged her shoulders. "Got any particular date in mind?"

"October first."

"That's today, silly." In the kitchen, a buzzer screamed for at-tention. "Today, I'm busy making coffeecakes and éclairs for the fair tomorrow."

"Okay, after the fair, then. October fourth, it is!"

The kitchen was perfumed with sweet cinnamon. Hannah pulled the raisin bread out of the oven, "Where will we have the ceremony?"

Gabe scratched his head and a cowlick sprang to life. "Here, I guess. Does that work for you?"

"And who will officiate?"

Gabe tugged on his left earlobe. "Father Donor."

"Who?"

"Father Donor, from Floddigarry. He married my parents."

Hannah put the oven mitt away and closed the drawer. She leaned against the cabinet, elbows resting on the counter. "Has he visited here, in the village?"

"No."

"Does he know that you live in a faerie raft?"

Gabe shuffled from one foot to another. "Not exactly."

"Did he know your mother was a selkie?"

"Oh yes!" He nibbled his thumbnail, rubbed the bridge of his nose and winced. "Maybe. Da swears they told him. It's just not a certainty that Father Donnor actually believed them."

"Uh huh. So how will you explain that some of our wedding guests can fly through the air and are small enough to land in the palm of your hand?"

Gabe stood in front of Hannah. He spanned her waist with his hands, thumbs almost meeting in the center. "Trust me. He won't question it."

"He's daft, then?"

Gabe chuckled and flicked her nose with his finger. "No, he's very canny, actually. But, the faeries have special methods to deal with humans. Ewan, Mairisi and Father Donnor will all remember coming to America for our wedding. They'll remember you as a beautiful bride and me as a besotted groom. They'll leave here with happy memories; but they won't have any recollection of the actual travel, the faeries, elves or pixies."

"And Sean…will he remember?"

"Every moment."

Hannah rubbed her hands together. Bits of dried dough stuck in the creases of her knuckles. She swiped her palms across her apron. She thought of the baby growing inside her, thought of how her body would soon swell like the yeast bread she'd just baked. "Okay, then. October fourth it is. How will we get everyone here in time?"

"Leave it to Trog."

The oven timer bleeped again. Hannah opened the oven and Gabe sighed, "Gingerbread!"

"Ella's recipe."

"Don't take it to the fair. Consider it a pre-sale. Name your price."

Hannah laughed. "Trog's not the only one ruled by his stomach!" She inverted the pan, plopping the cake onto a cooling rack.

Gabe leaned close and inhaled, eyes closed as though in prayer.

"It's dark and dense, black like dark chocolate. Taste," he said, pinching a few crumbs that clung to the inside of the pan.

Together they ate three slices of cake, alternating between bites topped with lemon curd and those crowned with the thick whipped cream.

"You smell like gingerbread." Gabe kissed her necklace and nipped at her earlobe.

"You told me that Ella smelled like gingerbread and you loved her immediately."

"Even if I didn't love you, I'd marry you for the promise of this gingerbread on a weekly basis!"

Gabe cut one more slice.

Hannah pushed her chair away from the table. She carried her plate and fork to the sink and rinsed them, questioning him while water splashed the counter. "Could it be that simple? Could this attraction...this love...be a fascination like a craving for gingerbread?"

Gabe reached from behind her to turn off the faucet. With hands on her shoulders, he turned her to face him. "You do make the strangest associations. Are you scared of marriage after only a few hours of engagement?"

"No. I'd marry you anywhere, anytime and know that I'll love you forever."

"Then what's the problem?"

"You're getting a bad bargain."

Gabe crossed his arms and leaned back, eyeing her. "Looks pretty good to me."

Hannah wiped the countertop, wide looping circles becoming tighter and faster. "You know what I mean, Gabe. Not only has your bride been raped; but you'll be saddled with a bastard."

"The baby is ours – yours and mine." His voice was a quiet fire, anger flickering on the perimeters.

Hannah crossed her arms at her waist. She concentrated on the pattern of brown and white floor tiles. Although she was muddling the attempt; she felt it important to force Gabe to consider his options. "It won't be easy," she whispered. "Could be that I'll always freak out with some memory of the rape; nightmares and crying jags."

Gabe gathered her close and spoke into her hair. "Did you know that somewhere in America, a rape is attempted every two minutes? There are more rape victims living in the United States than combat veterans. Some of those women have lovers or husbands; some of them have children or parents or grandparents. The rape affects the whole family. Most of them deal with the problems."

"Some don't," Hannah whispered. "Rape ruins some lives; ruins some relationships."

"We'll manage it together."

"Wish I could be certain."

"Who told you that life comes with guarantees? Lives are affected by events, just like the earth is affected by the weather. After a hurricane, the landscape is devastated. Trees are uprooted. Tiny streams overflow and run like rivers pulsing with white water; washing topsoil downstream. Rampaging waters push debris to form dams.

Then the streams are re-routed and ugly washed-out gullies are left naked. In time, Nature heals. The land begins to rejuvenate. Birds drop seeds that grow in the relocated topsoil. Savagely sheared trees grow lush new foliage to replace the old. Downed trees rot and lichens grow on the deteriorated bark. Ferns and wildflowers germinate on banks eroded by the storm waters."

Gabe dabbed the tears on her cheeks with the damp dishcloth. She tried to smile, but her lips quivered. He kissed her cheek that now smelled slightly of dishwashing detergent. "The land recovers. Scars remain, but the land isn't diminished; only changed. Obviously, you and I were both affected by the rape. But in time, the pain will be less raw. Together we can forge a better, stronger bond through shared difficulties. Let me help you heal."

Hannah rubbed the pad of her thumb across his knuckles. "I just don't want to lose you. I've lost everyone else who was important; I don't want to lose you, too."

"Do I look like I'm going anywhere?"

Sean arrived the next morning. Hannah rushed out to greet him at the garden gate.

"Madain mhath," she called, practicing the Gaellic Gabe had taught her last night.

"Good morning to you, too, Lass." Sean pulled her close in a bear hug. "Madain mhath, mo ghràdh."

Hannah giggled and admitted, "I don't know what you said."

"My dear. I called you 'my dear.' With the wedding coming, you should call me '*m'athair.*' That means 'my father.'"

Hannah slipped her hand in his. "I'd like that very much, m'athair."

"We'll do well together, you and I," Sean said.

"Come in, come in. Gabe's inside and I have breakfast ready. You do like blueberry muffins, don't you? I can whip up pancakes, if you'd prefer."

"The muffins will be lovely, if you've a bit of coffee to go along side."

"Coffee, juice, tea, milk…you name it!"

Gabe was in the kitchen, pouring two mugs of steaming coffee. The men hugged and pounded one another's back. Then Sean noticed that the table was set for two.

"Aren't you eating, then, Hannah?" Sean asked.

Hannah rubbed her stomach. "I'm too excited to eat and too busy to take the time." She covered the basket of cakes and eclairs with a yellow napkin and braced the heavy load against her hip. "After breakfast, you and Gabe can meet me at the fair. I promised to help Ella set up the display tables."

Gabe opened the door for her, brushing her cheek with a kiss as she passed. Trog slipped into the kitchen as Hannah left.

"Trog, a charaid, maybe you can tell me what's going on here," Sean whispered. "The bride is not in the best of health."

Trog braced for an argument. His cheeks puffed and his face was scarlet. His eyes were squinted under his spiky brows. His stubby arms were crossed over his broad chest. "I'll not say a word, Sean. You'll have to bamboozle your answers from the boy, not from me!"

The 'boy' in question was like a Highland warrior, ready for battle. "What goes here, Da? You've only just arrived, and already you accuse me of secrets?" Gabe jabbed a finger at his father. "If you've questions, let me hear them."

Sean steepled his hands, as if in prayer, and rested his chin on the spire of his middle fingers. "I'm wondering how the lass acquired the cuts and bruises, son."

"What?"

"She's a lovely girl, make no mistake. A man can hardly help but stare at her. But, because she has such pale skin, a man with eyes in his head can hardly fail to notice the scars and fading bruises at her temple, and on her jaw. When she worked with the basket, the sleeves of her sweater slid to reveal a trail of bruises running from her wrists midway up her arm." He arched a brow, sat in a chair at the table and pulled on his lower lip.

Gabe clinched and unclenched his fists, arms tight at his sides. He stared at the hairline cracks in the plaster at the base of the ceiling light fixture. In two long strides, he was at the window. Lifting the sash, he inhaled the cool damp air. With his back to his father, he said, "Okay. I'll tell you; but it's a long story."

He straddled the chair beside Sean and sat. Each of his hands rested on a knee, and he scraped at a speck of lint on his pants. He looked at his fingers rather that at his Da.

"Yes," Sean answered. "Go on."

"I talked Hannah into coming here with me. I made her think I was offering her shelter out of friendship. Actually, I figured Tatiana would intercede; that Hannah'd have to agree to handfast."

"So you tricked the girl?"

"Yes. No. Sort of. I meant for our handfast period to give Hannah time to adjust, to me, the faeries, to our life together. Do you see?"

"I think so. But you never really intended to let her go, did you, son?" The question was asked without accusation.

"No. I didn't really think she would ever leave me." The answer was a hushed confession. "I told her she would always be free to go, but I tried everything in my power to keep her when she needed to leave."

"You did that to her?" Sean leaned forward, pushing his forehead against his son's. In a low growl, he asked, "You hurt that tiny lass?" His fingers were powerful manacles at Gabe's wrists.

Gabe blinked, then scowled. "No! I'd never hurt Hannah. What do you think of me that you could ask that question?" He shook his arms, breaking loose of Sean's grip. Both men sat back, breathing hard as though they'd fought with fists rather than words. Trog reached up to place a reassuring hand on Gabe's shoulder.

"Hannah had a commitment to paint a fresco for a children's hospital," Gabe said. He stood, walked to the sink, picked up a sponge and tossed it into a bowl of sudsy water. "She needed a few weeks to complete her task. Even a few days would have seemed endless to me.

417

I whined and sniveled and begged her not to leave." He shrugged one shoulder, as if he'd had a chill. Turning to face Sean, he cocked his head to one side and tried to smile. "My best groveling was inadequate, though. She left to do the fresco because she'd made a promise." Gabe's voice dropped to a whisper. "That's the kind of woman she is, Da. Once a promise is made, she will move heaven and defy hell to keep it."

Sean nodded. "Yes. I can see that about her."

"The rest of the story is terrible." Gabe puffed out a breath. He glanced left, then right, looking for the right words. "There is no other way to say it, Da. Hannah was raped. Kidnapped and raped."

Sean sat up straight again. "No." The word was barely more than an exhale. The 'o' lingered on the air. He scrubbed at his eyes with the heels of his palms. "Poor lassie."

"You can't imagine." Gabe shook his head. "Two men held her. They were unspeakably cruel. I found her, but it was too late." Gabe rubbed at his thighs. A breeze rippled the gingham curtains. A puppy barked in the distance. Sean put his hand on his son's arm. "They had abused her terribly." Gabe's voice broke, his shoulders hunched forward, he hung his head to hide tears.

His father let him cry. "I understand too well the pain you're suffering."

Gabe sniffed and swiped at his eyes with his knuckle. "She's healing. But, she still has wicked dreams, and wakes frightened and crying." He shook his head slowly. "I try to help, but at times I feel so inadequate. So inadequate."

"But you love her still." Sean's words were more a statement than a question.

"Only more than life itself."

As he stood, he patted his son's shoulder. *"Duine math."*

Gabe covered his father's hand with his own. "Sometimes I don't feel like a good man, Da. But I'm trying."

The fair wasn't scheduled to begin for another hour. However, a boisterous bevy of elves in gaudy spangled clothing had arrived early. "They're hill people," Ella explained. "Don't deal well with times or schedules. Days begin before dawn and end at dusk for them. Watch them carefully, they'll steal your buttons and baubles if you give them a chance."

Hannah tugged the neck of her sweater to cover her pearls. She smiled to see Gabe and Sean striding towards her booth. Trog was behind them, galloping to keep up.

When Gabe stood beside her, she touched the pearls at her throat. "I'm deliriously happy!"

"Good. I love to make you happy." He leaned close to whisper, "Just wait until later tonight. I promise to continue the delirium!" Wiggling his eyebrows, he winked.

She laughed and swatted at his hand as he tried to touch her breast. Behind her, someone cleared his throat.

"Is this a private party, or is everyone invited to sample this confection?"

"Aidan," Gabe grunted.

Suave as any European diplomat, Aidan took Hannah's finger-tips between his, and lifted them to his lips. "The fair Hannah. And here, I thought we might never be introduced." He released her hand. With his index finger, he tapped a pearl that gleamed at the hollow of her throat.

Gabe whispered a growl low in his throat. "You'd be wise to search for your treats elsewhere, Aidan. Hannah definitely is NOT for public consumption."

"Poor Gabe," Aidan teased. "You never did learn to share, did you?"

Hannah sandwiched one of Gabe's hands between the two of hers. "But, we will gladly share our wedding cake with you, Aidan."

"Wedding cake?"

"Yes," Gabe said, though he gritted his teeth while he spoke. "Hannah has agreed to marry me. The wedding's in two days. You must come to the ceilidh to celebrate."

Crowds had gathered; men and children sampling treats and women searching for bargains at the booths set up along the path that was the main thoroughfare of the Village. It was difficult to maneuver through the throng. Lynnar was already out of sorts when she spotted Trog, licking meringue from his fingertips.

"My brother; have you seen him, Little Man?"

"Aye. He's at Hannah's booth…she's selling sweets and sto-ries."

"How boring." Lynnar glanced in both directions, then held her hand out to Trog, palm down. "Take me to him, then."

Trog's face flushed and his nostrils flared. "Follow me." He stomped through the horde, leading Lynnar in angry silence. After being jostled twice, he was elbowed in the belly when he bumped an intoxicated Spriggan. He heard several merrymakers placing friendly wagers on Hannah's chances in the inevitable contest with the Siddhe siblings. He shook his head and mumbled to himself, "Oh, my bet's on Gabriel's feisty wee bitch."

Trog stopped about ten feet away from Hannah's orange striped canvas booth.

"Watch Aidan and Gabe strutting and preening like roosters to impress our Hannah."

"Our Hannah, is it? Do you delude yourself to think that Gabe will share her with you, Little Man?"

"It's no delusion at all," Trog snipped, glancing over his shoulder to watch Lynnar. "Gabe shares her with the whole Village."

Lynnar arched her left brow, clearly questioning his statement.

Trog chuckled. "The boys, the girls and even the oldest faeries all share a bit of her. She's considerate. She sings and laughs while she works alongside us."

"Oh please. Spare me the sappy sentimentality!" She waved her hands in the air, swatting at the elf as if he were a pesky mosquito. "Just go away. You always did annoy me with your squeaky idle chatter." With a regal flick of her wrist, she tried to dismiss him from her presence.

Lynnar tried to wedge between the two men. She fixed her hands at her waist, elbows jutting out like triangular buttresses. She bumped an elfin girl with a deformed leg.

"Why, you ugly, stupid, clumsy little imp. How dare you paw a Siddhe?" Hannah turned just in time to catch Lynnar's arm as she attempted to slap the girl. "Don't even think of harming this child!" Her voice was an icy and menacing. The women glared at one another, all hostilities bared.

"You bitch!" Lynnar spit. "You dare to challenge me!"

"Bitch I may be, but I'm strong. You're hollow and vain with no substance. You've only a thin coating, a candy shell of beauty covering a rotten core. You don't have the power to harm me."

Someone in the mass of faeries called, "Put me down for five more brass buttons on Hannah!" as he jostled for a better view.

One shove was answered with another. Elves and sprites bounced in jerky, comical movements. Elbows slammed into jaws, split lips bruised and puffed. A display toppled. Slices of cinnamon bread and éclairs fell to the ground and were trampled. Lynnar snarled; she crouched. A tigress assessing her prey. She lunged to snatch a fistful of Hannah's hair. The Japanese lanterns hanging low overhead bobbled. Crimson fingernails tangled in golden curls.

"You'll live to regret coming to our Village, Bitch!"

Lynnar jerked Hannah's hair, then slapped her face. The force of the impact threw Hannah backwards. She fell against the table, upsetting four pies, three dozen cookies and a pitcher of lemonade.

When Lynnar struck Hannah, Aidan was frozen; surprised. Now he moved like lightning. He grabbed his sister's arm, smiled when she gasped in pain. He pushed at her back, roughly propelling her forward. "Get out of here! Go now! We'll talk later."

He knelt beside Hannah, who was still buffered in Gabe's arms. She was covered with bits of grass and her sweater was ripped. The strand of pink pearls hung loose at her neck. The clasp had been broken. Aidan dabbed at a small cut above her left eye with the tail of his shirt, and asked, "Are you okay?"

She nodded mutely, still stunned.

Ella pushed through the ruckus. "Gabe, get the girl home and tend her cut. Mind the necklace, there."

Gabe slipped the pearls in his pocket and helped Hannah to her feet.

"What will your father think of me?" she asked, resting her head against his arm.

Gabe cupped the back of her neck. "He'll agree that you are a braw fighter, me fine wee bitch!"

"I suppose the wedding will be postponed now." Aidan was at Hannah's back. She could feel his words like breaths on her neck. "At least until Hannah's feeling well."

Gabe pivoted, maneuvering Hannah away from Aidan. "Two days. No postponement."

"Ah," Aidan sneered. "Of course, you're afraid to let the fish dangle too long on the line. She might just throw the hook and escape."

"Your humor hasn't improved with age," Gabe grumbled.

"You're not very trusting, Gabriel." The Siddhe words were soft and gentle as a cat's purr. With his finger, Aidan traced the shape of Hannah's cheek with one finger. He touched the finger to his lips and then gently dragged it across hers.

Gabe clinched his teeth and exhaled noisily. "Oh, I trust Hannah implicitly. Make no mistake. It's your intentions I don't trust, Aidan."

"What's not to trust? I'm not hiding my intentions. Your vows won't stop me. Virgin, single, married, widow or whore. Some women are a challenge, but, in the end, they willingly come to me."

"Hannah! You look awful! My mum sent me to check on you; but I didn't really think you'd been hurt yesterday." Tobias thrust a wilted bouquet towards her, while he bowed his head, examining his bare toes. He clutched limp stalks of Queen Anne's lace, goldenrod and a few spring onions gone to seed. "These are, um, these flowers are for you." He shuffled his weight from one foot to the other. The pointed tips of his ears reddened.

"Oh, Toby. They're beautiful flowers. Thank you. Come in. We're just finishing breakfast, would you like something to eat?" She buried her face in the sad little bouquet and inhaled as though it were an armful of long stemmed red roses. The pungent aroma of the weeds was a balm to her heart. She pulled a small blob of mud from the root of a goldenrod. "I'll put these flowers in a vase. Help yourself to a cookie from the jar on the counter, then sit and chat with Gabe. I'll get you a glass of milk, okay?"

Tobias' head bobbled while he grabbed a handful of oatmeal raisin cookies. With his mouth full, crumbs spilled over his lips. Toby mumbled, "Morning, Gabe."

Gabe tipped his hand towards a chair, inviting the boy to sit.

Hannah brought a large glass of milk and set it on the table. She stood behind Toby's chair, resting her hand on his shoulder. He gulped the milk and grinned, sporting a creamy mustache.

"Good ookies," he mumbled around crumbs. He held his last cookie just below eye level, turning it for a close examination at all angles. Having selected the appropriate spot, he nibbled an edge, breaking loose a single raisin with his prominent front teeth. He carefully positioned the cookie amid a circle of crumbs on the table. His hands were long and slender, unkempt with ragged cuticles and dirty nails. Now he lifted the raisin off his tongue, balancing it carefully between thumb and index fingers. With a concentration to be admired by laboratory scientists, he examined that raisin from every vantage point.

"Got something on your mind, Toby?" Gabe asked.

Toby smashed the raisin on the tabletop, giving all his attention to ironing out the wrinkles from the paper-thin brown oval with the ball of his hand.

"Just thought …you being human and all…I thought you should know that the Siddhes…well, fact is, the Siddhes are planning to scare you off. Lynnar, she wants to piss you off, actually. Word is that Aidan says he wants a piece of you before you go. They're not nice people, Hannah."

Hannah leaned close and whispered, "I know, Toby." She finger combed the carrot-colored hair that brushed his collar. Behind his earlobe was a streak of dirt. She kept a hand on his scrawny shoulder.

Tobias turned the color of a radish. The chair scraped with a loud grunt as he pushed away from the table. He stood quickly, drained the milk remaining in his glass, and shoved the half-eaten cookie into his pocket.

"You're not gonna fight him, are you Hannah?"

"Fight him?"

"Aidan. Don't fight him just 'cause he says he wants a piece of you."

Gabe pushed his chair back so that it rocked on two legs. "No, Toby. Hannah won't be fighting. Aidan will have to take a piece of me before he touches Hannah." He pounded one fist into the palm of his other hand.

Twisting his cap in both hands, Tobias bounced on the balls of his feet. "Well, I've got chores! Thanks for the cookies. Well, um, well. See ya."

"In just minutes, the whole Village will have a recap of our conversation. Hannah's fine, nothing broken. Gabe threatens to fight Aidan," Gabe laughed.

"Well, something was broken." Hannah tapped her neck. "Your mother's pearls. In only one day, I broke them."

"No, Lynnar broke the clasp; but that was easily repaired."
Gabe reached into his pocket. "It's all right, Love. They're here." He
tucked the pearls into her hand and closed her fingers around them.

"Yes." She took a deep breath. "Thanks." She opened her fist
slightly, and peeked at the pearls. "They're so precious. I never
dreamed I'd own such a priceless gift." The hand clutching the pearls
was held close at her heart.

"No dream."

"So we will be married tomorrow?"

He nodded. "No doubt about it. You've got yourself a date
with me and a preacher at noon."

Gabe bit a corner from the piece of toast Hannah held to his
mouth. Sean's face peeked in through the kitchen window. "Am I interrupting?"

"No, Da, what do you need?"

"Well, I thought we should tidy the wee garden before the doings tomorrow. Fluff the mulch and tend the grass, you know."

Gabe whispered, "Idle hands are the devil's workshop."

Hannah laughed, "And busy hands are happy hands!"

"Go. Change into work clothes, then Boy. I'll have a chat
with my new daughter."

Hannah tore the edge off the toast, and nibbled it. Sean poured
a mug of coffee.

"Tell me about yourself," he said. "I'm curious. Where did
you grow up?"

"I was born in Georgia, in southeast America. Do you know the south?"

Sean nodded.

"I grew up there, but went to college up north. My parents were both killed in a car wreck while I studying art." She answered quietly, barely glancing at him. She crumbled most of the remainder of her bread slice into tiny balls of tan dough.

"We don't have to speak of them, if it makes you uncomfortable."

"No, it's okay." She did look at him then. "I think that it's hard to be an orphan, whether you are eight, eighteen, or thirty-eight. A child needs parents."

"Ah. Weel now, that's a situation I can understand. Has Gabe told you how his mother was killed?"

Hannah nodded.

"I thought so. I grieved for Caillie something fierce. Grieving's not a bad thing in and of itself. But, mine was all consuming. I had scarce room left in my life for loving my son. More's the pity, more's the pity. He suffered from my neglect."

He touched her hand. Hannah turned her palm up, lacing her fingers through his. "He's a lucky man to find you, lass. You will treat him well, I'm thinking."

"I'm the lucky one. He's a caring, gentle man. A gentleman."

"Aye. That he is."

The cuckoo was clucking the quarter hour when Trog escorted Marisi, Ewan and Father Donor to the front door. Hannah tossed aside the large mitt she had used to lift the pastries, golden brown and oozing goat cheese, from the oven. Gabe pushed open the heavy red door.

"Gabe, my lad. Good to see you; it's been much too long since you've been home."

The lad he had addressed answered the gentle rebuke with a bear hug.

"Is this the vicar you are mauling, then?"

"Hannah, I want you to meet Father Donor McKierney. Father Donor, this is my Hannah."

"I've been squeezed like one of the Dundee oranges!" Donor bowed, his vest strained at his rather plump waist.

"Dundee oranges?" she asked.

"Have you never tried Dundee Marmalade, then?"

"Can't say that I have."

"Mores the pity. In the 1790's a thrifty merchant found that his imported oranges were too tart to eat. His canty wife boiled the fruit with sugar and weel, the rest is history!"

"Ah, the ingenuity of a thrifty Scot!"

Ewan grabbed Hannah's shoulder and spun her around. "Give us a hug, then, Lass."

"Welcome, Ewan…Mairisi. Come in, come in. I've made lunch."

"Smells delicious," Ewan boomed.

"All this running about; I'm starved," Trog grumped.

"Can I help you?" Mairisi asked.

"Yes, thanks." The women walked arm-in-arm to the kitchen while the men gathered beside the f ireplace.

In the kitchen, Mairisi whispered, "Later, when we're all alone, you must tell all."

"Tell? What should I tell?" Hannah asked.

"I knew when Gabe fell, he'd fall hard. I want you to spill your guts, tell me every romantic detail."

"Oh," Hannah laughed. "No problem." She pointed to a bowl. "Use that dish for the raspberries. They're in the fridge in a colander."

Mairisi chuckled, "Don't know about rasp-berries; but I found some lovely brambles."

Everyone settled around the food and chatted as the salad, cheese pastries, brambles, cream and shortbread disappeared. Donnor relaxed against the soft cushions piled at his back in the chair. He belched quietly into his fist and rubbed the pink skin protruding through gaping buttons on his tapestry vest and starched white shirt. Hannah reached for his glass to replenish tea. At the same time, Sean produced a decanter.

"And would you be wanting a bit o' Talisker to settle your stomach, man?"

"Ah weel. And it's a fine idea you'll be having, Sean Murray!" Donnor extended the glass, drops of tea still clung to the melting ice cubes.

Donnor swirled the whiskey in his glass, inhaling the bouquet as he closed his eyes. Hannah wondered if somehow his being sightless enhanced the aroma. He tipped the glass and relished a penury taste of the scotch. His stamina refurbished, the rector sat forward and rested a palm on Hannah's knee.

"So. The two of you plan to marry."

Hannah nodded and licked her lips.

"Most definitely," Gabe answered, patting Hannah's other knee.

She looked from fiancé to pastor. She chewed one side of her lower lip.

"Yes, weel now. We can't rush these things," Donnor reminded them. Hannah twirled a strand of hair just at her temple. Gabe clinched his teeth. A small vein in his neck, just below his right ear, jutted out a tad more than usual.

Turning towards Hannah, Donnor asked, "How did you two meet?"

Her green eyes rolled and her smile widened to include her whole face. "He was loitering at the place where I was working."

"Awk! Was he now?"

"Oh yes. Quite definitely. There was magic in the air."

"Hmmm. Or something, you say." Donnor winked at Hannah and turned his attentions to Gabe. "And what do you say?"

"No magic, Donnor, just a powerful attraction. Not long after I met her, she slept in my bed." Gabe crossed his arms over his chest.

Hannah gasped and choked on a bite of cheese pastry.

Without missing a beat, Donnor reached over to pound Hannah on the back. "She did, did she? And where did you sleep, boy?"

"In a chair."

"Kind of blows the image I was working on," Sean joked.

"Well, my house had just burned to the ground," Hannah explained.

Mairisi reached for the decanter and poured a dollop of Tallisker in her glass. "That's a hot romance for you." She tipped her glass towards Gabe and winked. Then, she drank a long gulp of Scotch.

"I brought her here and begged her to handfast with me."

"Handfast? That is romantic." Mairisi took another sip.

"You two don't really know one another," Father Donor interjected.

"I know that Gabe confuses and confounds me. He fills me with wild imaginings and fierce longings," Hannah said softly. "He recognizes my potential and pushes me towards my goals." She glanced at her lap, then up at Donnor, then to Gabe. "I trust him. And I love him with all my being."

Gabe nodded. "She was born to be with me." He took her hand in his.

Donnor closed his eyes for a second. He sighed a deep breathy exhalation. "Aye. I can see you think so." Cocking his head towards Trog, he sighed again. "Himself announced that the wedding should continue with all haste." He waggled his rather bushy white brows, wedged among the wrinkles on his forehead.

Gabe rested their joined palms on Hannah's belly, just below her navel. "With all haste."

"Ah. I see." Donnor chanced a glance at Sean, who had remained uncharacteristically quiet throughout the conversation. Total silence reigned for more than ninety seconds.

"A baby?" Sean sighed. Hannah wondered if he might faint. His mouth hung open and his eyes bulged just a bit.

Gabe's chair scraped when he stood. "Make no mistake, Donnor O'Kierney," His voice was quiet; but somehow it seemed slightly aggressive. "There will be a wedding tomorrow at noon. I would like for you to officiate, but that's not a requisite." He moved to Hannah. "There will be a wedding." He looked from Donnor to Hannah, assuring them both.

There was an awkward moment, no one speaking. Ice settled in one of the tea glasses, clinking the crystal. Sean shifted positions in his chair, crossing one leg over the other knee. Donnor cleared his throat and took a step towards Gabe, whose chest he punched with his index finger.

"I don't take well to intimidation, boy," another finger stab. "Not at all." Now he grinned. "But you do want to marry the girl. That much is obvious."

Mairisi popped a raspberry in her mouth, leaned towards Hannah and whispered behind her hand. "Details. I demand every single detail."

Father Donor stretched. He belched softly and rubbed his stomach. "I feel the need for a bit of a rest. Must be the time changes, don't you know?"

Gabe cleared several plates from the table. "Would you mind accompanying the vicar to Ella's, Trog?"

The two nodded their good-byes. Trog hefted Donor's tapestry valise and they left, chuckling. A whiff of scotch whiskey floated in their wake.

Ewan set up the chessmen when Gabe brought out the board. Sean sipped iced tea laced with Talisker's finest while he settled into the large chaise in the corner.

"When is the baby due?" Mairisi started the questions before the swinging door had stilled.

"In about eight months, best as we can figure."

"Are you happy?"

"With Gabe?"

"Yes, of course with Gabe. But are you happy about the baby?"

Hannah turned to the sink. She stirred soap into the warm water and reached for a plate. "This baby may not be Gabe's."

"I don't understand."

"Even I don't understand." Hannah sighed. Her knees turned to rubber bands, her face was ashen and her palms sweated.

Mairisi reached to turn off the water faucet. Then she held Hannah's elbow and led her to a chair at the kitchen table. "We're both sensible women, you and I. Let's try to puzzle this out together, shall we?"

Hannah closed her eyes and slowly shook her head. "It's a long, long story." "Bottom line, I was raped. By one, probably two, men. This baby could be Gabe's, but one of those awful men could easily be the father."

A single tear scorched a trail down Hannah's cheek.

"Gabe says…" she sniffed, and touched her knuckle to her nose. "He says that the baby is his, or rather ours, nevertheless." She propped her elbows on the table and dropped her head into her hands. "Do you know what else? He says he loves me, therefore, he will love this baby." She rocked back and forth, wrapping her arms at her waist and gripping her sides. "I can't make a claim like that truthfully. Would I be awful if I can't love this baby?" Hannah spread her hands over the small mound of her belly.

More tears followed the first. Mairisi dug into her pocket to retrieve a clean tissue. Hannah dabbed at her face, blew her nose, and shredded the tissue in silence.

Mairisi waited for a moment. "You will."

"What?"

"You will love the baby. You and Gabe and the bairn together will be family. You love the father; of course, you will love the babe. It's not in you to hate an innocent." She leaned close and kissed Hannah's cheek. "Make peace with yourself."

Hannah chewed her bottom lip. She nodded her head once. "That's it, of course. I do love Gabe. Maybe that bond between the two of us will be enough. I just wish I could be certain."

"Not many things in life are certain, though, are they?"

The early morning hours of October fourth were chilly and damp. Pixies peeked out from under mammoth rhododendrons in the backyard. Faeries flitted from one waxy leaf to another, balancing on drops of rainwater that trembled and shimmered, but never broke. Soft weather, Sean had called it as he slurped steaming coffee.

When he arrived, Ewan shook his head, flinging cold dewdrops from his hair. "Ella says I should entertain Gabriel for a few hours," he reported with a chuckle.

"She wants you to keep me out of sight, does she?" Gabe asked.

"Mmmm. She suggested that we wander towards Farwe's farm. Seems that one of the cows might have measles. Or maybe she said that one of the children was about to calf…"

Gabe laughed and grabbed his jacket. "Let's start walking, then." Turning to Hannah, he winked. "You have three hours."

"I'll be ready," she promised.

She had less than five minutes quiet before Hannah was inundated with orders. Ella and Nowatil had bustled through the front door just as the men left through the back. They were trailed by a dozen other elves who carried boxes, baskets or armloads of flowers.

"Hold still."

"Sit; drink this milk, fresh an hour ago."

"Stand up straight, Girl!"

"Lean this way."

Ull's three daughters bounced on the soft bed, giggling louder as the geriatric frame groaned. Mellie, authoritative at the ripe old age of eight, displayed a collection of sadly wrinkled hair ribbons. She elbowed her path to Hannah's side. "Sit so that I can brush your hair."

Ella immediately countermanded that instruction. Hands on hips, but eyes twinkling, she ordered, "Stand up, you'll wrinkle the petticoat."

Mairisi took the brush and re-arranged a couple of the bride's fly-away curls. "There, perfect."

Faeries fluttered around Hannah's face wielding powder puffs made of mimosa blossoms. Each of the diminutive females wore elaborate gossamer veils over conical headgear studded with gems. Each

437

faerie wore tiny bells. A faerie might wear golden bracelets at her wrists or ankles. She might close to sew a series of bells to her veils or her belt. With more than twenty faeries flitting about, the jingling and pinging was a syncopated music.

"Close you eyes, Hannah." Ella led her to the floor length mirror.

"Okay, open them," Nowatil and Ull chirped in unison.

Hannah gasped. She opened and closed her mouth, gulping air like a beached mackerel. She touched her cheek and watched the reflected image touch hers. She pivoted, wide skirt swaying to reveal a lacy petticoat sewn with tiny pearls and emeralds.

"What have you done to me?" Her green eyes were wide; startled-doe-in-the-headlights-wide.

The elves and faeries exchanged confused, hurt glances. Ella quieted their murmurs with a finger raised at her lips.

"What's wrong then, Girl? Tell us, so that we can change it."

"Wrong?" Hannah looked confused now. She tapped her mouth with fisted knuckles. "No. You don't understand. Don't change anything!" She pulled on Nowatil's shoulder because the tiny seamstress had knelt to inspect the hemline one more time. "Don't change anything," she spoke softly, words forming around the emotion clogged in her throat. "You've made me beautiful."

"Oh. That was easy. You were beautiful before we started." Ella looked around the room, daring anyone to disagree.

Nowatil tugged at the bodice of Hannah's dress, adjusting first one shoulder and then the other. She spoke while keeping six straight pins caught between her teeth. "All it took was a bit of pixie dust and the design Gabe selected for you!" She clapped her hands and a mist of silver sparkles glittered in the sunlight.

Hannah licked her parched lips a number of times before Tatiania, Queen of the Faeries, stopped her.

"My darling girl, you'll spoil the effect! Where is the romance of kissing cracked lips?"

Tatiania stilled her wings and glided like a ballerina to perch at the base of Hannah's thumb, shedding opalescent dust.

Hannah joked, "Shakespeare said 'Love looks not with the eyes, but with the mind.'"

"Gabriel's got a good mind; but he is a sensuous man." The Queen's voice was dulcet, "I would doubt that his love has destroyed his sense of touch!"

Faeries of the court tittered. Elfin women shared sidelong glances and sly winks. The children giggled, bouncing on the bed, tumbling pillows to the floor. The bed frame groaned, the faerie bells tinkled. Suddenly the room was confining. Hannah felt faint. She went to the window and rested her forehead against the cool, damp pane.

Ella clapped her hands. "Okay, everybody out. Let's give the bride a few moments, shall we? Meggy, Margy; help your sister carry flowers to the kitchen. Will you help us decorate?"

Then, miraculously, it was quiet in the disheveled bedroom. Mairisi touched Hannah's arm. "How about a spot of water, then?"

"Thanks." Hannah accepted the glass and sipped.

"We brought you a wedding gift, Ewan and I," Mairisi said. She proffered a brown box tied with twine. "It's a collection of bulbs for your garden. Plant them in the fall and watch the explosion of color in the spring! You, Gabe and the baby can enjoy the flowers together."

"Plant them in the fall and watch the explosion in the spring?" Hannah rubbed her temple.

"Yes. It's not a new concept." Mairisi joked.

Hannah struggled to smile at her friend. "A concept as old as time itself. Thank you, Marisi. It's a lovely gift."

"Wow! Never in my wildest dreams…" Gabe spoke from the doorway. He stepped into the room and Mairisi slipped out unnoticed. "Turn around," he said. "Let me see you."

The sheer dress billowed, then fell as Hannah swirled. The diaphanous material wreathed her body like a wisp of palest pink smoke. Although the neckline was hardly daring, it was cut low enough to show a bit of cleavage. The entire bodice was intricately beaded with pink seed pearls. Tiny emeralds winked between the tucks that molded the bodice to her body.

"You're gorgeous." He moved closer, stroked her cheek with his knuckle.

"I feel like Cinderella." She thought she sounded winded; as if she were panting for breaths. "And you, Sir, are more handsome than any storybook prince." She touched the pearls at her throat. "I am deliriously happy!"

"I hope I will always make you happy." Gabe toyed with one layer of her skirt, rubbing the sheer fabric between his thumb and fingers. "Do you like the dress?"

"Even the faeries are envious of this gown. I figure Nowatil will be busy creating tiny duplicates!"

"No other woman will do it justice."

"It's faerie glamour, I know. Still, I feel beuatiful."

Gabe fondled a couple of the pink pearls at her throat. "Are you ready, Love?"

"Yes."

He touched a fingertip to her lip. "I'll meet you in the garden, then."

He almost stumbled over Nowatil as he turned to leave.

The matron covered her eyes with age-freckled hands, and peeked through her fingers.

"Wasn't that the groom?" she squeaked.

442

"You know it was," Hannah giggled.

"Do you think he saw you, then?"

"Of course he saw me. Why?"

The elf shook her head back and forth with quick, jerky motions. "Oh no! That's terrible. Just terrible. It's bad luck, you know!"

Hannah laughed out loud. "Oh, that's just superstition!"

"Well of course, it's superstition; but that term covers what the humans call elves and faeries, doesn't it?"

"Well, yes, but…"

"But, nothing. Just as the wee folk are real, so is this danger. Something bad will happen, mark my words, something bad! Maybe not today, but someday!" She shook her finger at Hannah, then at the closed bedroom door. "You two should know better!"

A tiny voice in Hannah's mind mocked her. Something bad…maybe later, like in the Spring. Plant in the fall, see the results in the spring. She shivered although she could feel beads of perspiration forming at her hairline.

"Hannah, they're waiting," Ella called from the hallway.

At precisely eleven fifty-five, Hannah stood in the kitchen. Outside, over the gardens, a brilliant sun rose higher in the amazingly cloudless blue sky. Gabe had promised her a beautiful wedding day, though how he'd managed it, she'd likely never know. Summer flowers were in full bloom during these early days of autumn. Magenta blossom clusters bowed the rhododendron bushes and thousands of fallen petals dotted the stone walkway like confetti. Music bellowed from a calliope in the gazebo covered with ivy and vines lush with pink roses. She'd never seen either the gazebo or the calliope. Neither was in the yard a few hours ago when she'd eaten breakfast.

Da, da, da-da-da-da-da, daaa, daaa, daaaa. The bridal march! Ella nudged at the small of her back, and Hannah belatedly recognized her cue. Everyone in the yard turned, facing the porch to watch her. A few coughs; one sneeze and some muffled rustling; then a moment of complete silence. After a few seconds, the oppressive quiet was shattered by deep heart-thumping, ground-vibrating music.

The first step of her bridal march was monumental. She took a deep breath and smiled at Gabe, waiting at the far end of the white carpet. When had they carpeted the lawn? A wide silly grin was plastered on Gabe's face. Hannah touched her bottom lip with her tongue. Just testing for chapped lips.

The second step was much easier. Her own smile stretched. Third step, fourth and fifth. Several ladies waved or nodded a greeting as she passed. Hannah saw only Gabe. His grey eyes pulled her closer. Her smile stretched even wider.

I probably look like a Jack o' Lantern, she mused as she took her eighth and ninth steps. Her jaws were beginning to ache, but it felt good.

She was almost there. No more than three steps away. Gabe reached his hand to her. The Reverend touched her wrist, stopping her with no more pressure than that of a butterfly's landing.

"We are gathered here today to join this man," he inclined his head towards Gabe, "and this woman," he winked and nodded at Hannah, "in the bonds of holy matrimony." He looked out at the sea of faces, watched as the congregation settled into the wooden chairs. Children squirmed. Adults cleared their throats, crossed and uncrossed legs or whispered quietly.

Father Donor opened the huge Book of Common Prayer on the lectern; but without consulting it, he recited, "Marriage is not to be entered into unadvisedly or lightly, but reverently, deliberately, and in accordance with the purposes for which it was instituted by God."

Hannah's concentration floated, settling once again on Gabe's eyes. Donor touched her wrist one more time. She blinked and jerked her head back towards him.

"Who gives this woman to be married to this man?"

Hannah answered, "I come of my own free will."

The minister stepped back and Gabe edged closer, his right hand reaching to Hannah. She moved to him, turning her right hand to his. Every action seemed to be in slow motion, almost a freeze-frame sequence. The tips of their fingers touched. Hannah shivered and Gabe sucked air through his teeth.

Sensory overload, that's what it is, Hannah thought. My vision works perfectly well, but I can't hear or smell or think clearly. When he touches me, I practically black out. The sensation is almost too erotic to contemplate during a religious ceremony anyway!

She closed her eyes and smiled. A few words penetrated her consciousness. "I, Gabriel take you Hannah Marie…" He squeezed her hand gently and she opened her eyes. "…till death do us part, according to God's holy ordinance; and thereto I plight thee my troth." Her eyes drifted shut again.

She inhaled deeply. Father Donor's vestments held a lingering odor of incense burned days ago, the smell holding mystery and pious ceremony. Tall white candles burned in candelabras stationed around the garden. How do you describe the aroma of melting wax? She inhaled again. Gabe had his own signature smell; exotic clove and citrus; lemon, maybe, and the mint that he chewed. His kisses tasted like mint. She touched her tongue to her bottom lip again and opened her eyes.

He was smiling at her. Can he read my mind? she wondered.

With his free hand, he touched her lips very gently, very quickly with his index finger.

Does he know what I'm thinking of right now? she wondered as mentally she stripped him naked.

447

He squeezed her hand and titled his head towards Donor O'Kierney, who was obviously waiting for a reply.

"I do?" she hazarded a response.

"Do you, then?" the minister teased, wrinkles gathering at the corners of his eyes.

Hannah turned to face Gabe. She spoke quietly, but clearly. Persons seated in the first several rows could hear her words well. "Forever and ever, amen."

Gabe reached into his jacket pocket. He dropped a small golden circlet into the minister's hand. Donnor stared at his open palm, his lips pressed tightly together. He closed his fingers over the golden ring and laid his fist over his heart. Then, he nodded and smiled.

Donor whispered a blessing and waved his right hand over the ring in the sign of the cross. "Bless, O Lord, this ring that he who gives it and she who wears it may abide in thy peace, and continue in thy favor, unto their life's end; through Jesus Christ our Lord. And may their lives be touched by a love as enduring as she who wore it and he who gave it before. Amen."

He handed the ring back to Gabe and whispered, "Your Mother would be pleased to watch you give her ring to your bride."

Gabe slipped it on Hannah's finger. She glanced at the intricate design, interlocking porpoise, seals and starfish, circling her fourth finger. With her thumb, she caressed the band.

Donnor rushed through the blessing. Mr. Gabriel Edward Murray proudly turned to present his beautiful new wife to the congregation of close friends; smiling humans and tittering elves. His palm rested at the small of her back, warm and reassuring. His index finger wiggled between two covered buttons and insinuated itself under the silk of her panties, enervating but sensuous.

Ella orchestrated the reception. She bustled around the yard, instructing elves to set up tables and chairs, pointing to the lanterns that would be lit at sunset. Wiping her hands on her ruffled apron, she directed the food service, too. Trays of warm canapés were carried by a procession of pretty redheaded pixies. Ull hefted a four-tiered cake decorated with crystallized rose petals and swirls of creamy white frosting. Sean delivered a massive bucket, filled with bottles of icy cold ale. A pint flask peeped out of his back pocket.

"Follow me," Gabe whispered to Hannah.

He led her to the small entry hall closet, which housed a broom, several overcoats, a pair of muddy galoshes, two umbrellas and a poncho someone had forgotten. Stepping inside, he put his finger to his lips. "Ssssh."

Before Hannah could chuckle, his mouth had covered hers. He held her cheeks, his thumbs tickling the corners of her mouth.

"If we stay here in the dark much longer, we'll miss the reception entirely!" she said.

"That's okay with me," Gabe answered as he bent his head for another kiss.

"Ella and the others would be disappointed, don't you think?"

"Probably," he said although he continued his sweet assault on her neck.

"Hmmm," Hannah muttered, craning her neck to allow him better access. "That would be irresponsible behavior," she said, circling his ear with the tip of her finger. "I've never known you to behave irresponsibly." She traced her lips with her tongue.

"I've never had a wife who harbors lascivious thoughts during solemn ceremonies." He mumbled because his lips were busy planting rows of kisses across her collarbone.

"I've never had a husband who inspires them," she laughed.

That laugh was their undoing. Suddenly the door flew open! The cramped closet was illuminated by bright sunlight. Mellie shouted, "Found 'em!"

"If it's hide and seek, I guess you're 'it' now, Gabe," Hannah told him as she straightened his collar.

"Don't worry, I'll catch you again later!" his laugh rumbled as the elfin girls grabbed his hands to lead him outside.

Almost like magic, Sean materialized at Hannah's side.

"Where did you come from?" she teased.

Sean casually wrapped an arm around her waist, chatting as he escorted her to the reception, which was well underway without either the bride or groom.

"I had a feeling that there might be a bit of mischief afoot." He winked. "Being Gabriel's da, I thought I'd best see to his woman!"

"Oh, I see," she quipped. She quickly scanned the multitude gathered at the buffet tables, looking for possible scamps who might decide to try a prank or two. Heaven only knew what the pixies might try!

"Will there be bawdy wedding toasts?" she asked with noted apprehension.

Sean held both sides of his stomach and chuckled. "Can a Scot drink whisky?" he asked rhetorically.

He flicked the tip of her nose with his finger, and smiled when she blushed.

Across the lawn, Gabe watched his father tease his bride. A sea of friends and neighbors crowded close to congratulate him. Old David pumped Gabe's hand and slapped him on the back. Brian Gregory, a good-humored young elf, elbowed Gabe's side and offered an off-color joke about sheep. Winnie, Carwig's young sister, wrapped both arms and legs around his left thigh. Now, she clung to him like a baby opossum to a mother. But Gabe granted them only cursory attention. He watched Hannah.

He watched as she accepted a limp daisy, pulled up by the roots, from a red-haired boy with grass stains on his best knee-length trousers. She sat for a moment to listen to a tale from Nigel, a white-haired elf who lost an arm during a disagreement with a raccoon. Three years ago, he lost his wife to cancer. Hannah kissed his cheek and left Nigel with a quivering smile and a tear in his eye.

Shaking his leg loose of the giggling elfin toddler, Gabe hurried to catch his new wife. He swung Hannah into the dance area and the elfin instruments generated an odd assortment of belches and tooting noises that somehow blended to become a pleasing sound approximating music.

They laughed, dancing together while sniggering elves cavorted in the flowerbeds, turning somersaults and swilling warm champagne. Hours later, the food was gone – even the crumbs had been eaten. The musicians had exchanged their instruments for a cup of ale. Mothers tried to corral drunken husbands and sleepy children.

Mairisi punched Gabe's bicep. "Be good to this woman or you'll answer to me!" She kissed his cheek and then she hugged Hannah.

"He's a good man, kind and gentle. But, bear in mind that he is a man, after all. You'll have to patient with him and explain things to him slowly. So many things women know inherently but men just never understand! Should he give you any trouble, let me know." She winked. "Together, I'm sure we can straighten him out!"

Hannah giggled, "I'll do my best, Mairisi."

"*Slainte mhath*!" Ewan shouted, raising his glass high overhead.

"*Slainte*," everyone answered.

Hannah patted her belly and whispered, "Good health to us all."

Ewan draped one arm over Hannah's shoulder. He cuffed Gabe's jaw with his knuckles. "Most of your guests have wandered off. Reverend Donor and I have polished off the Glenfiddich with Sean's assistance. A kiss for the bride and then I'm off to supper with these two rascals." He tipped his head towards Trog and Sean.

Sean hugged Gabe, pounding his back. "Congratulations, son." He pecked a kiss on Hannah's cheek. "God keep you both, and give you many happy years together. *A bheanachd*, my blessing."

"Alone at last," Gabe whispered. He dipped his head to her ear, tickling her with his breath.

"I will love you forever, Hannah Everett Murray. Maybe longer. Probably longer."

Two or three clouds hung low in the afternoon sky. Each pale blue cloud was outlined with light the color of molten gold. Hannah closed her eyes. "Can you hear them?"

"The angels? Yes. They're singing love songs just for us."

Hannah raised her arms. "Dance with me?"

Gabe wrapped his left arm round her waist and pulled her close. Her left hand touched his shoulder. Their joined right hands were tucked under the lapel of his jacket. They didn't really waltz, just swayed side-to-side. But, Hannah was dancing on air. For the first time all day, she felt at ease. Maybe it had been pre-wedding jitters, but she'd been nervous. Like there was something important she'd forgotten. The anxiety was forgotten now. Gabe was here and he had promised to love her and her baby. They'd be all right. She sighed and snuggled even closer.

"Sun's gone. Concert's over for tonight," he spoke soft breaths into her hair. "Let's go inside."

"Just a minute more." She climbed atop his shoes, stood on tiptoes to kiss him. "I don't want the moment to end." She nibbled his neck, just below his left ear.

Gabe twirled, Hannah still perched on his shoes. Her dress drifted around her like a vapor. "Then, this moment will go on and on and on," he chuckled. She threw back her head and laughed.

"And there in the wood a Piggy-wig stood, with a ring at the end of his nose. His nose. His nose. With a ring at the end of his nose."

"What are you doing here, Aidan?" Gabe's velvet voice barely sheathed the steely daggers of his eyes.

Aidan lounged in the darkened gazebo, a half-empty glass of champagne in one hand, a small chunk of cake in the other. "I was invited, you remember?"

Gabe bunched his fingers into fists. "The party's over. Eat your cake and be gone."

Aidan ate the piece of cake and drained the glass. "But I haven't kissed the bride."

Gabe growled and Hannah held his sleeve. "It's good of you to come and wish us well," she said although she didn't think the sentiment rang true.

Aidan sauntered closer. He touched her arm, circled her wrist with his fingers and leaned close to her face. He inhaled, his breath moving hairs at her temple. She turned her head at just the right time and his lips merely brushed her cheek. "May I have this dance?" he asked, stepping back a bit.

"Perhaps another time," Hannah answered.

"Probably never," Gabe grunted through clenched teeth.

"There will be another time, another place." When he left the garden, Aidan let the gate slam shut.

"We cannot dine on mince or slices of quince like the Owl and the Pussy Cat, but we can dance by the light of the moon. The moon. The moon. We can dance by the light of the moon."

And so they did.

Streams of morning sunlight shot through the lace curtains, dappling the bedroom floor with wavering patterns.

"What will you call our daughter?" Hannah asked when Gabe stroked the small tight bulge low on her abdomen.

"*A leannan.*"

"Lianne?"

"No, *a leannan means* sweetheart, sweet baby daughter."

Hannah rubbed the tiny mound of her baby and smiled.

"That's wonderful. *A leannan.* What would you call a son?"

"That's easy. I'll call him what Da calls me. *Mo ghille*, my boy, my lad."

"*Mo ghille,*" she repeated, practicing the taste of the words on her tongue.

Gabe squeezed her shoulders. "You will always be *Mo chridhe.*"

She smiled, "My heart." She covered his heart with her palm. "I love you," she whispered.

"I know."

Breakfast was a quiet affair. Just the two of them, for a change. Trog was escorting Sean, Ewan, Mairisi and Father Donnor back to Skye. Hannah wondered about the stories they would report to

458

Floodigarry. How would they explain travel without passports or airplanes? Did they have no memories of the magnificent faerie court or the raucous elves? Could she could stay here, cocooned in the safety of the faerie raft, forever?

"Daydreaming Hannah? I asked what you'd like to do today."

"Go back to Carver's Hollow."

Gabe dropped the saucer he was drying. It hit the floor and cracked into splinters of porcelain.

"Repeat that!" he croaked.

"I need to confront my rapists," Hannah's mouth was a taut line.

She knelt to retrieve the broken pieces scattered at their feet. Gabe crouched to grab her arm.

"Leave that." He closed his eyes and took a deep breath. He whispered, "Just leave it for now." He stood. Her bottom lip quivered and he kissed her cheek. "Okay?"

"Okay."

Gabe sat in a straight-backed kitchen chair, and pulled her to sit in his lap. She sat; straight-backed as the chair, tense. He wrapped his arms around her waist, resting his hands in her lap. She relaxed and they both took a deep breath.

"Okay?" he asked, skimming his finger along her jaw.

She smiled weakly and nodded.

"You took me by surprise there. Start at the beginning, will you? Just spur of the moment, you decide to spend your honeymoon tracking rapists?"

"Well, of course I do. It's the only way I can close this whole ordeal. Don't you see?"

His shoulders flinched slightly. His nostrils flared. His eyebrows scrunched together.

"NO. NO, I don't see. Why don't you explain?"

Hannah rubbed her knuckles. She picked at the ragged cuticle of her left thumb. She licked her lips and squirmed, shifting her weight from her right hip to the left.

"The idea came to me yesterday, sort of in bits and pieces."

Sorry. I had other things on my mind yesterday, Hannah."

She touched his lips with her fingers.

"Wait, let me tell you."

He nodded. "Okay."

"It really started when Mairisi gave me the box of flowers bulbs."

"Flower bulbs?" She tapped his lips again.

"She said we should plant them in the fall and wait for the explosion of color in the spring."

"So?"

"Plant them in the fall and wait for the explosion in the spring…I remembered Scar saying almost the exact same thing. But he was talking about bombs, I think." Hannah stood. She twisted the dishtowel around her knuckles. She paced to the sink and turned around. "I think he plans to plant some bombs around the university in order to draw attention to his group." She polished a damp mixing bowl with the dishtowel, then tossed the cloth on the counter. "Then Nowatil said that if the groom sees the bride before the wedding, there would be bad luck. Not right away, she said. Maybe in the spring." Hannah knelt between Gabe's knees, hooked her fingers through his belt and pulled it. "I've got to warn someone…the police, I guess."

"All right."

Hannah sniffed away annoying tears that threatened to escape. She blinked twice and stared at the ceiling for a few seconds.

461

"I suffered during my captivity. But, Gabe, it doesn't end. Even now that I'm safe, I can't stop the memories."

Gabe shuddered and she turned to look at him. The track of a single tear glistened on his cheek. He cupped her chin between his palms. His corduroy voice scratched like sandpaper. "I'm so sorry, Love." His head rested on hers. "I would take your pain if I could."

"I know that. I know," she whispered. She lifted his hand that lay limp in her lap. Turning her left palm up, she sandwiched his hand between the two of hers. "You share my pain. That's enough. That's more than enough."

He kissed her temple.

"The way I see it, we need to clear away the past to make room for our future as a family," she said. "I need to file a report with the police. I need to make the accusation and see if they can find the rapists."

Gabe nodded. "Okay."

"They're dangerous men," Hannah said. "Part of a hate group. I don't have any particulars; but I vaguely recall a conversation. I'm afraid they're planning some sort of bomb." She massaged her temples. "I just don't remember anything clearly. It's all so jumbled together."

She stood again, this time wandering to the window. She stared out at the garden, where several faeries taunted butterflies.

Gabe placed his hands on her shoulders, and she turned to face him.

"Whatever you decide, I'll be with you," he said. "I'll face Satan himself if that's what you want."

She rubbed his stubbled jaw with her palm. "Let's hope that isn't necessary!" She started to smile, but covered her mouth with her hand. "Satan...hell...That's it! The group. It's Hell's something. Hell's Demons. Hell's Minions. Hell's...ummm...I dunno. I can't remember!"

"It's all right, Hannah. We'll leave today. We'll make the report and get you some answers." Gabe traced the wrinkle between her brows. His thumbs massaged her temples. "Go pack a few things. Rest your mind a bit."

When Ella waddled into the bedroom, Hannah was trying to fold a sweater. She just couldn't make her hands work properly. She shook the sweater, smoothed out the wrinkles and began again. The elf settled herself in a comfy chair near the window. She pulled a ball of yarn and a pair of knitting needles from a pocket in her cloak. As the needles click-clacked, the yarn became a tiny yellow cap.

"Are you ill, then, Hannah?"

As if shocked by the question, Hannah turned abruptly.

"No. Of course not, why do you ask?"

"You've been staring into the drawer for several minutes. Looking for something in particular?"

"Ummm… What? No. I'm distracted this morning. That's all. Thank you for your concern, though, Ella."

The elf rubbed the circle of gold dolphins that Hannah wore. "We all love you, Hannah. Let us help you; give you strength when you need it."

Hannah nodded. "I know. I will. I do. Thank you."

"I understand your need to make this trip. Hopefully, you'll be able to purge the awful memories." Ella's fingers were like oak branches; gnarled but strong. She gripped Hannah's wrist. "Find the men who hurt you. Their punishment will be justified. But remember this. Revenge will never be sweet. It's a bitter taste that can poison your heart and mind."

"I have to make a report to the police, incomplete as it might be. Until I make a formal statement, this nightmare will never end." Hannah rubbed her eyes. "Whether or not the police believe my story, whether or not they find the rapists, I need to tell them."

Gabe was behind her. He supported her when her shoulders shuddered. "It's a brave thing you do. So many rapes go unreported because the victims are too scared, too embarrassed, too traumatized by the ordeal."

Ella shook her finger at him. "You care for Hannah and the bairn."

His deep voice rumbled through Hannah's whole body.

"*Mo chridhe.*"

Autumn was burgeoning in the North Carolina foothills. Poplars were a riot of bright yellow leaves and maples blazed crimson. Curbsides in Carver's Hollow were piled with leaves that rambunctious boys found captivating.

"Magnolia House," Gabe said. "Appropriate name!"

Together, he and Hannah negotiated the walk that was littered with leathery leaves. Flowerpots on either side of the steps were overflowing with bright magenta-colored mums.

"The house is charming. Looks like it's made of gingerbread," Gabe chatted.

Hannah answered with a small smile. "Gingerbread. That would be a plus as far as you're concerned, wouldn't it?"

"Especially when the porch has been decorated with curlicues of white frosting." Hannah nibbled her bottom lip. She fretted with her tousled curls for a moment.

"We probably should have called for a reservation."

Gabe smiled and pressed the doorbell. Hannah stepped back, stood behind him. She threaded her fingers through his belt and held on tight. They heard a voice call from the back of the house.

"Coming!"

"I doubt they're full up right now," he assured her.

A tall, slender woman opened the door wide. "I'm Maggie. Can I help you?"

Hannah peeked around Gabe's arm. " Maggie, do you remember me? This is my husband, Gabriel."

Maggie pumped Hannah's arm with each statement, like punctuation.

"Of course! Of course, I remember you! Got married, did you? That's grand. Just grand."

She turned to clutch Gabe's hand.

"Con-gra-tu-la-tions. My, my. How grand!"

She turned from one of them to the other, smiling. Gabe cleared his throat and started to speak, but Maggie interrupted.

"Sit. Sit."

She patted the plump chintz cushions arranged on the antique love seat.

"Sit."

Gabe sat. He appeared comically large on the small furniture. Hannah stood at his side and asked, "Do you have any rooms available? We have business here in town that should take a day or two."

"Oh. How grand. Of course, of course I have a room for you. It's a bit more expensive than before, since there are two of you now.

But, the room is big. There's a queen-sized bed and large windows that face the backyard. I think you'll like it."

"That sounds lovely. Thank you, Maggie," Gabe said.

"Come along then," Maggie answered as she started up the staircase. "While you two get settled, I'll get you a bite to eat. I've got soup simmering just now. How 'bout I ladle a bowl for each of you?"

Hannah stared into the dressing table mirror. Her eyes were more gray than green, her mouth was drawn into a tight smile, and she was flushed. She dabbed her forehead with a damp tissue. She feared she would be sick.

"Maybe some soup would be nice," Gabe smiled to Maggie. "Thank you."

"No. No, I just don't think I can eat a thing. Thank you for the thought, though. We really do need to see to our business as soon as possible," Hannah interrupted.

Gabe shrugged his shoulders and winked at Maggie.

"Later, then. Okay?"

Maggie left while Hannah rearranged the figurines on the dressing table.

"Hannah?" Gabe's voice was just above a whisper.

She faced the mirror, but looked at his reflection there.

"Oh, Gabe. I'm so very scared." She covered her mouth with her hand, almost as if she tried to recapture those words.

He opened his arms wide and she turned into his hug.

"I'll be right there with you. You're not alone anymore, Love. There's the two of us now."

She held him tight for a few seconds, then pushed away. She rubbed a place low on her abdomen and said, "Two for now. Soon to be three."

About an hour later, they stood in front of a neat one-story brick building. Mulch was carefully piled at the base of the boxwood bushes lined up under a row of windows at the front. A cheerful orange and yellow striped awning hung above the glass doors, which swung open to release a cluster of uniformed policemen. A traffic officer, dressed in drab green, parked her odd three-wheeled vehicle at

the curb. She pulled her notebook from her front pocket and jotted a
few notes.

"Are you ready?" Gabe's fingertips touched the small of Hannah's back.

"As ready as I'll ever be." Hannah chewed her bottom lip and
smoothed the blouse over her abdomen. Inhale. Exhale. Inhale. She
took a giant step and pushed through the glass doors, marching up to
the information desk.

A pleasant officer, someone's genial grandfather, sat behind
the bank of noisy telephones and radios that blinked red, yellow and
blue lights. In such a small, peaceful town, Hannah was surprised that
the police station would be such a bevy of activity. She waited until
the pleasant gentleman had recorded a caller's information regarding a
stolen bicycle.

"How can I help you, Miss?"

Hannah cleared her throat. Her fingers twitched at her side.
Gabe twined his fingers around her left hand.

"I want to report a rape," she squeaked. Her words were barely
audible. She cleared her throat again.

The gentleman had stepped around the desk, moving to her right side. He leaned his ear close to her.

"A rape," she stated clearly. "I want to report a rape."

Activity in the busy room halted. It was as if someone had pressed the mute button. The teenager stopped making excuses to his mother about a traffic ticket. His mouth dropped open and the pink traffic violation floated to the floor at his feet.

A man with uncombed hair was collecting his belongings after a drunken night's antics sent him to jail. A penny rolled across the Formica as he raked the handful of coins off the counter and stuffed them in the pocket of his wrinkled khaki slacks. He stared at Gabe and Hannah with bleary eyes.

Two men were laughing at a cartoon poster taped above the coffeemaker. The fellow with dark circles under his eyes scratched his neck said, "Breaks over. Gerald, go help that little lady, will you?"

The taller man crumpled his empty soda can and arched it towards the wastebasket. "Sure thing, Cap'n."

Gerald ambled across the lobby. He cocked his head, signaling his partner to join him. Together, the men approached Hannah and Gabe.

"I'm Detective Gerald Wurst," he said, extending his hand to Hannah. "This is my partner, Richard Wright."

Detective Wright nodded. The overhead light bounced reflections on his bald head.

"Maybe you'd be more comfortable if we continue this discussion in private."

Gerald pointed to a room with tinted glass walls. Hannah decided that it might be sound-proof, but it was definitely not private.

"I doubt that there is a way to make this conversation comfortable," she said under her breath as she followed the detectives.

"Take a seat," Detective Wurst mumbled as he dragged a heavy metal chair, bumping the badly scarred table leg.

The sound set Hannah's teeth on edge. When she sat, she pressed her palms flat on the table. Gabe moved his chair closer to her's. He leaned close and whispered, "I'm right here with you, Love. Right here."

She glanced at him and gave him an almost imperceptible nod. She scraped her bottom lip with her front teeth and released a long, slow breath.

Detective Wright leaned a shoulder against the wall, next to the closed door. He appeared relaxed, arms crossed just above his stomach, where the buttons of his faded blue denim shirt strained to meet. Gerald Wurst straddled his chair; his long legs spread wide. He reached long arms over the chair's back, which faced the table.

"Need anything? Water? Coffee? A smoke?"

Hannah shook her head. "Let's just get started, shall we? This is very difficult for me."

"Okay, then." Gerald leaned forward, swirling designs in the sweat of the soda can he'd placed on the table. A puddle had formed. He opened a ring binder. Looking at the blank page, he rolled a ballpoint pen between his palms. "Name?"

"Hannah. Hannah Everett Murray." She glanced at Gabe. "This is my husband, Gabriel."

Gerald did not even look up from his yellow pad. "Right. Address?"

Hannah shifted in her seat. She pushed on the tabletop so hard that her nails gouged tiny pocks in the wood. She looked to Gabe who winked at her.

"Well, up until late May, I lived at 303 Marsh Lane in Beaufort. North Carolina. Beaufort, North Carolina. I still own the property, but my house was destroyed. I've been staying with friends for the past few months."

"House burned, you say?"

"Yes. There was an awful lightning storm. Luckily I was outside on the deck, it all happened fast. I think my propane tank got hit. I don't know. There was some sort of explosion and the house burned to the ground."

Detective Wurst turned to Richard Wright and jerked his head, implying, "Check the facts later, will you?"

"Go on."

"I'm an artist. My work is handled by Pierside Peddler Gallery, in Beaufort. But, I have done several large canvases and some frescoes for corporations up and down the East coast." Hannah shrugged her shoulders and rocked her head side to side. She hissed out another long breath. "Just last month, I was in Carver's Hollow to paint a fresco in the Children's Wing of University Hospital." She

looked from Wurst to Wright. It was as if each of them wore masks;

neutral faces. Neither of them showed any sign of interest whatsoever.

"While I was here, I stayed at the Magnolia House, over on

Dayton Drive. That's where we are staying now."

Wurst scribbled in his legal pad. "Okay."

"After working for several weeks, I had finally completed the

fresco. It was early evening. I was in the pedestrian tunnel. You

know, the tunnel beside the book store that ends up at the backside of

the subdivision." Hannah shifted in her chair again. She fidgeted with

a thread that had sprouted from a seam in her pants leg.

"Why were you in the tunnel?"

"I was leaving town, heading home."

"Walking?"

"Walking to the highway. Yes."

"Why not drive or take a bus?"

"Is it against the law to walk?"

Gerald pursed his lips, shrugged his shoulders. "Nuh huh."

She crossed her ankles, then immediately separated them and

wrapped each foot around a chair leg.

"You'd just finished several weeks' work. Did you have the paycheck in your possession?"

"The work was gratis, Detective."

Gabe massaged a small circle at her shoulder blade.

"Okay; so you were in the tunnel," Gerald said.

"It was dark, not pitch dark, but darker than usual. Maybe a bulb had burned out; I dunno, but the tunnel was very dim. Lots of shadows." She looked up at the detectives again.

"Go on," Richard Wright said. It was the first time he'd spoken. His voice was deep and rough, like he was a chronic smoker. Sort of a Kris Kristopherson voice - lazy and soothing.

"This is very difficult," Hannah said softly. She hung her head. "Very difficult." She inhaled and sat up straight. "I heard a commotion, an argument, outside the tunnel. Voices got louder. Closer. I was frightened and I hid behind one of the pillars, in the shadows. It was a pretty big group of people..."

Gerald Wurst looked up from his paper, pen in hand. "How big? How many people...approximately?"

Hannah counted silently, moving her fingers in her lap. "I'm not sure, fifteen, maybe eighteen."

"Okay."

"Anyway, a fight broke out. People were being shoved. I really don't remember too much, because I got hit on the head. I remember feeling the jolt. After that, nothing."

The detectives exchanged looks. Richard Wright shifted positions to sit at the table, opposite Gabe. Gerald Wurst rubbed the bridge of his nose. Then he leaned back a bit and scratched his underarm.

Hannah exhaled a long stream of anxiety. "I must have passed out. I came to in what I think is a dorm room."

"Out in the lobby, you mentioned a rape."

"Yes. Although it's been a bit more than a month, I've come forward to report a rape."

"You're telling me you woke up today and suddenly recalled being raped?"

Gabe shifted in his chair, leaning forward, resting his forearms on the table. His eyes were very dark. His voice was steely calm.

"Let my wife tell you what happened, Detective. It's a long, frightening story for her. She's brave to come forward. I'm certain you policemen realize that very few rape victims do. Because rape is a stigma to its victims, the rapists frequently go unpunished."

Wurst shrugged his shoulders, held his palms out to his sides. "You're right, of course. My apologies, M'am. Continue, if you will."

Hannah reached for Gabe. She tucked her fingers into the bend of his elbow. She cleared her throat. "I think I was held in a dorm here on campus."

Richard Wright proded, "Can you describe the room?"

"Dirty. Littered with fast food wrappers and soiled clothes. There was a big poster - a picture of a drooling dragon with orange eyes – day-glo orange. He was crushing a school bus filled with terrified children. Anti-religious poster. I remember a menorah and a crucifix and the dragon."

Again, the detectives exchanged a knowing look.

"Okay. Go on." Wurst was filling page after page with his scrawling cursive.

"Um. Well. It took me a while to wake up. I was confused. I had no idea where I was." Hannah shook her head. "I still don't know! I was stripped almost naked. Lots of cuts and bruises."

Hannah touched her mouth, rubbed her lips. She struggled to swallow. Richard Wright poured water into a Styrofoam cup and offered it to her. She sipped the tepid water and placed the cup on the table. She was intent on placing the cup exactly in the center of a pre-existing water ring.

"My underpants were missing," she whispered.

Gerald Wurst tilted an ear in her direction. "Can you repeat that statement, please?"

Gabe arched a brow and exhaled noisily.

Hannah stared at the ceiling for a moment. She blinked a few times, then she leveled her gaze directly at the detective.

"My underpants were missing. My crotch was lacerated. A sticky white residue dried on my inner thighs." She glared at him, daring him to question her further. "Is that what you wanted to know, Detective Wurst?"

Silence followed. Hannah's heart raced. A thin line of perspiration dotted her forehead and upper lip. Gabe chewed his tongue. Gerald Wurst drummed the yellow legal pad with his pen. Richard Wright jotted a few words on a slip of paper and slid it across the table to his partner.

The chair groaned when Detective Wurst stood to pace. Nibbling the tip of his ballpoint, he whirled to face Hannah.

"You talk about rape, but you haven't mentioned a rapist."

She glared at him. "Rapists. Plural. There were two men."

Wurst bent over his paper, writing. "Go on."

"One of the men was stocky, his head was shaved. He had a very distinctive scar."

"Distinctive-how so?"

Hannah licked her lips again. She took another sip of water. "Well, it was very long. A very long, thin white scar." She touched her upper lip, just to the left of center. "It started here and went across his jaw." She moved her finger, mapping the route of his scar. "and up into his left earlobe."

Richard Wright was nodding as she spoke.

"Tell us what you remember about the other man, Hannah."

"Leonard. His name is Leonard. He was smaller, more slender. His features were almost delicate; not pretty, but somehow more feminine than Scar's. He had limp, dirty blond hair. About this long." She touched her shoulder. "He wore it in a ponytail bound with a dark leather thong." She took a deep breath. "He didn't say much, but he watched everything."

Richard Wright rubbed his shiny head. "That description could match about three hundred students on campus. Nothing significant to identify him?"

"He had a tattoo."

Richard sat on the table facing Hannah's chair.

"Where?"

"On his right hand. He had a snake tattooed on his hand. Here." She tapped the back of her hand near her thumb.

Gerald tapped his legal pad. "Okay. You come to, you're in the room with these two men who rape you. Then what?"

"I blacked out several times. I only have pieces of memories."

She slumped in the chair. Gabe reached to wrap his arm around her shoulders.

"Do you want to stop, Love?" he whispered.

"No. I've begun. I have to finish this. Once and for all." Her words were breathy and soft.

"I remember being assaulted by two men at the same time. I was forced to take one man's penis in my mouth while the other man entered me from behind."

She scrubbed at her eyes with her knuckles. Richard Wright produced a large box of stiff white tissues. Hannah grabbed a handful and dabbed at tears.

"And then…"

Hannah glared at Gerald Wurst.

She spoke each word slowly and succinctly, "and then I guess I passed out. When I was next conscious, I was alone."

"Alone? These two men kidnap you, rape you, then leave you alone?"

"Yes."

"And that's when you escaped?"

"No. I tried to escape, but I couldn't."

"Couldn't?"

"That's right. I couldn't. I tried to open the door. I crawled over and pulled myself up because I heard people outside, in the hall. The knob turned; but the door was bolted from the other side. I beat on the door and called out to them, but apparently no one heard me.

Next I went to the window and banged on it. I wrapped my hand in a quilt from the bed and hit the window as hard as I could. The glass bent, but wouldn't break."

"Plexiglass," Richard Wright explained. "The college replaced a lot of window panes with plexi to avoid damage."

"Well, it doesn't break," Hannah agreed. "I tried to raise the window, but it had been painted shut."

Hannah shredded the tissues in her hand, dropping the debris in her lap. Her throat ached and her head was pounding. She lifted her hair from her perspiring neck and breathed slowly, in and out.

"I found a scrap of paper. I wrote a note. I slipped it under the door, out into the hall."

"What'd the note say?"

Hannah rubbed her temples, shook her head and pursed her lips together.

"Umm. I can't remember exactly. Something like SOS I'm being held in a room with a lock outside. Help me. I signed it, too. Hannah Everett." She looked at Richard, "I wasn't married then."

Gerald Wurst resumed his pacing. He popped the tab on his soda. Hannah watched the tiny sparks of effervescence leap through the opening. The detective slurped loudly as he swallowed. His Adam's apple bounced with each gulp. He crunched the can and spun around, aiming for the wastebasket in the far corner of the room. It clattered against the rim of the basket and dropped on discarded paper wads.

Gerald straightened up and turned back to the group at the table. "Okay, now." Hand in the air, he folded down a finger each time he recounted a fact. "You came to town to paint a fresco at the hospital."

"Yes."

"You hid in the darkened tunnel when you heard the angry crowd approaching."

"Yes."

"You got hit on the head."

"Yes."

"You wake up minus most of your clothing in what you THINK is a dorm room."

"Yes."

"You THINK you remember being violated."

Hannah nodded.

"You THINK you passed out."

She nodded again.

"You THINK you were locked inside this room. You tried unsuccessfully to escape. Am I right so far?"

"Pretty close."

"Your story is filled with more holes than a colander. You don't even remember much about the fire that destroyed your house."

"What does the fire have to do with the rape?" Gabe asked.

Gerald shrugged. "You passed out in the tunnel."

"I was hit on the head; but yes, I passed out."

"And you blacked out periodically during your alleged captivity."

"Yes."

"Very convenient." Gerald scratched the bridge of his nose.

Hannah stood. She squeezed her hands together and her knuckles were white. "Convenient? You think so, do you?" She was close to tears and her voice was shrill and cracked.

"Just telling it like it is." Gerald shook his head, held up his hands. "Okay. I'm just curious here. How did you get away?"

Gabe pushed his chair away from the table and stood beside Detective Wurst. The detective was over six feet, but Gabe was a good two inches taller. The detective had wide shoulders and a trim waist; Gabe was younger and a bit more muscular.

"That's where I come in, Detective." He crossed his arms at his chest.

"White knight gallops in, huh?"

"Something like that."

"How'd you know where she was?"

"I have my ways, Detective." Gabe backed up one step. He rested his hands on Hannah's shoulders. "Even before we were married, Hannah and I lived together. We are very close."

Gabe and Detective Wurst stared at one another for ten long, long seconds. Hannah reached up to touch Gabe's wrist, rested her cheek on his hand.

"Hannah was scheduled to return from Carver's Hollow. When she didn't arrive on time, I was worried." He touched his forehead with his index finger. "I could feel that something was wrong."

"You could feel that something was wrong? You could feel it?"

"Yes. We have a connection. I could feel it." He tapped at his breastbone. "I searched for her."

"Sounds like you'd make one helluva detective."

Gabe shrugged.

Wurst flipped the pen, twirling it like a baton round and round his fingers.

"So, using your psychic powers, you determine she's in this unspecified dorm room. What'd ya do? Knock on the door?"

"Not exactly." Gabe looked at his hands. "I went to the dorm. I was in the hall when I heard Hannah cry out. I kicked the door in. Pretty sure I broke all the hinges."

"Bet that was quite an entrance. What happened then?"

"Two men left in a bit of a hurry. One fellow left without his trousers." Gabe smiled a wicked smile. "Hannah was my main concern. She was in bad shape."

"Where'd you go? To the hospital?"

"No. I'm trained in medicine. A friend and I cared for her."

"Um hmm. Can I talk to this friend?"

"If necessary." Gabe reached into his back pocket. He withdrew a folded paper and flipped it open. He gave it to Gerald. "This is her statement."

Richard Wright came to stand alongside his partner. Together they read Ella's notes.

"Dr. Ella, huh? Where's her practice?"

"Not doctor. Not a physician. She lives close by. I can get her, if necessary. She's very knowledgeable."

"Uh huh. Contusions, lacerations, traces of semen, stitches, swellings, concussions... Seems like a pretty thorough statement."

Richard Wright tapped Hannah's shoulder. She flinched under his light touch.

"Have to ask you one more thing," he said. "What made you wait so long? Why report the deed now?"

Hannah used a few moments to collect her thoughts. She took a breath and said, "I, um, I needed..." But, then she stopped. She looked at Gabe. She looked at Richard. She avoided Gerald's eyes. "Flashes of recall are almost worst than the deed. I need to close this ordeal. I can't go on this way."

Richard Wurst interrupted. His face was mere inches from hers. "Do you think making this report will make your life any easier?"

She closed her eyes, squeezing out two big tears. She collected the mangled tissue pieces and blotted at her cheeks. She touched her nose with her knuckle.

"I fight those two men night after night in my dreams. I wake up screaming! The most innocent thing can trigger a flood of horrible memories!" She whispered, "I'd try most anything to escape … to return to my normal life." She buried her face in her hands. Her shoulders shook as she sobbed.

Gabe urged her to stand. "Go wash your face, Love. Take a break."

He led her to the door, opened it and pointed to the ladies room across the hall. "Go on. I'll wait for you." He kissed her cheek and she nodded.

As soon as she'd left the room, he closed the door. His hands were fisted at his sides. His eyes were cold and hard, flinty gray.

"What's going on here, Detectives? Hannah is the victim. V-I-C-T-I-M. What are you implying?"

Gerald rubbed his chin. Richard looked embarrassed.

"You gotta admit, this story has more than a few missing chapters," Richard offered.

"And so the victim is guilty until proven innocent – is that the way it is?"

Gerald Wurst raised his arms and stretched. He dropped his arms and clasped his fingers together behind his head. "That about sizes it up. You and the lady might just be telling the truth. It's all a bit sketchy; but it could be true. Don't think we've heard the whole story yet."

He rocked to the balls of his feet. He arched his back and put both hands in his pockets. He jingled keys and coins, and pulled out a quarter. He tossed it in the air and caught it.

"Or there could be another story. One she hasn't told you."

Gabe pressed close, jabbed his finger into Gerald's sternum. "I don't like your implications."

"Didn't expect you would." Gerald tossed the quarter in the air. The silver glinted as it spiraled back to his palm. "Could be that she met someone while she was here working on that fresco. Could be she married you after this guy jilted her. This whole rape scenario could have been manufactured."

Once more, he tossed the coin. Gabe reached out to snatch the quarter as it flipped. "You'd loose, Detective. My wife does not lie. She was viciously beaten and raped. Repeatedly."

As he turned to leave, Gabe flicked the quarter over his shoulder. It landed on the table right in front of Gerald.

"We'll be at the Magnolia House. You can contact us there when you have information."

The walk back to Dayton Drive was far from pleasant; they trudged nine blocks. Hannah felt like a stranger to her own body. Her breaths were shallow and her feet, leaden. Her ankles were swollen and her head throbbed with an unholy rhythm. She went to bed without dinner.

At six fifteen the next morning, Maggie rapped on the bedroom door.

"Hannah? Can you hear me? Gabe?" Her knuckles beat a steady rat-ta-tat while she spoke.

Gabe struggled to sit up in bed. He scrubbed his sleepy face with his fingers. His hair stood at odd angles to his head. Hannah was tying the belt of her robe when as she opened the door.

"Good morning, Maggie. Can I help you?" She hoped she had a smile in her voice.

Maggie whispered conspiratorially. "There are two men, two policemen, downstairs. They have information for Gabe." Her eyes were wide with curiosity and maybe just a touch of fright. "You're not in trouble, are you?"

"No. No trouble. "

Maggie fluttered her palm above her heart. "Oh, good. I told them that you're nice young folks. Newlyweds, I told them." She touched Hannah's cheek. "Such happy young people, I told them."

Richard Wright sipped coffee at a small table in the breakfast room. Gerald stood beside the buffet table. His hands were jammed deep in his pockets while he eyed the selection of pastries. Hannah thought he looked like a boy struggling to avoid forbidden treats. Both men turned to her when she said, "Good morning."

"You know, a hall on the third floor of Morrison dorm was very busy one night in September."

"Morrison Dormitory?" she asked as she sat at the table adjacent to Richard's.

"Ever visited Morrison?" Gerald questioned.

"No. My work was at the hospital."

Richard turned, angling his back to Hannah as he questioned Gabe. "How 'bout you? Ever visited Morrison?"

"Only once, the night of September 2nd. My visit that night was very brief."

Gerald cleared his throat. "Right after you left the station yesterday, we had a visitor, Richard and me. Right, Richard?"

"Yep. Right after you left. Couldn't have been more than five minutes later."

"Yeah. Well." Gerald coughed into his hand. "This guy comes into the station. He asks if anyone has reported a rape recently. Desk sergeant sends him to us. Nice looking guy, wouldn't you say, Richard?"

Richard cracked his knuckles and nodded.

"Real nice looking guy. Curly blond hair, blue eyes, real good-looking guy, almost pretty. Tall. Maybe almost as tall as you." Gerald pointed to Gabe with his thumb. "Real smooth guy. Uptown, you know what I mean?"

Hannah stepped forward. "Did he give you his name?" she asked.

Richard, Gerald and Gabe all answered her question simultaneously.

"Aidan. Aidan Siddhe."

Richard and Gerald exchanged puzzled looks. Gerald sat at the table across from his partner. He flipped a spoon from one hand to the other.

"How'd you know that?"

"Good guess," Gabe replied.

The toothpick in Gerald's mouth worked double-time. He scratched the back of his neck. He pulled his right earlobe.

Gabe muttered, "Damn" under his breath.

Hannah ran her tongue along the edge of her upper teeth.

Richard puffed out a breath that might have been a soft belch. He rubbed his solar-plexus. "Well, anyway. This Aidan guy came in.

He told us he had been visiting a friend at Morrison Dorm back in early September. Said he saw this big guy, dark hair, dressed all in black."

Richard eyed Gabe, who was dressed in his characteristic black tee shirt, black slacks.

"This suspicious guy in black broke down a door in the dorm. He threw things around and yelled a lot. A few minutes later that same guy left carrying a blonde woman who was crying."

Richard burped. He knocked his ribs with his fist.

"Sound familiar?"

Gabe sounded calm when he answered. "Yes. Very familiar. It's the same thing I told you yesterday. Aidan's story only verifies my own."

Gerald stood up. He circled the table and stopped just behind Hannah's chair. He placed his palms on her shoulders, pinning her to the seat.

"Well, yes and no. Yes, he verifies that you were there. Both of you. However, that's where the similarities end. Aidan claims that Hannah had been there for days."

"Yes. We've told you that..." Gabe began.

Gerald raised his hand to silence him.

"According to Aidan, Hannah was partying. Said he and several of his friends had sex with her. Consensual sex." Hannah gasped and bit her knuckle.

Gabe growled, "You don't believe that ridiculous story, do you?"

Gerald took a defensive step back. He bumped another breakfast table, rattling small jars of jam.

"Do you?" Gabe snarled.

"It really doesn't matter whether or not I believe him. Question is, do you?"

Hannah made a sound. It wasn't exactly a moan, not really a sigh. Maybe it was more of a whimper. She slumped in her chair; propped her elbows on the table and dropped her head in her hands.

Gerald turned to her. "Your description perfectly matches a John Doe who's been hospitalized since the night of September 2nd. Broken collarbone, broken elbow, compound fracture of the left leg, cracked skull, right kneecap crushed, a few broken ribs, punctured lung. Bad injuries."

Gabe muttered, "Not bad enough. He's still alive."

"John Doe?" Hannah asked. "I don't understand."

Gerald Wurst tapped the tablecloth with a sugar cube. "Yeah, well. There's a whole helluva lot of shit I don't understand." He tapped Gabe's arm. "Let's take a ride. Go see if you recognize this guy or if he recognizes you."

Hannah laced her fingers through Gabe's when they walked out to the sidewalk together. A mud-splattered truck and polished sedan were parked at the curb.

"You can ride with me, Mrs. Murray," Richard said, opening the front door of his dark green Dodge.

Hannah caught Gabe's sleeve. "What do you mean?"

Gerald answered, "Your husband and I are going to the hospital. See if he can identify Mr. Doe as one of your assailants."

Richard was buckled into the driver's seat of an unmarked Dodge; a car so innocuous, it was obvious. "I've got a couple of questions for you at the station, Mrs. Murray."

Gabe leaned inside to kiss Hannah's cheek, to tuck that errant curl behind her ear again. She squeezed his finger.

"I'll meet you at the police station, Love." He raised her hand to his lips. "Soon."

Then he joined Gerald in a jacked-up SUV parked in a handicap space. Gerald gunned the engine, flicked the air conditioning to 'max' and unwrapped a stick of chewing gum. Tim McGraw crooned through the radio, making plans for his next thirty years. Both men stared through the dirt-speckled windshield while Gerald maneuvered the winding streets of Carver's Hollow.

Gabe gyrated the louvers on the air vent. Sweat dotted his brow. His shirt stuck to his spine.

"Nervous?" Gerald glanced at his passenger. He blew a bubble with the gum and when it popped, a potpourri of cinnamon flavored the close warm air in the truck.

"Anxious, not nervous. There's a difference, you know."

"Yeah. Right."

Gerald tapped out the Dixie Chicks' melody on the steering wheel with his thumbs. At a stoplight, he turned to watch Gabe's reaction. "Guy's not right in the head, you know?"

"I would think all rapists are skewed," Gabe answered dully. He continued to stare through the front window, not really watching traffic, just avoiding Gerald's eyes.

"Yeah, well, this particular guy screams and yells about demons coming for him. Rants about a dark devil shoving him out a window. Evil retribution and the wrath of hell…"

Gabe turned then. Unblinking, he met Gerald's eyes. "I never touched the son of a bitch." The car behind them honked a horn.

Gerald shifted his foot from brake to accelerator. The car moved forward. Neither man spoke again. An uneasy truce held while the vehicle snaked through the hospital parking lot. Gerald whipped the vehicle into a vacant space outlined in yellow. Large block letters read 'NO PARKING. LOADING ZONE.'

The detective grunted and slammed his door. "Let's get this over with." Without further preface, he hurried down the canopied walk, heading for the hospital entrance. In the lobby, he flipped his badge to the white-haired receptionist who smiled and touched the visitors' registry.

Gerald did not even break stride. "He's with me," he said pointing to Gabe with his thumb. They wedged into a crowded elevator. An orderly whistled quietly, eyeing a stained spot on the acoustic ceiling tile. A young man straightened his grease-splattered tie and tugged on his belt. He licked his fingers and tried in vain to plaster a cowlick of hair into position. Gerald shuffled from one foot to another and jabbed uselessly at the control buttons. A bell tone chimed, the doors whooshed open and Gerald stepped out into a busy corridor. Gabe followed him down the hall to a darkened room.

A plump nurse, whose nametag identified her as Mrs. Anna Marie Humphries, was leaving the room. Her rubber soled shoes exhaled with each step. She nodded to them.

"Any changes?" Gerald asked.

Mrs. Humphries looked briefly at the chart she carried. "Not really. He's sedated, so he sleeps mostly. If he's awake, he's panicky. Wild-eyed and sweating, muttering about devils and demons." A chime sounded at the nurses' station.

"I have to go," she said. "Do you need any more information?"

"Go on," Gabe said. "We won't be long."

The two men stood together in the doorway; surveying. The blinds were drawn, but thin stripes of light glowed at the windows. The decor was Spartan. There were none of the expected fruit baskets or flowers from well-wishers. It was standard-issue hospital fare: bed, rolling nightstand and an uncomfortable plastic chair. In the bed, a man slept restlessly. "University Hospital" was stamped in black ink along the top edges of sheets and blankets tucked around him with precise, tight corners.

The patient's leg was balanced in a mesh sling suspended from a metal contraption bracketing the bed. Even in the dimly lit room, his thin scar was illuminated, glowing evil and sinister on his cheek. Dark hair about a half inch long sprouted from underneath a white turban of bandages. One arm was set in a cast from shoulder to wrist. The other was secured to the metal cage with straps lined with lambswool. He grimaced and tossed his head side-to-side, muttering "bitch...shit...blow 'em...hell!" Saliva dripped from one corner of his mouth.

Gabe growled. It was a breathy, whisper of a snarl rising from his gut. "Do you smell it?" he asked the detective.

Gerald sniffed, testing the air. "I smell ammonia, alcohol, disinfectant...hospital smells."

"I smell evil. Unadulterated evil."

Gerald arched a brow and asked, "Wanna change your story? Still say you didn't touch the guy?"

"I never touched him."

"Somebody threw him out of a sealed plexiglass window, three floors to the concrete portico."

"I never touched him." Gabe didn't raise his voice. His mouth was drawn in a thin, rigid line. His fists were clenched at his waist.

Back at the police station, Richard Wright escorted Hannah into the glass interrogation room. He took the position at the head of the table, where Gerald Wurst had presided yesterday. Hannah sat to his right. Richard uncapped his pen and held it to the light, examining the nib. Satisfied, he flipped to a fresh page on the legal pad. He carefully aligned the pen, laying it parallel to the faint pink line on the left margin of the paper. Only then did he look up at Hannah.

She jostled her knees so that they bumped the table edge.

"Why are you so nervous, Hannah?"

She crossed her arms at her breasts. She watched Richard as if he were a snake poised to strike her. "I'm terrified!" she snapped. "Being here in Carver's Hollow brings back memories that horrify me." She covered her mouth with both hands. She shook her head, back and forth time and again. "Scar...or John Doe... or whoever he is… is evil. Her mouth was still hidden behind her fingers. "He thought I was some sort of spy, searching for secrets about a group he called 'Hell's Wrath'."

She stared at Richard; she was surprised by her own words. She dropped her hands to her lap. Her knees bounced even faster now. "I just remembered that name. Have you ever heard of them? Hell's Wrath?"

Richard nodded. "Go on," he encouraged.

Hannah ran both hands through her hair. She massaged her temples with her thumbs.

"I wish I could be more helpful. I…um… I can't remember much; just little snippets of conversations. Scar…John… complained that no one took them, the group, seriously." She pursed her lips and squinted, picturing the squalid room, recalling Scar's raspy voice and his wicked laugh. "He said that one day, everyone would listen." Hannah hugged her sides. "Boom," she whispered. "He said they'd hear the boom." She dropped her head forward, her chin rested near her collarbone. "I think they plan to set a bomb."

The detective stopped writing although his pen remained poised ready.

"What makes you think so?"

Hannah caught her bottom lip in her teeth. She shook her head.

"I don't know. Something Scar said. Ummm…He said 'It's like planting bulbs in the fall. Then, later the flowers come.' He laughed then, ummm, he yelled, 'BOOM! They'll listen to us then.'"

"Who are 'they'?"

She hunched her shoulders and shook her head.

"Did he give you any idea about where the bomb might be set? Any time frame?"

"Only said that it was like planting in the fall and waiting 'til spring for results."

Richard bounced the pen on the page half-filled with notes. He rubbed the side of his nose. "Yeah well. We'll get back to that later."

His abrupt change of subjects hit Hannah like a pellet gun. "How well do you know Aidan Siddhe?"

"Not very well at all. He's a childhood acquaintance of my husband."

"Acquaintance, but not a friend?"

"No. Aidan's not a friend."

Richard buttressed both elbows on the table. His eyes were level with his hands as he watched her across the expanse of the table. The air crackled with tension while he popped each knuckle.

Richard persisted. "He claims to have heard that you met our John Doe in a bar over on Franklin Street. Says you were flying, high on drugs. You fell down some steps, got pretty scraped up. John and his buddy brought you back to the dorm."

Richard twirled the pen on the pad of yellow paper. As it spun in drunken circles, he watched for her reaction. Hannah sat motionless, absolutely still except for the tensing of her fingers on the chair arms.

"His buddy-the guy you called Leonard-is a junior, majoring in political science. You gave a pretty accurate description of his dormitory room. No one has seen him since John Doe took a flying leap out of his window. Know anything about his disappearance?"

"No." Her voice was barely louder than a shudder.

Richard shrugged. He continued, "Anyway, Aidan says he was staying with a friend in Leonard's suite for the weekend. Claims it was one helluva party. He says you had pills and pot stuffed in a back-pack full of drawings, pencils and paintbrushes. Aidan said you told 'em you'd been paid a bundle and deserved a little relaxation."

The detective stared at Hannah, searching her face for some hint of deception.

Her jaw dropped, she breathed through her mouth, dragging in long, long breaths and panting them out again.

"Aidan says he had sex with you. He was next in line after Leonard."

Richard wiped his lips with his hand. A trace of perspiration dampened his tidy narrow mustache. "Why would he lie about those things?"

Hannah hung her head. She rubbed her stomach, closed her eyes for a minute. Her throat hurt. It was torture to compel her mouth to form words.

Richard leaned back in his chair. He locked his fingers behind his head. His elbows jutted towards opposite walls.

"Tell you what I think," Richard interrupted her concentration.

She opened her eyes.

"I think you met those guys, just like Aidan claims. I doubt you had the drugs, though. Maybe you'd had too many beers or wine. Let's suppose the fellows took you back to dorm to sober up. Maybe you were all drunk; who knows? Maybe things got out of control. Date rape."

"You disgust me!" She spit her words at him, venom aimed straight at his eyes. "Policeman. Servant of the people! HA!"

"Your story just doesn't add up. One man is missing, another is in bad shape over at the hospital. Then, pretty as you please, you and your big, bad husband come in more than a month after the fact to cry rape. Now you tell me something about bombs." Richard shook his head. He tugged on his belt and settled it under the flab at his belly. "I dunno. Just doesn't tally."

Hannah jumped up. Her chair flipped backwards and clanked to the floor. She bolted, sparing no thought for direction. It hurt when she slammed her shoulder against the swinging glass door at the station entrance. She blinked blindly in the noontime glare. She cupped her hands to shield her eyes and ran towards the street.

Horns blared. Someone screamed, "Crazy woman!" as she darted between parked cars and burst into a lane of traffic. A startled motorist slammed his brake pedal. There was smoke, the odor of scorched rubber and the horrific squeal of the locking brakes. Her body crumpled over the fender of a red Toyota coupe. Hannah couldn't breathe. Fiery pain blazed in her shoulder. She slid to the asphalt and sprawled beside the tire on the passenger side of the car. Her brain shrieked "Gabe!" but no one heard her say a word. A steady stream of blood dribbled down her left leg.

Richard Wright was only five or ten seconds behind her. He held his arms out from his sides, screening her body from curious pedestrians, concerned motorists and policemen streaming onto the sidewalk.

"Shit! Somebody call an ambulance," he yelled over his shoulder.

At the hospital, Gerald took a step into the quiet hospital room. The patient groaned and flinched his shoulders; but did not open his eyes. Gerald didn't notice when Gabe staggered.

"Oh, God!" Gabe doubled over, clutching his stomach.

Reflexively, Gerald reached under his arm to touch his holster. He spun to face the door.

"What?"

"Hannah. I have to go."

The detective reached to catch his elbow, but Gabe sprinted out of the room. Gerald ran out into the corridor, searching up and down the hall. He shrugged his shoulders and tipped his palms. "I can give you a ride…" His pager beeped.

A man stood beside his red Toyota. He slipped his driver's license out of his wallet. "I never had a chance to brake," he explained to a policewoman wielding a notebook. "Honest. She ran right into the car!"

Gabe raced towards the crowd massed in front of the police station. Two women with baby strollers stood on tiptoe to peer over the men crouched in the street. Drivers honked their horns, a few abandoned their vehicles, others talked on cell phones or consulted Palm Pilots. Cars snarled in a knot at the intersection. Sirens pealed as an ambulance wove through the labyrinth of traffic.

"My wife," Gabe said, nodding towards the inert body at the center of the crowd. "Let me through," he muttered. The throng was like an amorphous body, impenetrable in its curiosity. He spread his elbows, forging a path. Bystanders made comments like, "Fool …

running outta the building like a bat outta hell," or "…drugs, maybe."

Even though Gabe's hands were shaking, his voice was calm

when he knelt beside Hannah. He touched her cheek and lifted a

strand of hair that fell across her eye. "I'm here, Hannah."

Her eyes moved behind lids that were too heavy to lift. Her

words were soft, more quiet than a breath. "…knew you'd come."

Richard Wright squatted at Gabe's side. He winced and swal-

lowed hard. "Move aside, Mr. Murray. Let the medics help her.

Okay?"

Gabe stood, but he didn't back away. The team of emergency

personnel worked quickly, cautiously and efficiently to connect an IV,

check vital signs and move her into the ambulance. Gabe grabbed the

door, ready to boost himself inside when Gerald rushed alongside.

"Wait," he panted.

"No." Gabe climbed aboard the ambulance. He curled his fin-

gers through Hannah's. The siren's screams screamed. "Hold on,

Hannah," he whispered close to her ear.

"Ummm," she murmurred.

Gerald paced the waiting room with Gabe. Hannah had been in examination area for more than half an hour. The hospital staff bustled, pushing patients on gurneys through the swinging doors. Richard Wright sprawled uncomfortably in a plastic chair. Beside him was a wood-grained table littered with paper cups of cold coffee and dog-earred magazines.

"You knew she'd been hurt." Gabe ignored the comment, just as he had the ten previous times Gerald had made it.

"You got ESP or something?"

Gabe continued his circuit of the waiting area. "Or something."

"How'd you know where to go?"

Gabe stopped. Slowly, he turned. Hands in his pockets, he shrugged. "I just know. With Hannah, I just know. We've got a connection. I can't explain it. You'd never understand."

"That how you found her before?"

"Yes."

A doctor in surgical scrubs pushed through the swinging doors. "Mr. Murray?"

"Yes."

"Your wife is going to be all right."

Gabe closed his eyes and blew out a huge breath. "Praise be." When he opened his eyes, the doctor tipped his hand towards the red leatherette sofa with vinyl tape covering cracks on both arms. "But..."

"Sit down, Mr. Murray." The physician was middle-aged, approaching his mid-fifties. His voice was modulated and he spoke slowly. "My name is Ben Abrams, I'm head of ob-gyn."

Gabe sat on the edge of the seat. "My wife?"

"As I said, your wife will be fine. She separated her shoulder and fractured her wrist when she fell."

"And the baby?"

"Protected by amniotic fluid. At seven weeks, the fetus is still very small, its trunk would be approximately the size of a raspberry. There is every indication that mother and child will be fine."

"Then she didn't miscarry?"

"No. We detected a heartbeat with ultrasound."

Gabe slumped against the cushions. "Thank God. I saw blood."

Doctor Abrams patted Gabe's hand. "Bleeding during pregnancy isn't normal; but it's not unusual, either. Bleeding doesn't mean miscarriage is imminent. She needs bedrest. We're going to keep

your wife here for a few days, just to monitor her."

"Here? Here in the hospital?"

"Yes."

Gabe shoved both hands through his hair. He glanced across

the room where Gerald was flipping through a *Car and Driver* maga-

zine circa 1975. "I'll see that she gets plenty of rest, Doctor." When

Gabe and the doctor stood, Gerald and Richard came to join them.

"Mrs. Murray sustained a separated shoulder. She will be in

terrific pain. I've prescribed something. We've fitted her with a

sling." Dr. Abrams turned to Richard, "There isn't much else we can

do now. Physical therapy might help later, after the swelling has sub-

sided."

"I want to see my wife, Doctor..."

"Abrams. Ben Abrams."

Gabe accepted his hand and covered it with both of his.

"Thank you for treating my wife. I need to be with her now. I need to

see her."

"Setting her shoulder was a painful procedure, so she was se-

dated. She'll be in the recovery room for another half hour or so. Wait until we bring her to the private room, where she'll be for a few more days."

There was an uncomfortable silence in the room, littered with discarded coffee cups and people sprawling uncomfortably on furniture shielded by clear plastic slipcovers.

"Your wife will be fine. She's bruised. Her shoulder and wrist will be painful for quite a while. But she'll heal."

Gabe turned away from Dr. Abrams and walked to the windows that lined one long wall. "Why are hospital corridors always painted green? Is green supposed to be a soothing color? It's not, you know." He stared out at rain falling in big drops from a gray sky tinged yellow, like a bruise.

Across the room, someone coughed. The metal legs of a chair squeaked when Gerald sat. The doctor nodded silently and hurried back through the swinging doors. Over his shoes, he wore green surgical covers that muffled his steps to a soft shush.

Gerald and Richard watched Gabe at the windows, studying drops of rain as they dripped from leaf to leaf. He held his head in his hands and muttered to himself.

"Strange guy," Richard commented.

"Intense," Gerald added. "Very intense."

Gabe pivoted, facing Gerald. "I want to show you something," he said. He moved to the door in three long strides. He looked over his shoulder and asked, "Coming?"

"Uh, yeah. Yeah." Gerald quirked a brow at Richard and followed.

At the nurses' station, Gabe asked directions to the children's wing. The men silently navigated the maze of corridors; all painted a pale institutional green.

Then, there is was – an oasis of color! They gaped at the fresco Hannah had created. It was a floor-to-ceiling panorama. Faeries and pixies cavorted across the long wall, peering at the viewer from under fern fronds, hiding beneath toadstools. In the leafy branches, more faeries balanced 'en pointe' atop delicate dewdrops. Their wings glowed opalescent in the early morning sunbeams that shone through the forest canopy. There! Up high in the trees, nestled like pinecones, were the elves camouflaged in umber, cinnamon and drab green clothing. Gabe and Hannah were there, dancing in a faerie circle. And so were Trog, Ella, Nowatil and Tobias.

Gabe stepped closer. He touched Hannah's self-portrait. His fingertips traced the curve of her jaw, the bridge of her nose, her slender neck. He bit his lips together.

"Uh,hmmm," Gerald cleared his throat. "She's good," he complimented.

"Oh yes. She is the essence of goodness. Sentimental, caring, loving and truthful."

"Uhh… that's not… I mean, she's talented," Gerald stammered.

"I know what you meant. I'm telling you that she gave you the truth, the whole truth. She can give you no more."

Gabe turned to face the detective. "I'm taking Hannah home as soon as possible. We won't return here, to your town, again. She's already paid too high a price delivering the truth." He stepped closer; the men stood eye-to-eye. Gabe poked his index finger at Gerald's chest. "Find this group she mentioned. Stop them. They'll kill people and revel in their success. Hannah has given you all the information she can. Do your work now. Leave her alone."

Gerald jammed both hands in his pockets. He lifted his shoulders and stretched his neck. His shoulders drooped.

"Well, Mr. Murray…Gabe. It's like this, you see. What we've got is a John Doe who's been laid up here in the hospital for several months, ever since he fell, jumped or was thrown out of a dormitory window. We've already established the fact that those windows are plexiglass panes, painted shut. It would take a considerable force to propel a person through those windows. Don't you agree?"

"Is there a point to this discussion?"

Gerald found a toothpick in his pocket. He took a moment to peel the white wrapper off. He positioned the wooden pick 'just so' behind his canine tooth, left side. He slid the paper between his thumbnail and his index finger, smoothly creasing it in half. He pleated the strip, accordion-style, and dangled it between two fingers for a moment. Then, he tossed the paper in the air and caught it, crumpling it.

"Oh, yeah. There's a point. I believe you can explain how old John Doe ended up outside on the sidewalk, face first."

"Detective Wurst, I've explained this to you before. I knew Hannah was in that room. I could hear her crying. I burst through the door to find a man forcing her to perform fellatio."

Gabe squeezed his eyes shut. He scrubbed his hands over his face. His words were succinct. "How... would you... have reacted?"

He watched Gerald. "What would you do if she were the woman you love? If she was beaten and abused? If you saw that...that animal...that bastard...ramming his penis in her mouth? If you had heard her begging him to stop? If she was cut and bruised and half naked, what would you do, Detective?"

Gerald clamped his jaws together. His teeth grated against one another. His eyes narrowed to thin slits, barely any whites visible. He exhaled long and hard. "I'd probably want to kill the son of a bitch."

"The thought crossed my mind," Gabe admitted.

"But you didn't act on the thought?"

"No, I never touched him."

"So you say." Gerald mouth curled at the corners, not quite a smile, but close. "But,..."

"I never touched him. He was agitated when he saw me. He shouted an obscenity and charged past me, ran head first out the window."

Gabe crossed his arms across his chest and leaned against the wall. "The other fellow, Leonard, the one with long blond hair, peed on the floor and bolted. Umm,… through the door."

Gerald scratched his earlobe, ran his palm over his hair. "…And that's your story, huh?"

"That's it."

Gerald glanced at his watch. He stuck his hands in his pockets and wiggled them up and down, jingling the keys and coins.

"Well, I gotta head back to the station soon." He started to leave, but turned to face Gabe. "Don't leave town without checking with me, okay? I may have one or two more questions."

"You know where to find me, Detective. Right now, I've got to run. Hannah's awake!"

Before Gerald could respond, Gabe had sprinted around a corner and vanished.

"Strange guy," Gerald muttered.

When the nurse pushed Hannah's rolling bed through the swinging double doors, Gabe was pacing the corridor outside the recovery room. The tail of his shirt was only partially tucked into his trousers. Because he had been running his hands through his hair, tufts stood straight up. Since he hadn't taken time to shave that morning, his cheeks were bearded and scruffy. The nurse slowed her pace.

"Hannah."

Her name was spoken softly, hardly more than a heavy breath; but to her, it sounded like a prayer. Her smile was crooked; her lips wouldn't cooperate. She tried to lift her free hand to clasp his, but she had energy to raise it only three or four inches off the gurney. He covered her fingers with his palm.

"So sorry, Gabe," she whimpered.

"Ssssh. Not your fault, Love." He leaned over the bed, striding with the nurse who continued wheeling her patient down the hall. "You're safe, *mo chride*. Thank God, you're safe."

At room 524, the entourage stopped. The nurse efficiently maneuvered the bed with its attached pole that held a jostling medication drip bag. After a cursory check of the IV and a brief demonstration of the call button, she left the room.

Hannah closed her eyes, simply too exhausted to lift her lids. Gabe inspected the room, peeking into both the locker-sized closet and the handicap access bathroom. He had to turn sideways to pass between the bed and an ugly chair upholstered in tan vinyl. "Guess this is my bed." He lowered the window blinds and adjusted the louvers. The fluorescent lamps buzzed overhead. "Bad ballast," he mumbled when he flipped the switch "off." He dragged the small turquoise plastic chair close to the bed. He sat, resting his elbows on the mattress. Hannah's injured shoulder was immobilized by a canvas sling that strapped her right arm across her ribs..

She turned her head towards him and opened her eyes. Both of her hands rested on her abdomen, cupping her belly.

"I was stupid to think I wouldn't love this baby. What if I've killed him?"

He smoothed her hair away from her face. "It was an accident, Hannah. It wasn't your fault. Sssh, now, Love."

She stroked his cheek with cool fingertips.

"I bring you such heartaches," she whispered, closing her eyes again.

He covered her lips with warm fingers.

"You bring me joy." His voice was a rough whisper. "I can't imagine life without you."

"...for better or worse, for richer or poorer, til death do us part. Remember?"

"Of course."

A tear slid down his cheek unchecked.

"I'm here, Hannah. Lean on me."

Hannah's thoughts were jumbled, her emotions too huge to fit into words. She nodded. "I love you."

"I know."

"He's our baby. Did the doctor tell you? Conceived before I left the village."

"Yeah. I spoke with the doctor. He said you'd both be fine. You and our baby."

"But I'm bleeding. What if I miscarry?"

"Close your eyes and rest, Love."

She felt as if she were sliding into a narrow, dark tunnel. "Woozy. Doctor gave me a shot. Powerful stuff." She groped for his hand, grabbed his wrist.

"Don't leave me," she begged.

He leaned over her; his stubbled jaw scratched her cheek.

"I'll be right here, Love. Right here beside you, always."

She patted the narrow bed. "Room enough for two?"

Even before he could answer, her head lolled. Her shoulders slumped, her hand fell open and her fingers curled slightly, her breaths were slow and even. She slept.

About a half hour later, Trog coughed softly. The room was dark and he was silhouetted, backlit by the bright lights in the corridor. Gabe motioned to the chair upholstered in ugly vinyl. Trog ambled to his side, magic hat in hand. He shoved a paper sack into Gabe's lap.

"Brought the razor you wanted. Got Hannah a hairbrush, too."

"Sit with me for a while."

"Been chatting with a few of the lads," the elf began.

"Oh, been chatting, have you now?"

"Yes, with a few of the lads."

"...And which lads would they be?" Gabe asked.

Trog climbed into the armchair. Even though he sat forward on the cushion, his feet dangled about a foot off the floor. "When I went to the cafeteria for a wee bite, I happened to notice a few imps sticking green peas into the blueberry muffin batter. 'Twas them who introduced me to the Spriggans."

"Spriggans…here in the hospital?"

Trog nodded. "Blighters came to the hospital to terrorize a human." He lifted one shoulder, tipped his head and smirked.

Gabe shrugged. "No surprise there."

Trog covered his chuckle with his hand. He glanced quickly at the bed, making certain that Hannah was still sleeping soundly. Gabe quirked an eyebrow and the elf continued.

"Seems the manager at the bus station called the police because of the hullabaloo going on in the locker. After the police broke the lock, the guy fell out, naked, so I hear. Ranting about demons who'd kidnapped him!"

Gabe rubbed his lips with his index finger. "Lots of ranting about devils and demons in Carver's Hollow recently."

"So, I was talking to the lads about Hannah's ordeal. I mentioned how the rapist ranted about a demon throwing him through a window."

Gabe stood and stretched. "I see," he said.

Trog rubbed his palms down his shirt. "I thought I'd encourage the lads to pay a visit to your John Doe."

Gabe rocked back to his heels. He shoved his hands through his hair, massaged the crown of his head. He glanced towards the bed where Hannah slept.

"He's kept medicated to keep him calm," Gabe whispered. "Nurse told me that he drifts in and out of consciousness. He mumbles about demons and flays his arms around terribly if he's not sedated."

Trog nodded his head. He rubbed the end of his nose until it was bright red. Tugging his earlobe, he conspired, "Bad conscience, maybe. Spriggans and imps could visit his sleep. Could be nightmarish enough to scare him into a confession."

"Couldn't hurt."

"What I thought meself." Trog stuck his fingers in the back pockets of his trousers. When he grinned, his bushy brows wiggled. He plopped the hat on his head at a jaunty angle and headed for the door.

"Thank you for your help, Trog."

Trog glanced over his shoulder, "That's what friends do."

The elf's chuckle echoed in the corridor for several seconds after he'd left the room.

Gabe tugged at the front of his shirt, raising it to his nose.

"Phew, wish there were something I could do about this smelly shirt."

He flinched hearing an answer.

"Why don't you wear this one?"

"Da?"

"It's me, son."

"But how...? You brought me clothes?"

"Ella came to get me," Sean boasted.

He stepped closer to the bed, dropping his voice as he asked, "How is she?"

"She'll do."

"Ella said Hannah was bleeding. "

Gabe nodded.

"Miscarriage?"

"No. The doctor tells me that although bleeding during pregnancy isn't normal; but it isn't unusual. It doesn't mean miscarriage is imminent. As long as she doesn't have cramping or abdominal pain, she should be all right. There are no clumps of tissue in the blood. The ultrasound and internal pelvic exam looked good. He checked the fetal heartbeat."

"Praise be." Sean rubbed his eyelid. He sat in the chair Trog had vacated.

Gabe touched Hannah's cheek with the back of his hand. "I would rage at God or bargain with Satan to keep Hannah safe."

Sean leaned forward, propped his elbows on his knees. "If the doctor had offered you a choice between the mother or the babe, who would you have chosen?"

Gabe stared at his father. Then his dark eyes riveted on the woman lying in the bed.

Sean tapped his lips with a fingertip. Then he fired another question. "Would you choose to save the unborn bairn you already love? Or would you protect the woman you pledged to love through your whole life - good times and bad?"

Gabe chewed his lower lip. He exhaled and opened his mouth, ready to speak.

Sean covered his ears with his hands.

"No, don't tell me your answer. Just keep it in your heart."

He covered his son's hand with his own. Gabe curled his fingers through his father's wrinkled knuckles.

"You are a wise man, Da."

"Aye, I am. Listen to this last bit of advice, son. Give her your strength. Love her. That love will heal you both."

"My babes will have a wise grandfather."

Hannah could hear hushed voices. Men speaking quietly as though they were in a library or at a funeral. Gabe's corduroy rumble and Sean's Scottish burr. Her men. What were they saying? Something about babies...

She flinched, trying to roll onto her side. Nauseating white-hot pain shot through her shoulder, down her arm to her wrist. She groaned. Gabe rushed to the bedside.

"Don't move, Hannah." He dabbed her perspiring face with a damp cloth. "Breathe slowly."

"Ummm," was all she could mutter. She sucked in a deep breath and let it escape. The pain subsided to a throbbing ache. "The baby?" The fingers of her free hand tensed on her stomach.

Gabe laid his hand over hers. "He's fine. Dr. Abrams detected a steady heartbeat."

"I dreamed our baby was gone." She gulped another breath. "I never got a chance to hold him. He never wrapped tiny fingers around one of mine. I never put him to my breast."

Tears fought for release. She choked them back. "We didn't even know the color of his eyes." She swallowed hard.

"A dream, Hannah, only a dream."

An orderly brought Hannah a dinner tray. "Clear liquids," he announced.

"I'd prefer Ella's recipe," Hannah mumbled as she stirred the nearly colorless, tasteless soup.

"That can be arranged," Sean announced, producing a thermos of steaming chicken broth.

Gabe ate three slices of the bread and a pear Ella had sent. He saved the apple for snacking later. He sent Sean off to Magnolia House. "You stay in our room tonight, Da. Explain the situation to Maggie."

Some six hours later, Trog reappeared. He thumped Gabe's toe. "Thought you were going to use that razor I delivered, wee scoundrel," he teased. "You've the look of a pirate."

Gabe stretched. The chair's vinyl upholstery creaked. He scrubbed his eyes with the heel of his hand and rumbled, "This had better be good, Trog."

"Spriggans have spent the better part of the night dancing aboot in Scar's dreams."

Trog twitched with excitement, bouncing up and down balanced on his toes. "Hee hee hee," he chortled, "wicked devils were right at home in his black dreams, don't you know?"

"Yes, Trog, Spriggans can be perfectly wicked…"

"Ah, but that's the beauty of the whole plan, don't you see?"

"Which plan is that?"

Trog clasped his hands behind him and began pacing.

"This John Doe, this…Scar hurt our Hannah."

"Yes," Gabe agreed.

Trog quirked a wiry red brow. "He talked about Hell's Wrath. Am I right?"

"Yes."

Trog did a handspring, landing next to the bedside table. He grabbed the apple and tossed it in the air.

"…And there's the beauty of our plan! Stomping about in his dreams, our lads scared the beejasus of the Scar."

Trog bite the apple. He jumped and clicked his heels together.

"He mumbled threats in his sleep. Says he's got a bomb. Claims it's hidden somewhere safe."

Gabe held the elf in position with a firm hand on top of his head.

"Slow down. Back up. Tell me the whole story. From the beginning."

Trog's squeaky voice cracked, sounding either like a cricket chattering or a bullfrog croaking.

While he listened, Gabe cupped his chin in his hand. He pulled at his top lip. "It's a good plan, Trog." He rubbed his index finger up and down the bridge of his long, straight nose. "The key to the scheme will be insuring that a witness hears what Scar says."

"Don't fret," Trog assured. "The lads and I will handle that one! You be ready to call on your policemen, Boy."

Gabe nodded and stood. He arched his back and was rewarded by a series of satisfying little pops. He walked to the sink and turned on the water. He spoke to the mirror, "I need to finish this. I'm ready to take my wife home."

He bent over the sink, filled his hands with warm soapy water and lathered his face. He mumbled into his sudsy hands. "There are issues to settle with Aidan."

It had been an arduous session with the orthopedic therapist. Hannah was exhausted, achy and more than a bit out of sorts. The man had used her like a mannequin, manipulating her body into contortions while he explained techniques to Gabe. For all of his loving apologies, her husband seemed devoted to forcing her joints into restored health.

"What are you doing now?" she snapped.

Gabe was inspecting the hand on her injured arm, pressing on each fingernail, turning her hand, massaging her palm.

"Leave off," Hannah grumbled, jerking her arm out of his grasp. She winced, drawing her lips into a tight knot, expelling a flume of air.

"If your splint is too tight, the blood supply to your arm might be decreased or cut off. Just checking to see if your fingers are cold or pale."

"I'm fine!" She bit her bottom lip to keep from blubbering about the pain.

Gabe cupped his palms less than an inch above her injured shoulder.

"Don't tense, Love. The shoulder will only hurt more if your muscles are tight," he admonished for the twelfth time.

She squinted to peek at him. "How can one man be so patently annoying?" she snipped.

"'Tis a gift, to be sure," he chuckled.

She shook her head and tried to grimace, but fact of the matter was that his palms were generating a soothing heat that was relaxing the taut muscles in her shoulder better than any heating pad. She pressed her check against the back of his hands.

"Thanks."

"Anytime."

"Would I be interrupting, then?" Sean hurried to her bedside brandishing a dripping paper cup.

"For you," Sean said. Large globs of condensation quickly dribbled across his fingers to drip splotches on the starched sheet.

Hannah reached to accept the cup with her unencumbered left hand. She sucked on the straw and rolled her eyes. "Yummy! What is it?" She nodded a benediction to the sacred chalice.

"An ice cream float." Sean lifted the plastic lid and peered at the slush in the cup. He snapped the lid back in place and pushed the cup towards Hannah again.

"Drink up, Lass, before it's all melted and my good intentions wasted!"

Hannah sucked hard on the straw to produce an obnoxious *blatt* against the bottom of the now-empty cup.

"Well, ex-cu-use me!" Trog chuckled when he waddled into the room.

"Will it be time, then?" Gabe asked.

"Time?" Hannah asked.

Sean tapped her hand, took the cup and tossed it in the trashcan.

Trog nodded, but turned his attentions to Hannah. "Feeling better?"

Gabe flexed his hands open and closed a number of times. "Da, I need to leave with Trog for a bit." He squatted at the bedside, his head level with Hannah's. He touched her elbow that jutted out of the blue sling. "I won't be long, Love. Close your eyes and dream of me." He kissed the tip of her nose.

Passing Sean, he whispered, "Have a care for her, will you, Da?

Sean clapped a rough hand on his son's back. "As if she were my own, Son."

Hannah muttered, "What's going on?"

Sean quirked his brow as only a Scot can quirk a brow. Saying nothing, but acknowledging all.

"Close your eyes and rest, Lass," he lilted in a singsong. He stroked her eyelids lightly with his thumb. "*Oidche mhath, a leannan.* Good night, sweetheart.

Gabe hesitated in the dusky shadows outside the police station. Inside, a few officers milled in small groups. Gerald Wurst straddled a swivel chair, telephone receiver crushed against one shoulder as he drained a soda can. His Adams' apple bobbled when he swallowed. Gerald pitched the can towards a nearby wastebasket.

Gabe rushed forward, pushing his way past the blustering desk sergeant. "Gerald! Gerald Wurst!" he called. "You wanted proof! Let's go. Now!" He was almost shouting.

Gerald muttered something into the phone and slammed the receiver in place. He stood, checked that his gun was secure in his underarm holster and nodded.

"Let's go, then."

The trip to the hospital took about seven minutes. Gabe twitched in the passenger seat. He drummed his fingers on the dashboard when they were deterred by a red light. He tapped his right foot impatiently as Gerald accelerated through the quiet residential streets.

"So, what's up?" Gerald questioned.

"Scar...your John Doe... is talking."

"Oh. Yeah?"

"Yeah."

Ever the cop, Gerald questioned further. "You been to visit him?"

"Nope."

"How'd you know he's talking?"

Gabe cut his steely eyes. "Call it instinct," he said as he stared out at the lights sparkling on the windshield.

Both men were panting by the time they sprinted down the final hospital corridor.

"You set a mean pace," Gerald quipped. "Ever been a Marine?"

Gabe didn't answer; he just squinted at the detective.

A tormented scream tore through the hallway; terrorized soul-piercing anguish. Gabe nodded as he ran. The Spriggans were at work.

"Bastards!" Scar bellowed. "Don't mess with Hell!"

Three nurses sprung from their chairs at the hall station. One woman grabbed the patient chart and they sprinted towards Scar's room. While Gabe and Gerald watched, the duty nurse tried in vain to restrain her patient. She was no small-framed woman. Weighing at least one-sixty-five, she had thick biceps and shoulders quite capable of subduing either a small angry gorilla or a schizoid patient.

Scar trashed from side to side. He had successfully ripped the IV from his left arm. Although his eyes were wide open, it was obvious that he neither saw nor heard the crowd huddled around the bed. He shook a fist in the air, connected with an orderly who happened to lean too close. "Ga-damned fools! We're gonna blow your world apart!" Laughing manically, he kicked, bucking the hospital bed several feet across the room. "BOOM!"

The orderly rubbed his jaw and nodded to a nurse who thumped a syringe.

Gerald rushed forward to grab her wrist. She turned to watch his hand. Gerald flipped out his badge. "Police business."

She nodded curtly and stepped back slowly; both hands raised, the syringe held high.

"You're not under arrest, woman," Gerald grumbled. "Too much television."

Scar ranted, flogging the mattress with a clenched fist and one foot. He twisted his head side to side, shivering as he screamed obscenities. "Little shits! Assholes!"
Spit bubbled between his lips. "What the hell you doing? Who are you, takin' on Hells' Wrath?"

Gabe took one step. He raised his arms like a priest giving absolution. Noise in the raucous room quieted. "For you, Hell would be pleasant in comparison," he said in a stage-whisper.

Scar flinched. His eyes bulged. His head moved frantically. He turned his head this way and that, listening.

"Son of a bitch," Scar sneered, shouting to the ceiling. He fought with the bed covers, flinging sheets and blankets aside, struggling with his pillow. "Wait til we set the big one, asshole!" he yelled.

Gabe glanced at Gerald Wurst, who nodded in reply.

"The big one?" he asked.

"Oh yeah," Scar cackled. "Here to eternity. Say prayers, MoFo. Gonna blow this place from here to eternity!" He closed his eyes, but jerked his head from side to side, as if listening to ghosts.

"And when is that?"

534

Scar's head snapped in Gabe's direction. Unseeing, he stabbed a finger towards the disembodied voice. "Wouldn't you just love to know?" he taunted. "Nay na nay na nay na! You Fucker!"

Scar hurled his body side to side within the metal orthopedic cage that supported his leg in a sling. "Fucked the brains right outta your sniveling little bitch!" He groped at his crotch. "Hard to get it up with her crying all the time. Begging for us to let her go. Yeah, right. Like we'd do that! Had to knock her around some." He licked spittle from the corners of his mouth. "Tight piece of ass, that one! Duddn't give head worth a damn, though."

Gabe growled and lunged towards the bed. Three nurses and the orderly retreated in unison. Gerald snagged Gabe's belt and pulled him out of the room backwards.

"Easy, Murray. Easy," he muttered.

Guttural noises rumbled low in Gabe's throat. Gerald pushed him against the wall in the corridor, bracing a hand on each shoulder.

"I understand your feelings, man. But, you gotta control yourself. Okay?"

Gabe's fists clenched and opened at his sides.

"Okay?" Gerald repeated.

"Huh? Yeah, yeah,…Okay," Gabe agreed. "That bastard!" he spat in a hissing whisper. "You heard him talking about bombs."

"Bombs and rape," Gerald answered. "How'd you know he would?"

Gabe shrugged. "Just a hunch."

"Keep your cool, man," Gerald coached. "Keep cool."

Gabe nodded, took a deep breath and walked back to Scar's bedside. He leaned close to whisper. "I think you're all tough talk, man. You got no bombs!"

Scar grabbed a section of the sheet and wadded it in one fist. He rubbed his free foot up and down, running a mile in his dreams, held captive in the bed.

"You got no bombs. You got no power. Hell's Wrath is a joke!" Gabe sneered. "You're a bunch of weak assholes. Perverts. A big joke!"

Scar lunged, trying to bolt upright. His eyes popped wide open. He stared into Gabe's relentless gray stare. Gabe licked his lips and grinned a feral smile, all teeth. Scar screamed!

"Make 'em leave me alone!" he pleaded, shaking his head frantically. "Get 'em away from me!" Tears streamed down his contorted face. "Get the damned buggers away from me!" He rapped the side of his head with the ball of his palm. "They're taking orders from him!" He pointed a shaking finger at Gabe.

"They?" Gerald asked.

"They're in my head!" Scar beat his head against the mattress with such force that the bed crashed against the nightstand, toppling a styrofoam pitcher of water.

"Delusional," the head nurse murmured.

"Where's the bomb?" Gerald asked.

"Find it yourself, you SOB." Scar dragged his knuckles under his nose.

"Where's the bomb?"

"Fuck yourself, Pig," Scar mumbled through gritted teeth. He grabbed his head and screamed.

"Where's the bomb?"

"In the garage," Scar whimpered.

"Garage?" Gerald pulled out his notebook.

"Behind Pizza Shack on Coliseum. Old place, condemned building. Nothing there but rats and our supplies."

Scar clawed at Gerald's arm. "Get him away from me!"

The detective nimbly slapped a manacle on the offending wrist, hooking the other end of the cuff on the bed rail.

"Everybody out!" Gerald commanded.

As he marched out of the room, Gerald spoke to the hospital guard who had been called to investigate the disturbance. "Watch him! No one in or out until I return. Got it?"

"Yessir!" the guard saluted the detective's back.

Gabe walked to the parking lot with Gerald.

"You did good, Gabriel Murray. You did good work."

"Is it over, then?"

"Almost," Gerald rubbed his hands through his hair. "I'll call officers to meet me at the garage. Hopefully, we'll find the supplies and nab a couple of Hell's brothers."

Gabe nodded. He glanced back towards the hospital building.

"We're leaving tonight, then, Hannah and I."

"Your wife is a very brave woman." Gerald puffed his cheeks and exhaled a slow hiss of air. "It's not easy to cry rape."

"No, it's not easy."

In the hospital lobby, the florist was closing her shop. She had drawn the shade, and was flipping the 'open' sign to 'closed' when Gabe tapped on the glass door. "One red rose, please. Long stemmed and wrapped with a bit of fern."

He tiptoed into Hannah's room. Sean dozed in the vinyl chair. His chin rested on his chest, but he looked up. Gabe brushed his fingers across his wife's knuckles. She opened her eyes and smiled.

"I was having a lovely dream about you," she whispered.

"Good. Was I terribly romantic?" he asked.

"Terribly."

"Did I bring you gifts and say goofy things?"

"Of course."

"I love you beyond all reason," he said, handing her the rose.

"I love you," her words echoed in his mouth when they kissed.

"I'm taking you home," he said, scooping her into his arms.

He glanced to Sean, "Will you see to things here, then, Da?"

A gentle breeze lifted the hem of her hospital gown. Gabe straightened the terrycloth robe over her shoulders. She felt wonderful. Hannah curled her bare toes into the damp grass. "Twilight," she whispered. "Twilight in our own backyard." She flexed her arm, testing the canvas sling strapped across her chest. "It's good to be home." Two pinpoints of light blinked in the sky, stars that looked like faeries.

Gabe stood at her back. He wrapped his arms around her waist.

"My hero," she said. "I never could have faced the police without you."

"Sometimes, I pray that I could be the man you believe me to be," he said. "Those times, I could possibly move a mountain or fight Satan himself should you want me to."

Hannah drew a breath to speak, but Gabe covered her lips with both thumbs.

"But, fact of the matter is…" He glanced at the gray sky and then back to Hannah. "Fact of the matter is …there are times, times after we've made love…times that I lay sweating on top of you…times that you hold my head against your breast while we're still joined. I feel you shudder, I feel your womb hug me close." He was whispering now, his words like a sigh in a willow tree. "Those are the times I feel shattered. No; that's not right…not broken, but fragile like fine crystal; like I could break apart at any moment. Am I explaining it? Do you know the feeling? "

His thumbs brushed across her lips in a caress. She nodded. "But keep in mind that the best crystal is made with lead, Gabe. It's much more durable than it appears."

Hannah wrapped her one free arm tight around his waist. She buried her face in his shirt. "We'll do fine, you and I," she said. "Nothing can't hurt us when we're together."

Those autumn months were difficult. Around three every afternoon, Hannah would begin to fade – her energy drained. Gabe told her that the pregnancy had made her tired; that she'd recover in a few weeks. By mid-November she had regained much of her vigor. Now she was restless.

Her wrist was still tender; but it was improving. She struggled with her therapy, hating the unsightly bump on her shoulder. Even though Gabe said it was hardly noticeable, she felt deformed. Having one arm bound to her chest continually frustrated her. One afternoon she grumbled when a strap dangled into the pot as she stirred bubbling spaghetti sauce. Exasperated, she unhooked the Velcro closures and tossed canvas sling towards the trashcan.

"Belong to anybody you know?" Gabe quipped, holding the sling by one sauce-soaked strap.

"And you know it does," she snitted.

Gabe arched one eyebrow; a habit of his she found especially attractive.

"Well, I've a rchabilitation plan of my own, don't you see?" Hannah snipped.

"Really?"

"It's a sound theory," she began. "It really is."

"I believe you."

"Hmm, yes, well… hmmm. I'm not going to wear the sling anymore. I'll hug my side if my shoulder starts to hurt. That should immobilize the arm, shouldn't it? Yes, I'm certain that'll be fine. You think it'll work, don't you?"

540

"Trying to convince me or yourself, Love?"

"You. Trying to convince you, is all. I'm sure it'll work. I'll be fine, just you wait and see."

"Okay."

"Well, all right. I'll just hug my arm across my ribs if my shoulder starts to hurt. Meanwhile, I figure I've got to get some exercise. Right? The books all say that a pregnant woman needs exercise."

Through the window, she pointed towards Glyph Mountain, a long craggy rock perimeter at the northern end of the Faerie Village.

"Three times a week, I'll climb the hill."

She glanced at Gabe and flinched when she saw him frown.

"Climbing uses the legs, not the arms."

"Dr. Abrams suggested that you take it easy and 'tis no easy task you've set for yourself."

"Ahh, well. I'm married to a hill strider. Best that I learn to walk the mountains, don't you think?"

"Hmm, maybe we can do it without too much difficulty."

Hannah jerked her head. "Uh uh. Afraid there's a problem already. I'm going alone."

Gabe's mouth fell open. Hannah tapped his chin.

"There's no argument. This isn't a job for 'us.' I'll do it alone. I can and I will."

Three days a week; Mondays, Wednesdays and Fridays, Gabe held office hours at home while Hannah trudged up Glyph Mountain.

He'd told her that his attention was divided unequally between worry for her and for his patients. How could he be attentive to toddlers' teething problems or a teen's acne or a pixie's skinned knee? When the last patient had been treated, he would stand sentry in the garden watching her return.

"You're stronger," he said, coming to sit beside her on the stone bench outside their gate. She pushed the damp hair off her forehead and rocked forward, resting her palms on her knees.

"Right. And great purple pigs will be flying overhead soon."

Gabe laughed. "No. I'm serious. Look at yourself."

"A decidedly pear-shaped body streaked with sweat and red mud."

"You look great. The exercise has been good for you."

Hannah flopped to the mossy lawn, her legs had the consistency of soft pasta.

"Right now I feel like a beached whale," she mumbled. Her hands rested on the bulge of her belly. Turning her head towards him, she squeaked, "He moved! There, again."

Gabe crouched at her side, splaying his hands atop her abdomen.

"Did you feel it?" she whispered. "Just the tiniest flutter…kind of like a bubble popping. Did you feel it? There." She adjusted his palm over the right spot.

"He's swimming!" Gabe beamed. "Practicing his flutter kick."

Two days later, Carwig stopped by the cave.

542

"Are you ill, then, Carwig?"

"Nuh uh. I'm fine. Thanks."

"Is there something I can do for you, then?"

"No. Nothing you can exactly do," Carwig hedged.

Gabe crossed his arms and rocked back on his heels.

"What do you need, then?"

"I want Hannah, if you please sir."

Gabe spread his legs, propped his hands at his waist. "Perhaps you should explain yourself."

Carwig jumped to the side, hiding behind the wisteria vine that curled around the entry. "She promised to help me with my mathematics should I need assistance, sir," the boy stammered.

Gabe adjusted his belt buckle. He cleared his throat "She'd be up the mountain just now." Gabe tipped a thumb towards the gray rock face, now defrocked of its autumnal finery.

Carwig brightened immediately. "Climbing the Glyph yet again, is she?" He dropped the book he'd been clutching. He yelled to Tobias and Padraic. Together, the three fellows ran to meet Hannah, to escort her up the hill and back down again, laughing and singing most of the way.

It quickly became a routine. Three times a week, Hannah would toss her sketchbooks and pencils in her bag and swing through the garden gate in the early morning mist. Almost immediately she'd be met by a troop of the village youngsters.

Gabe complained to Trog with a smile, "The lads are all in love with my wife, wild with excitement for the tales she spins about sea captains, berserker pirates and whales. Of course, I understand how they're thrilled by the chance to stomp up the hill and down again!"

"It's a rare gift the girl has, to be sure," Trog agreed. "She can charm the birds from the trees and teach them to sing a sweeter tune."

"It sounds as if she might be an enchantress." Gabe pulled Trog's hair. "Has she transformed a great lion into a pussycat?"

It was early morning and Gabe was awake. A nighttime frost had left sparkling lace patterns designs plastered delicate and translucent on the windowpanes. In dawn's soft pink light Hannah's bare skin looked opalescent, like a cameo. She slept turned on her side, facing away from him. Both the yellow sheet with its crocheted edging and the brown velvet quilt were draped at her waist. He watched as her chest rose and fell with each breath.

He traced the bump on her shoulder where the bone was out of position under her skin. His fingertips skimmed over warm, smooth flesh that smelled faintly of hyacinths. He hesitated a few seconds, pressing his fingers to the bone, which skewed at an awkward angle to the graceful curve of her shoulder. He sucked in a breath.

"Does it hurt?" he asked quietly.

"No, not after those first few weeks," she answered as she rotated the shoulder in question. She rolled towards him, smiling. "Does it hurt you to see it?"

"Only because it reminds me of all you've suffered. How 'bout you?"

"Remember, orthopedists could do surgery to reconnect the separated muscles. Then, that bone would be held into proper position. Purely cosmetic, that's what Dr. Abrams called the procedure."

She pushed away from him so that she could watch his reaction when he answered. "Should I do it? Should I have that surgery?"

"Do you want to?"

Hannah pondered the question for a moment. She dropped a kiss just at his nipple, and nestled closer to him. "I don't want to look deformed. I want you to think I'm beautiful."

"To me, you are the definition of beauty," he whispered. "But, then, I think you know that."

His thumbs stroked small circles on her arms. Her hair was an amber cloud on the pillow; her eyes, sparkling emeralds; her skin, the finest ivory. The bed groaned when he moved over her. He sighed, kissing the hollow of her throat, the lobe of her ear, the crest of her cheekbone, the lid of her eye. She shivered. She arched against the very warm, very solid length of him.

Hannah kept necessities in the drawer of her bedside table. Saltines, gingersnaps and an apple and a booklet titled "Naming Your Baby." She thumbed through the book, stopping on an earmarked page. "What do you think of the name Roscoe?"

"You aren't serious, are you?" Gabe asked.

"I dunno." She rubbed her belly and grinned. "I've been thinking of him as Roscoe today."

"Maybe it will grow on me." He tucked a curl behind her ear.

Her stomach growled and she reached for a snack.

"Roscoe's grumpy when he's hungry," Gabe teased.

She bit into the apple, then offered him a bite.

"Why do you think Aidan told the police those lies?" she asked.

"I've wondered when you'd ask that question."

A drop of apple juice balanced at the corner of her bottom lip. Gabe caught it on his thumb. "Who knows," he answered.

"But, it doesn't make any sense. He gained nothing by lying."

"Well, you see, there's '*normal*' behavior and there's '*abnormal*' behavior and then there's this entirely different sphere called '*Siddhe*' behavior. "

Gabe plumped two pillows and leaned back, pulling Hannah to his side. "A Siddhe is motivated by his own desires, nothing more, nothing less. There's no use questioning his reasoning, because he'll simply fabricate a justification."

Hannah tried to speak again. Gabe touched her lips with his fingertips.

"I know it's illogical; but it's the truth. I swear. Aidan doesn't operate under your human dictates of truth and fair play."

"But..."

"Aidan thought that he could hurt me,… umm,… you, er… both of us, by lying. He knew that harming you would be the best way he could hurt me."

Gabe squirmed a bit and pulled Hannah closer. The half-eaten apple rolled off the bed and landed with a wet thud on the floor.

She curled her leg around one of his. She drew circles around his navel with her index finger. She smiled when she heard his breath hitch, when she felt goosebumps stipple his belly.

"My human dictates of fair play and truth, you say? Are those dictates different from yours, then?" she asked.

Gabe tracked the curve of her ear. As he spoke, his breath tickled her neck. "The half of me that is human understands and respects truth and fair play." He touched her chin, and lifted her face to look at his. "But, remember, I'm part selkie; still very much the animal."

Hannah grinned and nipped at his upper arm playfully. He recaptured her chin, "I'm serious, Love. Selkies mate for life. We're fiercely loyal, ferociously territorial. All's fair in love and war. There are no rules. You are my priority. Only you."

Hannah stared into the fathomless depths of his gray eyes. She tugged his hair, growing long and straight, shining black as a seal's pelt. Affecting a Scot's burr, she said, "And don't I ken the tales? Lucky's the human who hies up with a selkie come ashore in the light of a full moon, aye?"

"Awk, aye!"

"Mind you, I hear tell they're verra guid lovers, are selkies," Hannah teased. She licked his nipple and wiggled lower to dip her tongue in his navel.

It was late December. Hannah was preparing for her first faerie Christmas celebration. She had made presents for everyone. For Ull and Farwe, she'd painted tiny portraits of their children. She'd spent hours working to decorate eggshell ornaments for Nowatil and Ella. Gabe had carved slingshots for Toby and Padraic while Hannah braided multi-colored ribbons through hair barrettes for several elfin girls. Each gift was wrapped and carefully labeled, waiting under the cedar tree in their living room. Sean was coming to visit tomorrow and she was baking shortbreads as a surprise for him. She hurried through the market in search of the fresh nutmeg required for Ella's recipe. Unfortunately, she found trouble.

"Why Hannah! Oops, Mrs. Murray." Lynnar covered her lips with her hand. Her ring sported a ruby, the size of a pecan. Hannah thought the jewelry was well-suited for a Siddhe – ostentatious.

"Haven't seen you in ages! Gabe keeps you on a short lease, though, doesn't he, dear?" Lynnar grinned a wide smile that never quite reached her eyes. "The village is still buzzing with stories about your wedding. Nuptial bliss, is it?"

Hannah nodded and turned away. She pretended to inspect a basket of pungent ginger roots.

Lynnar stepped closer. "I guess you won the prize." She examined her nails. "Of course, I never wanted to actually keep Gabe. I just wanted to play with him," she snickered. "He always was a good playmate."

"It was never a contest, you know," Hannah said. "I had an advantage from the start."

Lynnar chuckled softly. She polished her ruby on the sleeve of Hannah's jacket. "And what is that?"

"Warm blood."

Lynnar rubbed her index finger along Hannah's injured shoulder.

"I heard about your latest misfortune. Are you prone to dizzy spells, or were you gawky as a child, too? It could be a hormonal deficiency."

Hannah grabbed a clove of nutmeg from the display basket. She plopped a rhinestone button on the counter as payment. "Merry Christmas, Feldstar! Give my regards to Magalise. " She thought she might explode if she didn't leave the shop immediately. Once outside, she took ten deep breaths. A toasted nut aroma floated in the crisp, cold air. Smoke from acorn fires wafted from every chimney in the village.

Christmas Eve, she and Gabe joined a humorous, but unharmonious, group to sing carols in the square. A male voice whispered at Hannah's ear, "Oberon, High King of the faeries, considers the pansy to be a love potion." A flat-faced flower with two purple and three bright yellow petals was dropped over her shoulder. She caught the pansy and turned.

"Aidan."

"Some of our wee folk call the pansy *'Tickle my Fancy'* or *"Heart's Ease."*"

Gabe spun towards the sound of Aidan's voice. In one smooth movement, he had corralled Hannah at his back and stepped closer to the Siddhe.

"Stay away from her, Aidan," he growled. "I'll not warn you again."

Aidan straightened the cuff on one sleeve. He inspected Hannah with a long, lazy look; his blue eyes shuttered behind curling lashes. He'd spoken low; but Hannah had heard him clearly, "Warn me if you must, Gabriel. Your bluster doesn't faze me. This time, I'll have your woman. You'll see."

A growl rumbled deep in Gabe's throat. He clenched a fist and took another step towards Aidan.

Hannah touched his sleeve. "He's goading you, Gabe. Don't fall into his trap." She slipped her fingers around his fist. "Let's go home. Just turn away."

Gabe glared at Aidan. His upper lip quivered in a snarl. But, he centered one palm at the small of Hannah's back. "Wise advise."

It had snowed on Christmas Day and the following week was cold. New Year's Eve sparkled with lacy frost patterns on the windows and long icicles clinging to the gutters. Hannah was content, bundled with Gabe in a nest of pillows on the floor near the hearth.

Flames danced in the fireplace and the walls seemed to sway in the wavering light.

Hannah stroked the mound of her abdomen. "Five months. We're over half way there."

"Our baby." Gabe tracked a finger down her nose. "I want to touch him, to count his fingers, to compare the shape of his ears to yours. I want to cradle him in my arms and brush my cheek across his fluffy eider down hair."

"What if he's born bald?"

"No matter. He'll be perfect."

"Pretty sure of yourself, aren't you?" Hannah said. "There could be problems."

"No problem could stop me from loving him."

Hannah cupped his jaw with her palm. She nodded and whispered, "I know what you mean."

"I'll keep you both safe, Hannah."

"I've never doubted you, Gabe." She put one hand on either side of her belly. Her fingers spanned her girth.

Gabe added an oak log to the fire and it sizzled, bright sparks snapped and sputtered. Hannah enjoyed the super-hot radiant heat. Her cheeks felt sunburned. She closed her eyes and smiled. The heat made her drowsy.

"We could move, you know."

Surely she had misunderstood him! Hannah blinked and squirmed to sit up straight. "What? Move? Why?"

"To get away from Aidan." Gabe sat cross-legged on a cushion. His shoulders were slightly hunched, his elbows propped on his knees and his hands dangled in between.

Hannah drew squiggly designs on his trouser leg with her fingertip. "Would it do any good for us to leave? Can't he track people the same way you do?"

"No." Gabe picked miniscule pieces of lint out of the carpet. He made a pile of dust on his knee. "Aidan's human. The Siddhe trained him to be charming and unscrupulous; he has no magic."

"You would be willing to leave your friends?"

"If doing so would keep you safe."

"If we left, Aidan would win. We can't allow him to bully us; to push us out of our home."

Gabe spread his arms wide. "Is this cave your home?"

Hannah hugged the pillow she had embroidered with sloppy remedial stitches. "Most definitely."

"What about the home you left behind? The one that burned?"

"That was a house, a building where I lived. It was never my home. I love this place; elves who live here are my friends. The humans in North Carolina were my associates. Friends were a luxury I thought I couldn't afford."

Gabe rubbed her neck, right at the base of her skull. She closed her eyes and felt like purring. "What changed your mind?" he asked.

"You. You dared me to trust you and I've embraced the challenge."

Gabe kissed the crown of her head. "Thank God for small favors."

Hannah slurped a sip of steaming cocoa. Gabe stretched out, resting his head in her lap.

"How do you propose we deal with Aidan's devilment, then?" she asked.

Gabe hunched his shoulders. "Ignore him."

"Not a very pro-active approach, is it?" Hannah twirled a strand of his hair around her finger.

"He can't cause problems unless we react, can he?" he asked. "It's all a game to him, isn't it? If we refuse to play; refuse to be upset, we destroy the game. It's really very simple. Ignore him."

"There are times when I can feel him watching us," Hannah whispered. "It's scary."

Gabe's fingers tensed on her thigh. He flexed his fingers, massaging her leg.

"Ignore him."

"His eyes... They strip me naked." Her words were breathy and low, more quiet than a deep breath. "He makes me feel exposed and ugly... dirty."

Gabe sat up, lifted her chin with his knuckle. She thought his eyes were the color of soft rain clouds.

"You're beautiful...loved and cherished," he told her and she believed him.

Hannah was well occupied during the next few days, and she had no time to worry about Aidan's unwarranted attentions. The new year had brought a flu bug to the community. Farwe's wife, Ull, was sick. Gabe had prescribed bed rest. He made her a tonic and told her to sleep. Then he sent the ladies of the Village to her house en masse.

The elfin women joined ranks to divide Ull's chores between them. Ella prepared a cherry pie, rolls and a stew. She filled a basket with jars of jam and pickles. Nowatil collected the family's dirty laundry. On her return, she delivered clothing that smelled faintly of soap and sunshine. Glendar, the baker, married Hilda, a woman shaped like a soufflé. She scrubbed the farmhouse with an evangelical zeal. Farwe teased that his wooden plank floor was now bleached three shades lighter than ever before! Hilda swatted his back with her dust cloth and rushed him outside.

"Tis no wonder poor Ull is suffering!" Hilda sang out as she batted a cobweb from a corner of the porch. "Her having to deal with all of your bairns and nary a help from you. Tracking mud all over the poor dear's floor. Grabbing biscuits off'n the counter and dribbling crumbs in your wake. Begone now, Farwe. Be about some project outside, man. Is there nothing to be done with your cows, then?"

Farwe shook his head, and turned towards the barn, where his eldest son, Niall, was finishing the morning's milking. Lian, the teething two-year old, gnawed his own pilfered biscuit. He stumbled over a wooden truck, one of many toys that littered the yard. Although his biscuit was crumbled, Hannah didn't think the boy was hurt. Rummaging in her pocket for a handkerchief, she murmured, "Are you all right, then, Big Boy?" She gathered him close, leaning him against her knee as she dabbed at his dirty hands with the cloth. He nuzzled his head against her shoulder.

"Can you smile for me?" she asked.

Lian chewed on his fingers and shook his head. A bead of saliva sparkled on his full lower lip.

She touched his cheek with her index finger.

"Are you sure you can't find a smile?"

"No got one," he answered.

Hannah pointed to the pocket of his coveralls. "What's in there?"

"Nuttin," the boy answered as he felt inside the pocket.

Hannah pulled the pocket and peeked inside. "Oh, I see something in there!" She patted the pocket and winked at him.

"You've got something in your pocket that belongs upon you face," Hannah sang. Lian pulled the lining of his pocket out, producing only a small wad of lint. Hannah grabbed at the air, closing her fist around an imaginary treasure.

"I'm sure you couldn't guess it, if you guessed a long, long while. So take it out and put it on, it's your great big elfin smile!"

She spread her hand over his lips, pushed the corner of his mouth to make a lopsided grin.

"There, you see, you had one all along!"

Hannah flicked his nose with her finger and Lian giggled.

Lian ran off towards the barn, calling to Farwe. "Da, I gotta smile in ma pocket!"

After lunch, Farwe pushed his chair back from the table. Rubbing his stomach, he belched softly. "I noticed a few late cranberries over at the bog." He tipped a finger towards the window that faced west. In the distance, past a row of cedar trees, the terrain dipped low, creating a sandy marsh at the base of the foothills. "I 'spect they're still good for picking."

The girls cajoled, "Can we go, Hannah, can we?"

"Only the ripe berries will bounce, Hannah."

"Some folks call 'em Bounceberries."

The day had been warm. Most of the snow melted; but in the shaded areas, a few patches remained. The sun was an amber orb in the winter sky when he found Hannah and the juice-speckled girls. Curled in Hannah's lap, Meggie sucked her thumb making contented slurping noises. Hannah finger-combed Margy's hair, fluffing the waves made by her braids. Mellie sprawled on her back, watching high clouds float past. Tucked close at her side was a colander full of plump cranberries.

"What a pretty picture," he drawled.

Hannah shivered and wrapped her arms across her chest like a shield. "What are you doing here?"

He sat beside her, bumped her shoulder with his. "Enjoying the view."

Mellie sat up. "Wanna cranberry, Aidan?"

He selected a berry and rolled it between his thumb and index fingers. "Hilda mentioned fresh chocolate chip cookies and milk when I stopped at your house, girls." He winked. "Why don't you take your sisters home,Mellie? Bet Hilda will help you make a cobbler with those berries."

Hannah stood. She shook grass and few dead leaves from her skirt. Aidan touched her arm and she flinched.

"Stay a moment," he said quietly.

"I... I can't." Hannah hated that she was flustered. She wiped her palms down her thighs. "The girls... I should go, too."

Aidan sucked air through his teeth in a long hiss. "Why are you so frightened of me, Hannah?"

"I'm not!" Her voice was high and shrill. She winced. "I'm not frightened of you, Aidan." She was frightened, though; like a toddler left alone with a new babysitter.

He arched a brow and smiled. She thought it was a patronizing smile, like an adult would give a child.

"All right then. Why are you afraid of the feelings you experience when I'm near?" he asked.

Hannah inched away from him. "Don't be ridiculous!" She grabbed her throat, bunching the neck of her sweater.

Aidan pivoted, leaning close, crowding her against the tree at her back.

"I make you feel desirable, don't I?" His nose touched her earlobe. She held her breath, trying to shrink into rough oak bark that prickled her spine. "I could make love to you for hours on end. Hot, wet, sex." She felt his words like condensation on her flushed face.

It was as if his hungry blue eyes pulled the sweater from her shoulders, stripped her naked. She hunched deeper into the cable-stitched angora.

Aidan moved closer still. Hannah was dizzy – almost intoxicated. She wondered if his musty herbaceous cologne was affecting her. He whispered, "Your body's humming, isn't it?" He touched the pulse just under her jaw. "There's a special thrill in the anticipation of pleasure; right?"

Hannah glared at him. She wished that she had Lynnar's knack for haughty stares. "I hardly think the lies you told the police were intended to please me!" She moved to the right, backed away from him.

"Pshaaa! Those little tales had nothing at all to do with you!"

"Oh really? That's not what the police thought."

"My grudge is with Gabe. You were a means to an end. Hurting you hurts him." He waved his hand. "He and I are something less than friends."

"So I've heard."

Aidan let his head drop. He peeked up at her through a tousled cowlick. She figured that was a practiced look; one that had gotten him out of trouble numerous times in his teen-aged years.

"I suppose I was wrong to involve you." His words were so quiet she had to lean closer to hear them.

"Yes, yes you were wrong."

He reached for the hand still clutching her sweater, gently circled her wrist with his fingers.

"But I'm not wrong about how I make you feel, though."

Hannah realized his face much too close to hers. She stared at his lips, watched them form words that made her pulse race.

"You're curious," he said.

Hannah gnawed her bottom lip.

"You can imagine yourself with me." He nuzzled her cheek with his knuckle. "Admit it," he whispered. "You'll dream of probing kisses; my hands on your breasts, exploring your sweet secrets."

Their hands were joined at the neck of her sweater. His warm breath tingled her lips.

Hannah pulled back with a shudder. "NO!"

Aidan tugged on her arm, she stumbled.

"The lady said 'No', Aidan!"

Gabe was seething. To Hannah the crackling energy of his anger was a tangible danger. Her voice was a raspy whisper that shattered and broke. "Gabe."

He seemed bigger than usual. She craned her neck to look up at him. She saw the same mouth, the same eyes that had smiled at her a few hours earlier. Only now those features were sharper, as if chiseled from stone. The warm eyes were cold as steel, hard and unblinking. Hannah wondered he could concentrate and hurl Aidan across the bog as easily as he could levitate a small rock.

Her fingers rested on his arm. His muscles flexed and he unclenched his fists. She marveled that she could restrain his anger with a touch no more restrictive than a tether made of spider webs.

He stroked her cheek. "Are you okay?"

She closed her eyes and nodded. She tipped her cheek into his hand.

"Leave now, Aidan," she said, pleased that her words sounded calm and assertive.

"Dream of me, Hannah," Aidan said. He brushed her cheek with the back of his fingers.

Gabe growled. She gasped.

"I'll be in touch."

"No," Hannah found a voice, but she didn't recognize the breathy whisper as her own.

Aidan smiled as he turned and walked away. His departure left a stifling silence. In that vacuum, Hannah thought her pulse was a sound loud enough to startle birds from their perches. She slumped. Her forehead rested on Gabe's shoulder.

"Hold me," she whispered. "Please hold me."

His arms crossed at her ribs. His hands circled her waist. His chin balanced on her head. They inhaled simultaneously, expelled their breaths in a collective *whush*.

"Why do I feel guilty? I didn't do anything wrong." A strange mixture of anger, humiliation and frustration clogged her throat.

"I want to believe you," Gabe answered

560

Hannah thumped her palm against his chest. "Don't think; just believe. Isn't that what you told me a long time ago?"

She thought it took him an unreasonably long time to respond. Her heart skipped several beats; but an electric current zipped straight to her brain when he lifted her hand to his lips. He kissed her palm and pressed it against his heart.

"I'm trying," he told her.

"Take us home. Both Roscoe and I are exhausted."

Dinner was leftovers. Neither of them had much of an appetite. Hannah stirred green peas through her tuna casserole and then let the concoction cool in an unappetizing lump. Gabe made a sandwich, took one bite and pushed his plate away. Neither of them had been in the mood for idle conversation. After several minutes of uncomfortable silence, Hannah had cleared the table. Now she shook out the dishtowel and draped it over the oven door handle.

"Do you want to talk about it?" she asked.

"Not particularly; but I guess we should."

"I took the girls to the bog to pick cranberries. Aidan found us there."

"Don't you think I figured that much?"

"Yes."

"Why did you stay there alone with him?"

Hannah shrugged, rubbed her nose and shook her head. "Don't really have an answer. I just did." She chose a glass from the rack and filled it with water. She rubbed her finger back and forth on the lip of

561

the glass until it squeaked. "I confronted him about the lies he told the police." She sipped the water.

"Did he make any excuses?"

Hannah pushed her hair away from her face and propped her hip against the counter. "Not really. But he surprised me when he acknowledged he was wrong to involve me in your disagreement."

"Oh Siddhes are good at keeping humans off kilter."

"Off kilter?" She scratched her head. "Yeah. I guess that's a good description. Aidan says things that throw me off balance, that's for sure."

"Like what?"

Hannah crossed her arms over her chest. "Ummm, sexual comments that make me uncomfortable."

Gabe stood close. "Like what?" His fists were clenched; his eyes, squinted.

Hannah tried to turn away. He held her arms to turn her to face him. "Like what, Hannah?"

"He asked why I'm nervous around him. Why I'm frightened of him."

"And…?"

Hannah drank more water. "Then he turned things around, said that I was frightened of the way he made me feel. He made outrageous assumptions."

"Like…?"

"That I wanted him to kiss me, to touch me. To touch my breasts."

"And what did you say?"

"Say?" Hannah rubbed her forehead. "Nothing. I tried to leave."

"So you didn't dispute him?"

She balled her fists on her hips. "His absurd comments didn't warrant validation. He makes me uncomfortable. I've told you that I don't like the way he looks at me." She turned away, put her hands flat on the counter. Her head was pounding and her stomach was upset.

"Maybe there's a grain of truth in what Aidan says," Gabe mumbled.

She whirled around, jabbing her finger in the center of his chest. "How dare you! What happened to that trust we're supposed to share?" She pushed him and he staggered backwards, bumping a chair. "Your battle is with Aidan; not me. I'm going to bed." She drank the remaining water and refilled her glass.

It was after midnight when Gabe tiptoed into the bedroom. Hannah lay on her side, a pillow tucked under the bulge of her belly. She had kicked the covers to the floor He pulled the sheet over her bare shoulder and curled around her backside.

"Hannah! You're burning up!" He sat up quickly and reached for the water glass on her bedside table.

"Hmm?"

"Here," he said, pushing the water into her hands. "Drink this water. I'll be right back."

Hannah sat up and sipped the lukewarm water. Her mouth was dry and scratchy, like it was lined with sandpaper. Her head swayed side-to-side, much too heavy for her neck to hold it upright.

Gabe returned with a steaming mug. "Here," he said exchanging the empty glass for the mug. "Drink this."

Hannah lifted the cup to her nose. The steam was herbaceous and lemony. Tiny bits of leaves floated in the brew. She slurped and swallowed a taste. "Lemongrass?"

He nodded and sat on the edge of the bed. "And tea tree and yarrow. A good combination for flu and fever."

Hannah gulped another mouthful of Gabe's concoction. "Do you think I caught Ull's flu bug?"

"Looks that way."

Hannah spread her palm over her belly. "What about Roscoe? Will he be all right?"

Gabe set the mug next to the lamp on her table. "He'll be fine. You just need to rest and recover." He kissed her forehead. "Go back to sleep."

When he stood, Hannah caught his hand. "You're not mad at me anymore?"

"I was never angry with you, Hannah. I was jealous."

"And now you're not?"

"Oh, I'll probably always be leery of Aidan; but I'll try to control it."

"I love you."

"I know."

Hannah was chilly. She pulled the quilt close to her face and wiggled over to Gabe's side of the bed, seeking his heat. Still half asleep, she rubbed the cool sheets and patted his pillow to search for him.

"Gabe?"

"Here, Love." His voice was deep, a soothing sound in the dark.

"Are you all right?"

"Yes. Of course." His baritone was closer. She could feel the air stir with his movements.

"What were you doing, there in the dark?"

"Watching you sleep."

"You've got a great bedside manner, doctor."

"Were you dreaming of me?" he asked as he trailed a finger down the bridge of her nose, across her lips and back again.

Hannah wrinkled her nose. "Was I smiling?"

"Yes."

"Then I was dreaming of you."

He buried his face against her belly.

"I love you," she said.

"I know," he answered. "I know."

His words were no louder than a heartbeat. She felt them echo in her pulse. She, brushed his hair straight back off his face.

Gabe took one deep breath, then another.

"Did you know that I watch you sleep? That I stand guard so that you aren't alone with your nightmares?"

"I haven't had nightmares in a long while," she said.

"But you did, when you first came home."

"Yes. Yes, I did."

Gabe spoke through gritted teeth. "Sometimes you'd scream, you'd cry out my name." He tilted his head to look up at her. "Do you know how I felt, hearing you call for me, hearing you whimper? Do you know how impotent I feel, knowing that you were scared and hurt and that I failed you?"

Hannah curled her fingers in his hair, grabbing handfuls and pulling hard. "Don't ever say that again! You have never failed me! Never. You found me there in Scar's room. Against all the odds, you came."

She jerked his hair once more. "Not even you can change the past, can you?"

"No; but Aidan plays a vicious game with no rules, no parameters, Hannah."

"Aidan isn't a magician. He could never make me leave you."

He grinned and rested his chin on top of her head.

"I'd find you if you tried."

"Promise?"

"Oh yeah. I promise." His words were lethargic, his voice a soft breathy whisper. "We're a family, Hannah." His hand was a warm cradle for tight ball of her belly. He curled against her backside

566

and spoke into the hair at her nape. "This little one will grow strong and happy."

Hannah snuggled deeper into her nest of pillows. She laid her arm over Gabe's.
She yawned, "You'll keep us safe."

He kissed the protruding lump of her shoulder bone. Hannah purred a soft "Mmmmm", but her breathing was instantly slow and steady. She slept.

But Gabe was awake. He stared at the window, looking past the sheer curtains that fluttered like apparitions, to the night shadows. An owl called and a small animal ruffled dried leaves in the garden. The willows whispered.

It was daylight. Sunshine was warm on her face; sunlight was bright even through closed eyelids. Hannah was achy. Her neck and shoulders felt bruised. Even her wrist and finger joints were stiff. Moving her head on the pillow was an effort. The bedroom door was closed; but she heard the velvet rumble of Gabe's voice. "It's the flu. Just stay here while she rests. There's soup on the stove."

Someone mumbled a soft reply and then there were footsteps and a few bumping noises. "Every family in the village has someone sick. I've got to make rounds."

"*Uisge beathe!*" was the squeaky reply.

"Thanks, but I've got my own potions. I'll be back by sunset. Take care of Hannah."

Moments later, Trog rapped on the bedroom door. "If you're sick, I'll make you a warm posset," he declared.

"All right," Hannah answered, trying to sound cheerful. "Fine. A posset, then." When Trog pulled the door closed, she wondered what a posset might be.

In less than five minutes he knocked again. "You don't have any milk."

"That's no problem. I hate warm milk anyway."

"Then how can I make you a posset?" Trog laughed. He snapped his fingers and winked. "I'll use my personal recipe. Leave out the curdled milk. Just double up on the Scotch and whip in the egg yolk and honey!" He proudly displayed a green jug, then he pulled the thick cork that came free with a satisfying 'pop'. A whiff of the pungent, burnt smelling whisky aggravated Hannah's nostrils. He poured a generous dollop into a mug. "For medicinal purposes," Trog chuckled as he quaffed the whisky in a single gulp. "*Uisge beathe!* Water of life!"

"You hellion, you bit me!"

Gnawing the gold coin snatched from Aidan's hand, the Spriggan cackled. Aidan swatted at him. Puffed into a grotesque shape, the Spriggan gleefully jumped out of his reach.

Aidan clutched his wallet, checking its safety in his back pocket. "So, you agree to kidnap the woman, Hannah?"

The Spriggan spat dialog.

"Yes." Aidan nodded. "Yes. Of course. Payment as we discussed. A bag of gold coins and bag of emeralds, green like her eyes. You'll collect after the kidnapping. Not before."

Another stream of barely intelligible words followed.

"Damned straight, I don't trust you! Does your own mother trust you?" Aidan's hair stood on end when the Spriggan answered. Static electricity crackled around them, small whirlwinds disturbed debris at his feet. "No? I didn't think so."

Hail fell within the circle where they stood warily, maybe fifteen feet apart.

"No need to get all pissy, is there?" Aidan brushed bits of litter off his shirt.

Mid-day, Gabe was one of many village males who stopped at Glendar's bake shop for a hot bagel and a cup of soup.

"I'd like to engage your professional services," Aidan said as he took a chair. He laid his hand on Gabe's table.

"It never pays to scheme with the Spriggans, does it?" Gabe muttered as he inspected the hand that was wrapped in a wet handkerchief. "Nasty punctures. Already infected." He poked the wound, oozing a drop of yellow pus. After rummaging through his bag, he held out a small blue vial. "This is an essential oil … produced from valerian rhizones."

"Ever the professional aren't you, Gabriel?" Aidan tucked the vial into his pocket. "Where's your little wife?"

"I think you should go home, Aidan. You need to start soaking that infected hand right away," he said. "Soak it in salty water, as hot as you stand it. Then, rub a drop of this oil on your wounds at least twice a day for a week."

By early afternoon Trog was on the sofa, curled in a tight little ball, sleeping off the effects of his own medicinal doses. The bedroom door creaked open. The bed dipped slightly when another body lay down beside her.

Hannah muttered, "Back so soon?"

"Sssh," he answered as he touched the crown of her head. "Sleep," he whispered, his voice soft as a night breeze. He covered her nose and mouth with his handkerchief soaked with the valerian oil

"Mmmm," she mumbled.

He lay quiet, waiting for her breathing to slow, waiting to be sure she slept deeply. After ten minutes or so, Aidan got out of bed. He plucked a couple of his hairs and arranged them across the indentation his head had made on Gabe's pillow.

"I'd love to be a bug in the corner when Archangel Gabriel comes home!" he snickered.

Aidan crossed the room and opened the window. Outside, four Spriggans were urinating in the garden. Flowers had already shriveled and turned brown. "Get ready," he hissed to them.

Eight beady eyes glowed red. Shrill cackles, like high-pitched static, answered his order.

Aidan lifted Hannah's limp body. He leaned out the window. His arms quivered beneath her. Eight hands reached up to relieve him of his burden. The Spriggans cooed with an evil glee. One cupped her swollen breast; another touched her protruding navel.

"Enough!" Aidan snapped. "Just stuff her in the bag and take her away." He pointed to the large black canvas bag he had hung on the dogwood tree earlier. "You know the agreement. You place her in the bed, and then you leave!" He stabbed his finger at the largest Spriggan, who had now inflated to a grotesque orb shape. "No rape! I want that babe born safe so that he can grow up without a father. More punishment to the almighty Gabriel!"

He pulled the window shut and left the cave quietly.

She shivered as sweat on her neck, arms and breasts dried to a cool damp film. Her heart was racing from the terrors of a nightmare she couldn't remember. Her fingers inched across the sheets, seeking Gabe. The sheets beside her were chilled. With a sudden jerk, she sat in the bed, disturbing mounds of lacy pillows. Stifling a scream of alarm, she was immediately awake; eyes wide and unbelieving.

She recognized this room; but it wasn't in Gabe's house. She was intimately familiar with each knick-knack clustered on the nightstand beside her. Across the small room, bits of sea glass danced on the mobile suspended from the curtain rod. Sheer white curtains billowed in the soft northerly breeze. Gulls laughed as they glided over

571

the bay, searching for breakfast. Breakers crashed ashore with a cadence as regular as a pulse beat. Her own heart raced. She gulped a deep breath, inhaling the smell of sea salt and seaweed.

She was in her own bedroom! The bedroom she had painted pale blue in her North Carolina bungalow! The paint smelled fresh.

Oh God! This bedroom was consumed by fire almost a year ago. I saw the fire, I felt the heat. I tasted the smoke!

She sat on the iron bed that had captivated her at the Unique Antique Market. She was sprawled on a patchwork quilt. She'd painstakingly pieced this quilt together with remnants from the Sew and Sew fabric shop in downtown Morehead City. As her mind raced, trying to understand, her fingers rubbed the soft fabric squares, tracking her own irregular stitches.

"How can this be?"

Her own words surprised her. The sounds echoed in her brain. Each heartbeat bounced in her ears. Even as she had asked the question, she knew the answer. She'd been dreaming. But it all seemed so real – frighteningly, mystifyingly, beautifully real.

She was frightened to leave the bed. This was a mattress island afloat in a sea of insanity. The radio at the bedside clicked on. The cheerful announcer began her hourly news report.

"Good morning, North Carolina. It's seven o'clock on this sunny Friday, August 3rd. Reports of out Palestine are grim. There appears to be no break in the on-going negotiations for the release of

American Embassy hostages being held by guerrillas. Secretary of State's comments were made to an international group of …"

Reflexively, Hannah reached over to shut off the radio alarm. Questions whirled.

August?

Mild panic was morphing into hysteria. She cautiously slipped off the bed and stood in the center of the room. Was it all a dream? My life with Gabe…was it a fantasy?

Outside the seabirds were quiet. The waves crashed soundlessly to shore. But, she thought she heard someone giggle on the porch.

"Gabe?" she called. "Gabe!" She was screaming now.

Her throat ached as if she'd swallowed pins. Her knees were rubbery and shook like Jello. She shivered although sweat ran in rivulets between her breasts. She had butterflies in her stomach. Little quivers that tickled from inside. She pushed on her enlarged abdomen. No butterflies! Roscoe! She sank to the floor, bent her head forward and fought to control her breathing.

She ran her fingers through her damp hair. Her ring caught in the tangles. A circle of dolphin that circled her finger …She knew tha the inscriptions inside read 'To Caillie, love everlasting. To Hannah, trust eternal.'

"My wedding band. Thank God!"

She rocked back and forth. She wrapped her arms across her ribs. Her baby woke and stretched. She rocked faster, tears pouring down her cheeks. She rubbed her   distended belly and crooned to her baby.

"It's okay, Roscoe. Daddy's coming. He promised. He's coming, Baby."

CPSIA information can be obtained at www.ICGtesting.com
Printed in the USA
LVOW10s2040131015

457961LV00014B/3/P